the
Weather Composer
Rise of the Mahdi

Also by the author

The Ancient Arrow Project
The Dohrman Prophecy
Quantusum
Collected Works of the WingMakers Volumes I & II

the Weather Composer

Rise of the Mahdi

James Mahu

Planetwork Press
Egg Harbor Township, NJ

ISBN 0-9641549-8-6

ISBN 978-0-9641549-8-8

First Paperback Edition, 2013

Library of Congress Control Number: 2013906968

Manufactured in the United States

Planetwork Press

403 Gravel Bend Road, Egg Harbor Township, NJ 08234
planetworkpress.com

Abbreviations:

12F	Grade Level 12
12M	Grade Level 12
AK-47	Assault Rifle Soviet-designed gas-operated magazine-fed rifle
AK 103	Assault Rife— Modernized Incarnation AK- 47 system.
ALIGN	Advanced Learning Institution of the Greater Nation
AM	Ante Meridian Latin meaning "before midday"
AMK	Assault Rife upgraded from the AK-47
BG	Board of Governors
CIP	Curriculum Institute Program - graded levels test for male and females
CROW	Common Remotely Operated Weapon Station
DNA	Deoxyribonucleic acid
D.C.	District of Columbia
ES	Emergency Services
FR	Faculty Research
FRC-HR	Faculty Research Center-Home Personal Base
GN	Greater Nation
HQ	Head Quarter
HCP	Human Cloning Project
ID	Identification
IQ	Intelligence Quotient
IVECO M65	Light Multirole Vehicles- an Italian armored vehicle
KH-100	Great Nation Satellite
L	Level - test, grade or buildings
LB	Left Brain- nickname for Atkins
LMV	Light Multirole Vehicle
MAV	Micro Air Vehicle
M1114	High Mobility Multipurpose Wheeled Vehicle, commonly called Humvee
M2	50 Caliber Machine Gun
M4/M5	Automatic Tactical Assault Rifles
MK 19	Grenade Launcher
MP5	Submachine Gun
MP5SD	Submachine Gun
MPH	Miles Per Hour
MRAP	Mine-Resistant Ambush Protected vehicle
NSA	National Security Agency
PA	Public Announcement
PI	Personality Index
PM	Post Meridian
RAM	Radiation Absorbent Materials
RF	Radiation Frequencies
RPG	Rocket Propelled Grenade
RPS-29	Russian antitank grenade launcher
SIG 510	Swiss Assault Rifle
SUV	Sports Utility Vehicle
UHIQ	Ultra-High Intelligence Quotient
U. S.	United States

Acknowledgements

My gratitude goes out to Planetwork Press who has been a wonderful partner to the WingMakers project. Darlene Berges for her unwavering support and commitment to bring these words to a global audience, and Tony Sakson for his integral role in the interior book design.

To my readers, thank you for taking the "path less traveled."

To Sarah, Mark and Ernest, thank you for your ongoing support and willingness to provide your inputs. They are always appreciated and heartfelt.

Sincerely,

James

PROLOGUE

Terran Kahn was small for his age, hosted in a body that seemed in no hurry to grow up. He possessed the rarest of all gifts, a mind capable of dissecting the formidable forces of nature. As wild and untamed as these forces seemed, he knew they were still governed by the same laws that extended from the smallest particle to the largest structures of the cosmos, and in that fact, that common modesty, that thread of creation and destruction that wound its way through everything, he could envision something that no one else had seen: how to compose the forces of nature, namely, weather.

His vision had begun when he was only three years old. The earth had been scorched by drought in the wake of cataclysmic storms, and every resource ripped open to shrivel beneath the merciless sun. The populations of earth soon imploded, from ten billion to a mere nine-hundred million in a matter of twelve years. *Twelve years!* Communities were decimated across the food chain. The word *extinction* was on everyone's lips.

Three classes of people emerged: the first class was the powerful leaders who curated and protected the remaining technologies after the crash of humanity; they were called Helios. The second class was known as the Faculty, and they were responsible for the critical knowledge of humanity, and to ensure its perpetuation. The third class was everyone who lacked the good fortune to be a member of Helios or the Faculty. This inauspicious class was known as the "third classers," but only those within the highest circles of Helios used this term. Third classers were disorganized by comparative measure, and yet they managed to survive like a willful seed whose roots could not be bound.

It was to this third class that Terran belonged, at least initially.

He was, by any measure, bright. An orphan, as was the case for most of his generation. Orphanages were as plentiful as Burn Posts—

the places where dead bodies were cremated. Most of the Burn Posts had been shut down by the fifth year, but the orphanages continued their expansion as children were herded into their care. Families had been ruined during the twelve years of drought, and it was at the orphanages that Helios leaders elected to build schools so the Faculty could transfer the salient knowledge to the next generation.

These orphanages were slowly retooled as boarding schools, and became known as Preserves. It was to these Preserves that Helios looked for humanity's new footing to prevail once again on earth and resume its stewardship of the planet.

There was a name for the twelve-year drought, though third classers seldom used it, and then, only in an expletive context. The name was *Sunrot*. The near annihilation of humankind came at the hand of an overly active sun. (Much later, it would be understood to be a gamma ray explosion from a star millions of light years away that interacted with the sun, causing the sun's energy to surge.) It had first taken down the power grids and satellite systems, plunging the world into chaos. That was its first bombardment of humanity. The ensuing weeks only got worse. Food supplies became choked. Mass riots erupted across the planet as people panicked for basic resources. Governments stepped in, clumsily as first, managing to subdue the initial riots, but couldn't produce food and water in ample supply.

Two weeks after the grids went down, as rioting began its senseless rampage, the first storms hit, and they were the strongest ever recorded—by a large margin. Unfortunately, they were followed by earthquakes. The storms showcased the power of nature in ways that no one had seen before. Two-hundred miles per hour straight-line winds attacked entire regions of the globe; hurricanes and typhoons changed shorelines and toppled coastal cities. The death and destruction was utterly mind-numbing. Those who survived walked around in a daze, unsure of their next meal, drink of water or shelter. Millions had simply lost the will to live. And the storms kept coming.

After those first two weeks, earthquakes began to rumble across the planet. Most were in remote regions, but scientists knew the signs were not good. When the first earthquakes struck Japan, the entire

Pacific Rim buckled, and tsunamis cut further into the coastlines of nearly every country. In Japan, the devastation was unimaginable. The entire west coast of the United States lost, on average, about forty miles of coastline—in a few places it was more than two hundred miles.

More earthquakes hit China, Turkey, Southern Russia, Egypt, Nova Scotia, Italy, Kenya and Pakistan. They crippled all hopes that the event which started the chaos would be short-lived, and the damage from the storms could be managed. This was an unmanageable, unimaginable event. In the first four weeks after the solar storms hit earth, nature had meted out over three billion deaths. The ensuing shock was absolute, constant, and crippling to everyone. The entire mood of the planet had been thrown into a deep well of hopelessness.

No country had been devastated more than China from the initial blows of Sunrot. Its citizens were completely overwhelmed by the resource constraints—especially water, but then disease swept in unseen, and made its march amid a starving and severely weakened populace. A strain of bird flu hit the Asian continent hard. It was like a third bombardment—following the storms and earthquakes—to the populations of both China and India, and no one could stop it. Travel had come to a grinding halt in those times. Nothing was imported or exported, and this was to the benefit of North and South America, because the bird flu never got a hold on its citizens.

A sinister withering of the food chain beset people in every area of earth. No one—fauna or flora—was excluded. Food stores were organized at the local level and nearly all societies were localized. Those that lacked resources—be it food or water—died, either from starvation, dehydration, or the onset of various diseases that quickly spread amid the breakdown of medical services. Suicide was routine.

By the second year of the Sunrot, most of the local citizenry had become self-sufficient in food production, but only those who were strong and enterprising made it that far. The weak and enfeebled died. There was no room for laziness. No refuge for the infirm. There were no social classes in those early days. Even the wealthiest were struggling to survive. All systems of law and order, in the first two years of Sunrot, were eroded to such a degree that murder for food was in the public domain. Fear and panic were the watchwords of those days, and no one wanted a return to that chaos.

In the third year of Sunrot, a global political presence emerged called Helios. Gradually, law and order returned to most local communities coincident with their ability to bring food production and water resources in balance to their populations. In years four and five, a degree of normalcy returned to many communities as they began to mature their food production. Helios continued to emerge as the global leader, helping to reshape humanity into a coherent system of commerce and local self-sufficiency.

They gradually took over the role of law and order, and began to have a local presence in major communities to help bring efficiencies to food production and water resources. After these areas were stabilized, the next gravest danger was the orphan communities. Children of any age were often left to fend for themselves. Families had degenerated into loosely organized communes, and children—especially young ones—were often seen as parasites that used up limited resources, and didn't produce anything valuable to the community.

A self-imposed birth control fell over the globe's human residents. When Helios came into power, the notion of birth control was already well established in most populations. But in year five, Helios began a forced sterilization program with woman over twenty-nine years old, and restricted families to one child. The institution of marriage was a requirement to have a child, and any child born out of wedlock was immediately taken and placed in one of the Preserves. Then offending parents were sterilized.

By the sixth year of Sunrot, the Preserves were a global phenomenon, and Helios instituted—through its Faculty—a comprehensive system to sort through the children in the Preserves in order to identify the brightest and most creative minds. Those selected were brought to special schools.

One of the major changes that occurred during the middle stages of Sunrot was the unification of the planet on the basis of language. English was chosen as the language of the realm, and all Preserves taught English, and only English. There were some exceptions, but these were in remote areas with limited populations that Helios had no interest in governing. Speaking English was considered the ticket to being inside the "tent" of Helios or what was called the *Greater Nation*.

The Greater Nation was the fusion of all nations, operating in cooperation to survive the Sunrot. Scientists of that time were struggling to understand the exact nature of the calamity's onset and most importantly, its duration. All they knew, was that intense solar weather caused the initial chain reaction that triggered magnetic disturbances so severe that the planet's weather systems changed overnight. Within six months, the lack of rain, coupled to a severely overheated planet, conspired to reduce crop productivity by 84 percent.

It was a lot less clear as to how long the drought would last. Helios had to assume the drought was a constant, and no one could relent on rationing and preserving resources. In years seven and eight, new agencies were created to oversee the water preservation and food production processes for the Greater Nation.

A form of state socialism pervaded the Greater Nation, and infrastructure was gradually created to support the fledgling global society. The two largest agencies were Technology and Communications. Most of the major population centers were able to connect to the Internet through their local government centers. Individual Internet access was unavailable. The Internet had gone down for nearly four years. It was one of the first priorities of Helios, and a major reason that no one challenged their authority—*they brought back the Internet*. The Internet was a symbol of hope that the world was still connected and would eventually find its way to every citizen, as it had been before Sunrot.

Helios effectively owned and operated the Internet, and the Greater Nation was connected therein. By year nine, the Preserves were established on the Internet, and the Greater Nation curriculum was largely distributed through it. Computers were solar-powered, and Helios created the computers. There were no private companies producing computers, they were only produced by Helios and distributed through their agencies, which included the Preserves.

The Preserves or state boarding schools, provided only a basic education. Their highest purpose was to identify the brightest of the bright, and bring those students—whatever their age—to the Advanced Learning Institute of the Greater Nation (ALIGN). There were six of the ALIGN Centers on earth in year nine, each accommodating approximately one thousand students.

By the tenth year, Helios was deploying its technology to rebuild certain defensive weapons systems. While there were no wars among the member states of the Greater Nation, Helios framed the weapons development program as a precautionary readiness in the event there was ever an aggressor who would rise up against the Greater Nation. It was commonly accepted among third classers that the *"aggressor"* that was feared were terrorist enclaves that had survived in the Middle East, and remained unattached to the Greater Nation. These terrorist outposts were few in number, but they had a reputation as "Old Schoolers" who would never join the global community, and would fight to remain independent with their own language, customs, religion, and culture.

In year eleven, a new economy was implemented within the Greater Nation. All of the world's great cities had fallen prey to entropy and disuse. The survivors were insufficient in size to manage the demanding infrastructures of major cities, thus, most of them had fallen into disuse and whatever resources could be stripped from them, had been taken and used to build rural, self-sufficient collectives that were more like communal farms than cities.

In most regions, a commune would grow by virtue of its proximity to a large city, the charisma of its leadership, and its complicity with Helios and the Faculty. These communities became cultural and economic centers. It was at these hubs that the ALIGN centers were established.

These communes became known as the New Cities of the Greater Nation and all of them were given names by Helios as identifiers of their unique stature. The capital of the Greater Nation was known as Olympia, and it was located thirty miles west of Washington, D.C. It was here that the major agencies of the Greater Nation were established and Helios made its headquarters.

The leader of Helios was a man named Trevor Stanton. He had been a senator for four years before the time of Sunrot, and was one of the surviving members of Washington's elite inner circle who had the resolve, education, connections, and sheer tenacity to become the leader of the new world. Ostensibly his leadership was neither singular nor supreme; each member nation had a leader that represented the interests of their particular nation. Each of these people shared power in the Greater Nation. Nevertheless, it was understood that Trevor Stanton was the voice of the Greater Nation and his power was undeniable.

Wynton Jennings was the leader of the Technology agency and Marsha Owen was the leader of the Communications agency. Both of these leaders reported directly to Trevor Stanton, so it was commonly acknowledged among the three classes that Stanton was the King of the Greater Nation. Realistically, Stanton was responsible for "righting the ship." The world had been unambiguously listing during the first years of Sunrot, and it was Stanton's dynamism that organized the formation of Helios and the lesser agencies that ultimately unified the global populations under the Greater Nation's umbrella.

Stanton was forty-eight when Sunrot began. He was enjoying the peak of his career as a politician, and after only four years in the senate, rumors flourished that he was on a fast track to be President. What had distinguished him was his fierce independence. He was unaffiliated with either of the main parties, and it was this distancing that won him admiration in the circles of the common man.

Per capita loss of life during the first year of Sunrot was the lowest in the United States, when compared to any other nation. Its systems of food production, food stores, water resources, and disease control allowed Stanton to exert his leadership across party lines and rise in stature quickly and visibly. He had seized the idea to enable communes to be developed by using the resources of the cities. He had placed disease control as a top priority. This single decision proved to be the most powerful of all, and was probably the key reason he was given the mantle of leadership within Helios.

Amid the ensuing chaos in the early days o, leadership was not a democratic proposition. Communications were down, no travel, no Internet, every man, woman and child—at least the strong ones— were on their own, seeking one thing: *survive another day*. There were no debates, no elections, and no party system.

To most, it was destiny, but for Stanton himself, he relished the idea of resetting the economy, trade, culture, religion, science, every not-so-shiny particle that comprised humankind. He liked the whole concept of a rebirth for humanity, and the fact that he was in the center of it all, only made his exhilaration all the more gripping.

Never before had the entire world's citizenry, been unified against a common enemy, and in this case, that enemy was an overactive plasma furnace some ninety-three million miles away.

In the twelfth and final year of Sunrot, Helios was a strong and vibrant organization that ruled the Greater Nation with growing competence. Communal cities were beginning to stabilize. New hope was abounding that a major change was afoot. Weather patterns seemed to be stabilizing. Food production was rapidly growing. Infrastructure was being built to accommodate people's comfort, and there was a growing sense of stability in nearly all regions.

The decaying presence of cities was the most vivid reminder that something was massively wrong. Gone was the expertise to run cities, airports, traffic systems, water- works—all of the hundreds of systems that intermesh. The populace of the United States was one-tenth of its former self, and it was better off than any other nation. The sheer loss of human knowhow forced humanity to retreat to a simpler life.

The Greater Nation, under Helios' encouragement, had elected to focus its limited resources on technology and communication, and develop a global educational system to identify the new minds that would bring humankind to a new understanding of its environment and once again, as it had done for centuries before, master it, mold it, and if need be, exploit it.

CHAPTER 1

The Faculty

The biggest disease today is not leprosy or cancer or tuberculosis, but rather the feeling of being unwanted, uncared for, deserted by everybody. The greatest evil is the lack of love and charity, the terrible indifference towards one's neighbor who lives at the roadside, the victim of exploitation, corruption, poverty, and disease.

- Mother Teresa

The words of Mother Teresa were etched over the main doorway of every Preserve. They were the words that Trevor Stanton and Marsha Owen had agreed would grace every school. It was the rallying cry of the new generation. However, these words were reserved for the Preserves, the six ALIGN Centers had a different message, though it was unwritten. It was the message that if you were so fortunate to end up at an ALIGN Center, then you were the vanguard of the new humanity. You were its leaders, its scientists, its politicians, its technologists, its teachers… its *hope*.

From a global society of nine-hundred million, about six-thousand of the brightest students were selected to attend the ALIGN Centers. The precise manner in which students were identified was a mystery to all but those within the highest reaches of the Faculty, the organization responsible for ensuring that the human species would pass from its darkest hour to once again reclaim its stature as the technological wunderkind of the planet. It was the Faculty's role to supply Helios with the brightest of the bright, so its Technology and Communications agencies were well stocked with prodigious IQs.

The curriculum of the Preserves was focused on three things: basic skills, learning a special skill, and readiness for a trade skill. By the time students graduated, they would be well-versed in the basic skills of reading, writing, humanities, and arithmetic; they would possess a "gift" for a special skill, like hunting, weaving, carpentry or local leadership; and they would be ready for an apprenticeship in their chosen trade.

In the case of the ALIGN Centers, the curriculum had a heavy emphasis on technology and the sciences—specifically, software programming, engineering, chemistry, medicine, physics, and all of the other right-brain activities that make the world a better and safer place. At least, that's what the students were taught.

Many of the pre-Sunrot technologies were sufficiently intact to enable reverse engineering, yet the simple fact was that too few experts remained to know how to fix the broken technologies or build new ones that were better. Helios was well aware of this problem, and its Technology agency was working to identify and collect the most critical, surviving technologies and work with the Faculty of the ALIGN Centers to fix or reverse-engineer them. It was the elite Faculty instructors of the ALIGN Centers whom Trevor Stanton held in the highest regard, because they were the ones who would sculpt the new generation of geniuses to repair—perhaps even improve—the pre-Sunrot technologies.

The Faculty was divided into those who served the needs of the Preserve, and those who taught and administered to the ALIGN Centers. The leader of the Faculty was a young professor from Yale. The professor had been the head of Yale's English department, and because Stanton wanted English to be the language of choice for the Greater Nation, he offered the position to young and ambitious Josh Sinclair.

Josh was a tenacious leader within the Faculty. In many ways, the Faculty was the single most challenging position because of its charter to provide a uniform, global educational program that was practical—in the case of the Preserves; and masterfully challenging—in the case of the ALIGN Centers. The goal to make English the global language had been a tough sell, but then Helios *brought back the Internet*, and Trevor Stanton had proven that his leadership was superior to any of his contemporaries.

Josh Sinclair was only thirty-two, but had been widely regarded as the most competent department head at Yale and certainly its most charismatic leader. He was as bold as he was brilliant, and nothing ever seemed to come between him and an opportunity to expand his personal influence.

CHAPTER 2

School

Mashhad was the second largest city in Iran with a community of nearly three million citizens before Sunrot, and only about six-hundred thousand in the twelfth year. It had fared better than Tehran—much better. Mashhad had always been known to be a protected city, and when Sunrot hit, true to its mystical reputation, it was spared the brunt of the storms, floods, and earthquakes that beset other cities in the Middle East.

It was the only major city in the region that had not lost its entire infrastructure, and its population, while reduced by 70 percent, had one of the highest survival rates on the planet. It was one of the reasons that a Preserve was established there in the eleventh year.

Iran, like many of the nations of the Middle East, had been reluctant to join the Greater Nation. Its new leader, Aban Molavi was educated at Cambridge and Harvard, and had previous relationships with both Washington D.C. and London as an attaché to the Iranian Ambassador to the United States. Trevor Stanton worked diligently to bring Iran into the Greater Nations. While he was ultimately successful, there were many tribes that condemned the decision and chose to live unaligned as "Old Schoolers"—their handle, courtesy of Helios.

It was a cool afternoon in Mashhad, mid-October in the twelfth year, when a young boy, dressed in scraps of linen cloth draped around his thin frame like a mummy, collapsed on a street amid a throng of people. The street bordered the market square in Mashhad, and people ignored the young boy, who was face-down in the middle of the dirt street. He was disheveled, dirty, dusty, and mostly unconscious. A few years earlier, he would have been left for dead, but on this day, a young woman knelt down and poked him in the ribs.

"Are you alive?" she asked.

The young boy could only manage a faint moan.

The woman turned the boy onto his back and held his head in her left hand. "Here, drink some water."

Behind the woman was a young girl, perhaps five or six years old, watching the scene with great interest. "Who is he, Mother?"

"I don't know. From his look I would say he's lost… maybe from one the Pashtun clans. It's hard to say for certain."

"Will he die?"

The woman poured some water into the mouth of the boy, most of it spilled down his chin. She poured some water into her hand and then splashed it on his face, softly slapping his cheek. "Wake up, boy. Drink some water."

His eyes flashed open for a brief moment, blinking uncontrollably in the bright sunlight. "I am Terran Ahmad Khan. Where is your school?" As his raspy words emptied into the open market, they were quickly absorbed by the din of bartering in the nearby market, and the boy lost consciousness.

Apart from his name, the only word the woman understood was school, as the boy had a strange dialect. She looked around for help, but seeing that no one shared her interest in the boy, she put her arms under him and stood to her feet, carrying the limp body, with her young daughter in tow.

CHAPTER 3

Listening

Parto carefully set Terran down on a concrete table outside the Preserve entrance. She looked around, worried that she may have done something illegal or unseemly by taking the boy. The streets were relatively quiet, and no one took any notice of her, so she told her daughter to wait by Terran while she went inside to find someone.

As she opened the door she glanced at some writings above it, and quietly cursed at them, *English!* She walked down a hallway and noticed an office to her right, its door open. A small, kindly looking man looked up and motioned her in. He was hunched over slightly, and looked to be in his mid-sixties.

"You look lost…" He observed. "I'm the office manager. Can I help you find something?"

Parto smiled awkwardly, feeling her face flush. "I found one of your students… or… I think he's one your students."

"You found one of our students?" The office manager repeated; his face suddenly perplexed. "I didn't know any were missing."

"Do you have a student… a Terran Ahmad Khan?"

The office manager glanced at his monitor, clicked a few buttons, and mouthed the words: Terran Ahmad Khan. "How's his first name spelled?"

"I… I don't know. I just met him. He's very frail… maybe even dying."

"Odd first name… where is this boy?"

"He's lying on a table just outside," Parto said. "I carried him from the market square. He'd collapsed in the middle of the street. He said something about a school… I thought perhaps he was a student here."

"No one by that name in our school," the man announced, standing to his feet. "And while there're many Khans, no one with that first name…"

"What should I do with him?" Parto asked.

"Let's have a look."

The two walked out to the entrance in silence, the sound of their shoes echoing against the cool stone walls of the hallway.

When they arrived outside at the entrance, they found Parto's daughter, who, like a sentinel, stood next to Terran's lifeless body. "He said something when you were gone," she said softly, studying the face of the Office Manager.

"What did he say?" Parto asked.

"I don't know... I couldn't understand it."

The office manager examined him for a moment, checked his pulse, and placed his ear on the boy's chest. "Hearts beating just fine." He pulled out a piece of paper and a pen and scribbled something on it, and handed it to Parto. "That's our doctor's address. Find him and tell him to come immediately. I'll see to this boy's needs in the meantime." He leaned down to pick up Terran, paused for a moment, looking at Parto. "Do you know the way?"

Parto looked down at the note, her face confused, then slowly nodded. "It's the old drugstore on—"

"Yes, yes, that's the place. Go, and please, be as quick as you can."

"He'll ask me your name... the doctor, he doesn't know me."

"Just tell him that Hamid from the Preserve needs his help—it might be an emergency, so convince him to hurry. Okay?"

Parto looked down the street in the direction of the doctor's office. "Wouldn't it be quicker if we took the boy to him? It's only three blocks away. The boy is light."

Hamid sighed, furrowing his brow. "I'm old, I can't walk fast... my back is lame, I can carry him to my office, but more than that, I'm—"

"I can carry him," Parto offered. "I already carried him from the market square—a longer distance."

"I can't let you carry this boy. It's a disgrace." In the next moment, Hamid snapped his fingers. "Wait one moment, I'll be right back."

A few minutes later two teenage boys came running through the entrance and stopped in front of Parto. "Is that the boy?" the larger of the two asked, pointing.

Parto nodded, hesitantly.

"We're supposed to run him to the doctor."

Parto put out her arms as if to say, *"Then, by all means, do so."*

The two boys grabbed Terran—one underneath his shoulders and the other his ankles, and began to trot awkwardly in the direction of the doctor's office. They were already a hundred feet down the block when Hamid came out of the school panting.

Parto looked between the boys and Hamid. "Should I go with them?"

"You seem to be his guardian angel… go." Hamid smiled.

Parto grabbed her daughter's hand and they walked off, following the boys who were already turning the corner down the street.

"Tell Dr. Najafi I said hello," Hamid half-shouted.

Parto glanced back and nodded, but kept her focus on the street. The streets could be dangerous to walk due to the debris, cracks, even the occasional clump of seemingly immortal weeds.

Before they arrived at the doctor's office, Terran's carriers were already running back to the school, and as they passed they waved politely. "He's with the doctor," the larger boy said, only slowing down for a moment.

Parto managed a weak nod and kept walking at a brisk pace. *Why am I getting involved? What can I do anyway?*

She entered the doctor's office and looked around for any signs of life. It was empty.

There was no sign on the door that said "Doctor's Office" or any indication that a doctor was inside, but the address that Hamid had written down was exactly where she was. This had been an old drugstore before Sunrot—mostly for ice cream and candies—Parto was sure, but it was now a dilapidated room with empty shelving and little else.

"Hello?" Parto said, her voice quivering a little. It was cold inside. There was one large window, but no lights, only unlit candles punctuated the shelves and an empty glass display. She thought she heard a muffled voice. "Wait here, Dorri," she whispered, "I'll be right back."

A door in the back of the room was closed, but Parto sensed activity behind it, and knocked gently on the door, opening it cautiously.

As she poked her head into the adjoining room, she saw the back of a large man, leaning over a table. Barren shelves bordered the upper reaches of the rectangular room, where a dozen candles shone their light.

A pair of feet could be seen, but nothing else, though Parto recognized the bare feet as Terran's.

Parto cleared her throat. "Excuse me, are you Dr. Najafi?"

Without turning around, the man spoke quietly. "I am."

Parto opened the door a little wider, but stayed on the threshold, quieting her voice to a near-whisper. "My name is Parto, and I found the boy in the market square, passed out. I carried him to the school, and Hamid told me to take the boy to you."

"Yes, well, I know how to fix him, but I have no equipment. It was all taken from me years ago. We'll have to pray that Allah has plans for this boy, for if he does not, he might be calling him home this very hour."

Parto frowned, not sure how to respond. "…is there anything I can do?"

"Pray. There's little more than that. He needs more than I can provide. I doubt he's had any food or water for several days. His body's shut down to conserve energy, but sometimes it reaches the point of no return, and I'm not sure if that point has passed."

Dr. Najafi straightened up and turned to face Parto. He was about forty years old, close-cropped hair with tinges of gray at the temple. He was tall and thick. His eyes were slow and methodical in their appraisal of Parto. "Are you alone?"

"My daughter, Dorri, is with me."

"Maybe she can pray, too."

Parto looked away from his stare. "My faith died with the Sunrot. I don't pray anymore. I'm sorry."

"I don't question your reason, just your timing. This boy… he needs something more than I can provide, and he needs it *now*."

"Mother, I can pray," Dorri announced.

Parto smiled thinly, looking down at her daughter who had, as usual, not listened to her instructions to stay in the outer room. Dorri's black eyes dominated her elfin face.

"If you want, go ahead," Parto whispered.

Dr. Najafi stepped back and motioned to Dorri to approach the boy's body, which remained motionless on the table. He was wrapped in a light blue wool blanket and occasionally his eyes would roll beneath his eyelids, as if he were dreaming. Dorri walked tentatively to his side and took his limp hand in hers.

"I am small. I am just a little girl, but I ask that this boy be made good again. I pray that he lives. Spare this one, Allah. You have taken so many… my brother and father… cousins, uncles and aunts. Leave him. He can be my brother. I would like a brother. Please… let him stay. He is good. I don't know how I know this, but I do. This one is good." She patted Terran's lifeless hand.

Dr. Najafi locked eyes with Parto for a moment and smiled, and then bowed his head as if he were praying, too.

"He wanted to know where the school was," Dorri continued quietly. "He wants to learn, Allah. Let him learn, please. He will bring something to this world that is missing. He will bring good. Please, Allah, let him live. Please spare him…" Dorri paused as if she were trying to find the right words. "If you want us to believe in you, make him good again… we'll believe in you again."

Dr. Najafi intoned in a whispered voice. "Ameen."

Dorri placed Terran's hand back on the table and kissed his cheek. Parto stepped forward and put her arm around Dorri. "That was a very nice prayer."

"Yes, very well done, indeed," said Dr. Najafi.

"Allah will not let him die," Dorri announced with a confident tone.

"Really… and how do you know that?" Parto asked.

"When I was praying, I felt it."

"Felt what?"

"That Allah was listening."

CHAPTER 4

Cafeteria

The day had barely dawned when Terran began to cough. The sound woke Dr. Najafi first, but soon Parto stirred as well. The two stood around the boy, offering him water, which he drank eagerly.

"This is a miracle," Dr. Najafi said excitedly. "I feared we'd awaken to a corpse. Allah listened!" He looked at Parto with fire in his eyes.

The boy spoke in a strange dialect. "Is this the school? Are you my teachers?"

Dr. Najafi and Parto looked at one another with vacant stares. Neither of them could understand what Terran said.

"The dialect is similar to Kurdish, but I don't understand it. Do you?"

Parto shook her head.

"Where am I?" Terran asked. "Who are you?"

They knew he was asking questions, but apart from the word "school" none of the other words made sense to them.

Dr. Najafi brought Terran a bowl of bread. "Eat?"

Terran took the bread and devoured it. His chewing brought his questions to an abrupt end.

Parto smiled, watching him eat. "He's very hungry. Where do you think he's from?"

"Pashtun… maybe some obscure Afghani tribe. Possibly he's Baluch. I don't know."

Dr. Najafi bent down and looked into the boy's face. "Do you understand me?"

Terran's eyes immediately narrowed in confusion.

"He probably understands us as well as we understand him." Dr. Najafi confided. "The Preserve is probably the best place to take him—someone there will know his dialect."

"Do you see, Mother, I told you Allah was listening." Dorri was awake, watching the boy eat his bread. She got up from the makeshift bed on the floor and went to Terran and put out her arms. He scrutinized her like someone who had never seen a child. He stopped eating; his entire face became motionless, staring at Dorri. "Don't you want a hug?" Dorri asked.

Terran put the bread down on the bed and spread his arms out, mirroring Dorri, who then leaned in and put her arms around him—mostly his knees, but it was the closest thing she could hug, because Terran was sitting on the table and she was standing on the floor. Terran looked bewildered by the gesture, unsure of what it meant.

Dorri stepped back, pointing to her chest. "You're my brother, now."

Terran stayed still, as his arms slowly descended to his sides, and then one arm, with its index finger extended, touched his chest. "You're my brother, now."

He spoke it in perfect Farsi, exactly in the same rhythm as Dorri had moments earlier. Both Parto and Dr. Najafi looked at one another in amazement.

Dorri chuckled. "No, I'm your sister. *You're* my brother."

Terran shook his head slightly. "School?" He pointed to the room's walls. "Teachers?" He pointed to Dr. Najafi and Parto.

"He thinks we're teachers," said Dr. Najafi. "Let's see if he can walk."

Dr. Najafi helped Terran off the table and supported him to see if he had the strength to walk. "He seems fine. I've never seen such a recovery before. But these kids from the mountains are built tough. I'll walk with you to the school."

At the mention of the word, "school," Terran grabbed Dr. Najafi's sleeve. "School?"

Dr. Najafi nodded forcefully. "Yes, we'll go there now." He took Terran by the arm and led him out the door, and the four of them made their way to the Preserve.

It was still early when they arrived, a little past seven in the morning and the school was just waking up. Dr. Najafi went inside to find Hamid. He knocked on the office door, and down the hallway he heard the shuffle of feet. "I'm coming. Hold on."

"Hamid, it's Dr. Najafi."

Hamid turned the corner and bowed slightly. "Ah, Doctor, it's good to see you. I hope you're here with good news on your lips."

"The boy, Terran Khan, lives. He's outside right now."

"Excellent, what's his story?"

"He's a mystery. He speaks a dialect we're not familiar with—"

"The woman and… the little girl, are they still with him?"

"Yes," Dr. Najafi said, nodding.

"What do you want me to do?" Hamid asked, unlocking his office door and motioning for the Doctor to follow.

"Who is your best student… with languages?"

"We only teach English. You know that, my good Doctor."

"You have no records of the language skills of your students?"

Hamid shook his head, and then snapped his finger and looked at his wristwatch. "The kids are having their breakfast right now, we could have the boy come into the cafeteria and say something, if anyone recognizes the dialect, we'd have ourselves a translator."

"Okay, I'll get the boy and you can lead us to the cafeteria."

A few minutes later, Dr. Najafi's group, escorted by Hamid, entered a large room consisting of long tables and about three hundred students of varying ages and gender. The Preserves—as part of their mission— were open to anyone between the age of six and sixteen. It was a ten-year curriculum, but most of the students, regardless of their age, were in their first year, because the Preserve in Mashhad was relatively new.

The noise in the room was mostly of utensils on metal plates. There were a few laughs and chitchat, but it was obvious to any astute observer that the students were trained for efficient eating so they could get to their classes on time. Hamid walked to a raised stage on the far end of the cafeteria and clapped his hands sharply. "Quiet, please. I'd like to gather your attention on a mystery we are trying to solve."

An immediate hush fell over the room, while the students craned their necks to watch Hamid speak.

"A boy has come to our school who speaks a dialect none of us is familiar with. I'm going to have him say something, and if any of you recognizes the dialect, raise your hand. Okay?"

A chorus of voices responded. "Yes, Mister Mokri."

Parto noticed a few teachers leaning against the wall, curious about the mysterious boy. Dr. Najafi led Terran to the podium and motioned to the assembled students, as if he was telling Terran to introduce himself. Terran looked between the assembled students and Dr. Najafi, but seemed to have no idea that he was supposed to speak. Dr. Najafi put his hand to his mouth and thrust it outward, signaling to the boy that he should say something. The boy mimicked the gesture, and the students instantly giggled. Dr. Najafi pointed to the students. *"School."*

Terran's eyes lit up. "School?"

Terran's body was still wrapped in the blue blanket, his face had been cleaned, but the rest of his body remained dusty and dirty. His hair was mostly straight and long, reaching his shoulders. His face was thin, as was his entire body, but there was a strength to his physique that was undeniable. Standing next to Dr. Najafi, he looked particularly small, but there was a quality about him that seemed authoritative. Perhaps it was his unaffected demeanor in front of the students or his square jawbone, or his wide-set eyes that looked unflinchingly at the world before him.

Terran walked to the edge of the stage on which the podium stood, staring out at the students. The room was absolutely quiet as he looked among them, as one would do if they were trying to select one person on the merit of a singular, unique characteristic. His eyes finally rested on a teacher who was watching him. Terran turned to the teacher and held out his arm. "You are my blood, are you not?"

The teacher, eyes locked with Terran's, nodded.

"You can understand him?" Hamid asked.

"I can," the teacher replied.

Hamid clapped his hands together sharply twice. "Okay, children, go back to your breakfast and hurry to your classes."

"Let's go to my office," Hamid said as he walked by the teacher. "You can come, too, if you want," he added turning back to Dr. Najafi, Parto and Dorri.

Hamid walked hand-in-hand with Terran, while the rest of the group solemnly walked behind them. Every once in a while Terran would look behind, seemingly to make sure the teacher was still following. The dark limits of language had finally been pierced, and Terran Khan was soon to become knowable.

CHAPTER 5

Revelation

Hamid's office was small, with one window that overlooked a barren courtyard. It had a desk and two chairs, but Hamid quickly pulled in three chairs from his reception area and then closed the door. "Please be seated." He turned to the teacher and bowed slightly. "This is Nouri Abbasi, one of our language instructors. He taught English at Ferdowsi University before coming here. This is Dr. Najafi," Hamid motioned with his arm in a sweeping gesture at the Doctor, "probably the reason we are even talking today."

"I can't take any credit for saving this boy. I did next to nothing, I assure you. Actually, I credit Dorri for his miraculous recovery."

"Really, and what did she do?" Hamid asked, turning his attention to Dorri, who squirmed on the lap of her mother.

"She prayed," Dr. Najafi replied matter-of-factly.

"Well... very good," said Hamid. "And this is Dorri's mother, Parto, who first found the boy and brought him to our attention."

Hamid cleared his throat and turned his full attention to Terran who was studying him closely. "And this is our mysterious traveler, who seems to have journeyed a long way to find our school. Nouri, could you please ask this boy to tell us his story?"

Nouri glanced around the circle of chairs and nodded faintly, never making eye contact directly with anyone, and then turned his focus to Terran. "My name is Nouri Abbasi. I am a teacher at this school. Please tell me from where you came, and who you are."

Terran immediately began to speak in a strange dialect.

Nouri looked at Hamid. "His dialect is a mixture of languages... part Sufi and part Kurdish. I don't understand some of it, some of it I recognize. I'm afraid my translations will be so-so. It's been a long time since I spoke anything similar."

Hamid nodded. "Just do your best."

Terran spoke again with great earnest and Nouri put his hands out to Terran, signaling him to stop, and then he turned once again to Hamid. "He says he is Baluch, and that he left his tribe in order to go to school."

"Are his parents alive?" Hamid inquired.

Nouri asked and then shook his head.

"Ask him if his tribal leaders know that he's here."

Nouri asked and a thin smile touched his bearded face when Terran answered him. "He says that they know very little beyond sheep and goats."

"Hmm," Hamid murmured. "Ask him why he doesn't look Baluch."

Nouri asked the question and Terran's face crinkled into puzzlement, and then he began to speak hesitantly.

"He says that his grandfather, whom he never met, was a Russian officer—a colonel. His tribe was nomadic... and... and in the early eighties when Russia occupied Afghanistan, this colonel was kidnapped, and he later became a member of their tribe. He has this bloodline."

Hamid sat back in his chair, contemplating what he had just heard.

"Why did he come here?" Dr. Najafi asked.

Nouri asked the question and then replied laconically. "To learn."

"What is it that he wants to learn?"

Terran became very animated as he answered the question, and when he finished, Nouri asked him something else. The two of them began to converse as if the rest were no longer present in the room. Hamid interrupted them, indignation showing in his voice. "Stop! What are you talking about?"

Nouri apologized. "I'm sorry, he's very bright. His intellect is not what I expected."

"What do you mean... what did he say?" Hamid questioned.

"He says he understands the elemental forces. He wants to learn physics, chemistry, astronomy... he wants to ensure that Sunrot never occurs again."

"Noble aspirations," Hamid said quietly, "for such a young boy who comes from the mountains—"

"Actually, he's from the desert—Turkmenistan, to be precise."

"It's just sand... how can anyone live there?"

"Do you want me to ask him?" Nouri said.

"No, no, ask him, instead, how many days he journeyed to get to Mashhad."

Nouri asked, and Terran held up seven fingers.

"Tell him that if he wants to go to school here, he can, but we don't teach physics and astronomy. There're only six places in the entire world that do, and none of those are in Mashhad."

Nouri explained, and Terran, visibly disappointed, asked a question.

"He asks where the closest of the six ALIGN Centers is."

"Tell him it doesn't matter. He has to be invited, and the only way that happens is if his IQ is a lot higher than I suspect it is…" Hamid sighed and shook his hands as if he were erasing his previous words. "No, just tell him it's a long way away, but he needs to be invited."

Nouri delivered the message, and then looked at Hamid. "He wants to know how he can be invited."

Hamid pointed to his head, just above his right temple. "He must be *brilliant*."

Nouri delivered the message, diligent to place the same emphasis as Hamid had, but Terran only smiled when he heard the reply and then asked another question.

"He wants to know," Nouri said, "why physics and astronomy are only taught in six places throughout the world."

Dorri whispered to Parto. "What's physics?"

Hamid leaned forward in his chair, focused on his veiny hands. A thin copper wedding band was their only ornament, and he spun the ring on his finger out of habit, as he spoke. "The young boy might not know that humanity has shrunk by 88 percent, and that the remaining world's populations have been unified so we can endure, and Allah willing, regain our former stature as quickly as possible. The needs of our communities are more… more about *surviving* than splitting atoms or photographing distant galaxies." Hamid let out a deep breath, glanced at Nouri, and then nodded sharply for emphasis. "Tell him."

As Nouri started to translate, Terran's eyes narrowed, and he began to shake his head. His eyes—a deep shade of bluish gray, suddenly downcast—seemed to retreat inwardly. When Nouri stopped, the room was suspended in an unnerving silence. A rosy glow had emerged on the far wall as the sun began to climb, lending some relief to the sobering revelation, but also a hint of the revelation's culprit.

CHAPTER 6

Innocence?

Pirdah was a holy man among the Baluch. His robes were pure, washed daily. His long beard was white, drawing to a fine tip like a funnel. His turban was a golden color with a tinge of amber-red at its base, adding to his already formidable height.

Javad was escorted into Pirdah's tent, and left in silence to stand like a spirit hovering in the air. Pirdah ignored him, too annoyed to acknowledge his presence. Javad stood silent like a sentinel, wondering if his fate was to walk on burning coals or proceed directly to a beheading. His body shuddered from fear.

"Are you cold?" Pirdah asked, suddenly turning his attention to the man standing before him.

As soon as his presence was recognized, Javad knelt down and touched the feet of Pirdah with great reverence. "No, your Holiness. I am most appreciative to be in your presence."

"You may sit there," Pirdah said, pointing to a red cushion on the floor. His tent was large, easily accommodating a bed, desk, chairs, washroom, and a small fire pit. Javad, like a trained dog, half-crawled to the cushion and sat in it, facing Pirdah with his eyes staring down. Pirdah was the Sardar of a constellation of tribes. He was the capstone of the pyramid of the Baluchian people in Iran, and the cornerstone of tribal loyalty.

"What news do you have for my ears?" Pirdah asked, stroking his beard, and for the first time, turning his full attention on Javad.

"Your Holiness, I have nothing new to offer you. I am sorry. I did not kill him; that is all I can say."

"We will let the coals decide that," Pirdah replied. "What I don't understand is that you offer no other explanation. Did he evaporate? Did a pair of eagles carry him off? Did our enemies abduct him? Tell me, Javad, why do you have no explanation when the boy was under your guard?"

The coals give me a chance, Javad thought. A glimmer of hope surged through his body. "Your Holiness, I do not know what happened to him. He took provisions for a journey, but his destination is unknown to me, and the storm that night, when he disappeared, made it impossible to track him."

"Look at me!" Pirdah demanded.

Javad raised his eyes, but no matter how hard he tried, he could not keep them focused on Pirdah's imposing stare.

"Terran was our best hope to have a leader who could protect our people from our enemies and unite the Arab world in these times. He was *your* charge. *Your* responsibility. How can you look into my eyes and tell me you know *nothing* of his whereabouts or his plans? How is this possible?"

Javad hesitated for a moment, biting his lip in a tortured conflict. "Your Holiness, he was smart—"

"Of course he's smart, that's why you were chosen to oversee him. He's a child; you're a man—supposedly our most learned, and you *lost* him."

Pirdah stared unflinchingly at Javad. "So that's it? No confessions. No clues. No suspects besides you. Nothing?"

Javad trembled at the tone of the Holy man that sat before him. Javad pushed his unkempt hair to the side of his face, and looked up momentarily. He was without a turban, wearing only a long-sleeved shirt that went down almost to his knees. He was barefoot and without pants—the standard attire of a Baluch prisoner.

He was the only one in his entire tribe of 14,043 people, who had ever been a teacher in the *outside world*. He had been both revered and reviled by his fellow tribesmen, but Pirdah had always been a supporter, until Terran disappeared two nights ago in the midst of a sandstorm.

"There is one clue, your Holiness…"

"Yes?"

"I had shown Terran how to build a compass the week before he vanished."

"And this compass is missing?"

Javad nodded, his unadorned head, feeling the lack of weight like an odd reminder of his sins.

"So you think the boy took his compass into the middle of a sandstorm and walked... *where?*"

"I don't know, your Holiness."

"But you think this clue, as you put it, points the finger of blame on Terran, and not your carelessness or our enemies?"

"Your Holiness, I only mention the compass because it seems unlikely he was abducted. It looks more like he planned to leave—"

"Did you provide the boy with any geography lessons?"

"Yes, your Holiness."

"And what cities or locations did he seem to find particularly interesting?"

"Your Holiness, his mind is like a sponge. Everything is interesting to him. I cannot say what stood out for him, but I know that he often asked questions about the surrounding cities, especially Tehran, Mashhad, Gorgan, Ashgabat, and Zabol."

"What kind of provisions were missing?"

"Three water flasks, a bag of bread and rice, and some goat meat."

Pirdah sighed. "These could have been stolen in his abduction. It doesn't mean he left of his own freewill. I don't believe he would leave his people behind..." Pirdah paused and adjusted his robe, as if it was chafing his neck. "Did he ever ask about his grandfather?"

"Only once, your Holiness."

"And what did you tell him?"

"Your Holiness, I told him..." Javad closed his eyes in recollection, "...that his grandfather was a colonel in the Russian army. That he had been an enemy of our people, and through our cunning, we captured him and brought him to our desert holdings. There we tortured him, but he would not die. Our elders were so impressed that they spared him for they wanted his bloodline. A year later he converted to our customs and married our chief's eldest daughter, and his father was born a few years after that."

Pirdah sat, deep in thought. "Does he know his grandfather's last name?"

"Your Holiness, I told him that we called him Nicolai Dushman, but I might have mentioned his real surname, too."

"You don't remember for certain?"

"No, your Holiness, I'm sorry."

Apart from the wind that was blowing against the flaps of the tent, the quiet of the desert hung over them like a crystal dome.

Pirdah cleared his throat and then shifted in his chair to grab a drink of water. After two loud gulps, he set down his glass and perched his fingers together, his elbows on his armrest. "I will be sad if the coals show you to be liar. I have placed all of my trust in you, to make certain that this boy would be protected. He is the *Mahdi!*" Pirdah took a deep breath and then exhaled slowly. His voice suddenly became quiet. "He was born on the night of the first storm… exactly as was prophesied."

"But your Holiness, he's not ummah—"

"He's second generation, three quarters of his blood is ours. That means he's ummah… and he was born *here*. You know better than anyone that his intellect is superior. If the Mahdi exists in our time, he is most certainly it, and you let him go… perhaps even encouraged it with your talk of cities, and building him a compass."

Pirdah looked away and clapped his hands loudly. A guard came in immediately and bowed.

"I want the Jirga assembled. We will test this man's truthfulness. Take him."

The guard grabbed Javad and pulled him to his feet, but Javad turned to Pirdah for one last word. "Your Holiness, regardless of how I fare on the coals, I assure you that I had no knowledge of Terran's plans, nor do I believe he was abducted by our enemies. I am guilty of only one thing; I wasn't able to stop him because I slept. If that is a sin, than, yes, I am a sinner. But if it is not, then I would like to help find him and return him. Please, I beg of you, let me be of help in this regard. I know him better than anyone else. Please!"

Pirdah stood up, his body stiff from sitting. He walked up to Javad appraising his countenance as only a judge can do. "One step at a time. If you pass the test, I will entertain your plea, but first the Jirga must have their say. If you are guiltless, you have nothing to worry about."

"Yes, your Holiness, but I have one fault in that I am educated, and when I walk over burning coals, my feet *will* burn. I'm not like those other men who believe in superstition. My feet will burn—"

"Then you are guilty and your burned feet will be the least of your worries. Take him." Pirdah walked back to his desk, and never looked back despite the persistent pleas of Javad.

"Someone has miscalculated the depths of my compassion." Pirdah whispered to himself.

A moment later, the sound of a throat being cleared caused Pirdah to look up from his papers.

"Your Holiness, I merely wanted to seek your advice on the Charbeli—"

"Moderate should do," Pirdah said distractedly.

"As you wish, your Holiness. Who do you want to monitor the test of innocence?"

"Moshen."

"And the schedule, your Holiness?"

"Tonight."

"Peace be upon you, your Holiness." The man walked backwards out of the tent, bowing low.

Pirdah held up his right hand, palm out. "And you as well." His voice trailed off into a whisper. His interest was on a map, and a city that he had circled. *Ashgabat would be the first leg of your journey to Moscow. Your father's blood was strong, too. I have a feeling that's where you're headed. May Allah shine down upon your journey and guide you back to us unharmed.*

*   *   *   *

The trench was twelve feet long, about two feet wide and two feet deep. The dry, splintered wood had been burning for three hours. The coals were a deep red-orange, and the high desert was painted in a twilight blue-violet. Stars were peeking through like silent, dispassionate observers. It was a cool evening, though the heat radiating off of the coals was palpable as Javad was led to the fire pit, his hands bound and his legs tethered—at the knees—to a leather rope that made it impossible to walk fast.

Moshen, one of the tribal elders, conferred with the spirits of the fire, chanting a reminder to the fire spirits to only burn if the walker is guilty. He wore a red vest over a long shirt, and beige-colored trousers, loose and wrinkled. He walked the length of the trench, chanting his religious prayers, invoking the cooperation of the fire spirits. When he finished, he turned to Pirdah and nodded.

Javad was led to the edge of the pit where his shinbones began to burn from the heat. His heart was terrorized at what loomed before him. The trench seemed impossibly long. *Do not fall. Do not fall.* It was all he could think. Falling was death. A terrible death. He took one more look at Pirdah. "Your Holiness, I am innocent. Please release me. I can help you find him. I think I know where he might have gone. Please let me find him. Isn't it a better use of my life?"

His whole body convulsed at the silence that returned, and then he felt a slight push on his lower back, guiding him to enter the *pit of pain*, as it was called. His legs began to shake uncontrollably, and he wasn't sure if he'd be able to even remain conscious. Then, suddenly, and from some inexplicable source, he had a strange desire to be part of oblivion. To be made from a substance that was preternatural. He curiously felt a sense of letting go. It was as if his mind had entered a labyrinth and his body was lost in a current that devoured him. He had no memory of actually walking over the coals. A magnetic power drew him to the other side. Hands pulled him from the pit, and he fell to the ground without feeling any pain.

He was in the grasp of something that he had never experienced— an alternate reality, sober, brilliant, inexhaustible, inviting and ancient. He felt it—not pain, not indifference, not oblivion—the stateless state. He looked up at the elders who were examining his feet, and he felt like an infant who had just been born into a bewildering night.

Under the sky's infinite roof he smiled the expression of innocence. He may have even laughed before he lost consciousness.

CHAPTER 7

Test

The citizens of Mashhad had remained inside the city, because its infrastructure—through those first months of Sunrot—remained miraculously whole. It was one of the few cities on the planet that had survived, and most of its buildings were intact.

It was only a day after Terran was discovered unconscious in the market square that his new mentor, Nouri Abbasi, began to appreciate Terran's unique gifts. Because Nouri was the only one in the school who understood Terran's native dialect, Hamid had assigned him to mentor Terran as much as his time would permit, and help Terran integrate with the student population. His initial focus was to help Terran understand English.

Most of the curriculum of the Preserves was delivered through the Internet. Instructors were more like assistants to the online experience. Nouri had been an English professor at a prestigious university in Mashhad, and was bored with his role as a "janitor of the curriculum." Terran represented a new challenge, though the communication was sometimes difficult.

On the second day of his schooling, the Curriculum Initiation Program (CIP) for twelve-year-old males was to be given to Terran. It was a timed test, administered through a remote website of the Faculty. There were twenty-two versions of the CIP, one for each age level from six to sixteen, and then one for male, and one for female. CIP 12M was the one Terran was to be given, and Nouri was setting it up on the computer while Terran watched.

"Forgive me," Terran said, "but the information inside this…this…"

"…Monitor," Nouri offered.

"This monitor… is actually being sent to me from a place on the other side of the world?"

"That's right," Nouri replied, his focus on the screen, setting up the first program and logging in.

"And when I take this test, someone on the other side of the world will see my answers and score them?"

"Yes."

"Why don't you give me the test and score me? You're right here."

"The results of the test indicate how you rank in the world, what your skills are relative to millions of other children your same age and gender. Based on that, the Faculty can provide you with a curriculum that will help you become a productive member of society."

Terran listened carefully. "So every child has a unique learning program?"

Nouri nodded his head. "Look, the CIPs come in two parts: the first is general problem solving, the second is math and language skills. I'll stay with you the whole time to help you with translations, but I won't answer any question other than to help you *understand* the question. Okay?"

Terran nodded his head.

"Are you nervous?"

"No."

"Good. Are you ready to start?"

"Is it a race?"

"You'll be timed, but it's not a race. If you run out of time, the CIP will simply move to the next question. Understood?"

"Yes," Terran replied. "If I do well, will they invite me to the ALIGN Centers?"

"Don't worry about that for now. The CIP is just to locate your current knowledge and identify your strengths and weaknesses. If you answer correctly, the next question will be harder. If you answer incorrectly, the next question will be easier. That's how it works."

Nouri rolled his chair back, and brought Terran closer to the monitor. "Now, when I click this button, the program will start. Are you ready?"

"I'm ready."

The first question came up and Terran looked at the screen expectantly, but didn't understand anything, and looked at Nouri with an expression of instant frustration.

"It's a word problem—"

"In English?"

"Yes."

Nouri quickly nodded as he read the problem silently to himself, and then translated for Terran. "Omar's father is forty-five years old. He is fifteen years older than twice Omar's age. How old is Omar?"

Without a single hesitation, Terran answered. "Fifteen."

Nouri smiled. *The first question is always hard.* He never understood why the CIP was designed this way, but the student never received feedback—right or wrong, though most students could sense the easier question on the second try.

Nouri took a quick glance at Terran, expecting him to ask if he'd gotten it right, but he was simply waiting for the next question. The questions got harder and harder. On the seventh question, he noticed a green light blinking on the lower right portion of the screen. He'd never seen it before. Already the questions were beyond Nouri's ability to answer, even with a calculator, and he was convinced that the questions were getting exponentially more advanced.

The ninth question asked the student to rearrange 28 numbers in a grid so that the total number was 558 in every direction. It took five minutes to translate the number values and once the translation was complete, no more than twenty seconds transpired and Terran had arranged the numbers to his liking and leaned back in his chair.

"Go ahead and hit 'Submit' if you think you're done," Nouri instructed, not able to concentrate well enough to know if Terran was correct in even one direction, let alone eighteen. *He's a genius.* Every cell in Nouri's body was screaming that this was not an ordinary human being. This was something else. Something else entirely. *I am in his presence!*

Terran clicked the "Submit" button. A long delay ensued. Suddenly a new screen popped-up and a webcam video came on, showing a man sitting in a high tech room with eight large monitors in the background. Below the video were the words: "Live Feed: Faculty Operations."

"Hello, can you speak English?"

The man was about fifty years old, and looked slightly uncomfortable. He had short blond hair and wore a t-shirt with strange writings on it.

"I'm Dr. Sorenson. Can you understand me?"

Nouri leaned in, his heart racing. "I am an instructor here, my name is Nouri Abbasi, and the student's name is Terran Ahmad Khan."

"Glad to meet you. Terran, is it?"

"Yes," Nouri replied. "He can't understand English. He's new to our school. This is his second day."

"If he can't understand English how did he take the test?"

"I translated for him."

"Even the numbers required translation?"

"Yes."

"I see," Dr. Sorenson said, scratching his shoulder. "He's a new student… from where?"

"We don't know precisely. He's Baluch; his tribe is from the high desert across the border in Turkmenistan."

"Sorry, I'm a mathematics teacher, never had much of an interest in geography… give me a moment."

Dr. Sorenson was typing on his keyboard and then looked into a monitor that seemed to be to his left side. "Yes, I see it now. He's from a tribe?"

"Yes, but I can't say much more than that. Usually these tribes are nomadic, so it's hard to pin them down to a city or specific location."

"You said he's been a student at your Preserve for only two days?"

"Yes."

"And before that he lived in a nomadic tribe in the desert of Turkmenistan? Do I have that right?"

"Yes, you do," Nouri said with an irrepressible smile spreading across his face. He knew to a Westerner this would seem impossible.

Terran looked at Nouri and put his hand on his arm. "I will accept their invitation."

"They haven't extended one yet," Nouri whispered.

"What did he say?" Dr. Sorenson asked.

Nouri squirmed in his chair, seeking an appropriate response. "He's new to the world of computers; he wanted to know if you were a real person."

Dr. Sorenson smiled and then quickly frowned. "Mister Abbasi, don't take this question the wrong way, but I have to ask it, did you provide any of the answers to Terran, or assist in anyway... especially the last three?"

Nouri grimaced slightly. "No, Sir. I am an English professor from Ferdowsi University. I was lost after the third question. I couldn't have provided help if I had wanted to, and as Terran is a new student, I have no relations with him."

"I see..." Dr. Sorenson said. "How long did it take him to produce the answer for question nine—after your translation was done?"

"Less than a minute... perhaps thirty seconds," Nouri replied.

Dr. Sorenson wrote a note to himself and then looked back to the camera.

"I have one more question I'd like to personally ask him, if you can translate for me. Is that okay?"

Nouri glanced at Terran, who just shrugged his shoulders wanting to know what was happening. "Yes, but let me explain to Terran. One moment please."

"Sure, take your time," Dr. Sorenson said, taking a sip from a coffee mug.

Nouri turned to Terran, who had been waiting patiently. "This man is Dr. Sorenson. He's from the Faculty, the organization behind the Preserves throughout the world. They also manage the ALIGN Centers. He wants to give you one more question, and I'll translate for you. Okay?"

Terran nodded and glanced at the monitor, smiling at Dr. Sorenson, who seemed to be fixated on a computer monitor to his side.

"Dr. Sorenson, we're ready."

"Good, I'm sending you a new program. Tell me when it opens up."

There was a 10-second delay, and then a new screen opened up, and Dr. Sorenson's video pop-up was reduced to a thumbnail in the upper-right corner of the screen.

"It's open."

"Good. What you see is a grid of boxes—twenty-four in total. Inside each box is a unique, complex design. To the right of the grid are six boxes. The goal is to choose from the six boxes which one completes t' pattern of the grid…" Dr. Sorenson's explanation trailed off to silence, as he squinted and leaned forward. "Which box is he pointing to?"

Terran had already pointed to a box as Dr. Sorenson was speaking.

"He's pointing to the third box," Nouri said.

"Ask him why he's pointing to it."

"Terran, why are you pointing to *that* box?" Nouri asked.

"It is the next box in the pattern. Isn't that what he wanted to know?"

When Nouri explained Terran's answer, Dr. Sorenson excused himself and returned a minute later with a woman who had long gray hair, tied back in a ponytail, and wore wire-rimmed glasses. She was dressed casually in jeans and a yellow sweater with elbow patches. "Mister Abbasi, this is Dr. Eleanor Sinclair, she heads-up our recruiting office for the ALIGN Centers."

Dr. Sinclair was standing, and she leaned down to look into the monitor. "I believe it's 'Good morning' in your part of the world."

"Yes, good morning, Dr. Sinclair."

"Dr. Sorenson shared with me Terran's scores, and we'd like to have him visit our ALIGN Center in Delhi, India. It's the closest one we have to your location. Does Terran have a guardian?"

"Yes, but she's not a blood relative."

"And what is her name?"

"Parto Jafari. She found the boy, here in Mashhad only a few days ago. He was unconscious. We believe he walked from the border some eighty kilometers."

"Are you certain of his age?"

"He says he is twelve."

"He looks younger…" Dr. Sinclair observed.

"He's small for his age, that's all."

"It seems to be the trend. So Terran has no parents, I assume."

"He says they died when he was young," Nouri reported.

Dr. Sinclair frowned slightly. "It's a great honor to be invited to one ʕ ͻur ALIGN Centers. Do you think his new guardian would have ⁕rns?"

⁕ think so, and I know that Terran is very excited to study ⸱stronomy. He has big plans."

"Does he speak any English?" she asked.

Nouri shook his head. He only started learning this morning—about two hours ago."

"One moment, please," Dr. Sinclair asked, holding up her hand. The video screen went black with a message: *Please Hold.* Terran immediately turned to Nouri. "What did they say? I heard her say Delhi, India. Is that where they have an ALIGN Center? Is that where they want me to go?"

Nouri couldn't hold back his smile. "They have invited you!"

Terran put his arms up in jubilation. "When do I go?"

"I don't know—"

The video turned on again, and Dr. Sinclair was now sitting in front of the monitor, and Dr. Sorenson sat behind her and to her right. "Mister Abbasi, we'll have to get back to you on the specific arrangements, but we believe we could find a position for you in our ALIGN Center in Delhi, if you would like to accompany Terran. I know these decisions take—"

"Yes, I would love to," Nouri interrupted, trying to control his excitement, but not doing particularly well. Terran's eyes were lit up as Nouri glanced at him.

"You have no attachments there? Family, spouse, children—"

Nouri was shaking his head back and forth, smiling. "No attachments."

"Great. Then we'll see to your travel arrangements, and contact your Director, Hamid Mokri, and explain our plans. We want his support for this, so for now, we would ask that you keep our conversation private, because we'd like to secure his cooperation in our own way. Is that acceptable Mister Abbasi?"

"Yes, yes, of course."

"How soon could you be ready to travel?"

Nouri stole a quick peek at Terran. "Tomorrow?"

Dr. Sinclair smiled. "We'll need at least a week to arrange everything, Mister Abbasi, but we'll keep you posted through Mister Mokri."

Nouri leaned forward, eagerness written on his face. "When will ⋅ talk with him?"

"Give us twenty-four hours."

"Okay…"

"Mr. Abbasi?"

"Yes?"

"Please convey our excitement to Terran that he'll be joining us. We'll make sure that he has access to our finest physicists and astronomers. And Mr. Abbasi?"

"Yes?"

"Do take good care of him, and let us know if you need anything. My personal email is being sent to your file right now." Dr. Sorenson was busy typing on a keyboard behind her, and looked up momentarily to the camera and smiled faintly.

"I will see to it, Dr. Sinclair."

"Very good. Nice to meet you, and we wish you a very pleasant day."

"Thank you—you, too."

The video screen went blank, and Nouri let out a long sigh of relief, and turned his chair to face Terran who was still smiling expectantly.

"When?" Terran asked, holding his arms out, palms up.

"Soon, very soon… perhaps a week or so," Nouri replied. "And I will be going with you!"

Terran hugged Nouri with joy. It was the best Nouri had felt in thirteen years. Delhi was far away, but he had wanted a new start for so long. His wife had died from pneumonia shortly after the Sunrot, after the first big storms assailed Mashhad. The memory had settled deep in him as she had faded from his life in three dark days while riots raged outside his home, and bullets whined their chorus of fear. That was his deepest decent into hell, and now, a strange boy had entered his life and brought him a ladder from which he could ascend, and he hoped, reclaim a debt that life had taken from him.

CHAPTER 8

Journey

The main headquarters for the Faculty was in a hardened facility that had been part of the National Security Agency (NSA) before the Sunrot. It was based in Denver, Colorado. The local citizens decided to keep the name Denver even though there was some pressure from Stanton's office to change it. The Faculty headquarters were very modern, utilizing the finest computer network that remained on earth.

Often referred to by its senior directors as *schizoid*, Faculty Headquarters were completely destroyed on the outside and had never been cleaned up—the task simply too daunting. However, a quarter mile underneath the surface, where the crown jewels of the NSA's computer network had been stored, the offices were mostly intact. When visitors came to the compound, they followed a carefully constructed path through debris piles to what most would perceive as a bomb shelter, guarded by a small, but lethal unit of armed guards who patrolled the vicinity.

It had taken five years to restore the network, but once it was completed, it was one of Trevor Stanton's first decisions to reengineer the NSA facility in Denver to become the Faculty, a global educational system.

With Josh Sinclair heading the Faculty, his older sister, Eleanor, was immediately put in charge of recruiting the finest minds wherever they might be. In year twelve, she had assembled, with her team of nearly seventy recruiters, the brightest and most capable students from across the world. It was the Greater Nation's global brain trust.

Eleanor and her team had developed the CIP format. It had become the primary tool through which the world's best minds were funneled into the six ALIGN Centers. The goal of the ALIGN Centers was simple: build a communication and learning channel between the most experienced technical and scientific minds and the best students on the planet—wherever they lived.

The stated goals of this massive effort were threefold:

1. Restore humanity's technology for peaceful purposes
2. Protect earth's limited resources for the use and betterment of the surviving populations, and
3. Improve the way of life for all members of the Greater Nation

Dr. Eleanor Sinclair and Dr. Liam Sorenson walked briskly down a wide, windowless hallway, entered her office, and went directly to her desk. Eleanor clicked her keyboard and waited, watching the monitor screen with interest. "It's late out East, he may not be available."

Suddenly the screen came up, and a man, sitting gloomily in a chair, stared back at them. His brown, uncombed hair seemed suitably matched to his wrinkled t-shirt and tired expression. "Hi, Sis."

"Hi, Josh, I hope we didn't wake you."

He shook his head. "Whatever sleep I get these days, it's never enough, so don't worry about it. It's good to see you. Who's that behind you?"

"Liam Sorenson—my little brother, Josh Sinclair." Eleanor motioned with her arms as if they were in the same room.

"An honor to meet you, Sir," Liam said with a light nod.

"Just call me, Josh. It's good to meet you, too." Josh sat up a bit straighter in his chair. "So what's the reason for your call?"

Eleanor glanced at her associate, cleared her throat and sat down in her chair. "Remember our discussions that the CIP was biased because it was in English?"

"...Yes..." Josh said, looking a bit perplexed and curious at the same time.

"We just found a twelve-year-old boy who doesn't speak a word of English, and using a translator, was able to finish L9 in record time. Liam administered L10, and the boy completed it before he finished explaining it to the boy's translator."

Josh leaned forward. "How's that possible?"

"We don't know."

"And where is this boy now?"

"In Mashhad, Iran, at one of our Preserves—"

"Today was only his second day there," Liam added.

"And where did this boy come from?" Josh asked.

"We don't know exactly," Eleanor replied. "But somewhere in the deserts of Turkmenistan. He's from a tribe—the Baluch—just wandered off... a woman found him unconscious in a Mashhad market, and brought him to our Preserve. Not much else is known about him."

"What's his name?"

"Terran Khan."

"So what's your plan?"

"We'll have his translator and the boy transported to our ALIGN Center in Delhi. I'll need your authorization to transport them from Mashhad to Delhi."

"What about guardians?" Josh asked.

"He doesn't have any."

"And his tribe?"

"They're not members of GN."

"You checked?"

"Yes."

"Okay, I'll send you my authorization code. Have you uploaded a Project File yet?"

"No, I'll do that right after our call."

Josh swept his hand through his tousled hair. "All friendly in Mashhad?"

"We haven't spoken with the Preserve Director yet, but we'll make it worth his while to assist us."

"So once the boy gets to Delhi, then what?" Josh asked.

"We'll bring him here."

"You'll need authorization for that, too."

"I know."

"Let's leave him in Delhi for a while and just make sure he's the real deal. Okay?"

"Oh, he's the real deal," Liam said, mostly to himself.

"Josh," Eleanor said, "only two students have ever gotten to L7 with perfect scores in the allotted time, and they both knew English. No one has ever gotten to L10. When we show an L10 question to our brightest physicists, most will get it right, but they need time to work it out. This boy solved it instantly. Liam saw it."

"And again, I have to ask…. how is that possible? How is it possible that the intellect of an uneducated twelve-year-old boy—who's only known the chaos of Sunrot—trumps our highest educated scientists? It makes no sense."

"You think he cheated?" Eleanor asked.

"I think it's possible… or maybe the translator—"

"Sir, I understand your suspicion," Liam interrupted, "but I saw him and his translator, and I believe his intellect is one in a billion… possibly greater. The CIP is designed to find clear intellects whether they're polished by an educational system or not. We need to bring this boy here as soon as we can. We need to have him surrounded by our best minds—teach him our most advanced knowledge, and then we can see what he'll do with it. He might be our best hope for recovery."

Eleanor turned around to look at Liam. "So you think we should just bring him here directly?"

"I do," Liam said, his response punctuated with a sharp head nod.

Josh drummed his fingers on his desk. "How soon can you get him to Delhi?"

"I'm not sure," Eleanor said. "I need more time to research it."

"Okay, well, it's an exciting development," Josh said. "Let our ALIGN Center director in Delhi know what's coming so he can be prepared. Let the boy stay there a minimum of a week while we arrange transport to Denver. I assume a week will be sufficient for them to assess his skills and capacities…"

"It'll only take a few minutes if they know what to ask, in my opinion," Liam said.

"Okay, so we're agreed?" Josh said, ignoring Liam's remark.

Eleanor and Liam replied in chorus. "We're agreed."

"Excellent. I'm off to bed, unless there's anything else?"

"Any limits on our offer to our Mashhad Director?"

"Start low, he'll want to negotiate… but, no, there're no limits."

"Okay, thanks, Josh."

"All my love, and tell that nephew of mine to email me."

"Will do."

"And Dr. Sorenson?"

"Yes?"

"Good job identifying this boy. I hope he's everything you think he is."

"Thank you, Sir. I'm sure he'll be a great asset for our work."

"Goodnight."

"Goodnight."

The computer monitor suddenly went blank, and the room was quiet for a moment.

Eleanor tapped some keys on her keyboard and then leaned back in her chair. "I just sent you the email for Hamid Mokri. Set up a meeting so we can talk as soon as possible. I'll tackle Emergency Services and requisition a Support Travel Convoy from Mashhad to Delhi—which should be an interesting conversation."

"Okay," Liam said. "Should I hint at our agenda?"

"No, just tell him it's urgent and we need to speak immediately. You know where to find me, and I don't care what time it is."

Liam headed for the door. "I'll keep you posted."

Eleanor turned her attention to her computer monitor and opened up a secure channel. She typed one word: *Emergency*, and hit "Enter."

She leaned back and waited for the connection. She checked her coffee cup, but she saw that the coffee she had remaining was cold and stale. She took off her glasses and rubbed her eyes.

"This is Carol Langley, Badge ID 100892, how can I help you?"

An elderly woman, in her late sixties, was sitting in front of her computer with a headphone set, trying to look alert and friendly. She had on a blue blouse with frayed sleeves.

"Hi Carol, this is Eleanor Sinclair, Director of Recruiting at Faculty Headquarters in Denver. I have an emergency requirement to escort two GN citizens from Mashhad, Iran to Delhi, India. Is this something you can help me with?"

"What are the requirements?" Carol asked, while typing into her computer.

"First, any chance of an airlift?"

"Not in that part of the world."

Eleanor looked down at her desk and saw some of her scribbled notes. "I think we'll need armed personnel, full supplies, three vehicles, gas truck, mechanic, spare parts, and full side-support on call."

Carol was typing, and then stopped and looked up at the camera. "And your timetable?"

"As soon as possible."

"Cargo is two people and nothing else?" Carol asked.

"That's correct."

"Give me one moment, Ms. Sinclair, while I check availability of resources. Do you have an authorization code?"

"My brother, Josh Sinclair, will be sending me one, I don't have it yet. This situation developed within the past hour." Eleanor tried to sound casual about having a brother who controlled the world's educational system, but she knew it was a good trump card to any resistance.

"Okay, please hold one moment while I make an initial assessment of our resources in the target arena."

The screen went blank and a "Please Hold" message faded in, replacing Carol's face and her surrounding cubicle.

Two minutes later the screen opened up again, and Carol and a new person were smiling back at Eleanor. "Ms. Sinclair, this is Mister Andrews. He has some questions."

"Good evening, Ms. Sinclair, I'm the Director of ES for the Middle East Region. Carol mentioned your requirements, and I must say we've never had any experience in extracting anyone from Mashhad... so... our resources are slim to none. Realistically, I think even with a Level One authorization code... we're... we're looking at three weeks to organize an extraction, especially of the scale you're talking about."

Eleanor let the silence fill the room and then let out a long breath. "Is that what you'll tell President Stanton when he calls you?"

Mr. Andrews glanced at Carol with a subtle frown. "I didn't know the requisition was from his office."

"It isn't, but when you tell me it'll take three weeks, I'll bring this project to his attention and then it *will* come from his office, I assure you."

"Can you tell me what the cargo is?" Mr. Andrews asked.

"A young boy and a man. That's all."

"Is the cargo dangerous?"

"No."

"You realize that the only way to travel that part of the world is through truck... special trucks and personnel. The roads are still dreadful in Pakistan. It's a dangerous journey... about fifteen hundred miles on roads that will barely support more than—"

"What about choppers?" Eleanor interrupted.

"We have none in that vicinity."

"None?"

"Not at our disposal."

"This is a top priority mission for the GN, and you're telling me that we can't find one fucking helicopter to fly to Mashhad?"

Mr. Andrews suddenly looked uncomfortable, and then forced a smile. "We'll do our best, but lack of parts, mechanics... there's nothing within a thousand miles that would enable an airlift. I think a truck convoy is our best bet, but even with President Stanton's authorization, it'll still take a week, maybe two, to organize a team. I'm sorry, but I'm just trying to be realistic. Our resources in that area are limited."

"What happened to all of our military installations in Afghanistan?"

Mr. Andrews was a large man. Not fat, just large like an old-world farmer with thick sausage-like fingers, huge forearms, burly shoulders, and wide neck. His short-cropped hair was solid black, and he had a thin mustache that seemed oddly delicate on his otherwise stout frame. He leaned forward, propping his elbow on the tabletop, and nervously twitching his pen back and forth. "Look, I'm just speaking off the top of my head right now, so you can't hold me to this, but we have some resources in Kandahar that I might be able to acquire... but I'd need President Stanton's authorization."

"Choppers?"

"I'm not sure. I'll check and get back to you. It's still a five hundred mile journey from Mashhad to Kandahar, but we can skirt the mountains, and in that part of the journey, the roads are passable. I think we'd want a larger convoy though."

"How much larger?"

"I'd recommend a small team of long-range sharp shooters, four

Humvees, two supply trucks, and a minimum of ten armed guards. We might be able to deploy from Kandahar and send our convoy to Mashhad and do a round trip."

"And from there? What?"

"Ideally, we'd try and get a Chinook A-47. There's no landing strip in Delhi, and the roads from Kandahar to Delhi... like I said, it's too treacherous to try. With a light payload, a Chinook could make it to Delhi. We don't need a landing strip, we'd just land it at your destination—which is what?"

"The ALIGN Center just outside of Delhi."

"Can you send me those coordinates?"

"Yes, of course. How long before you'll know?"

"We're night shifters; by the time you get up tomorrow, we'll know."

Eleanor smiled. "I'm an early riser."

"I'll send you the update myself, but I can't guarantee this plan will work."

"Do your best to make it happen," Eleanor said. "I'm sure the entire GN will appreciate your efforts."

"Tell me, Ms. Sinclair, what's so special about these two people that President Stanton's involved?"

Eleanor leaned back in her chair. "The most important resource we need right now—extraordinary intelligence."

"I see. Okay, we'll do everything we can, and I'll send you a report status in the next three to four hours."

"Excellent. Thank you for your help, Mister Andrews."

"You're welcome. Have a good night."

"You, too."

The call came to an abrupt end. Eleanor felt relieved that the meeting had gone as well as it had. Her world was like living in molasses—everything moved slowly. Every strategy and tactic was thwarted by the reality of an apocalyptic Sunrot. Nothing was easy. Time seemed the enemy in every project, and she hated it.

CHAPTER 9

A Shepherd

Pirdah wiped his mouth and the edges of his beard with a cloth napkin. The lamb was very good. He had the company of three elders, and was enjoying a hearty lunch when a young guard entered his tent and bowed. "Your Holiness, a man has arrived with news he claims is vital to you."

"When we're done, show him in," Pirdah said, his tone dismissive.

"Your Holiness, I told him that you should not be disturbed, but he said it's about the boy, Terran Khan. He claims to know—"

Pirdah thrust his right hand up, the guard instantly stopped talking. Pirdah stood to his feet. "My friends, I will only be a minute, please, continue your meal."

Pirdah followed the guard out of the tent and across the courtyard to a small tent where visitors waited to gain an audience with Pirdah. He motioned to the guard to wait outside, and entered the tent. Immediately a man fell to his knees and touched Pirdah's feet, repeating over and over again. "I come in servitude of Allah, Your Holiness."

"Please, stand, what is your name?"

"Your Holiness, I am Omid Khadem. I am a shepherd… a humble man of earth."

"And what news do you bring me?"

Omid wore a tattered white shirt and tan colored pants. His turban was also white, though it was stained from sweat at its base. He had a nervous manner, but Pirdah was used to the uneasiness he aroused in men. Omid bit his lip. "Your Holiness, two men approached me very early this morning and asked me for water. They were travelers. I had never seen them before. I told them I had only one flask of water, and they could only have a small sip. When I asked them where they were going, they said they were shooters. My curiosity, your Holiness, was great… though I was afraid of them when I learned of their trade. I asked them why they were walking in the direction of Mashhad, and they said they had been recruited to escort a boy and a man to Kandahar. They were going to be rich for their services, and they bragged that they could pay me twenty toman for my flask of water—"

"Why do you think the boy they refer to is Terran Khan?"

"Your Holiness, they said the boy was Baluch. Who else could it be?"

Pirdah folded his arms across his chest. "They were going to Mashhad, you're sure?"

"Yes, your Holiness." The man stared into the chest of the revered spiritual leader, his voice clear, without a hint of hesitation or doubt.

Pirdah reached out with his arms and placed them on the shepherd's shoulders. "Whosoever belongs to Allah; all his gifts are of grace. Do you belong to Allah?" Pirdah stared into the man's eyes unflinchingly.

"I do, your Holiness," the shepherd nodded, looking down at his feet.

Pirdah stepped back and stroked his beard for a moment. "Is there anything else you can tell me?"

Omid closed his eyes and slowly shook his head. "No, your Holiness." When he reopened his eyes, he was careful to avoid eye contact with Pirdah.

"Did these men say when they were going to escort this boy to Kandahar or why?"

"No, your Holiness."

"Did they mention anything as to why this boy had a companion?"

"Only that he had one… I think they referred to him as the boy's teacher. They were both being escorted to Kandahar."

Pirdah sighed and looked at the young shepherd. "Is there anything I can do for you?"

Omid smiled broadly in a sudden flash, and then quickly composed himself. "Only a blessing, your Holiness."

Pirdah narrowed his eyes, softened his tone and walked clockwise around Omid as he spoke. "Life is a constant process of striving. Striving for the one thing that matters: *Light*. *Light* in its purest state. Let that be your single effort—to find light in its purest state and to hold it *here*." Pirdah reached out and touched the man's chest. "You have my blessings, son. Go now, and be this light to all you meet."

Omid knelt again and touched Pirdah's feet, and then backed away out of the tent in silence.

Pirdah called the guard and whispered three words while his mind was deep in thought. "Bring Javad here."

CHAPTER 10

Just in Time

Hamid was startled by the message. A Director from Faculty Headquarters wanted to meet with him? His mind turned to a dozen possibilities—all of them undesirable. The English scores of his students were lagging. Student enrollment was trending down. His budget request was too high due to shipping and installation costs associated with the Preserve's technology infrastructure. Perhaps he was getting too old?

When he'd gotten the invitation from Dr. Sorenson, he immediately set the time to meet for noon. It would give him a chance to bathe and change into his best shirt, and groom himself so he could look deserving of his post. Hamid had been an assistant dean at the University of Tehran before Sunrot. His scholarly achievements had provided him access to the Faculty when it was first organizing its Middle East initiatives.

Tehran had been hit hard by the Sunrot, but Hamid had survived, though his family was less fortunate, suffering from a wind storm that all but obliterated vast portions of Tehran, even burying large portions of the city. Hamid had been at the University when the storm hit, and managed to hide in a bomb shelter with a collection of teachers, administrators, and even a few students. They were trapped there for two miserable weeks, struggling to dig their way out through the debris.

There were rumors that Mashhad had been spared the worst of the storms, so a Caravan of Survivors walked, rode camels, and even managed to find a few working vehicles, and together—about two-thousand desperate people—clawed and scratched their way to Mashhad.

I lived through the Caravan of Survivors, I can manage this meeting just fine, he thought to himself as he sat down at his computer and waited for the video transmission to start. One minute after the appointed hour, the video screen opened up automatically, and a woman, who was writing something at a desk, looked up at the camera and smiled. "You must be Hamid Mokri? I'm Eleanor Sinclair, Director of Recruiting at the Faculty Headquarters. Good afternoon."

"Good afternoon…"

"How are you today?"

"A little nervous, to be honest."

"Ah, well, this call, Hamid, is actually good news, so please relax, you have no reason to be nervous, I can assure you."

Hamid smiled and a curious expression formed on his lined face as he adjusted his spectacles. "Then why *are* you calling, ma'am?"

Eleanor set her pencil down and looked directly into the camera. "You have a new student by the name of Terran Khan. Earlier this morning he took our CIP test, and did so well, that we've extended an invitation to him to come to our ALIGN Center in Delhi. I'm calling you to inform you of this invitation and would like your support to transfer him to our oversight, and prepare him for his trip."

Hamid blinked several times, his eyes squinting in disbelief. He glanced at the footer of the video transmission. It said: *Live Feed: Faculty HQ—Eleanor Sinclair.* It was really happening. It was his first student who had been invited to an ALIGN Center.

"But he can't even speak English!" Hamid blurted out.

"We understand. A teacher helped him, a… Nouri Abbasi. We'd like him to accompany the boy to Delhi."

"You want my teacher to transfer, too? For how long a period?"

"Only as long as it takes the boy to learn English."

"That could be many months, even if he's as smart as you think he is."

"Is it so hard to replace Mister Abbasi?" Eleanor asked, tilting her head slightly.

"English teachers with his credentials are non-existent in Mashhad… I… I don't have any applicants with his expertise."

"Hamid, I'm sure you understand that it's not only that he's a good English teacher, but he knows the language of the boy, Terran Khan. We have other English teachers in Delhi, but none of them knows Baluch. We could do an exchange perhaps?"

"I have a very limited budget… I can't afford to bring in replacement teachers, especially from as far away as Delhi—"

Eleanor chuckled. "We weren't expecting you to undertake those costs. The Faculty will take care of everything. We will even include a small bonus for you."

"A bonus?"

"Yes, in gold."

"What exactly are the arrangements?" Hamid asked, trying to sound casual.

"The details aren't clear at this time," Eleanor began, "but we know that Terran Khan and Nouri Abbasi will be escorted to Kandahar, and from there, transported to Delhi. We need you to make arrangements with the boy's guardian, who is a brand new relation, I understand. Make sure she feels good about Terran's move to Delhi. We think the transportation arrangements will take a week or two to coordinate, but they're already in motion."

"And the replacement teacher for Mister Abbasi?"

"Yes, well… we don't have anyone in mind at this exact moment, but this whole thing just happened a few hours ago. We'll need a week, maybe more, to find a replacement, but don't worry, we'll find one."

"Have you already told them?" Hamid asked.

"The boy and Mister Abbasi?"

"Yes," Hamid said.

"We extended the invitation only a few hours ago, and they both seemed quite pleased."

There was an awkward pause, and Eleanor leaned a little closer to the camera. "Hamid, were you going to say something?"

"I don't really care about your gold," he whispered. "I want to teach again."

"But you're a good administrator. The Mashhad Preserve is successful—maybe its English scores could be better, but your mathematics scores are first rate—"

"I want to be with students. Not sit in an empty office and push papers around all day."

"Okay, we can set up a transition plan and move you into teaching. It might take a while, but if you can be patient, and help us in this situation with Terran, we'll figure something out. Okay, Hamid?" Eleanor smiled warmly, hoping she was done with negotiations, but she sensed a quiet melancholy in Hamid.

"Okay," Hamid nodded slowly. "How long would a transition like this take?"

"Do you want to stay at your Preserve?"

"I want to teach in Riyadh... I have relatives there."

"Eleanor typed on her keyboard for a moment. "We have three Preserves in Riyadh. We can arrange that. As for time, it would take us a few months to make all of the arrangements, but if that's want you want, we'll make it happen."

Hamid smiled broadly, nodding his head. "This is no dream?"

Eleanor returned his smile. "No dream."

Hamid brushed his eyes quickly, wiping away some tears. "I'm sorry, I'm an emotional man... this is the best thing to happen to me in..." he looked down at his hands, "for a very long time. Thank you. Thank you very much for your help."

Eleanor took it all in, feeling the emotion of Hamid some 7,000 miles away, and marveling at how the connection between two strangers with a small video window could be so powerful.

Hamid took a deep breath of composure, and looked directly into the camera. "What do you need me to do?"

"Talk with the boy's guardian and make sure she's okay with his move. We want her to be supportive. Okay?"

"Okay."

"Let her know that Terran will have the best education possible. He has a special intellect, and we intend to develop it to its best capacity. Let her know this. Okay?"

Hamid nodded.

"I'll send you a form for both you and his guardian to sign. It's just a formality, but we take the transfer of a child seriously, especially when it's out of the country, and we need to have the proper papers signed. Okay?"

"Yes... yes, I understand."

"I'll be in touch on the timetable when I know more about the details—"

"What about my replacement teacher and my transfer to Riyadh?"

"Yes, we'll keep you informed about those as well. I'll assign a project coordinator on your transfer, and I'll have them set up all the details and keep you informed. Be patient, Hamid, it'll take some time to arrange it, but you have my word, it will be done."

"I believe you."

"Good. Any other questions?" Eleanor asked.

Hamid slowly shook his head. "No, I think I understand what I need to do. I'll wait for the papers and talk with his guardian—"

"Hamid, we can help you if you get any resistance. I'm sending you my personal email address right now, so please keep me posted if you need anything, anything at all. Okay?"

"Okay…"

"Excellent, thank you, Hamid. We'll be in touch very soon."

"Yes, thank you, too." Hamid said as the video window disappeared.

Did that really happen? He asked himself in the silence of his office. Does every administrator of a Preserve get a personal call from a Faculty Director when they find a candidate for one of their ALIGN Centers? Do they get job transfers? He was never a fan of the Greater Nation, but here, finally, was proof—at a personal level—that there was tangible value in being a member. A smile spread across his face as he spun the copper wedding band on his finger. The darkening mirrors that had crowded around him, stubborn and miserly—suddenly offered a truce. A new hope had entered him, and it had come just in time. Just in time.

CHAPTER 11

Prophecy

Javad was third in a small caravan of four camels, winding its way to Mashhad. Camels were one of the rarest animals on earth, and in the far eastern region of Iran in which the Baluch lived, after water, and possibly lamb meat, camels were considered the greatest asset.

The day was still breaking. The sun was minutes from peeking over the sand dunes that stretched in every direction. The red haze behind them cast the sand dunes a blood red color even while the stars gleamed in the highest parts of the sky.

There were twelve men and four camels—three of which were rotation camels, which meant that eleven men would rotate between walking and riding. The lead camel was ridden by the tribe's equivalent of a sheriff, Moshad Adali, and his camel was never shared. Moshad was a powerful man among the Baluch tribe of eastern Iran. He was known to be loyal and cunning, fair and ruthless, peaceful and vengeful, and which of his traits you invoked was an outcome of your fastidious or derelict attention to the behaviors of agreeability and submissiveness.

Any tribal member charged with criminal action, had come to know the vengeful and ruthless side of Moshad's personality. Those persons were rare in the Baluch tribe—in part, because of his reputation. Also, because the tribe's culture was to provide for all. Everyone worked for the good of everyone else, or they were ostracized, and that was tantamount to a death sentence.

Moshad had hand-picked ten of his best fighters—their goal was to find and return Terran to his tribe. Javad would simply lend his expertise to find Terran, and once found, assure him that he would be much better off with his own people than with infidels, who, once they understood Terran's true purpose, would surely kill him. It was the prophecy, and everyone within the Baluch tribe knew this prophecy by heart. It was taught at an early age and most within the tribe believed that Terran was the Mahdi. If Pirdah said it, that was enough. Those who wavered or were uncertain of his stature as Mahdi were doubtful only because his bloodline was not pure.

The journey to Mashhad was extremely difficult. The sand dunes were steep and seemingly unending.

How did Terran cross this on foot? Javad thought. As soon as he had been summoned to Pirdah's tent, he knew Terran was alive. He had felt it, but now that they were traveling the path to Mashhad, he doubted it was possible, especially in a sand storm at night. When Pirdah told him Omid's story, his heart had initially sunk. *He already had a new teacher? They recognized his brilliance.*

Javad knew that Terran's intellect was unusual in every dimension that intelligence could be measured. The way Terran could ask questions that would so quickly exhaust Javad of his own knowledge. If Terran went to Mashhad, it was to go to school. He knew that would be the only place to find him.

"Why would he go *there?*" Pirdah had asked him. "Are you not his teacher? Perhaps he finds you dull?"

Javad had tried not to take offense, but it was difficult. "I am one man… he needs… variety. More expertise in subjects I have not mastered."

"But if he chose Mashhad," Pirdah insisted, "why would they be transferring him to Kandahar—in only a few days? The only possible explanation is that these travelers lied or were misinformed."

"Your Holiness, if Terran made it to Mashhad, and entered a school there, if they had only one student who could understand our dialect—well enough to communicate, it would not take them long to see his intellect and feel his spirit. He is the Mahdi."

"Yes, yes, I know of your certainties," Pirdah replied. "I share them, but if he falls into the hands of the infidels, they will kill him. They will surely kill him just as the prophecy warned. We must find him, return him to his people, and shelter him until his mission is properly revealed, and all those who are here to help him are prepared."

Pirdah paused briefly and stroked his long white beard while his arms were partially folded across his chest. "I'm sending Moshad to find and return him. I want you to go with him. When they find Terran, assuming he's there, he'll need your comfort and support. You must convince him that this is in his best interest—"

"Your Holiness, what if he refuses—"

"He can't refuse!"

"But what if he does? Are you suggesting we'll *force* him to return?"

"What else can we do, Javad? He is the Mahdi. We must protect him… it's for his own good. He has no experience in the world of the infidel, he has no idea what evil lurks there. He is but a child. We *must* not allow him to be tainted… either by their supposed education, culture or seditious ways. *You must convince him!*"

Pirdah had sat down hard after he spoke, slumping in his chair with an anxious look. "Can you do that for me?"

"Your Holiness, every cell in my body wants him back. I will do everything in my power to convince him, but if he sees Moshad, he will know we are prepared to force him to return. I want to speak with him alone first—"

"Your wish is granted. Moshad will do nothing unless you fail." Pirdah waved his right hand, as if it were a trifling request, and then pointed his index finger squarely at Javad, and bore into his eyes. "But you must listen to Terran and find out what it is he desires to achieve by running away from us. He is the Mahdi; his reasons need to be heard. Once you understand, you must convince him that we will provide whatever it is he wants, and the infidels will not. They will only use him for their own purposes, and we both know what the prophecy says on that subject."

"I understand, Your Holiness. Your words are wise and proper. Allah shines in you, and in this light, I see."

Pirdah nodded gently and smiled. "You must be successful. There is no other way. We have tribes all over the sacred lands that are ready to unite, but he is too young, and if he falls prey to the infidels, they will never follow him. His mission will be doomed before it even starts. This is precisely what Shaitan desires. If I were in better health, I would descend into Mashhad myself. I send you in my stead. Do not disappoint me."

Javad recalled the words as they echoed in his mind, as the image of Pirdah's index finger wagged back and forth. Javad knew that he had to persuade Terran that the infidels would only use him for their own purposes. They could not be trusted. He rehearsed his pleas to Terran and hoped they would be compelling enough to convince him, because the alternative was to forcibly abduct him and return him against his will. Terran was the Mahdi, and anyone who would go against his will…

Javad tried not to think about it.

Suddenly the first rays of the sun lit the sand dunes, turning them from red to gold in a single instant like an all-powerful alchemist.

CHAPTER 12

Negotiation

Dorri looked up and smiled. "They're called checkers, and they have to be placed like this."

Terran watched as she ordered the checkers in neat columns over the triangles. Backgammon was a very popular game throughout the Middle East, and even in Terran's tribe, it was a staple of leisure time. It was the perfect blend of strategy and chance, but very few would play him, because the result was that they lost. Chance seemed to play a weak hand whenever Terran commanded the board, and so he was seldom invited to play unless his mentor, Javad, would indulge him.

Terran liked Dorri. She was unaffected by him. Her large, shining eyes played beneath thick eyelashes, and her dark curly brown hair, defiant of any hejab, bobbed uncontrollably as she moved her head. After the Sunrot, the dress code in Iran dissipated into the reality of survival. No one cared, nor was there anyone left to police the incompliant—like Dorri's mother, Parto. But now, the only dress code was in the Preserves, and Dorri was too young to attend.

Parto, a single mother, tended a communal garden and worked on an irrigation system that was being developed in the outskirts of Mashhad. She lived in the outline of womanly archetypes—possessed of an intuitive imprecision that, at its core, was the single thought that God was deceiving her. Her husband had been killed during the second day of the Three Day Storm, as he was trying to save an elderly neighbor who had been trapped underneath a collapsed roof. As he had been clearing a path, following the moans of their neighbor, the rest of the roof fell on him. In the chaos that surrounded the storm, Parto ached for her husband, but didn't know where he was. His body was found a week later, buried under cream-colored, sundried bricks.

His death had unleashed a rage in Parto, and everything she had been taught, to honor the Shahadah and proclaim a life of a good

Muslim, had vanished in that storm. It was as if the Three Day Storm had unleashed every memory of injustice and indignation she had encountered growing up in Mashhad as a beautiful girl, teenager, and woman. Now Allah, and even to some degree, Muhammad, were the targets of her rage. But unlike the storm, her rage persisted well beyond the three days.

Parto's eyes were thin, but full of meaning. They were quick and intelligent eyes, yet there was a tension in them that seemed incapable of relaxing. She looked at Nouri and Hamid, wondering why they had come to her home.

"More tea?" she asked.

"No, no, this is fine," Hamid replied, leaning back against the wall.

They sat on the floor atop red cushions that had been salvaged from a sofa. Parto lived with her father, two uncles, and an aunt from her mother's side. It was her father's home, and he had allowed them to use the rooftop patio to meet. Their home was a two-story vertical apartment, with small rooms and very little furniture. It had a rickety wrought-iron staircase on the outside that went to the roof where there was an outside patio that overlooked Mashhad. Nouri, Hamid and Parto were sitting together. Terran and Dorri were on the other side of the patio playing backgammon on the floor.

Parto felt a change from Hamid, an agenda of some kind that was waiting to unfurl.

"So, why don't you tell me why you stopped by," Parto asked, turning to Nouri.

Nouri looked to Hamid, and stayed quiet.

"What is it?" Parto asked.

"Terran took a test yesterday," Hamid began, clearing his throat, "and did so well that the Faculty headquarters invited him to one of their ALIGN Centers in Delhi. It is a great honor."

"Delhi?" Parto said, her face wincing.

"It's the closest one," Hamid said.

"It's two thousand kilometers away... how will he get there?"

"The Faculty has resources, they're arranging everything."

"And how soon?"

Hamid glanced in Terran's direction. "We don't really know. Maybe a week, maybe three."

"He's just a boy. He doesn't speak *our* language let alone Hindi or English—"

"Nouri will go with him," Hamid said, raising his hand as if to suggest they lower their voices.

A long pause ensued, and Hamid looked nervously between Nouri and Parto.

"I will take good care of him," Nouri offered. "I believe he is very special. His mind... it's... it's brilliant... it's—"

Parto waved her hands and Nouri stopped mid-sentence. "So they will just take him and use him as they desire? I have no say in this?"

"Parto, you found him only four days ago, you're not his guardian—"

"Then who is?" Parto shot back, her eyes glaring. "Maybe I'm not his legal guardian, but I did find him, carried him to your school, took him to the doctor, and stayed with him overnight to make sure he would be okay. I'm the closest thing he has to a guardian, and just because it's only been four days, doesn't mean he isn't important to us."

Parto wrapped her arms around her legs and rested her chin between her knees, and looked keenly at Terran and Dorri as they played backgammon. "Dorri wanted a brother, and Terran's the closest thing we have..."

Nouri reached out and touched Parto's forearm. "*He* wants this."

"Then let him tell me," Parto whispered.

Hamid let out a sigh, and then leaned in, keeping his voice low. "The boy needs what we can't provide. The Director of Recruiting at Faculty headquarters called me—she's the sister of the man who manages the Faculty."

"So?"

"Don't you see, if she called, they must believe that Terran holds great promise. She said they would make sure he has access to their best teachers. Their very best."

"Why are you trying so hard to persuade me?"

"Yes, well, the Director of Recruiting—Eleanor Sinclair—asked me to meet with you and get your approval."

"Why?"

"Because he's a minor, and you're the closest thing he has to a guardian. They just want to be considerate—"

"I don't believe you."

"We all want the same for Terran," Nouri offered. "He might go on to become a great scientist or inventor, and bring all of us honor."

"And what of his home?" Parto protested. "He came from somewhere. He didn't just wander out of the desert from a sand dune. What about *his* people? Shouldn't their permission be sought?"

Hamid removed his glasses and rubbed his eyes. "You know his people are Old Schoolers. The GN won't bother with them. The boy ran away from them. He knew he needed teachers they couldn't provide. He risked his life to come here. The Faculty discovered him—they see his promise. The boy's destiny can't be fulfilled as a simple shepherd."

Hamid put his glasses back on and took out a contract, passing it to Parto.

"What's this?"

"A release form for your signature."

Parto looked at it briefly, and eyed Hamid with suspicion. "Do they *want* my permission to move Terran to Delhi, or do they *need* it?"

"Why are you being so difficult, Parto? This is a life-changing opportunity for Terran. You should be overjoyed."

"…And yet I'm not," Parto said, quietly. "Can he stay with us tonight?"

"Are you going to sign it?"

Parto put out her hand. "Do you have a pen?"

Hamid smiled, and handed Parto his pen. Parto signed the release form and handed it back.

"I won!" Dorri suddenly shouted. "I beat him!"

Terran was clapping and smiling, while Dorri twirled in what could only be called a victory dance.

"Our genius just lost to my daughter," Parto quipped, standing to her feet. "She's five; will they want her in Delhi, too?"

Hamid tucked the paper in his shirt and forced a smile.

"Do you want me to stay?" Nouri asked.

"If you can," Parto replied, stretching out her arms. "You can sleep out here. We have blankets."

"Then I'll be on my way," Hamid said, rising to his feet with a little unsteadiness. "Thank you for your cooperation," he said, bowing slightly.

Parto walked Hamid to the stairs and gripped his arm. "I noticed your signature on the release form, too. What did they give you for that?"

"What makes you think they gave me anything?" Hamid said, looking indignant.

"You seemed a little too eager to get my signature. What did they give you?"

"Even if they had given me something, it's none of your business."

"It's my business, because they didn't give me anything. Instead, they're taking the one good thing that's crossed my path in a long time."

"I have your signature, now is not a good time to be negotiating—"

"You have my signature," Parto leaned in closer, "but *they* don't know that. Tell them I want…seven… no, ten mesghals of gold."

"And if I don't?"

"Then I'll refuse to cooperate."

"An Iranian woman against the GN Faculty?" Hamid patted his chest where he had placed the signed release form, and smiled timidly. "To be fair, I will try and get you something in exchange for your cooperation, but I can't guarantee it will be gold, and certainly not in that quantity."

"Try!" Parto spoke the word with intensity, but held her voice to a whisper. "Do I have your word?"

"Do I have your word that you will cooperate with less?"

"I'll go as low as five, but anything less than that is an insult, and I expect you to start at ten. Agreed?"

Hamid leveled his eyes with her and nodded, and then went down the stairs without another word.

Parto knew she had no leverage. She had nothing, but as is often the case with those who have nothing, they also have a heightened sense when destiny beckons a new path.

CHAPTER 13

Oasis

It was small, about the size and shape of an amphitheater. Moshad cautiously scouted the oasis to determine if they were alone. Once he was satisfied, he gave the all-clear signal by whistling into his hand, creating a haunting bird call. Javad and his compatriots emerged from behind a sand dune with their camels in tow. They were tired and hungry. The night air was warm and the smell of the water and vegetation was a welcome change to the men, who half-jogged to the edge of the spring and began to drink and douse their dusty faces with water. They filled up their flasks, and then led their camels to the water's edge, though only one camel bothered to drink.

The palm trees were large, but weathered. Even in the dim light, their scarred trunks revealed the tough times they had witnessed, but water has a strange way of keeping alive the things that should be long dead. When the rest of the men arrived, Moshad was already lowering one of the huge clusters of dates and hacking at them with his imposing sixteen-inch knife blade. It looked like a piñata breaking open and spilling its candy to the floor.

Date palms were the perfect vegetation. They provided ample shade from the heat, and a nutritious, good tasting, high-energy fruit. Each cluster of their fruit contained at least one-hundred dates, and most of the date palms had three or four clusters, so each tree could feed thirty-to-forty adults, and the oasis had at least twenty date palms.

This specific oasis was not on the road that bound Saraghs and Mashhad. It was a lesser known path, but it was also notorious as a hangout for rebel caravans that consisted of drug smugglers and bandits. Often they were criminals from Baluch tribes that had been ostracized. They tended to band together and operate as gangs of thieves, extracting their recompense from unsuspecting travelers. Moshad, in particular, had to be careful, because many of them he had caught, convicted and sentenced, and their burned feet reminded these criminals of their nemesis every day. The reward would be sweet for any of their members to find Moshad and exact their revenge.

After a dinner of lamb meat and dates, the men sat around the fire, enjoying a drink of hot tea. Alcohol was strictly forbidden, but it was impossible to find anyway. The Baluch had their own tea, and it was the most popular drink, especially when combined with date juice.

As they were drinking and laughing, Moshad suddenly stood to his feet and took out his gun—a semi-automatic Glock 19. The camels were snorting, a warning that Moshad took seriously. A few seconds later, two men, each riding camels, entered the oasis and stopped thirty meters from the fire pit where the men were enjoying their tea. They both dismounted their camels and stood with their arms raised above their heads in submission, and walked slowly towards Moshad, whose gun, like a compass needle, was tracking them.

"You are Baluch, we are friends… I know your tongue. Please, in the name of Allah, let us drink the cold water." The man was tall and very lanky, with a long frazzled beard. His face cast a longing look at the natural spring to his right.

Moshad eyed the men with suspicion, but lowered his gun slightly, because the taller of the two spoke his language, though not well. Moshad's men were still sitting, but all were turned to face the two visitors.

"Do you have weapons?" Moshad asked.

"Only knives." The tall man answered. Their hands were still wavering in the air above their heads.

"And what are you doing out here?" Moshad asked, narrowing his eyes.

"We journey to Saraghs. We are Turkmen. There we live."

"And from where did you come?"

"Sellers we are," the shorter of the two tried to say, patting his chest, but the Baluch did not understand his term, and Moshad leered at him.

"Importers really…" interrupted the taller of the two strangers. "Can we put our arms down?"

"No," Moshad barked, and then turned to one of his men. "Josid, check them for weapons."

A strong-looking man sprung to his feet and immediately began searching the two strangers. Josid was easily six-and-a-half-feet tall and, while not large in girth, even beneath his baggy shirt his muscular shoulders and arms were unmistakable.

The two strangers kept their arms in the air, and complied with the heavy-handed search by Josid, who eventually turned around and showed two knives—one in each hand. "This is all they have, Sir."

"You never told us where you came from," Moshad said.

The taller man stepped to his side a few feet, as though to get a better view around Josid's massive frame. "We are merchants, like I said. We come from Mashhad where we went to find new... new things to sell to... to... customers in Saraghs. That is all," he said, struggling to find the right words.

"And why would merchants travel this road, known to be the haven of lawbreakers?"

"Then you are thieves?" the tall man asked.

Moshad ignored the question and walked towards the two men, keeping his eyes focused on the tall one who seemed to be the leader. He walked up to them slowly, sizing them up, occasionally glancing to the black perimeter that surrounded their camp. The two strangers stood silent and still, only their hands moved from fatigue and possibly fear. Moshad walked past them and examined their camels. "You didn't find anything in Mashhad worthy of your customers?"

"We import clothing, Mashhad was not good. We only found a few dozen hejabs."

"Not much to sell for such a long trip. How do you stay in business?"

"We struggle like everyone else. Some trips are better than others. This one was not so kind." The tall man shook his head back and forth as if to punctuate their meager results.

"You can put your arms down," Moshad said. "But we'll keep your knives until you're ready to leave."

"Thank you. My name is Sanjur, and this is my business partner, Hafez. May we stay the night so we can rest?"

"If you show me your hejabs, and you can prove your word is true, you may stay." Moshad kept his gun trained on Sanjur, and noticed the camels were moving their feet, pawing at the ground. He motioned to his men to rise, which they all did with the exception of Javad, who was transfixed with what he saw. *Why does he fear these two, unarmed men?*

"You want to see the hejabs we purchased in Mashhad?" Sanjur asked, his voice rose in pitch and volume.

Moshad walked behind Sanjur, with his back to the cool and inviting waters of the spring. He signaled to his men to be prepared to fight. He looked carefully in the dark that surrounded them, and suddenly, he saw what he had feared: the iridescent flash of their campfire in a human eyeball, which meant they were not alone, and the two strangers were probably scouting them for weaknesses, but had now become the prey of Moshad, who leaned in directly behind Sanjur. "Call your men off, and I will let you live."

"What men?" Sanjur protested, putting his arms out, palms up.

"The men who wait for your signal to attack. The men out there. Call them off, or you will die. You have five seconds."

Moshad released the safety on his pistol and placed its barrel directly on Sanjur's spine, between his shoulder blades.

Sanjur raised his arms, and shouted in Turkmen. "Stay where you are! These men are friends!"

Moshad turned to Javad. "Do you understand what he said?"

Javad nodded. "He told them to stay and that we are all friends."

Moshad spit on the ground. "We are *not* friends."

He grabbed Sanjur's turban and yanked his head backwards and spoke directly into his right ear. "Tell them to leave and when they're a kilometer away, in the direction of Saraghs, they should fire three shots into the air—"

"But we have no bullets," Sanjur pleaded in a hushed voice, and in doing so, confessed his deception.

Moshad knew it was plausible. Guns were fairly plentiful, but bullets were very rare. "Tell them to shoot a flaming arrow into the night sky— three times. When we see that, we will know you are on your way, and we will release you and your friend. If we don't see the arrows in the next ten minutes, we will assume they wish to fight, and we have guns *and* bullets, and you two will be their first targets."

Sanjur cleared his throat and shouted into the surrounding darkness the message that Moshad had commanded him to deliver, but only silence returned.

"Tell them to answer that they understand our arrangement and they will submit to it. If they don't answer I *will* kill you, and then we will hunt them down and kill each of them as well. Tell them!" He jabbed Sanjur with the barrel of his gun.

Sanjur stepped forward a few inches, hoping to relieve the pain of the gun barrel thrust against his spine. He cupped his hands around his mouth and shouted loudly into the night air. When he finished, a grunted sentence in Turkmen returned a few seconds later, and Moshad turned to Javad. "Did you hear it?"

Javad nodded. "They want proof we have bullets, they want us to fire our guns in the sky."

In one quick motion, Moshad directed his gun at the shorter of the two strangers and shot him in the back of his head. The man immediately crumpled to the ground like a puppet cut from his strings. Sanjur gasped and his body began to tremble uncontrollably.

"Ask them if they need more proof," Moshad said in an eerily calm tone.

The gunshot rang out across the desert floor, and the camels shook their heads and snorted in contempt of the terrible sound.

Moshad returned his gun barrel to Sanjur's spine, who immediately felt the heat of the freshly discharged barrel. Sanjur gulped a few breaths of air, trying his best to compose himself, and then cupped his trembling hands around his mouth and repeated the message, his voice cracking in several places.

As Sanjur spoke, Moshad motioned with his hands to his men to lie flat on the ground. "Be ready," he said in a loud whisper. "Make yourself a small target."

Some of the men slinked behind the date palms. Some flattened themselves against the ground and readied their rifles.

Unprovoked, Sanjur spoke again into the silent desert, and when he'd finished, Moshad motioned to Javad to tell him what he had said.

"He told them we are strong. To leave and do exactly what you had asked them to do."

Moshad leaned forward and whispered in Sanjur's ear. "Do not speak again unless I tell you. Now, I want you to tell your friends to confirm their submission. If they do not, I will kill you, and then we will kill every one of your comrades. Remind them that they have ten minutes to fire their flaming arrows from a kilometer's distance. Tell them, *now!*"

Sanjur immediately shouted the message. His voice was now stronger and held more conviction.

Moshad turned to Javad, who simply nodded.

A grunt from a distance of about a hundred meters sounded, and Sanjur turned his head to the side. "They agree."

Moshad held his hand up to quiet any whispers of his men and turned to Josid. "Take three of our best shooters, follow them, if they are less than fifteen in number, kill them all."

Josid nodded and gathered his men, and ducked behind the palm trees and disappeared into the night's shadows.

Sanjur turned to Moshad. "And what of me? Please, let me live. I can be of service to you."

"Your camels can be of service to me. You are just another mouth to feed."

"I know Mashhad like the veins of my hand. That's where you're going isn't it? I can be your guide... even your translator. I speak many dialects."

Moshad pointed to the ground. *"Sit and be silent."*

Sanjur looked down at the lifeless body of Hafez, and moved away as far as he could without upsetting Moshad, and then sat down with a sigh.

Moshad motioned for one of his men to come to him. "Bind him."

The man went to one of the camels and removed some rope and began to tie Sanjur's hands and then his feet.

"I also know a place you can stay in Mashhad for... free..."

Sanjur's voice trailed off as Moshad's angry glare fell upon him like a sudden, deep shadow.

Moshad knew that Sanjur's pleas were a subtle admission that his band of Turkmen ne'er-do-wells was small—less than fifteen.

Moshad gathered his men. "I want sentries there and there—a hundred meters, straight line. I'll send replacements in four hours. If you see anything suspicious, fire a sky-shot immediately and retreat back here."

The men nodded and talked among themselves, and then elected two men for the first shift. After getting some supplies, the two men left in opposite vectors at a light jog. Now Moshad and his men were down to six, and one of those, Javad, was not a fighter, nor did he have a gun, or knife, for that matter.

Moshad turned to the remaining men. "I want you and Afshin to inspect these camels, if you find anything of interest, bring it to me. Shaheen and Jalil, move this body over there and bury it. Navid, you stand guard, there." He then turned to Javad. "Come with me."

Moshad sat down near the fire and tucked his gun underneath his crossed legs. Javad sat down close to him, uneasy from the events of the last ten minutes.

"What just happened?" Javad asked.

"We were being scouted for weaknesses by a band of thieves. They send in their least suspicious members, they befriend their victim, break bread with them, maybe drink a little wine which they miraculously have in their camel packs; they drug their victims and steal everything, including their camels, even their clothes. These are the most unscrupulous of men. *I hate them.*" Moshad turned to Sanjur as he spoke, knowing in the quiet of the desert night, he could hear his words.

"And if they shoot the three flaming arrows into the night sky?" Javad asked, hoping he didn't sound too naïve.

"It only proves they are stupid," Moshad replied. "My men will kill them. If they are smart, they are running away as fast as they can. They know I won't release him," he said looking in Sanjur's direction. "Their only hope of surviving the night is to take advantage of their head start and move as quickly as possible. If they are thieves, and good ones at that, every man will have their own camel. They will be able to move fast. That's their only advantage."

"I've seen Josid run," Javad remarked. "He can outpace a camel who's fully packed with a man aboard."

"That's why I sent him," Moshad said with a smile.

Moshad paused briefly. "You see, the oasis is like a spider's web. When people come here, they vibrate the silken web and alert the spider—"

"How?"

"The birds let them know... or tracks. If you hunted around this place, you'd find the bones of men buried everywhere. Some old, some new. Many people say these oases are haunted. I feel it sometimes—"

A sudden barrage of gunshots could be heard in the far distance, and Moshad's hand immediately went up. He tilted his head in the ensuing silence. "Those were all our guns."

"How many men, Sanjur?" Moshad shouted.

Sanjur squirmed nervously. "Not including my deceased partner and myself... seven."

"One got away..." Moshad said.

A moment later a seventh gunshot sounded in the distance.

"I spoke too soon." Moshad grinned. "It seems you're alone, Sanjur. Would you like to join your friends?"

Sanjur immediately shook his head. "I would like to join you."

Moshad grunted disapprovingly, and then laughed. "We'll see. We'll see."

Moshad looked at Javad, and his voice softened in a whisper. "What do you think of this man? Could he be helpful?"

"If he can find us a place to stay in Mashhad, yes, he could be helpful, especially if it's free. My Persian is okay, but his might be better."

"Go find out," Moshad said, glancing in the direction of Sanjur.

Javad stood up and walked slowly over to Sanjur's position. "Do you speak Persian?"

"Yes, of course. How could I be a merchant if I didn't?" Sanjur answered in flowing Persian.

"We know what you are, so stop the—"

"I really was a merchant at one time," Sanjur exclaimed. "Everything I told you was true... for the most part. Just... not... now."

Sanjur cast his eyes downward. "I *can* help you."

"How?"

"First, you must tell me what you want in Mashhad—that is where you're going, correct?"

Javad nodded, but hesitated, unsure how much he should divulge. "We seek one of our children?"

"He or she was stolen?"

"He was… lost there."

"How old?"

"Twelve."

"He'd almost certainly be at the Preserve then… did the boy like school?"

"Very much."

"The best place to find him would be at the Preserve. I can take you there. I know exactly where it is."

"This place you said we could stay… in Mashhad. How far is it from the school?"

"Three, maybe four kilometers," Sanjur answered.

Javad squatted down to level his eyes with Sanjur. "Are there any other skills you have?"

Sanjur looked up to the stars for a moment. "I am a very good negotiator. I understand human psychology."

"Then why are you a thief?" Javad asked.

"I lost everything in the Sunrot… everything." Sanjur's eyes instantly glistened. "The mayor of Saraghs is a mad man. He abandoned the city, and it became lawless. Merchants were raided, and everything that wasn't destroyed by the storms was stolen by the citizens of Saraghs. I met these men when I was starving. It was a way of surviving. I'm not a bad man. If I could find an honorable job, I'd do it, but there isn't one to be found."

Sanjur looked up at Javad with pleading eyes. "Don't let him kill me, please. I promise you, I'll be useful to you."

Javad backed away. "We'll see what Providence brings."

When Javad returned to the fire pit, Moshad was going over some of the stash that Afshin had brought from Sanjur's camel. It looked like gold lace and some ivory buttons of various sizes.

"So?" Moshad asked, glancing at Javad.

"His Persian is better than mine. He believes he knows where we can find Terran—"

"We can find the school on our own, we don't need him. What else?"

"He can find us a place to stay that's about three kilometers from the school."

"What else?"

"He says he's a good negotiator."

Moshad smiled. "He's still alive... I would agree with him."

CHAPTER 14

Why?

Parto remembered a time when she would sleep on the rooftop patio of her parent's home, watching the stars and planets shift their positions in the sky. But now, she would see a star and imagine that it was rotting another planet in some distant solar system, torturing its hapless inhabitants for no particular reason. (Just the physics of a cold universe.)

The night air was cool, but there was no wind. Parto, Terran and Nouri were each wrapped in blankets, drinking hot tea beneath the starlight on the rooftop patio. Dorri was sleeping inside. It was late—almost midnight, but Parto wanted to spend some time understanding Terran.

"Ask him why he wants to go to Delhi?" Parto said, turning to Nouri.

Nouri asked, and then looked at Parto. "He said that he desires to be a channel for the one God, that is all. Delhi is a step in that process."

Parto looked surprised and slowly shook her head. "Really? He still believes in God?"

Terran touched her arm, smiled, and pointed to the stars and spoke, and then looked to Nouri to translate.

"He says to tell you that the stars are not indifferent. The slum, the mosque, the wicked, the wise, they all live inside you. They're part of the one force that enters our universe and swirls around in the hearts of all beings. Some feel this force as separate from themselves, and when bad things happen, they blame it... some even hate it."

He read my mind? Parto thought.

Nouri stole a quick glance at Parto, and then Terran, signaling he was done with his translation. Terran immediately began to speak again, gesturing with his hands, his voice soft and resolute.

"He wants you to know that this force is present most strongly in the heart, where it never dies, but sometimes sleeps. It can be reawakened at any time. Sometimes the awakening can come from outside, sometimes from inside, either way, it requires that you seek it. That you reach for it. Desire it. Call it to yourself."

"These are his words?" Parto asked in a disbelieving tone.

Nouri grinned. "They're not mine. I don't speak like this."

"These are not the words of a boy..." Parto whispered, mostly to herself. "Ask him what he hopes to accomplish by going to Delhi."

Nouri smiled. "I know the answer, because I've already asked him."

"Then tell me."

"He wants to develop a way to ensure that the world will not have to undergo another Sunrot."

"He wants to control the universe?" Parto asked sarcastically. "How can a boy even have such thoughts?"

Nouri smiled at Parto's comment. "I'm an intelligent man. I have an advanced degree. I taught at the University, but when I saw him take this test, it was as if I was in the presence of an intelligence that doesn't belong in a human body."

"What do you mean?" Parto asked, suddenly curious.

Terran tugged on Nouri's sleeve and asked a question, to which Nouri shook his head and simply grinned.

"What did he say?" Parto asked.

"Nothing. He was just feeling left out of the conversation."

"What did you mean... about his intelligence?"

"Only that I've never seen an intelligence like his, and from the reaction of the Faculty Director, I believe she felt the same way."

Parto set her tea cup down and pulled the blanket around her more tightly. "There were too many of us, and nature decided to thin us down. It's as simple as that. No one can control the universe. Nor should we want to. If he's so brilliant, it seems to me that this would be obvious."

Terran began to speak, and then Nouri translated.

"He says that you have darkened your heart, but this is only... um... polishing your pain. It makes you feel shunned when you're not, and now you feel shame for seeing only one reality—one layer, when you know there are many."

"Again these words, are you sure you're a good translator?" Parto asked.

Terran spoke again before Nouri could defend himself. "He says he's not interested in controlling the universe, he wants to compose its effects on earth. He has seen this…"

Nouri asked a quick question, and Terran shook his head and spoke passionately for about twenty seconds, while Nouri nodded his head.

Parto watched Nouri. He was average looking, a slightly graying beard, softened features, but there was something about his presence that never seemed to fray or spread adrift on wild speculations, and she admired it. There was, however, an enormous sadness that she felt, and in that sadness, it was as if his wings were held down by an unseen hand. His face was kind, but there was an unmistakable kindred quality to his persona, and Parto was alarmed and curious at the same time. In some ways, she felt like his twin.

Nouri looked into Parto's eyes, searching for a moment to find the right words. "It's hard to explain, for me, at least. He feels that he can tune nature in such a way that as the energies from cosmic sources like the sun come within our earth's magnetosphere… we can modify their impact, so it's helpful and not harmful. He keeps using a term that I can only translate as composing—it has a musical meaning to it, but I'm not sure that that's what he means."

Parto suddenly realized that she was less interested in the nuance of Terran's mission, than the sound of Nouri's voice. It was a difficult admission for her. She was tired of men and their superior airs, and possibly, because he had been a professor, Nouri was no different, but his voice had a tone that seemed to dissolve in her bones. This was what attracted her to him. Now that she realized it, she wondered if it was at all reasonable to expect it to be mutual. He was leaving soon. She closed her eyes, wondering why she allowed this impossible spark to suddenly consume her.

A simple tone of voice. The vast complexity of two people. The charity of a compass needle that points to the strongest magnetic pull, whose rule extends to the farthest paradise and most tortured fire. *Is this the stirrings of love?* Her eyes moved star ward: maybe Terran was right, and the stars were not villainous creators of human misery.

Love, even when it was a mere seed, still had the power to see everything anew.

CHAPTER 15

Address

S anjur and Javad had been walking for nearly thirty minutes, and according to Sanjur, they were within a few blocks of the Preserve. They were followed by three of Moshad's men, who remained fifty meters behind as inconspicuous protectors. The streets of Mashhad were empty, except for an occasional homeless person suffering from the restlessness of an empty stomach. Usually they were too tired and hopeless to even beg, but all of this was new to Javad. He'd only been to Mashhad once before, and that was before the Sunrot. It had changed dramatically for the worse. Weeds grew everywhere, no city lights, rubble filled the streets. No cars or trucks moved. There was the misery of compounded silence layered like swords fallen in a massacre.

"When's the last time you were in Mashhad?" Sanjur asked.

"Almost fifteen years."

"School?"

"No, it was for health reasons."

Sanjur paused. "How long were you here?"

"Four weeks."

"Must have been serious," Sanjur remarked, and then suddenly stopped. He disappeared into the black shadows of an alley, but not before he grabbed the jacket of Javad, pulling him behind a concrete wall.

"What's wrong?" Javad whispered.

"They have guards."

"How many?"

"I think two, but I ducked away so fast, I'm not sure."

"Where do they get guards?"

"Parents. They rotate in shifts."

"Are they armed?"

"If you mean guns, probably not… but they'll have knives and metal rods… which still hurt like hell."

"What do we do?" Javad asked.

"Moshad asked us to have a chat with the director, and we'll do that." Sanjur nodded, as if convincing himself to move forward.

"Why are you afraid?"

"I'm not afraid." Sanjur pointed out. "I'm cautious."

"Okay, we'll ask the guards if we can meet with the director—"

"What if they say it's too late?" Sanjur asked.

"It's only around nine, that's not that late. Let's try, but you'll have to do the talking, your Persian's better than mine."

"Okay, okay. But if they're nasty guards, I reserve the right to run away."

Javad grinned, and shoved Sanjur in the direction of the Preserve. "Let's go."

Javad glanced down the street, but didn't see any signs of the protectors that were following them.

The first guard they encountered was a short man with spindly arms and legs who was holding a book.

"Salaam-Alaikum…can I help you?" the guard asked.

Sanjur cleared his throat in an official manner. "Salaam… Yes, we're here to see the director."

"The director?"

Sanjur and Javad both nodded in unison. Another guard drifted over, this one was more rotund, but equally short. He was holding a water bottle. If they were guards, they certainly didn't seem threatening.

"It's late," said the approaching guard, "is he expecting you?"

"No, I don't think so, but could you call him down just the same?"

"And what's the nature of your visit?" the first guard asked, setting his book down on the steps.

"It's… it's of a personal nature," Sanjur explained. "It will only take a minute or two."

"Does the director know you?"

"No, we believe he knows the child we're looking for… we're only looking to confirm the boy's safety. That's all."

"The boy's name?"

Sanjur looked at Javad, hoping he had been able to follow the conversation.

"His name is Terran Ahmad Khan," Javad said timidly.

"And you're his father?" The first guard asked, looking directly at Javad.

"No... I am his teacher."

"I'll see if the director is available. You can wait at that table."

A few minutes later the guard returned with Hamid by his side, dressed in a long night coat. Hamid immediately began to shake hands with Javad and then Sanjur. "Which of you is Terran's teacher?"

Javad raised his hand tentatively. "I am, my name is Javad, and this is my friend, Sanjur."

Sanjur bowed. "It is a great pleasure to meet you..."

"Hamid Mockri, just call me Hamid."

"Wonderful to meet you, Hamid."

"Likewise," Hamid replied. "It's a little chilly out here; would you men prefer to meet inside?"

"That would be great," Sanjur replied.

"I didn't get your relation to the boy?" Hamid turned to Sanjur.

"I am the boy's uncle... on his mother's side."

"Ah, well then, follow me, gentlemen, and I'll make us some chai to warm us up."

The three men sat down in Hamid's office, and Hamid immediately went about the business of boiling some water for hot tea. Hamid kept the conversation light, asking questions about their journey to Mashhad mostly.

As he made tea, Hamid couldn't resist a little bragging. "One of the advantages of being in the Preserve is that we have a generator, and it stays on all night, so we have electricity for essentials like a hot cup of chai, even this late."

Hamid poured some tea into a glass tea cup about half full, and then checked its color and returned it to the pot and then poured out three cups. When he'd finished, he passed tea cups to his guests, and sat down. "So, how can I help you, gentlemen?"

Sanjur took a quick glance in the direction of Javad. "We just wanted to make sure that Terran made it to school, and that he's alright?"

"Not only is he alright," Hamid replied, "but he's our most prized pupil."

"Really? So soon he has made this impression. How?" Sanjur asked.

Hamid took a long sip of tea, his face struggling to create a smile whose origins could not be traced. "You see, we have tests that new students take to ensure that they're properly challenged—academically speaking. Terran took this test, did so well that he has been rewarded with an invitation to one of the six most prestigious schools in the Greater Nation."

"And where is this school?" Sanjur asked.

"Delhi."

"India!" Javad exclaimed. "No, no, no… it cannot be. He… he must stay with his people."

Sanjur leaned in towards Hamid, speaking calmly, but with exquisite conviction. "I think we have a problem. When was this decided, and by whom?"

Hamid looked nervously between the two men, and sat back in his chair, his hands cupping his teacup for warmth. "Do either of you smoke?"

"Whenever Providence allows it," Sanjur nodded.

"I'm going to have a smoke. Would you join me?"

Sanjur nodded his head, trying to look casual, but he couldn't remember the last time he had a cigarette. Tobacco was one of the rarest crops around.

Hamid opened a drawer in his desk and pulled out a pack of hand-rolled cigarettes and handed one to Sanjur, and then held one up for Javad, who shook his head faintly.

Hamid struck a match and lit Sanjur's cigarette and then his own, and took a long drag and exhaled. "First, and I'm being very honest with you, you must understand that we had no idea where Terran came from, who his guardians were, or if they even cared about him. After all, he collapsed in our market, and if not for a kindly woman who carried him here, he would probably be dead."

Hamid turned his eyes to Javad. "If you are his teacher, you know that his intellect is superior. The boy wants to be taught by the best teachers… physics, astronomy, mathematics, he needs the best instruction, and the Faculty—that's the GN school system—has the best teachers. It was Terran's decision to go to Delhi. No one forced him, the invitation was extended and he accepted it. It's as simple as that."

Sanjur took a long look at Javad who seemed speechless, flicked his cigarette ash in his cupped hand, and took a long drag on his cigarette. "My nephew, where is he now?"

"He's staying with the woman I mentioned—who literally saved him from—"

"We would like to see him..." Sanjur blurted out. "We would like to see him and make sure he's okay. You understand?"

"Of course, but he's probably sleeping at this hour. Our lessons start early. I can let you see the boy tomorrow. Where're you staying the night?"

"We have lodging a few kilometers away—to the south," Sanjur replied. "What time in the morning?"

"We could say ten. Is that early enough?"

Sanjur turned to Javad and spoke in Baluch. "In thirty seconds, I need you to ask to use the bathroom."

Javad narrowed his eyes for a moment and nodded.

Sanjur turned to Hamid and shook his head slightly. "His Persian, with regard to numbers, is always messed up. Yes, ten o'clock will be fine. By the way, I can't tell you how much I appreciate your sharing a cigarette with me. It's been a long time since I've enjoyed a smoke. In my nephew's regard, at least speaking for me, it's a great honor to have one of our own receive such an invitation. Your help is appreciated there as well." Sanjur bowed his head, as Javad watched and listened in suspended awe. Sanjur's real talent was that he could act. He could act masterfully.

"Ah, you're very kind with your praise. You're welcome," Hamid said with a broad smile.

Javad cleared his throat, and in stilted Persian, asked his question about using the bathroom.

"Of course," Hamid replied. "Follow me, I'll show you where it is."

"If it's okay, I'll finish my smoke," Sanjur offered.

Hamid did his best to cover any uneasiness, but there was a pause of hesitancy, and Sanjur knew he wouldn't have much time. "Certainly, I'll be right back."

As soon as Hamid and Javad shuffled out of the small office, Sanjur rifled through all of the papers on Hamid's desk, and found one with two signatures. He looked carefully at the paper, and the address underneath the signature. Speaking Persian was easier than reading it, but he caught the name: Parto Jafari. On the top-left corner was a paper-clipped note that said: *Scanned and sent 4–21.*

Sanjur memorized the address and took the last drag from his cigarette, wincing slightly as he burned the tip of his index finger. As he exhaled, he repeated the address twice, burning it into his mind. He then made a quick assessment, opened the desk draw, and withdrew—with swiftness and dexterity—two cigarettes.

Hamid, his absence measured in the span of one minute, returned to find Sanjur perfectly composed in his chair, taking his last sip of tea with relish.

CHAPTER 16

Arrival

Moshad had been impressed with Javad's report. Sanjur had turned out to be a good asset. The night was late, and they had been searching for the home of Parto Jafari, but maps were hard to come by, and Sanjur's knowledge of Mashhad did not include Parto's street address. It was midnight when they finally found the home, a two-story vertical apartment that looked dilapidated in every respect, except the door, which was covered in a fresh coat of red paint, though in the darkness of the night, it was the color of Bordeaux wine.

Moshad, Josid, Shaheen, Sanjur, and Javad were huddled across the street, watching the home carefully. "I heard laughter... up there." Moshad pointed to the roof. "They're up there, on the roof."

"Remember, I get to speak with him alone," Javad said, his voice barely a whisper.

Sanjur looked at Javad cautiously. "If the boy's awake, as soon as he sees you he'll know why you're here. If Hamid is right, and he wants to go to Delhi, he'll run from you, or this woman, Parto, will protect him from you. Who knows maybe she has a gun or a bodyguard. We only have one chance to get him, and that's tonight."

Moshad held up his hand before Javad had a chance to respond. "What alternative do you propose?"

"No one knows me here," Sanjur whispered. "I could pretend I'm lost... looking for a friend who lives in the neighborhood... maybe I'm little drunk, and I hear things and decide that's my friend's house. I go up there and check things out. Worst case, they'll throw me out in a few seconds. But that's all I'd need to see what they have in weapons, whether Terran is there, how many others are there—"

"It's a good plan," Moshad said. "Go."

Javad grabbed Sanjur's shirt as he moved away. "He'll sense you... if he's awake, he'll know why you're there."

"He's a boy, maybe brighter than most, but he won't see through me," Sanjur said, and then cocked his head to his side. "Does he even know Persian?"

Javad released Sanjur's shirt, shaking his head. "No, but the longer you stay, the more you'll be exposed. Just be quick about it."

"Go!" Moshad ordered.

Sanjur walked across the street, drifting in and out of shadows cast by the buildings and trees. As he came to the home, he looked up, examining the roof, and then went to the side of the home, and disappeared.

CHAPTER 17

A Different Vision

A slight rattling sound trembled in the night air, spreading the fear of human intrusion. Parto looked over to the stairs, wondering why her father would be coming up to see them. It was late. He should be asleep. *Perhaps we're talking too loud*, she thought, but then a strange face appeared and stumbled onto the patio.

"Where's Saeed, and why is the party so small?" Sanjur asked, his voice aptly slurred for the drunkard role he was playing. "Either I'm too late or too early. Which is it, if I may ask?"

Parto and Nouri both rose to their feet, while Terran remained in his place, silently observing the stranger.

Nouri stepped forward, brushing Parto back slightly with a protective arm. "There's no party here, or anyone by the name of Saeed. You have the wrong address."

"Ah, I heard laughter when I walked by, I figured this must be the place. I just came from a party and probably drank a little too much. Sorry about that. Now..." Sanjur pointed his thumb behind him, "I have to climb down those miserable stairs again... which—in my current state—could very well be the end of me."

Sanjur paused and looked around, catching the eyes of Terran for a moment, and then looked up at the stars. "Beautiful night... a little cold, but the stars look friendly, do they not?"

Terran spoke quietly to Nouri, believing him to be the only one who would be able to understand. "This man is not honest."

Nouri glanced back at Terran.

Sanjur pretended not to understand. "What does the boy say? Strange dialect..."

Nouri came closer to Sanjur. "I'll help you down the stairs."

"Ah, thank you, my good man. Too bad the party isn't here; I could really use a drink."

Nouri took a quick glance at Parto who was watching more out of curiosity than fear, but she could tell that Nouri was troubled by something that Terran had said. Nouri grabbed Sanjur's arm and helped him onto the rickety, wrought-iron staircase that was bolted onto the side of the house. They proceeded slowly and amicably, and when they made it to the landing at the bottom of the stairs, Sanjur turned to Nouri, holding his arm as if they were best friends. "You are very kind to help me, but can I ask you one question?"

"Sure…" Nouri said.

"Do the numbers get smaller that way or that way?"

"What's the address?" Nouri asked.

"8210…"

"This is 8313. You need to go down one block in that direction."

"Ah, thank you for your humanity. It is most appreciated."

From behind him, Nouri suddenly felt a sharp knife blade against his throat, and then a whispered voice in Baluchi. "Move or speak, you die."

Nouri let the words register in his mind, watching the strange drunkard walk behind him and whisper something to one of his accomplices.

"Gag him, bind his hands," came the whispered orders from the man holding the knife.

Nouri remained still and compliant. A large man suddenly appeared in front of him and gagged his mouth with a tight cloth that tasted bitter. Nouri's hands were tightly bound together, and then he was pushed to the ground behind a tree.

Sanjur explained what he had seen in a whispered voice to Moshad.

"Go. You have ten minutes to convince him," Moshad said, turning to Javad.

Javad walked up the stairs—one teacher replacing the other. He was nervous. Sanjur had just told him that Terran and Parto were on the roof. With each step he took, he prayed for Allah's help.

When he arrived at the top of the stairs, Parto started to speak, but then caught her words in a hushed gasp, realizing it wasn't Nouri. Terran immediately rose to his feet and rushed to his teacher's waiting arms.

"I knew you would come," Terran gushed. "I knew you would find me."

"It's good to see you," Javad said, stroking Terran's tousled hair, and looking into the eyes of Parto who could only stare in silent bewilderment.

"Where's Nouri?" Terran asked, looking up into the smiling face of Javad.

"He's okay, don't worry. We need to talk about other things."

"Tell her." Terran nodded in Parto's direction.

Javad looked at Parto and spoke in his best Persian. "I am Terran's teacher. The man who was here, he's okay. I just wanted some time to talk with Terran."

"I want you to leave now," Parto said, her voice trembling. She pointed to the stairs. "Leave now!"

Terran stepped between them, his hands raised slightly. "Tell her that I want you to stay for a while."

Javad delivered the message, and Parto shook her head slowly from side to side. "I want you to leave, now. You're trespassing. Leave."

"Then I will take Terran with me," Javad said.

"No!"

"Then I will stay and talk with him."

Parto stepped forward and grabbed Terran, pulling him gently to her side of the patio. "You have five minutes, but when you're done, you leave alone. Agreed?"

Javad nodded, and then turned his attention to Terran as if Parto had suddenly vanished. He knelt down, and in Baluchi, with a pleading tone, spoke. "You are the Mahdi. You cannot leave your people. Why Delhi? What do you possibly hope to achieve there?"

"How do you know about Delhi?" Terran asked, his countenance darkening.

"We met with your school's director."

"Is he okay?"

"Yes."

"No harm must come to any of these people. They are family to me."

"I understand," Javad nodded. "But Moshad does not."

"And what of Pirdah?"

"I'm not sure." Javad admitted solemnly.

Terran stood wrapped in Parto's arms. She stood behind him like a sentinel with her arms draped across his chest.

"I've known that my life has been planned since I was two years old," Terran said. "But there are many planners. Pirdah is only one, and his plan for me is not the plan I want to realize—"

"What plan could be a higher mission than being the Mahdi?" Javad interjected, disbelief forming his words.

Terran started to speak, and then paused, pointing upwards to the stars. "I know that there are energies coming from space that can destroy us—Sunrot is proof of that. I also know that we can devise a way to compose these energies so they can never hurt us again. I have seen this. This is the plan I wish to make visible."

"But what of the spiritual welfare of your people?" Javad asked. "Do you not care for their well-being?"

Terran pulled free from the grasp of Parto and stepped closer to Javad, who remained kneeling. He touched the side of Javad's face tenderly. "You have been a loyal teacher. I realize my actions have left you in misery, and they must look selfish to you, but you must know that I am not motivated by selfishness—"

"Of course I know this, and it is not *you* I distrust, it's the leaders of the Greater Nation who will use you for their own agenda. It's only a matter of time, and they will know you are the Mahdi, and when this realization dawns on them, they'll seek to destroy you and our people. We live outside their new, global economy, educational system, language, culture, trade. They seek to eliminate our kind. You *know* that. We need you to protect us. To unify us. Please, return with me to your home."

"My people are all people. Not only the ones who speak my language. They are animals, insects, trees, all life—the very planet. These are all my people. I will either help all, or I will help none. It is the way I am designed, Javad. You and Pirdah cannot force me to limit my mission.

"You asked me if I care about the spiritual welfare of my people, and I'll answer you, *no*. Their spiritual welfare isn't my concern. It's every individual's concern, but it is not mine. No man should be burdened with the spiritual progress of another—their own is enough. Do you understand me?"

Javad slowly shook his head, looking into Terran's eyes like a man whose best friend suddenly altered into a complete stranger.

Terran walked to the edge of the patio and looked down. "Moshad is with you?"

Javad nodded. "Yes."

"His orders?"

"Do I need to tell you?"

"And you're here to convince me, and if I refuse, Moshad is here to abduct me? Is that true?"

"Yes."

"If you force me to return, I will only try to return here. Is your plan to hold me in a cage? If you believe I am the Mahdi, then how can you make me your prisoner?"

"It is contemplated only for your own good. You are too trusting. We, your elders, are only trying to protect you from those who would destroy you."

"And to do this, you're willing to abduct and imprison me. You refuse to trust my vision over your own—the one that was handed down to you from generations of men who conspired to build an army for their God to make one religion. Tell me, Javad, how are they different from the founders of the Greater Nation?

"Do you really think I could be used by anyone? Do you think I'm so naïve that the leaders of the Greater Nation could dispose of my talents in service to their own agenda? Do you understand me in such a limited light? And Pirdah, too? You're supposed to be the wisdom of our people, and yet you look upon me as a simple child, and I stopped being a child when I was six years old, you—more than anyone else—know that. You're stuck on a legend, a myth, invented by men in different times and circumstances that ordered a battle and demanded a leader, and now their distant hopes point to me."

Parto cleared her throat, interrupting the long silence that followed Terran's remark. "It's time for you to leave," she said, guiding her stare in Javad's direction, but avoiding direct contact with his eyes.

"You know what I want," Terran said. "And now you need to allow me to do it. You need to release me."

Javad stood to his feet, slowly, looking down at the tile flooring. His mood troubled, as a great debate raged inside his head. He knew that Moshad would be unmoved by anything Terran had said. Terran was little more than a possession of the Baluch tribes of Iran, and Moshad was hired to find this possession and return it to its rightful owner— the Baluch people. Terran was a symbol. An embodied hope owned by every member of the Baluch nation. What Terran really wanted was to raise his middle finger to his own people and walk away. Moshad would never concede that. Not from a twelve-year-old boy who held the hope of his nation.

Javad shook his head as he turned to leave, then paused and turned around. "You know what will happen next... I cannot change it. Not even you can change it. If it were in my power to release you, I think I would... I think I could. But Moshad... he will never release you. I'm sorry."

"Send Nouri up here," Terran said in a resigned voice. "Give me a minute with him, and I will come down on my own. Moshad must promise to leave here when I come down, and these two remain unharmed. Those are my terms. Tell him."

Javad nodded, paused, and then looked into Terran's eyes. "And if he doesn't agree to your terms?"

Terran looked up to the stars. "Then I will resist in every way that I can."

Javad walked down the stairs with a heavy heart, his mind gripped on the fact that he was unable to convince Terran, and now he must convince Moshad.

I am powerless, he thought.

CHAPTER 18

An Exchange

Eventually every single thing withers into a regret, and Javad, as his feet reached the bottom of the stairs, knew he regretted being the first of his people to attend university. It had been the most joyous of times. He bloomed in every way, but now, nearly twenty years later, he saw how this pinnacle of his life had brought him to this place where he had to be a traitor to greatness. A bar in its prison.

*   *   *   *

"Where is he?" Moshad asked.

Javad looked in the direction of Nouri, who remained bound behind the trunk of a tree. "He's asked to have this man returned, and then he'll come down."

"There're no escape routes up there?"

Javad shook his head, deep in thought, searching for consolations, but finding none.

Moshad took a long look to the rooftop. "What will stop them from following us?"

Javad went over to Nouri and began to unbind him. "He's a teacher, she's a mother... how would they follow us?"

Moshad turned to Josid and whispered in his ear. "Hide. When we've left, go back up there and bind them and then find us. We'll wait down the street so you can follow us—but stay back so Terran can't see you. Understood?"

Josid nodded and then backed into the shadows of the surrounding buildings, and in a few seconds, had vanished.

Javad removed the gag from Nouri and helped him stand up.

"Please, don't take him!" Nouri blurted out. "He has a calling that—"

"Shut-up!" Moshad ordered. "Take him up there, and this time, return with Terran."

"That wasn't the deal," Javad protested. "We were to send him up, and Terran would come down on his own."

"That *was* the deal you negotiated. I wasn't a part of it. Bring him down. Now!"

Javad looked between Nouri and Moshad. "He said that if we didn't abide by his terms, he would resist with every power he has."

Moshad crossed his arms over his chest and spat on the ground. "Do it."

Javad walked right up to Moshad, within inches of his face. "He's the Mahdi. It would be better to grant him this wish in return for his compliance."

"Do what I say," Moshad said, "*or I will.*"

Sanjur stepped forward, and touched Moshad's sleeve, tugging on it gently. "I have an idea…"

"What?" both men asked, turning their frustration to him in unison.

"The boy probably wants to say goodbye to his teacher in private. So we'll let his teacher go up, and we'll bring down the woman. Once the boy comes down, we'll send the woman back up—sort of like an exchange. That works, doesn't it?"

Moshad nodded his head. "I will agree to that. It is a good compromise. Javad, you bring him up and exchange him for her. Terran will know that we're serious—no tricks."

Javad grabbed Nouri by the shoulder and pushed him ahead. "Let's get this over with."

As they started up the stairs, Nouri looked back. "You're his teacher?"

"Yes."

"Why do you want him to return… to be a shepherd? Don't you want him to realize his full potential? His intellect—"

"You don't know his mission. Among our people, it is the highest one could possibly hope for. Someday the whole world will understand."

Nouri looked over his shoulder again. "They will want him back…"

"They can't have him."

When they got to the top of the stairs, Terran looked disapprovingly at Javad. "I wanted to speak with Nouri alone."

"I came to get the woman. We will hold her until you come down. That's the only deal Moshad would accept. I'm sorry."

Nouri looked to Parto and explained the situation in a hushed voice. She was reluctant at first, but Nouri persisted, explaining he would only be a couple of minutes, and then Terran would come down, and she could go back up.

Javad was nervous that it was taking so long. "Come on," he whispered. "We need to get going."

Nouri glanced back and held up his index finger. "Parto, these men are tribal. They're not civilized like us. Please, do as you're told." He squeezed her shoulders together lightly and gave her a pleading look, to which Parto could only nod.

Javad held out his hand, but Parto refused it, though she did follow him down the stairs without another word. She looked back at Terran and wondered how she would explain Terran's absence to Dorri in the morning.

Nouri looked over the edge, watching Parto descend the staircase. "Your teacher told me that you have a high mission. Is it true?"

"To some of my people it is true, to some it is untrue, and to some it is uncertain."

"What about to you?"

"I'm in the middle group," Terran said quietly with a faint smile.

"What will happen to you?"

"I will be a prisoner for a while until they decide they can trust me."

"How long before trust will return?"

"Once it is broken, it can only be reclaimed when our Holy One decrees it. It could be a day; it could be a year or two. It depends on the needs of the Holy One."

Nouri kept his eye on Parto as best he could, but the darkness was thick below them, and the tree branches were plentiful.

"Is there anything we can do to help you?" Nouri asked.

"Yes…"

Nouri turned to Terran, a little startled at his response. "What?"

"Don't follow me. Don't let them send anyone after me. It will only bring death to innocents. I'll find my way back when I'm able. I'll never give up."

Nouri was silent for a few seconds. "I'll do my best to honor your request, but I don't know what influence I will have…"

"Just do your best, I can't ask for more."

Terran looked over the edge. "I should go down there now. Please express to Parto my appreciation for everything she's done, and to Dorri… give her this." Terran reached behind his shirt and unhooked a silver necklace and handed it to Nouri. "Goodbye. I hope to see you again… soon."

The two embraced beneath the black sky in the blindness of closed eyes.

Just before Terran began his descent, Nouri, emptied of all but one question, spoke. "Your teacher, down there, used the term *Mahdi*. What's a Mahdi?"

Terran paused for a moment, considering his response, and then shrugged his shoulders. "There is no proper way to answer you in the time I have, but I am not one. Goodbye."

When Terran's feet touched the ground, he nodded to Javad, and returned Moshad's stare who was watching him with cold, judging eyes. He walked to Parto and took her hand, and led her to the staircase, and then turned to Sanjur. "I want you to translate for me."

Sanjur looked to Moshad who nodded. "What would you like me to tell her?"

"Tell her that I love her." Terran glanced upwards to the roof. "That she and Dorri both saved me, and my gratitude is endless."

Terran's voice trailed off into silence, and Sanjur's voice, speaking eloquent Persian, relayed Terran's words. When he finished, Parto embraced Terran, and kissed his cheek, and she spoke in Persian for a short time, until Moshad cleared his throat.

Sanjur was about to begin his translation, when Moshad grabbed Parto by her shoulder and spun her around to face the staircase, pointing his harsh finger. "Go!"

Parto flashed an angry look and walked up the stairs, slowly at first, but as she got to the first landing, she picked up her pace, almost running up the remaining steps.

Terran thought he heard her crying, but he clenched his jaw, and tried his best to subdue the feeling of loss that flooded his heart.

"Let's go," Moshad whispered, leading the way to the street.

Javad took Terran's hand and pulled him lightly, and together they followed Moshad without a single look backwards, while both of their minds sought to delete the past seven days, to make dust of history, and pretend their grief was from a dream.

CHAPTER 19

Conjuring

Darkness, true darkness, can only be seen from the side, and with a pure eye, but few are the men or women who possess the ability. The vast majority stare into the blackness, and it only swells and distorts, becoming possessive of the few photons that—like winged birds—soar and explore. Only the pure eye can see the light within the abyss, and know it as the hope that comes from love.

*　　　*　　　*　　　*

After a long walk, the tired men came to a warehouse, long abandoned, but dry, cool, and flickering in dim candlelight. The rest of Moshad's men were inside, most were sleeping, but there were two who were guarding the premises and made their secret calls, evidence that all was clear.

The camels were outside, and Terran knew one of them well and instinctively went over to it, murmuring some soothing words like a meeting place of old friends. Javad stood back and watched.

"If he gets any ideas, you know what to do," Moshad said, walking behind Javad like a ghost.

Javad ignored him. Moshad was a warrior who had gone deep into the beast, and when he found that one voice, he stopped listening to anything else. He had a narrow sense of what Terran represented. Terran was simply a possession to protect, like a wealthy collector who acquires a great painting, and then locks it away in a vault in the bowels of a bank.

It was almost two in the morning, and the men were exhausted. Javad walked over to Terran, who was still petting the camel, and sat down to rest his legs. "There's some bread and soup if you're hungry."

"I'm not hungry."

"Are you tired?"

"No."

A long, uncomfortable silence ensued, and Javad reclined on the ground and closed his eyes. The smell of the camel was his last memory before he drifted off into a drained, dreamless sleep.

Sanjur finished his last drop of soup, and went outside to relieve himself before getting some rest. He chatted briefly with one the guards who stood by the door. As he positioned himself to relieve his full bladder, the deep breathing of Javad caught his attention.

He wondered about the shadowy figure who stood by the camels. Judging from its size, he had no doubts that it was Terran, who was a growing curiosity to Sanjur. So much effort, so much risk associated with securing this boy. They were locked in a tug of war with the Greater Nation. This thought was exciting to Sanjur. It was also sparking his curiosity about Terran's identity and why did the powers of an evicted tribe and the world's most elite educational system want this boy so badly? He'd heard the term Mahdi before, but never paid much attention to it. He'd always considered it the equivalent of some messiah who would wield his magic wand and make the world a better place. Then Sunrot happened, and the idea of a messiah seemed an absurd hope, held only by feeble-minded zealots, of whom he was definitely not one.

Sanjur squinted into the dark, and walked over to Terran's shadowy presence. "Aren't you tired?" he asked.

"What did she say?"

"Parto? Ah, she told me that she loved you… that you would always be her son."

Terran smiled invisibly in the darkness. "From where do you come?"

"I am from a small town called Saraghs… in Turkmenistan."

"You're a hired soldier?"

"No… no, I am a merchant, but lately more of a… a tradesman."

"And what trade is that?" Terran asked politely.

"The trade of staying alive, I suppose." A soft chuckle accompanied his response.

Sanjur sat down. "It's okay if I sit?"

"I am a prisoner; it's not for me to say…"

"I can bring you food, if you'd prefer to eat out here..."

"I'm not hungry."

"What makes you so valuable?" Sanjur asked awkwardly. "I don't mean to pry, but this whole thing about being the Mahdi, how did you get that title?"

There was a long pause as Terran thought about how to respond to such a question.

"The man sleeping could answer your question better than I."

"Perhaps, but, as you say, he's sleeping..."

Terran sat cross-legged on the ground near Javad. He leaned forward, putting his elbows on his knees, studying Sanjur in the dim light. "I will answer your question, but first tell me how you came to be associated with Moshad?"

Sanjur told a shortened and slightly more favorable version of the affairs from the previous night, and Terran shuddered at the telling of the fate of Sanjur's compatriots. There was something about Sanjur that he liked. He was resourceful, intelligent, a survivor, and certainly an animated storyteller.

"I'm sorry about your friends' fate," Terran said after a long pause. "In some way, I'm responsible."

"There is no fault on your side. They were thieves and murderers, they—we—all know where that leads." Sanjur crinkled his brow, and then looked at Terran. "Why did you leave your home for Mashhad?"

"I wanted to find the teachers who can help me assemble the knowledge I need to build my inventions."

"Why are you, a boy, interested in such things?"

"Because I have seen how to help... everyone. Once you see this, it's your responsibility to do everything in your power to manifest it. Another Sunrot will occur, and it will come swiftly and more will suffer."

"You know how to control the sun? Is that what you're saying?"

Terran could hear the smile on Sanjur's face, but could not see it. "No. I know how to compose weather, and weather is the effect of the sun... in theory."

"How do you know of such things? Did he teach you?" Sanjur nodded in the direction of Javad, who was now snoring.

"I just know... I have seen it."

"And so what does this have to do with being the Mahdi?"

"When I was two years old, my parents were killed—"

"How?"

"I was told it was an accident, but there are rumors they were killed so I could be raised by Pirdah—he's our Holy One. I was born on the night of the first storm of Sunrot, almost twelve years, four months from today..."

"I remember it well," Sanjur whispered.

"The prophecy was that the Mahdi would be born on the first day of the end times. My grandfather was Russian—"

"Ah, it explains the eyes."

"Yes... but it was also part of the prophecy that the Mahdi would be pure blooded, so there are those within my tribe that doubt my entitlement, as do I."

"What of the Greater Nation? Why do they want you in Delhi?"

"I scored well on their tests."

"You don't even speak Persian or English... how could you have done so well on their tests?"

"The tests were like puzzles, and I had Nouri to translate."

"And they saw your test results and invited you to Delhi? How? They're no roads. Nothing flies anymore. How were you going to get to Delhi?"

"They were bringing a team to escort Nouri and me."

"They must have really wanted you."

Sanjur looked around at the guard who was about twenty meters behind them, leaning against the wall next to the door. "What if I could get you out of here... would you be interested?"

"Why would you take that risk?"

"The reward could be great if I could get you safely to Delhi."

"How would you do that?" Terran whispered.

"I don't have all the details in my mind, but between your brain and mine, I think we could do it." He turned around again, and lowered his voice ever further. "See that guard?"

Terran nodded, "Yes?"

"He's the only one who's watching us. The second guard is on the other door, on the other side of the building. It's dark. Everyone else is sleeping. I just need to take out that guard. I know my way around here, I can find us a hiding place where we can sleep the night and in the morning, we can find a safer place. Mashhad is a big city, there's no way they could find us. Do you know the place where your teacher lives?"

"No."

"Do you know his last name?"

"Yes."

"They don't. And they'll never be allowed back to the Preserve. They'll put new guards around the Preserve. We can find where your teacher lives—"

"Nouri."

"—Where Nouri lives and we can stay with him until we figure out the whole journey to Delhi... it could work. What do you say? We'll never have a better chance than right now."

"How would you take out the guard?"

Sanjur picked up a large rock, weighing it in his hand. "Watch... and be ready to run."

Terran began to feel the rush of adrenalin as Sanjur stood to his feet. He could sense the world shift like a massive pair of lips conjuring the imprisoned to run free.

Terran watched, wide-eyed, as Sanjur walked to the guard and said something that Terran strained to hear, but it was unintelligible. Sanjur stayed talking with the guard and then a light momentarily flared up and the faces of the two men could be seen for a moment, and then they were gone. *Cigarettes, they were smoking cigarettes.* Then Sanjur disappeared inside the building. About a minute later he saw the guard collapse, and a few seconds after that he saw Sanjur running towards him. Terran stood up, like a runner in a relay race, waiting for the baton.

"Follow me," Sanjur said in a loud whisper, not wanting to awaken Javad, but just as Terran started to run, Terran felt Javad's hand grip his ankle.

"Where are you going?" Javad demanded; his voice still groggy from sleep.

Terran struggled, trying to shake lose his grip, but only managed to fall to the ground where Javad overtook him. "What are you doing? Are you crazy? Stop this, now!"

Terran struggled quietly with all his strength, but Javad was too strong, and sat across his chest holding his arms down at the wrist. One of the camels started to bellow.

"Stop it!" Javad said, trying to convince Terran to stop struggling. "Where do you think you could go?"

Terran held his tongue, watching a dark shadow rise over Javad, and then he heard a dull thud, and Javad went limp, falling on top of him with all of his weight. Terran could feel Sanjur pushing Javad off of him.

"Get up! We have to go, *now!*" It was in Persian, but Terran knew what Sanjur was saying anyway, and he began to run as fast as he could to keep up. Sanjur was holding his hand and pulling him along. A few times he stumbled, and Sanjur literally pulled him up as if he were a doll.

They ran for ten minutes never looking back, and then Sanjur stopped abruptly, as they ducked inside an alleyway, his lungs heaving. "Are you okay?"

"Yes." Terran nodded, struggling to find enough air for his lungs. "Do you know where we are?"

Sanjur held his hand up for a moment, and Terran knew he was listening with all his powers of concentration.

"No idea... but then, neither do they." Sanjur looked down at Terran. "Can you jog?" Sanjur asked.

"Yes, I think so."

"Okay, we'll go at a comfortable pace. Ready?"

Terran held up his hand for a moment as if he were asking a question in school. "Among Moshad's men, is there one who is very tall?"

"Yes, yes, Josid."

"He's here..." Terran lamented. "Then we have to keep running... he's a tracker."

"First of all," Sanjur whispered. "I've picked a route that is untraceable. Secondly, we had a huge head start, and we've been running the whole time, and third, he's one man in a city of two hundred thousand—"

"You don't understand. Josid is a tracker, and not only a tracker, the best tracker of all our people. Perhaps the best of—"

"This isn't the desert... there's no sand here..." Sanjur beat his shoes against the ground. "This is pavement—it's hard. There's nothing to track."

"Josid doesn't track footprints..."

Terran looked around; a new form of fear was written on his face. "We have to keep running," he said, as he ran off down the alleyway.

Sanjur swore in Persian, and then followed.

The streets of Mashhad were empty and dark. Silence engulfed them. It was about 2:40 A.M. They ran at a comfortable pace for another twenty minutes. Sanjur was picking his route intuitively, making every effort to put as much distance between them and Moshad's camp. Suddenly, he stopped and put his hands on his knees, trying to catch his breath.

"I think we can walk now, let's focus on finding a place where we can rest."

"Where?" Terran asked looking around. They were in a residential neighborhood, reasonably well kept.

"I don't know, just keep your eyes open."

A few minutes later, Terran pointed to a teahouse. "Wouldn't it be better to try a business? No one would be there."

"A teashop... good choice. They should have water."

Sanjur went to the side of the teahouse and looked through a window, but couldn't see anything. They went around to the back and found a cellar door that was half underground. It had two panes of glass, and Sanjur pulled out a handgun, poised to break one.

"Where'd you get that?" Terran whispered intensely.

"Borrowed it from the guard. He didn't seem to mind at the time."

Sanjur struck the glass with the butt of his gun—a short, but decisive strike. The breaking glass, when it fell on the cement stairs, seemed horrendously loud against the deep silence of the city streets, and they waited for a minute before they moved again. Sanjur crouched on the steps with his finger to his lips the whole time, and then slowly stood up.

The sound of footsteps running nearby broke the stillness and he immediately crouched down again. There was only one pair of feet, but they were from a large man, and Terran knew they had to be Josid's. He was the only man who could have closed the distance so quickly. Terran's heart was pounding in his chest as he slowly looked over the ledge of the stairwell they were hiding in. He heard the crunch of pebbles as Josid walked within ten meters of their position, but he couldn't see anything, until suddenly, in a glimmer of the faintest moonlight, a shadow fell against the building next door, revealing Josid's inimitable physique.

Terran quickly ducked below the stairwell's ledge and silently mouthed the words to Sanjur's waiting, nervous face. "He's right there." Terran pointed.

Sanjur gripped his gun, his fingers pulsing with adrenalin.

Suddenly, off in the far distance, a gunshot rang out, echoing its terror like a whisper from a ghost.

CHAPTER 20

Trapped

Sanjur, to his own disgust, moved his right foot slightly after the distant gunshot and a scraping sound jumped out of the stairwell—the solemn strains of a tired body, cramped in a small space. The scraping sound projected outward as if they were in an amphitheater, which, in many ways, they were. One of the unique characteristics of a concrete stairwell is its amazing acoustical properties, none of which were fully appreciated by Sanjur, until it was too late.

Terran slowly raised his head over the ledge of the stairwell to see if Josid was visible. Terran could hear shouting way off in the distance, but he wasn't sure if it was real or imagined. His eyes moved on an otherwise perfectly still head—like a periscope he studied the street and the neighboring buildings. Then he heard the slightest of sounds. Someone was walking—slowly. One step, and then another, like someone walking a tightrope suspended above a steep canyon.

The problem was that the sound—subtle as silk on silk—was definitely coming closer. They were trapped. If Josid had a gun, he would use it without hesitation, and while he was a legendary marksman among his tribe, Sanjur and Terran were essentially one target, entwined in the confines of a narrow stairwell. As the footsteps came closer, Sanjur grabbed Terran's arm and motioned to the door. Sanjur stuck his arm inside the open pane, and unlocked the door as quietly as he could, but the sound was still noticeable, and he grabbed Terran's arm and the two went inside.

They were found, and they knew it. They all knew it, including Josid, who immediately surged to the stairwell, noticing the broken glass. His quarry was trapped, but he was still one man, and he didn't know what weapons, if any, he was up against. He knew only one thing: *capture Terran alive.* Sanjur was not to be so lucky.

Josid ducked down into the stairwell, trying his best to avoid making any sound. His knife drawn, he walked through the open door. It was even darker inside the cellar. The scent of jasmine and lavender were the first things he smelled, but there was also the lingering odor of sweat that even the pungent aroma of loose tea couldn't cover.

"You can put the knife down, Josid. I'll come out. I'm alone," Terran said quietly.

"Show yourself," Josid ordered.

Terran shuffled carefully through the barrels of tea that were stacked on top of one another, and presented himself to Josid, his hands at his side, palms open and facing Josid.

"Where's Sanjur?"

"We split up, when he couldn't keep up with me. I don't know where he is."

"His legs are long—"

"Yes, but his lungs are small. He's a merchant... rides camels. He's old."

Josid quickly frisked Terran for any weapons, and not finding any, and satisfied with Terran's explanation, turned around to leave. "Come with me, and stay right by my side."

"Can we at least see if there's any water in here? I'm so thirsty. Aren't you?"

Josid stopped. "Water would be good."

"I think I saw some over there... it looked like a huge jug." Terran pointed to a wooden shelf that was hazy in the blackness. "It looks heavy."

Josid walked over to the shelf, set his knife down, and started to pull the jug from the shelf. Sanjur, with surprising speed took one quick step and slammed the butt of his handgun across the back of Josid's head, and Josid immediately bent over, but didn't go down.

"You must hit him again!" Terran shouted in a half-whisper.

Sanjur couldn't compute how any man could stay conscious from such a blow, but he heard Terran's order, and with robotic precision, struck Josid a second time. This time he fell to his knees, but he was still miraculously conscious, covering his head with his hands, and moaning in pain.

"I can't hit him again," Sanjur exclaimed. "I can't kill him... I'm not a murderer."

"At least take his knife," Terran said, consciously keeping his voice quiet.

Sanjur grabbed Josid's knife, and with his leg, shoved Josid into the wood shelves. And in that decisive kick, the large jug fell on his chest, and a welcome silence spread throughout the cellar.

Terran went to the stairwell and poked his head outside. All was quiet. He pulled the door closed, and locked it.

"We need to find some rope," Sanjur said nervously. "I doubt he'll be out for long."

"We need to find some light," Terran said. "There must be some matches around... let's look."

Sanjur tucked Josid's knife in his back pocket. "We could just run—"

"He'd track us down," Terran quipped. "Our best move is to secure him, and then we can decide our next move... and maybe rest for a while."

"You're right," Sanjur said. "I'll check this side, you take that one."

The search for a rope or matches was unnerving. A six-and-half-foot warrior shared the small cellar, and in the pitch darkness it would be impossible to know if he had awakened, or where he could be if he had.

After a minute of searching, Sanjur let out a long sigh. "Anything?"

"Nothing..." Terran replied. I think you should watch Josid. I'll do the searching."

"That thought occurred to me, too," Sanjur admitted.

A minute later Terran announced he'd found a candle.

"Check all around it," Sanjur offered, "there could be some matches nearby."

A moment later there was a loud snapping sound, and Terran winced and swore.

"What happened?"

"Something pinched me... hard! Ow!"

"Sounds like you met a mousetrap."

"What's a mousetrap?"

"Can you get it off? Sanjur asked.

"Yeah, it just got my hand good. How does it trap mice? It seems like it would kill them."

"Sounds less violent I suppose when you call it a mousetrap," Sanjur replied.

Terran walked to the other side of the cellar, carrying the candle he'd found. "I'll try this side, maybe it makes sense to check his pockets and see if he has any matches."

"Cigarettes!" Sanjur suddenly exclaimed in Persian.

"What?"

"I gave the guard a cigarette to get him to relax and trust me," Sanjur said, as he rifled through his pants pockets, "he gave me a match box and told me to keep the matches that were left. I've had matches this whole time... I must be getting old."

In a few seconds Sanjur had struck a match and instantly the cellar became known to them. Terran brought his candle over and they both lit it.

Terran pointed to a barrel on the top shelf. "Rope. Use his knife to cut the rope off, and we can at least bind his hands and attach the rope to this support post. That should hold him."

Sanjur cut the rope from the barrel top, and then handed his weapons to Terran. "Cover me... just in case he wakes up while I'm binding him."

"Check to make sure he's alive," Terran said.

"I can hear him breathing, he's alive."

"Good."

Sanjur finished tying his hands behind his back, and then put the rope around the support post and tied it snug, while Josid lay on his side. "If he's as exhausted as I am, he'll probably just sleep."

Terran was feeling more relaxed now that they had Josid tied. He allowed his eyes to roam a bit, and saw another rope that was clad in vinyl. He used Josid's knife to cut a length of about ten feet, and then handed it to Sanjur. "Insurance."

"You think he's that strong? That rope is tight and very strong."

"His legs?"

"You really don't trust this guy, do you?"

Sanjur grabbed Josid's legs and began to wrap the rope around them.

"Give me his boots," Terran said. "Socks, too."

"I like the way you think," Sanjur remarked, handing the sand-colored boots and mostly white socks to Terran, who promptly hid them behind a barrel in the deep recesses of the cellar. As he was doing that he suddenly heard a scuffle and Sanjur crying out for help. As he returned, he saw Sanjur held between Josid powerful legs that were squeezing him in a vise.

"*Do something!*" Sanjur screamed.

Terran held a gun in one hand and a knife in the other.

Terran pointed the gun at Josid's head. "Let him go, or I will shoot!"

Josid looked at Terran and continued to crush Sanjur's chest. Sanjur was like a gazelle in the grips of a lion, and he was being suffocated. His head was turning a purplish-blue-red, and Terran knew he didn't have more than thirty seconds, before Sanjur could die from asphyxiation.

"I said let him go!"

"You won't shoot me," Josid said with a madman's glare. "This man isn't worth saving—at least let me kill him, and then you can shoot me if you must."

"Terran, please…" Sanjur was straining to speak.

Terran went around to Josid's feet and took his knife and slit the soles of Josid's left foot. Josid winced in pain, but refused to let go. Seeing no other option, Terran took the knife blade and slipped it between Josid's ankles and then rotated the knife blade with all his strength until it was cutting into Josid's ankles, and suddenly Josid had no other option but to release his crushing grip. Sanjur, with the little strength he had remaining, freed his left shoulder and struck his elbow into Josid's groin.

Josid curled into the fetal position and began moaning. His hands remained tied behind his back, and the rope was still tied to the support post, but in the struggle to crush Sanjur, it had become taut.

Sanjur hobbled far enough to get out of Josid's range, and then collapsed on the floor. Josid was bleeding from his foot, ankles and head. Terran looked between the two men and wondered how his next move could possibly bring him a step closer to Delhi.

Suddenly a thought, or feeling, or some form of vision, burst into his consciousness, and he went over to Josid, pointing the gun at his head.

"The gunshot we heard earlier. What was it?"

Josid opened his eyes at the sound of Terran's voice, but stayed silent.

"Where is Moshad?"

"How would I know?"

Terran looked at Josid from head to toe. "You're bleeding. If I don't bandage you, you could bleed out and die. If you tell me what you know... or what you suspect, I'll bandage your wounds and get you some water to drink."

"Tell me, Terran, why would the Mahdi, if that's what you are, try to run from his people, draw their blood—even aid their enemies? Is it your impurity? You are no more a Mahdi than I am." Josid paused and spit a mixture of blood and saliva. "Keep your bandages away from me, my body is strong. Your help is not wanted. You're an enemy and nothing more, and anyone who will listen to me... that is what I'll tell them. I have seen it with my own eyes. You are not the Mahdi. You're an enemy of my people, and because you're an enemy, I'll tell you nothing. If I die here, let me die in silence."

Josid closed his eyes, signaling his intention not to cooperate. Terran was an enemy in his eyes, and once a Baluch warrior condemned you as an enemy, it was usually your death sentence.

Terran picked up the jug of water that had fallen on the floor, and took a long drink, and then crouched down to Sanjur and poured some water over his face.

"I pray that's water..." Sanjur whispered.

"It is."

"Am I alive?" Sanjur asked feebly.

"Yes."

"And our friend?"

"He's not our friend."

"Sarcasm."

Terran managed a thin smile. "Can you drink?"

"I'll try." Sanjur struggled to roll over and then sit up. Terran helped as much as he could, especially considering his own state of exhaustion.

Sanjur drank several large gulps of water, and then waved his hands. "Can you pour some in my hands?"

Terran poured some water in Sanjur's hands, and he splashed it over his face. "That feels better, thanks."

Sanjur looked in Josid's direction. "And thanks for that, too."

Terran nodded.

"Now what?" Sanjur asked.

"Can you walk?" Terran asked.

Sanjur nodded. "I think so."

"Let's go outside."

They walked outside and sat down on the steps of the stairwell, keeping their voices at the level of a faint whisper, making sure that Josid could not hear them.

"He won't cooperate in any way. We need to bandage his wounds, or he could die."

"Him? I doubt it." Sanjur said. "I think we should just leave him here. We need to keep going—"

"He's a tracker... as long as he's alive, he'll track us. Only Moshad can call him off."

"So what are you saying—we kill him?"

"No, we need him detained."

"How?"

"Whoever owns this teashop will come to work tomorrow and we need to make sure they find him and arrest him for trespassing and destruction of private property. Josid doesn't know a bit of Persian. He'll be detained. They'll take one look at him and know he's not your typical citizen—"

Suddenly they heard two loud, concussive thuds, like someone kicking against a wall, and then a large commotion in the cellar, and the light went out. Terran and Sanjur instinctively backed away and then turned to one another. Terran handed Sanjur the gun, but held onto the knife.

"He kicked out the support post," Terran whispered in awe.

Sanjur heard Terran's whisper, and started to shake his head. "Look, he's got no weapons, no shoes, he has an eight-foot-long post tied to his arms, he's bleeding, what can he do? Let's leave him."

Just then, the support post, like an eight-foot battering ram, came hurtling through the back door, missing Sanjur's head by an inch.

CHAPTER 21

Four Inches

In the perpetual realms of change, in the briefest pause, the filmstrips of lives lived can warp when they get caught in the lens of heat and light. They can begin to distort, and sometimes, an entire life is burned and wasted. Parto worried that Terran's life was like this. It was being warped by those who could only see him as the Mahdi, and anything else was a lesser part to be deleted from the script.

*   *   *   *

Parto and Nouri had been bound by Josid back-to-back with rope. Their legs tied tightly at their ankles. Their mouths gagged. When Josid had arrived, shortly after Moshad left with Terran in tow, he had suddenly appeared on the patio, having climbed the back wall unnoticed. He had first taken Parto from behind and held a knife to her throat, and using only hand movements, made clear his intent.

Nouri bound his own feet first, and then Parto. Once their feet were bound, Josid had them sit back-to-back, and he flung a rope around their chests, circling them many times, tightening it with each turn, as if he were a spider wrapping his prey in silk. When he had finished, he re-tied their legs to his standards, and then placed gags around their mouths—twice. Josid never spoke a word, but if either Nouri or Parto said a single word, he would immediately grab his knife and stare at the offending person with cold eyes that knew well how to paralyze vocal chords.

Almost two hours after Josid had left, Parto and Nouri heard the stairs creaking and immediately began their muffled cries, but instead of a friend or relative, it was the strange man that they had seen at the bottom of the stairs, who appeared to be the leader of the men who abducted Terran.

Moshad was powerfully built, about forty years old, and moved like someone accustomed to preferentialism. He came over and pulled down the gag around Nouri's mouth so Nouri could speak.

"Have you seen anything since we left?" Moshad demanded.

"I presume you ordered this... where's Terran? Why are you here?"

"Keep your voice down," Moshad ordered. "I'm tired, and I'm in no mood to tell you anything." He pulled the gags upwards over Nouri's mouth, sat down, and then stood up again and pulled the gag back down. Nouri winced.

"Do you live here, too?"

"No…" Nouri shook his head.

"What is your address?"

Suddenly, Nouri understood. "He got away didn't he?"

"Tell me your address!" Moshad raised his gun for the first time.

"Terran has never been to my home, and he doesn't have my address."

Moshad brought the gun barrel within a few inches of Nouri's face and then slowly swept it behind him to Parto's profile, who instantly began to fidget and fight with her ropes. Muffled yelps danced in the air.

Nouri spoke in Persian. "Parto, he's just bluffing. He doesn't want to wake anyone up by firing his gun. Terran escaped—"

A moment later a gunshot, so loud, that Nouri lost his hearing for several seconds to a loud ringing sound. He was in shock. Parto was in hysterics, screaming through her gag. Someone was shouting out their window from below. Parto was cut from a bullet graze—a four-inch lesion all the way across her forehead.

Moshad brought his mouth to Nouri's left ear. "This is what we do to women who refuse to dress properly. The next bullet I fire will not be for atonement. It will be for pain. Now, tell me your address!"

The stairs suddenly began to shake, and far below, Parto's father was asking something, but Nouri's hearing was still compromised. All he could do in the pressure of the moment was to speak his address and close his eyes.

He heard some scraping sound. Moshad went over the side of the house, disappearing into the darkness. When he opened his eyes again Parto's father and another man were standing over Parto, wiping blood from her face.

"Cut the ropes," Nouri repeated over and over again.

The men had no knives, they were wearing simple bed clothes, so one ran down the stairs to get a knife and something to use for bandages. Her father consoled Parto the best he could, repeating the only words that rise to the tongue when one is asked to console the inconsolable: "It'll be okay…"

Nouri could see blood stains all over the father's bed shirt, as he craned his neck to see. "How bad? How bad is she hurt?"

"She's cut across her forehead… I don't see anything else… there was only one gunshot, yes?"

"How deep?"

"It's okay… it's okay, you'll be okay." Parto's father held his sobbing daughter, ignoring Nouri's question.

CHAPTER 22

Warning Shot

Hamid paced his office like a leopard in a cage. "Are you sure they were the same men?" he asked.

"From your description, I have no doubt," Nouri replied. "They seemed so civil..."

Nouri was describing the affairs of the past night. It was almost 11:00 A.M., and Nouri was still wearing the same blood-stained clothes from his ordeal in getting Parto to a doctor, and other than to wash his hands, he hadn't had a chance to clean up. Parto had been taken to the doctor by Nouri and her father to see if stitches would be necessary, but she had gone into shock, and was mostly unresponsive.

The doctor had insisted that she stay for observation, so it was decided that Nouri would go to the Preserve and update Hamid on the recent, terrible events. Parto's father would stay with her at the doctor's clinic.

"What about the police?" Hamid asked.

Nouri snorted a sarcastic chuckle. "The Baluch scare the hell out of them. They want nothing to do with them. These are not gangs of knife-wielding drop-outs looking for some thrills, these are cold-blooded killers..."

"It's their job!" Hamid shouted. "We're teachers, we can't defend ourselves... what do we do?"

"I only know I can't go home," Nouri said in a resigned voice. "They'll be there. Safest place is probably right here..."

Hamid crossed his arms across his chest and abruptly stopped pacing. "So you've given up on the boy? You're just going to let them have him?"

"What do you suggest, Hamid? I have nothing to defend myself with. We're over our heads here."

Hamid went to his computer, sat down and started typing. "I have permission from the Director of Recruiting at the Faculty to call her in an emergency. If this isn't an emergency, I haven't seen one."

An automated message opened up: "The person you have called is unavailable at this time, please leave a message. If this is an emergency, click the emergency link below. Thank you."

Hamid clicked his mouse and waited.

A man with reddish-brown, short cropped hair came onscreen. "Security Officer, Franklin, Badge ID 100728—please identify yourself."

"Yes... ah, my name is Hamid Mokri, I am the director of the Preserve in Mashhad, Iran. My authorization number is... 12009-33."

The man typed into his computer and then looked to the camera, after studying what came up on his screen. "Yes, Mister Mokri, how can I help you?"

"Would it be possible to speak with Eleanor Sinclair?"

Franklin glanced at his computer screen. "One moment please, Mister Mokri." The screen immediately went blank with the standard "on hold" message.

Nouri squirmed in his chair. "Do you have anything to eat in here?"

Hamid opened a drawer and tossed a bag of sunflower seeds on the desk. "It's all I have. Sorry."

Nouri glanced at the bag. "It's better than nothing. Thanks."

A minute later, the screen came back on, and it was Eleanor Sinclair sitting in front of her computer. "Hello, Hamid. How are you this morning?"

"I'm fine, Miss Sinclair, but we have a problem... and... and I'm not sure what to do, so I thought I should call you and..."

"Hamid, just tell me what happened."

"The boy, Terran Khan, was taken by his tribe—"

"What do you mean... *taken?*"

"They abducted him, by force, from his guardian's home, and they tied up his teacher and guardian. Actually, they shot his guardian—"

"Is she okay?"

"She's at a clinic right now; we think she'll be okay... but we don't know."

Eleanor leaned forward in her chair, looking very concerned. "When did this happen?"

"Last night... actually early in the morning..." Hamid clicked his fingers to get Nouri's attention.

"Which part—the abduction or the shooting?" Nouri shrugged.

"The shooting... I apologize, Miss Sinclair... I have Terran's teacher in my office and I'm trying to get the most accurate details."

"That's okay. Can the teacher join the conversation?"

Hamid motioned for Nouri to come around to his side of the desk. "This is Nouri Abbasi, Terran's assigned teacher—"

"Yes, we've met before. Hello, Nouri."

"Hi. The time was around two in the morning... it's now about eleven in the morning, so about nine hours ago."

"Do you have any idea where Terran is right now?"

"Somewhere in Mashhad," Nouri said, "But he escaped—"

"From the men who abducted him?" Eleanor asked.

"Yes."

"How do you know that?"

"One of the men who took him came back to our place about two hours later, and I could tell he was looking for him."

"How?"

"He wanted my address, thinking that that's where Terran might go."

Eleanor sat back in her chair and crossed her arms and legs. "Hamid?"

"Yes?"

"We have a team that's being assembled in Mashhad right now. Men started arriving yesterday, and they're assembling at a site we leased to stage the caravan in the outskirts of Mashhad—about ten kilometers from your location. Three Humvees, a gas supply truck, and two armored vehicles equipped with serious fire power are being readied there along with a team of ten of the best security personnel we could find. The armored vehicles are on their way and should arrive tomorrow evening. They're coming up from Kandahar. The Humvees are already there, and most of the security detail is there, too."

Eleanor paused and rubbed her forehead. "This new development throws all of our plans... everything... in a new direction. We have to find Terran and secure his safety. I'll contact our mission leader.... a Captain..." Eleanor looked at her computer screen "... a Captain

Carson Brunel."

Eleanor began to write a note, and took a long pause. Nouri poured out some sunflower seeds in his hand and swept them in his mouth. Hamid opened his drawer, eyeing his dwindling stash of cigarettes, but decided to wait, and slowly closed the drawer.

"I'll be right back gentlemen." Eleanor disappeared from the monitor, and the two men looked at a metal bookcase, mostly filled with three-ring binders, and an empty leather chair with a sweater slung over it.

Hamid opened his desk drawer again and decided that fate had offered him an opportunity to smoke. He quickly selected a cigarette and lit it. "My smoking won't spoil your appetite will it?"

"Actually, I like the smell. Reminds me of my father, when we used to go to cafes."

"Do you want one, too?"

"Maybe later. Thanks."

The movement of Eleanor returning drew their attention back to their fourteen-inch monitor. "Thank you for your patience, gentlemen.

"I'm going to have Captain Brunel visit you so he can make a thorough inquiry into what exactly happened in the abduction… did they say—the men who abducted Terran—why they were taking him back?"

Hamid looked at Nouri.

"They think that Terran is the Mahdi."

"I'm not familiar with that term," Eleanor said, typing something on her keyboard. "Are either of you?"

Eleanor's computer search returned a definition before either Hamid or Nouri could respond.

Mahdi n. Islam: The messiah prophesied to appear at the world's end and establish a reign of peace and righteousness.

Hamid took a drag from his cigarette and then exhaled with his definition entwined with smoke. "To me, the Mahdi is a messiah who comes to unite the world's people in one religion—the one, true religion: Islam."

"He doesn't want this," Nouri said quietly.

"Doesn't want what?" Eleanor asked.

"He told me that he isn't the Mahdi, and that he would do everything in his power to return so he could continue his education. He also said that we should not send anyone to rescue him, as it would only cause the death of innocents."

"That's why we need to find him before they do," Eleanor said, sitting up straight as if she was late for an important meeting and had to go. "I'm sorry to hear that Terran's guardian got in the middle of this conflict, I hope she's doing better very soon. If she needs anything... anything at all, please let me know so we can help. We have resources in Mashhad now. Captain Brunel can be of help. We'll do everything we can to find Terran. Just cooperate with Brunel's team; they'll help. Okay?"

"Okay..."

"Anything else, gentlemen?"

Hamid cleared his throat for a moment. "These Baluch tribesmen are as clever as they are ruthless. We're vulnerable here. They'll assume that Terran will try to return to the school—they're probably out there right now, and I have over five hundred students in this complex. The police are worthless in this city, a few of our wealthy residents have private security, and we have nothing... a few parents patrolling at night with sticks and pocket knives—"

"Got it. I'll have Captain Brunel post some guards outside your school. Gentlemen, I want to get a message to the Captain, so I'm going to have to say goodbye. Thank you for your help with this. Keep vigilant, and keep me posted."

She grabbed her mouse. "Goodbye, gentlemen." The video window disappeared, and the monitor screen suddenly reflected the slatted window shades in Hamid's office.

Nouri went back to his chair and sat down, grabbing another mouthful of sunflower seeds. "Do we have any guns—with bullets— anywhere in this school?"

As if on cue, a gunshot rifled through Hamid's window shattering the upper pane and spraying glass throughout his office. Both men lunged for the floor. It was the start of a war they were ill-prepared for.

"No." Hamid's answer held an eerie irony.

"No, what?" Nouri asked.

"No, we don't have any guns… with bullets."

"I hope this Captain gets over here fast."

"I hope we're still alive when he does."

CHAPTER 23

Awakening

When the support beam had been hurtled through the cellar door, Sanjur and Terran took flight, and had they been gifted with wings, they would have flown as far from that place as possible, but their legs were already tired, and their bodies exhausted. They ran full speed for about one kilometer and then Terran saw a grove of pine trees, and suggested that they hide in it.

"I like the idea of being outside," Sanjur said, gasping for breath. "I don't want to be trapped... inside again with that crazy man. He's... he's not human. I'd rather take my chances outside. Besides... I think I could outrun him."

Terran laughed to himself. "No, you couldn't."

"He has a telephone pole to drag around; I think I can outrun him now."

"Don't count on it. The only solution with Josid, if you're his enemy, is to kill him. Anything else only delays the inevitable—your death."

"Well, the good news is that he doesn't have either a gun or a knife, and we do."

As they walked into the pine grove, the scent of pine trees was suddenly abundant, and Terran could feel the ground soften from the cushion of fallen pine needles.

Sanjur sat down and leaned against one of the trees. "If I snore too loud, know that I am very sorry."

"Shouldn't we have a guard?" Terran asked.

"We should, but it can't be me... I'd be a lousy guard... only stay awake for a minute or two. Have to close my eyes..."

In a matter of a minute, as he had predicted, Sanjur was breathing in the rhythm of deep sleep.

Terran struggled to stay awake. He knew that Josid was out there and would be searching for them as soon as he could free himself and bandage his wounds. The only question was whether he would first go back and seek help from his team or move immediately to track them. Now that Terran had sided with their enemy—he was unsure of his own safety. Once a Baluch conspires with the enemy, they, too, transform into the enemy. His only saving grace was that Pirdah saw him as the Mahdi and had convinced the Baluch elders of this as well. It was the only thing that might keep him alive in the event Josid found him.

It wasn't long before Terran fell asleep, too. Perhaps the intoxicating scent of pine or the utter exhaustion of his body and mind, whatever the cause, took him from the world of banality to a world where kinship with eagles, circling in wild space, brought him a measure of peace.

*   *   *   *

It was the light that woke Sanjur, and while he could have slept longer, the light activated his remembrance of a certain Baluch warrior that was searching to kill him, and even though the pine tree grove was thick, in the early morning light, they would be visible to a trained eye looking for a flash of white in an otherwise green shelter. The other element that had stirred him to wakefulness was the hunger in his stomach and the thirst in his throat.

Sanjur winced as he sat up, his ribs were very sore, and the recall of how close he had visited death's door in the vise grip of Josid's legs brought him to full wakefulness. All of the events that had transpired the past twelve hours came crashing through his consciousness, like vandalizers searching to degrade purity.

His arm reached out to poke Terran. "Wake up. We need to move on."

After a few moans, Terran stretched his body, and forced himself awake. "Good morning." His squinting face hid his attempt at a smile.

Even in the weaker light of an early dawn, it gave their location a vulnerability that Terran immediately sensed. "This isn't as well-hidden as I had thought. I think we should stay down… you especially."

Sanjur lay as flat on the ground as he could. "I could fall asleep again like this."

"Don't," Terran said. "We need to get to the school. If we can get back there, I could disappear—"

"And where do I disappear?" Sanjur mused, looking up through the branches.

"We'll figure that out once we get to the school."

"And don't you think your friends will be patrolling the school just waiting for us to appear. I can't imagine they'll just let us walk in."

"What if we went to a police station?"

Sanjur chuckled. "You mean if we just walked in and announced that a band of wild Baluchians were hunting us down, and we'd like them to escort us to the Preserve for refuge?"

"Why not?"

"First of all, and I'm by no means guilty of any offense, but the police have a record on me—" Sanjur held up his hand to quiet what he presumed to be a question from Terran, "—secondly, the police don't see themselves as an escort service, unless you have something valuable to give them in return for their assistance."

"What if I went to them and tried?"

"Do you speak Persian? Oh, and then there's still the matter of me, your rescuer, or did you forget that?"

Terran stayed silent, knowing that Sanjur's questions were rhetorical.

Sanjur held up his left hand and looked at it admiringly. "One thing about Mashhad is that it has a lot abandoned buildings, and these buildings house people, people who have nothing. I can use this ring... perhaps... to... to get some people to help us. Maybe they could create a distraction long enough to get us into the school."

"Sounds like a good idea," Terran said. "This ring, is it valuable?"

"It is to me..."

"To others?"

"It's solid gold... I should think so."

Terran turned to face Sanjur, lying on his stomach. "Then we have our plan."

"Can we include in our plans some food and water?" Sanjur asked with a smile.

"We'll make that part of the deal for the ring," Terran replied. "Let's go."

CHAPTER 24

An Unwelcome Return

Mashhad began to sound more like a city as people awakened and walked outdoors to greet the day. Its citizens were tough, gritty souls, wearing lean, muscular bodies. Old people were rare, but occasionally one would appear on the streets, serving notice to the younger generations of their future state—if they were lucky.

Terran and Sanjur cautiously made their way through the streets, attentive to the telltale flash of a white shirt accompanied with a red belt. An old man, walking with a cane, passed by, and Sanjur went up to him and explained that he and his "son" were looking for the Preserve, and needed directions. He pointed with his cane, and spoke Persian with a raspy, but friendly voice. Sanjur thanked him, and they adjusted their path further north, cutting across an abandoned strip mall of tiny shops with boarded windows.

"He said it's about two kilometers north on Daneshgah Street. I know the street, and we should be crossing it in a few more blocks."

"If we're getting that close, maybe we should find our... helpers."

"Yes, I agree," Sanjur said, looking around. "Maybe that one."

Sanjur pointed to a large storage building where two young kids were playing in the front with a deflated soccer ball. As they walked up to the boys, one ducked inside and the other one picked up the ball and stood and watched them, waving his hand tentatively. Sanjur and Terran stopped about ten feet short of the boy and lightly bowed. "I am Sanjur, and this is my son, Terran. Are your parents around or an adult perhaps?"

A middle-aged man came to the open door, a boy trailing him. The man was dressed in gray pants, but was otherwise shirtless as it appeared that he had just been washing his face, and had a white towel wrapped around his shoulders. "Salaam," he said, with a light bow. "I'm Rostam, can I help you find something?"

"Actually," Sanjur said, "we're on our way to the Preserve—"

"Ah, it's just down this street about a kilometer and a half." Rostam turned around to gesture behind him.

"Yes, we know the way," Sanjur said, nodding his head. "The problem is that we come from a small village where we fear that there may be those who will try to block our entry into the school. We need someone—preferably a small group—who could create a distraction at the school so we could sneak in. I know it's an odd request... from a stranger no less, but we don't know a soul in this entire city, and you can call it fate or randomness, but here we are." Sanjur put his arms out, palms to the sky, and smiled as warmly as he could.

Rostam put his hand to his beard, and looked contemplatively between Sanjur and Terran, sizing them up. "I don't know..."

"I can pay you for your trouble." Sanjur took his ring off and handed it to Rostam. "It's solid gold."

Rostam looked into Sanjur's eyes, never even looking at the ring, and then looked down at Terran, smiling slightly.

"There are three families who live here," he said. "We have five boys and two girls at the Preserve, and two more on the way. Why would your people care if he goes to school? Isn't it an honor?"

"It's a very complicated situation..."

Rostam pointed to Sanjur's side. "Are you bleeding?"

Sanjur looked down at his right side and saw the blood stain. "I know we look messy... and yes, that is blood... my blood, but I'm okay."

"From where do you come?" Rostam asked, his eyes squinting as the sun broke over the surrounding buildings and suddenly made its presence felt.

"It's a very small village to the northeast. About sixty miles away."

"And you just arrived?"

"Yes."

"Are you hungry?"

Sanjur smiled and nodded, looking at Terran. "He's starving... I was hoping that the ring could pay for a meal *and* your help with getting Terran safely inside the school."

Rostam handed the ring back to Sanjur, and motioned them inside.

"You don't need to pay us. It's a wedding band. Keep it. We were just making some breakfast. Come, you can eat with us... we have enough."

"You are most kind," Sanjur bowed. He took Terran's hand, and the two walked inside, and immediately smelled eggs frying. The interior was open with a few compartments in the back. They walked for about sixty feet to a back area that opened to a courtyard of sorts where two women were preparing a breakfast of eggs and rice. Rostam made introductions. The two women were a bit somber, but kindly in their gestures, though they never spoke a word. Another man, tall and angular like Sanjur, came from one of the compartments and stretched his arms behind him. He looked about thirty, his head perfectly bald with a full, black beard. He seemed unconcerned with the strangers as if it were a common practice to invite strangers in for breakfast.

Rostam glanced at the man. "These are travelers from the north. This is..."

Sanjur pointed to himself. "Sanjur, and this is my son, Terran," Sanjur said in his best Persian.

"Salaam. I'm Ahmad."

"Salaam, Ahmad." Sanjur looked to his various hosts. "Thank you for your hospitality. It is most appreciated."

"Are you looking for work?" Ahmad asked.

"Actually, I'm trying to enroll my son in the Preserve—"

"Is he old enough?"

"Oh, yes, he's just small for his age."

"How old are you, Terran?"

"I'm sorry; he doesn't speak Persian."

"English?"

Sanjur shook his head. "No, not very much."

"Where are you from?"

"A tiny village about sixty kilometers to the northeast."

"And what do they speak there?"

"It's a Baluch dialect..."

"Shiite or Sunni?"

Terran had a sense of the question and detected that Sanjur was rapidly getting over his head. "Tell him that after the Sunrot, few care about the past anymore—differences dissolved in the shared misery that we all felt in the passing of so many. The Baluch are one people now; we see a new future together."

Sanjur did as he was told, and Ahmad nodded when he finished his translation. "This is true throughout Iran. Your son... he seems older than he looks..."

"He hears that a lot," Sanjur remarked diffidently.

Rostam cleared his throat, signaling his interest to join the conversation. "Our adopted son mentioned that a Baluch boy came to the Preserve about a week ago. He described him as similar to your son, but he never came to school... seemed he was given a private tutor who could speak his native language. Do you know of this boy?"

Sanjur shook his head. "No, but we are a large ethnicity..."

"My son," Rostam continued, "said that a rumor existed that this boy was brought to the school half-dead. He had walked through the desert for eighty kilometers all by himself without food or water. He was tested and he was invited to an ALIGN Center—the first from our city. His name was..."

"...Terran Khan," one of the women whispered, who had started to listen to the conversation.

Sanjur instantly wished he had had the foresight to use fake names. Even he, with his quick tongue and agile mind, would not be able to deny this turn of events.

"So it is you, Terran Khan?" Rostam asked, looking at Terran.

"How do they know my last name?" Terran asked.

Sanjur managed little more than a shrug and then faced Rostam. "Yes, it's him. I'm sorry to have lied to you nice people. Deception is not something I do easily... my humble wish is for your forgiveness."

Suddenly, from somewhere in the shadows of the great room, they heard a child's whimper, and then a loud scream. Then, from out of the shadows, a towering man, limping in blood-spattered clothing, carried a child. The young boy, only four years old, was held by a massive hand whose grip was holding the child's shirt, dangling him in the air like a mobile. The young boy was crying as he was suspended helplessly in the air.

Josid looked around and spoke one word in terrifying purity. *"Terran!"*

Sanjur reached from behind his back and pulled out his gun. "Release the child."

Rostam and Ahmad were speechless, though the women were suddenly gasping in hushed cries as they cowered, unsure of what to do.

"I will spare this child when I leave here with Terran. Drop your gun or this child dies."

"What's he saying?" Rostam screamed.

Sanjur kept his eyes on Josid, and dropped his gun gently to the floor. "He says he'll release your child when he and Terran are allowed to leave."

Terran stepped forward, in the direction of Josid, but Sanjur stuck out his hand and grabbed his collar, pulling him back. "How do we know you'll release the child and leave in peace?"

"You have only my word... Terran, pick the gun up and come here. Now!"

"You are a coward to use a small child—"

Josid's forced laughter filled the room, and the boy—dangling in despair—suddenly quieted down as he craned his head to examine the giant that held him.

"I will go with him," Terran whispered. "These people should not suffer any penalties from my doing. Let me go. I'll be okay."

"No, you won't," Sanjur whispered.

Rostam grabbed Sanjur's arm. "Tell me what's going on—"

"Not now" Sanjur said. "This is my problem—"

"That's *my* child!"

"No one will be killed," Terran said, and then darted away from Sanjur's grip with a sudden shrug.

"The gun!" Josid shouted.

Terran bent down and picked up the gun, and then solemnly walked towards Josid. As Terran walked he dispatched the gun's bullets. Five bullets fell to the concrete floor in a brittle, metallic melody.

"Pick them up!" Josid shouted.

Terran kept walking, ignoring Josid's orders, and then angrily threw down the gun.

Josid's arm was getting tired of holding the child, and he shifted the child to his left hand.

As Terran made his way to Josid, Josid backed up towards the door from which he'd come. The whole group followed, like iron filings drawn by a powerful, but invisibly distant force.

With his free hand, Josid motioned for Terran to hurry, but Terran kept his pace, careful and deliberate.

"He won't hurt you," Terran said to the young child who was whimpering, but everyone in that room knew he was really talking to Josid.

"Release him," Terran said. "I'm here."

"When we get outside," Josid countered, in a tone of voice that didn't invite discussion.

"Don't move!" Josid ordered, looking in Sanjur's direction with contempt. "When I get outside, I'll release the child. Everyone stays inside."

Sanjur was forty feet away, and his sightline was slightly obstructed with wood beams that crisscrossed between himself and Josid, but he noticed a blurred flash of clothing, deep in the shadows, behind Josid. Was it more of the Baluch clan? He squinted and then suddenly saw a man step forward with a large wooden beam, swinging it with full force against the shoulders of Josid. A loud whack shuddered through the room, and Josid dropped to his knees in a loud, gasping breath. The young child fell to the ground, and in one moment, all was chaos.

Josid fell to his knees, gasping for breath, his face in shock.

Sanjur ran to the scene with his knife out. The man with the wooden beam, swung again, and this time is was sufficient to knock Josid flat on the ground. "Do you have rope?" Sanjur asked, turning to Rostam and Ahmad. "Rope?"

Ahmad ran to a back room and returned with a section of rope about twenty feet long. One of the women clutched the terror-stricken child in her arms and went out to the courtyard to console him. Terran sat down and watched as the men lurched into action to tie Josid up, hoping to contain him before he regained consciousness.

"What... who is he?" asked the man with the wooden beam. He turned to Terran. "And who are you? What's going on?"

Amid the chaos, the questions just hung in the air, unanswered.

Between Sanjur and Ahmad, Josid was neutralized. Rostam stood up, believing that the giant was subdued and under their control, and went to the gun and picked it up. "Grab those bullets, and bring them here." He pointed to the bullets scattered on the floor some ten feet away.

The man, short, but powerfully built, leaned his improvised weapon against the wall, squatted down and began collecting the bullets one by one.

Rostam pointed the empty gun to where Josid lay, bundled tightly in rope from his shoulders down to his ankles. "Who is this man?"

Sanjur stood and wiped his brow, staggering slightly to catch his balance. "His name is Josid. He's one of those who're trying to abduct Terran, and return him to his people. He's also, and I mean no disrespect to his family, the very definition of terror in a human body. I hate him." Sanjur kicked Josid on his side, but not so hard as to wake him.

"Who are these people?" the short man asked with the bullets in his hand.

"Arash, this is Sanjur, and his son, Terran."

Arash nodded dutifully. "And their business here?"

Josid moaned a little, and moved his left foot—wrapped in thick bandages. Josid only wore one boot.

"Give me those bullets..." Rostam said.

Arash reached over and dropped them into Rostam's cupped hand.

"These are travelers from a Baluch village," Rostam said, "the boy is the one Danush told us about a few days ago."

Arash looked astonished. "The one who crossed the desert and was invited to the ALIGN Center? This little one?"

Rostam finished reloading the handgun, flipped the safety on and stashed the gun in the back of his pants. "I'll hang on to this for the time being. I was in the army... I know how to use it."

Sanjur flicked his hand, signaling his relief.

Terran looked up, seeking Sanjur's eyes. When he found them, he glanced at Josid and whispered. "We found our distraction."

CHAPTER 25

A New Plan

Eleanor tried her best to avoid her brother's help—nepotism was definitely on her short list of pet peeves—but without doubt she needed his influence. The computer "rang"... for too long. *Where is he? He picked the wrong night to turn off his computer.*

On her second try, the screen suddenly lit up, and a tired looking face, squinted at the screen. The man was almost unrecognizable to Eleanor, except for the green plaid robe. It was definitely her brother, Josh Sinclair.

"This is becoming a habit, Sis," Josh said.

"I wouldn't call this late unless it was an emergency. Thanks for answering."

"Give me a second," Josh got up and returned about a minute later carrying a glass of water. "So, what's the emergency?"

"The kid in Iran, remember him?"

"Yes..."

"He was kidnapped by some rogue elements in his tribe. They shot his guardian and tied up his teacher. Almost killed them."

"Why?"

"They believe this boy is their messiah."

"Messiah?"

"They probably think that an education will corrupt him, that he'll lose interest in his supposed mission, which, by the way, the boy thinks is bullshit."

"What do you need, Sis?"

"Josh, I want this boy—"

"We can't take him. It's his tribe. If they want him to stay, it's their call, he's a minor. It was one thing when he ran away, we didn't know if he was a runaway or a reject. Now, it's clear."

"The only thing that's clear is that the boy wants to learn. After he was abducted, he ran away again, and right now, he's in Mashhad, and our Director at the Preserve doesn't know where... but then, neither do his pursuers."

"So the boy is missing?"

"Yes."

Josh leaned back in his chair. "You really can't call them pursuers, Sis. They're his people; hell...one of them could be his father. We don't know."

"We know that he wants to learn. He's demonstrated that much. He's risked everything to come to us. His intellect may not show up on our planet for another thousand years, and you're willing to let him be smothered by tribal elders who want to dress him up as a messiah... like ... like he was a fucking doll? We *need* him."

"Okay... so what exactly do you propose?"

"I need more resources—"

"Specifics..."

"An airplane. I need a team that can go in there and extract him and bring him directly to Denver, and I need this team assembled and ready to leave in twenty-four hours."

"I said specifics, not dreams... look, you know I can't get a plane for this mission. We have three working planes that *maybe* have a range that could make it to Mashhad. Three planes for the entire GN! How can I go to Stanton and make a pitch that we should risk one of our most important assets to rescue a twelve-year old boy from a backwards tribe of Old Schoolers in the deserts of Iran? How can I do that?"

"Josh, I already told you. We could wait another thousand years before we see an intellect like this. All we need to do is bring this boy in, get him our best teachers, and see what he does with this knowledge."

"It's that simple?"

"I studied the video tape—when Terran took the CIP—I've never seen anything close to his intellect. The inventions, the insights, the value that he could bring to Helios... it could take a year or two, but after that, *he* will be our greatest asset. It's well worth the risk of an airplane. I'm sure of it."

"He's still one person," Josh observed, "and a twelve-year-old at that.

It's a hard sale to Stanton."

"I've never felt as strongly about something as this. We need him. Every risk we could possibly make is worth it. Please, Josh, do everything you can to convince Stanton. You can take over the project if that would help. I don't care. I just want to get Terran here. Okay?" Her plaintive tone made clear her seriousness.

Josh let out a long sigh, and put his hands on his knees. "I'll call Stanton and see what I can do—"

"When?"

"First thing in the morning."

"Now..."

"No, not now, it's after one in the morning."

"He'll know it's important if you call him now."

Josh looked around his room, exasperation showing on his face. "Look, don't push it. If I call him now, he might think I've gone crazy. This isn't national security. This isn't some Saudi prince who needs emergency bypass surgery, and needs a plane to—"

"No, this is much more important," Eleanor interrupted, her voice taut and intense. "This is the future of our planet—our entire species, condensed into a small boy who just happens to have scored the highest on our CIP by an order of magnitude! He could be the source of new technologies that help humanity crawl out of the deepest pit it's been in since the Middle Ages... call him, now... *please?*"

Josh stared at the screen. His sister was the most determined person he'd ever met. He suddenly knew it was going to be a late night. "I'll put on some coffee and call him."

"Thanks, Josh. Call me afterwards... okay?"

"Do I have a choice?"

Eleanor kissed her fingers and touched them to the screen. "Thanks."

"You're welcome... and I'll call you as soon as I'm done."

The video screen faded to sudden darkness, and Eleanor took a deep breath. Now she had to wait.

CHAPTER 26

War Room

Peter Lucas was anxious. He was an ex-Navy lieutenant who had survived the Sunrot only because he had been a student at the Naval Academy. Peter was a favored student of his engineering professor, who happened to have access to the Naval Academy's underground bunker system, owing to the fact that he had designed it.

When the first storm hit, it caught most people by total surprise. Unbeknownst to the masses, the Director of Science and Technology within the U.S. Department of Homeland Security had lobbied for a media blackout. Even government websites which distributed space weather data through their live feeds were shut down for national security reasons. The mainstream media, complying with orders from Homeland Security, ignored the subject, while astronomy and science blogs lit up about the issue.

To those who could read the "tea leaves," there was little doubt that something extraordinary was about to happen. A few brave scientists spoke out, but they were ignored by the media, and their messages—like ghostly images—soon faded to all but a small fraction of concerned citizens. Even entire universities were gagged by the media, and the blackout covered not only the U.S., it was global. Those who were fortunate to have had both the information and quick access to an underground shelter were the lucky ones. Everyone else, if they survived, were "walking miracles," as they were known in those early years of Sunrot.

The first storms hit much harder than anyone expected. Sustained winds in excess of 200 miles per hour surprised even those who were predicting harsh storms, and the speed, at which the storms grew, was unlike anything seen before. Darkness engulfed the entire world as the power grids went down. No one was spared. Peter was one of the fortunate who were able to get to reinforced, underground shelters quickly, hunker down, and ride out the storms, which lasted nearly two weeks. Then, as if to ravage any hope, the storm only led to worse destruction in the form of earthquakes and floods.

It was just after 3 A.M., and Peter had been summoned by Trevor Stanton's office. The message had been cryptic:

"New mission. Orders at Helios HQ. Come ASAP. No Further Communication."

Peter was one of the leaders of what was known as the Advance Guard of the GN. He was thirty-six, reasonably handsome, but not your typical square jawed, crew-cut Navy officer. He was more of an intellectual, top of his class in engineering at the Naval Academy, and preferred longer hair. He seldom exercised—at least physically, preferring the exercise of books. He was known as a skilled problem solver. Stanton took notice of Peter's leadership when Peter had been involved in a series of dangerous and successful rescue missions of important dignitaries and politicians during the first year of Sunrot.

As Peter entered Stanton's offices, inside Helios' headquarters, he was met by an aide who escorted him down a long corridor to an elevator. They descended three stories to a war room, in which two men sat chatting and drinking coffee.

One of the men stood up and invited him in, thanking the aide for the escort. "We have coffee if you need it," he said, shaking hands. "I'm Josh Sinclair, and this is Bill Jennings. We're leading a new mission to rescue some people who are important to the GN, and are currently stranded in Mashhad, Iran." Josh let the words hang in the air, and then sat down, pointing to a chair for Peter, encouraging him to do the same.

"Mashhad? How... how would we get there?" Peter asked, not hiding his confusion.

"As it turns out, we have a Boeing 777-X that's on its way here as we speak."

"From where?"

"Berlin..."

"So it's flying from Berlin to here, and then back to Mashhad? Why not just fly to Mashhad directly?"

Bill Jennings stirred and sat up a bit in his chair. "Because it's a more complicated mission than being a taxi."

Bill was a diplomat. He had been stationed in Baghdad as an attaché to the American Embassy. He knew Iran well—better than anyone at Helios—and Stanton had required his involvement when the mission had been begrudgingly approved.

"That's why you're involved as the field manager," Josh explained. "The *complication*, as Bill refers to it, is not really too complicated, because our cargo is a twelve-year-old boy and his teacher. The real issue is that the boy is trying to run away from his home to pursue his studies, and at the moment, we're having a little trouble finding him."

Peter looked perplexed as he pondered this new dimension. "Sir, I don't understand." Peter looked around with a nervous smile, as if he were the victim of a practical joke. He knew Josh Sinclair by name only. He'd never heard of Bill Jennings. Josh was known to be one of the smartest people in Helios, but his explanation was incoherent and impossible. *Sleep deprivation, perhaps?*

Josh poured some coffee into an off-white, bone china teacup, and slid it over to Peter, who lightly nodded his appreciation, but remained silent.

"I realize it sounds crazy," Josh said, "but the fact is that this is no ordinary boy. He tested off the charts on our CIP tests, and we want him here, at our ALIGN Center, as soon as possible."

"But what did you mean when you said you were having trouble finding him?"

"This boy's name is Terran Khan," Josh said, turning to a computer screen that showed a satellite image of northeastern Iran. With a laser pen in hand, he pointed to the screen. "We believe he left his village, which was somewhere in this vicinity, and walked—alone, mind you—across this desert area to Mashhad. Eventually he found his way to our Preserve. Now, the issue is that his tribe sent a team to abduct him from the Preserve, and return him—against his wishes—to his home village.

"This abduction team forcibly took the boy from his guardian and teacher, shooting his guardian, and making off with the boy to an undisclosed place. From there, according to our information, he escaped. He's now somewhere in Mashhad, and is being sought by his abductors."

"And the police?" Peter asked quietly, taking his first sip of coffee.

"In Mashhad, the police are indifferent to such things," Bill responded. "To them, it's a domestic dispute between Old Schoolers, and they'd prefer that the Baluch stay in the desert. They don't get involved."

"Even if the GN pressures them?" Peter asked.

"We don't have time to grease the wheels there... and there's one other thing to this story we haven't mentioned... the boy is widely believed to be a messiah to his people. We really don't want that story getting out. It complicates things, so it's in our best interest to keep the story simple: boy leaves Old Schoolers for the Preserve, Old Schoolers abduct him, he escapes and the GN helps him regain his freedom to learn. Simple, like that."

"A messiah?" Peter asked.

"Supposedly, it's the reason they're pursing him. I'm sure a kid with that kind of intellect stands out, and they probably assume, as smart as he is, that it's a gift from God. I don't know the details, and I don't think it's important to our success."

Josh took a sip of coffee, and glanced in Bill's direction. "What is important is that we're putting you in charge of the task. We want you to assemble your resources, and be prepared to leave..." Josh looked at his wristwatch, "in five hours."

"What resources will I need?"

"The plane's equipped with a staff. We're working on potential landing strips with the right kind of fuel. We have some options in Tehran, but that leaves you with a five-hundred mile drive."

"Excuse me, Sir," Josh asked, "Can a plane fly all the way from here to Iran... that's what, six-thousand miles?"

"About that... to Tehran. It's tight, but with a light payload, our plane will do it just fine."

"Okay," Peter said, "so once we land, how do we find this boy?"

"We have a team on the ground in Mashhad. It's a bit of a rag-tag team assembled from our base in Kandahar, and some of the members of that team are mercenaries, but they'll provide ground support and supplies. They have everything you'll need once you get to Mashhad. We have a Colonel… or Captain there—one of our own, from Louisiana I believe. Something of a cowboy, according to his profile, but he was the best we could find that was anywhere within five-hundred miles of Mashhad."

"So he's searching for Terran Khan, too?"

"I think it's more accurate to say he's staking out strategic locales where the boy might go for refuge, like the Preserve."

"Do we have com channels open in Mashhad with this Colonel or Captain?"

Josh nodded. "We do. By my estimate you should be on the ground in fourteen hours. Chances are, even if they can get Terran to a safe house of sorts, it'll still be hard to secure his transport to the airplane. His abduction team was probably carefully chosen to be good fighters. Bill, what can you tell Peter about the Baluch?"

"Not a lot, to be honest. We don't know their numbers. They're an ancient people with roots in Mesopotamia. They're a collection of tribes—some nomadic, some settled in villages and even small cities, stretching across Iran, Afghanistan, and Pakistan. They're a tough lot, raised in tough environments, and they have social laws that would make your head swim—brutal people… certainly can be. If this boy is seen as their messiah, the fact that he ran away… well, he probably knows what's in store for him if he becomes christened a messiah…"

"What?" Peter asked.

"Unite everyone in Islam. That's it. That's everything." Bill shook his head, and stared down at his empty coffee cup.

"Everyone?"

"Yup, that's what any good messiah is tasked to do… establish the one, true religion and get everyone on the planet to salute the same God, religion, morals, the whole ball of wax, you know, the covenant."

"That's a tough job after Sunrot," Peter observed.

Josh nodded. "You got that right, and it's probably one of the reasons the kid wants out."

A deep silence filled the room for the first time since Peter arrived. He took a sip of coffee, and swallowed hard. "Would it be possible to talk with this Colonel or Captain?"

"Now?"

Peter nodded.

"We can try." Josh grabbed a keyboard and punched some keys. A password field popped up, and he entered his password to access the project file. "It's *Captain* Carson Brunel. Looks like a good chap. He's been in Kandahar for six years. Should know something about the Baluch, I would think... right, Bill?"

"Maybe..."

"I'll make the introductions, but you and the good Captain should do the talking. Bill and I will step aside. Okay?"

Peter nodded.

"You ready?"

"Yes."

Josh pushed a single button and a video window opened with a single word on the screen: *Calling*.

Josh pushed a folder across the table to Peter. "It's all there. Access codes to the project file, everything we have. I'm your only vertical report, so if you need anything, you come to me. Understood?"

"Yes, Sir."

A very choppy video suddenly materialized at one frame per second. The audio was filled with static, but a voice was recognizable, though it had a thick Middle Eastern accent. "Hello? This is basecamp Mashhad, I am Farzad Ghorbani."

"This is Josh Sinclair, calling from Helios. Is Captain Brunel available?"

"Sir, Captain Brunel is on his way to the Preserve."

"Has there been any progress in finding the boy, Terran Khan?"

"No, Sir. None that I can report."

"We will be making a complete update to the project file in the next hour," Josh explained. "Please review it and make sure that Captain Brunel is aware of these plans as well. I expect that the project file will be changing on the hour over the next ten hours or so. Please keep a steady eye on it."

"Yes, Sir."

"What is your role, Farzad?" Peter asked.

"Technical Operations Director—communications mostly."

Josh leaned in, pointing to Peter. "This is Peter Lucas, he's the Director of Strategic Projects within the Advance Guard of Helios. He'll be visiting you in about fourteen hours. Peter will be the project leader on the ground."

"You said you would be here in fourteen hours? Did I hear that right?"

"You did," Josh answered. "We're deploying a plane."

"Yes, Sir, I understand. It will be good to meet you, Mister Lucas. We will take good care of you."

"Thank you, Farzad." Peter opened his notebook, his pen poised to write. "Are there any resources you need that would improve your operational efficiency?"

Farzad's face lurched into a questioning look, as if no one had ever asked him such a question. "Batteries... if you have them. Our remote communicators have a range of only a few hundred meters when the batteries are low. I'll upload the kind of battery we need to the bulletin board on the project file. That's about all I can think of for now... unless you can bring cheeseburgers." The next frame caught Farzad grinning, his teeth clearly visible for the first time.

Peter and Josh grinned, too.

"I'll see what I can do," Peter said.

Josh leaned in again. "Okay, Farzad, thanks for your time. We'll keep in touch through the project file. Oh, and one thing I need your commitment on..."

Farzad looked eagerly into the camera and smiled expectantly. "Yes?"

Josh paused for a conspicuously long time, letting the gravity of his comment build. "The project file is for your eyes only. Do not share it with anyone other than Carson upon his return. If for some reason Carson doesn't return, contact us for further instructions. Under *no* circumstances, are you to share this file. Understood?"

Farzad blinked a few times nervously and glanced behind him, moving closer to the camera. "You have my word."

"Good. Your discretion will be rewarded."

"Thank you, Sir."

"One last thing… let us know as soon as you have any updates on the boy's status."

"Yes, Sir."

"Goodbye, then."

"Yes, Sir… goodbye."

The video instantly faded to black, and the room was suddenly quiet except for the whisper of a ventilation fan.

"I'll leave the project file open, but close it when you're done. Study what's in that folder when you get on the plane. For now, focus on the project file."

Josh stood up. "Anything else you need?"

"Is deadly force authorized?"

"Josh looked at Bill and chuckled. "I'm an educator. Never fired a gun in my life, but if I were in Iran, and I had Old Schoolers shooting guns at me, I'd say yes, deadly force is authorized. The key element of this mission—how your success will be measured—is one thing and only one thing: the boy shakes my hand in the next forty-eight hours. Understood?"

"Yes, Sir."

"Excellent. Have a good trip, Peter."

"Thank you, Sir." Peter half stood up and shook hands with Josh and then Bill, who promptly left him alone in the war room.

CHAPTER 27

Wheelbarrow

It had taken three men to deposit Josid in the wheelbarrow. Unfortunately, the effort to do so woke him up.

"Where are you taking me?" Josid asked groggily, struggling with his ropes.

"Gag him," Rostam ordered.

Arash grabbed a strip of cloth from Josid's torn shirt and wrapped it around his face.

"Terran!" Josid yelled. "Come here!" He kept turning his head from side to side, fighting Arash's attempts to gag him.

Terran came over and put his hands over Josid's mouth. "Be quiet. There may be others nearby. We have a gun, there are children around, it would make no sense to fight here. We're taking you to your people—"

"*Our* people!"

Terran shook his head. "They're not mine anymore. If they were, they would let me go."

Josid turned his face away from Terran, anger filled his words. "You can't escape. We will kill you before that happens."

Sanjur walked up to Josid and slapped his hand on his shoulder. "Again, you talk like a man with a loaded gun pointed at someone's head, and yet, you're bound up, sitting on your ass in a wheelbarrow. Oh, that's right, *we* have the gun. Consider yourself lucky that Terran convinced us to return you to your thugs. If it were up to me, you'd be dead."

"I am not stupid," Josid muttered, his eyes glaring at Sanjur.

"We're going to gag you," Sanjur said, "so you can either cooperate or resist. If you resist, we'll knock you out again. Any preference?"

Josid closed his eyes with a frustrated sigh.

Terran caught Sanjur's eyes. "We should give him some water before we gag him—"

"He's a camel—let his own water him," Sanjur said, spitting on the ground.

Sanjur nodded to Arash who then tied the cloth strip tightly over Josid's mouth, securing it with a knot. While Arash did that, Sanjur walked the length of Josid's body and checked the ropes to make sure they were snug and secure.

Rostam came up behind Sanjur. "We should blindfold him, too."

Sanjur nodded again, as Arash looked to him for confirmation. Arash began to put a blindfold around Josid's head and felt resistance. Josid held his head flat against the back of the wheelbarrow, making it impossible to put the blindfold on.

Sanjur took the beam that Arash had used and pushed it firmly against Josid's face. "Remember our deal?"

Josid closed his eyes again, uttered something indistinguishable, and became still, and lifted his head up slightly.

A few minutes later, the men wheeled Josid in an industrial-sized wheelbarrow stained in the grayish white color of cement. Arash held one handle while Ahmad held the other. Rostam led them, while Sanjur and Terran walked behind by about twenty feet. A few people watched them as they wheeled their bound, bloody giant through the street like hunters wielding their quarry, but most turned away afraid that their gaze could involve them in some clandestine treachery. Terran and Sanjur were surveying the streets with great care, ultra-vigilant for any movement. They were within a mile of the Preserve, and they knew Moshad and his men could be lurking on any corner or rooftop.

Josid would occasionally wince as the wheelbarrow hit a bump. His 260-pound frame was feeling the effects of exhaustion and wounds, of which Sanjur was quick to dismiss as self-inflicted. After three more blocks, Rostam held up his right arm and stopped, pointing to an alleyway where they convened in a tight huddle.

"I think this is close enough," Rostam said. "The Preserve is three blocks down, then one block to the right. We'll wait ten minutes. That should give you enough time to get in position. Okay?"

"Thank you," Sanjur said, shaking hands with the men.

"I'm only firing one shot," Rostam said.

"It should be enough if you can get him to roar," Sanjur said, smiling.

"Ten minutes…"

"If only I had a watch," Sanjur lamented.

"Good luck," Rostam said.

Terran waved goodbye, and he and Sanjur walked briskly down the street. They hadn't gotten more than a block away when a gunshot rang through the air, but not from behind them—from the direction of the Preserve. They quickened their pace, their breath short, their hearts leaping, almost fleeing their chests. They could feel something drawing them inexplicably to the Preserve, but the gunshot could only mean one thing: Moshad was waiting for them. With guns.

CHAPTER 28

Distraction

Rostam looked at Ahmad. "It's almost time. Put him on the street."
Ahmad and Arash pushed Josid into the middle of the street, and slowly backed away, watching the rooftops and streets carefully as they retreated to Rostam's position in the alleyway. Rostam, gun ready, watched for any threats as well.

Ahmad nodded. "It seems okay."

Rostam relaxed a bit, and walked out to Josid, who was lying helplessly in the wheelbarrow, and yanked the gag down onto Josid's neck, but left the blindfold on. He had learned one Baluchi phrase before Sanjur left. It had been part of Terran's plan, and now he hoped his pronunciation would be enough.

Rostam crouched down and leveled his mouth with Josid's right ear.

"Call your friends!" Rostam whispered in an intensely controlled command.

Josid immediately turned his head to face the voice he heard. "Who are you?"

"Call your friends!"

Josid resumed his blind-eye view of the sky, and suddenly looked introspective, as if the voice that was ordering him to speak was inscrutable, and he had given up.

Rostam raised the gun slowly and positioned the end of its six-inch barrel on Josid's sweaty temple. Josid flinched a little from the touch, and again when he heard the percussive click of the cocked trigger.

"Call your friends!" Rostam repeated a little louder.

In a city that has no electricity, and hardly any cars, the ambient noise level is unsettlingly low. Even neighborhood dogs were virtually extinct. Sound soared great distances, carried by the silence like a muscular wave. Ten minutes ago they had heard the gunshot near the Preserve as if it were a block away, and now it was their turn to make noise, and draw Moshad away from the Preserve.

Rostam pulled the gun barrel an inch away from Josid's temple and pointed the gun into the air. "Call your friends!" Rostam looked around, nothing. The streets were eerily quiet as a result of the gunshot ten minutes earlier. He could feel Josid thinking, trying to sort out the puzzle that he was a part of. Rostam closed his eyes and squeezed the trigger. A loud blast exploded and Josid flinched wildly.

Rostam put the hot gun barrel back on Josid's temple, pushing hard. His voice, this time, was twisted in the darkness of a murderous villain. *"Call… your… friends!"*

Maybe it was the sound of a gunshot inches from his ear, maybe it was the smell of gunpowder, or maybe it was Rostam's voice that struck terror in Josid, whatever the reason, Josid responded with an eruption of Baluchi phrases at an astonishing volume—a "roar"—just as Terran had said. Every fiber of stress and rage that had been hoarded inside Josid like a black hole, suddenly released itself, and the gunshot felt like a staccato undertone in comparison.

Rostam, Ahmad, and Arash ran in the direction of their home like teenage kids who had just completed their vandalism when the neighbor's porch light came on. They never looked back, careful to take back streets and lesser known paths.

Josid's yelling quieted as the distance between them grew, and each time he yelled out, the involuntary inflection in their gut was a little less. The winged energy of their legs began to weaken, and they started to half-walk, half-run, laughing to one another that they'd done it. They'd triumphed. They had slain Goliath.

CHAPTER 29

Fight

It stood out from the silence of the morning, a gunshot that sealed the city in another wave of panic. Terran and Sanjur waited.

"Why isn't he screaming?" Sanjur whispered. "The gunshot isn't enough!"

"He's refusing—"

And then they heard it, the blood-curdling scream, and the words, even four blocks away, were clear: "Terran is near! Terran is near! Help me!"

Sanjur looked at Terran. "I was really hoping he'd just scream."

They were crouching on the flat roof of a building behind the Preserve. They watched carefully as they saw two men running in the direction of the Josid's shouts, one was Moshad, the other, Terran couldn't identify.

"I think we can go," Sanjur said.

Terran pointed to the two men he'd seen running away. "I only saw two."

"We're in the back, maybe the rest are in the front or the side we can't see."

No sooner had Sanjur spoke, and they saw another of the Baluch men walking only fifty feet from their position, down an alley just below them. Sanjur put his fingers over his lips and turned to Terran. Fear was written on his face, and though he tried his best to hide it, Terran had no trouble detecting it. They were without a gun, and Sanjur knew how vulnerable he was.

They flattened themselves against the rooftop and waited.

Sanjur leaned over to whisper in Terran's ear. "I don't think the distraction worked. Moshad didn't fall for it. He's got too many men here. Soon they'll have Josid back in their ranks. We need to go before they get back—it'll only get harder if we wait."

Sanjur looked over the edge of the roof and then instantly retracted. He pointed down. "He's right below us," he said, mouthing the words silently.

Terran understood and stayed quiet. They couldn't run for it. They had to get into the Preserve undetected. It was the only way to ensure that no one got hurt. The biggest concern on Terran's mind was to keep the Baluch henchmen away from the students and teachers of the Preserve. If they observed him getting inside, they would follow, and there was nothing that the parents guarding the front entrance could do about it.

After another ten minutes of waiting. There was a strange bird call or whistle, and the guard below them suddenly jogged off in the direction of the front entrance.

"I'm betting that Moshad's back," Terran whispered.

"Do you think we can make it now?" Sanjur asked.

"I'll go alone," Terran announced. "You stay here. Once I get inside, I'll figure a way to get you in, even if it takes till nightfall. You stay right here. Okay?"

"Why?"

"If they see me, they won't fire; they'll just try to capture me. If they see you, they won't hesitate to shoot. If I make it, we'll get you next."

"We can both make it," Sanjur insisted.

"It's possible, but what if they spot you?" Terran asked, raising an eyebrow. "I won't leave you out here. I promise."

"I won't seem like much of a rescuer if I come in last..."

"Your life is more important than your ego," Terran said. "Sometimes patience is the best strategy, wouldn't you agree?"

Sanjur stared for a few seconds into empty space, feeling his head nodding, but wondered how a young boy could make life and death decisions with such certainty.

Terran put his hand on Sanjur's shoulder as he got up in a crouching position. "I'll make sure you get full credit for my return. Don't worry. Just stay here, no matter what. Agreed?"

"Agreed... be careful."

Without another word, Terran shimmied down the side of the

building and dropped to the ground softly. From his new angle on the ground he noticed a broken window. He was almost certain that it was Hamid Mokri's office. *That's what they shot at*, the Director's office. It was about fifty meters to the outside wall that housed Hamid's office. If he could jump to the window ledge, he could scurry through the broken window, and get in without being detected. All he needed was something to protect against the broken glass so he wouldn't cut his hands.

Terran took off his shirt and held it in his hand, and then took one last look in every direction, and not seeing anything, he ran across the street as fast as his legs would carry him. His eyes focused on the window, deciding the best angle to take a running jump at the ledge, which was about four feet from the ground.

He was within ten meters of the window ledge when he saw a blur in the corner of his eye, running towards him. Whoever it was they were running at full speed on a path to intercept him. Terran made it to the wall, but in the time it took him to climb the ledge, he was pulled down by the man, and they both fell to the ground in a one-sided struggle.

"Settle down, Terran. It's over. It's over."

Terran looked up at the man who sat on top of him, it was Navid, one of Moshad's fighters. He was strong with a fierce expression engraved on his face. Terran was clearly overmatched. Suddenly he saw another man running towards them incredibly fast. He delivered a powerful kick across the chin of Terran's assailant that literally caused him to fly off Terran.

Sanjur immediately went down on the ground, wincing from the pain of the kick, holding his ankle. "Damn, his jaw is like a rock..."

Sanjur turned to Terran. "Go, get inside, I'll be right behind you."

Just then they heard pounding above them. They looked up to see dozens of students pushing their face against glass windows in the third and fourth floors. They were pointing to something that neither Terran nor Sanjur could see, but they assumed it wasn't good.

Sanjur glanced at Navid who was starting to regain consciousness and was moaning, face down on the ground, a mere six feet away.

Sanjur struggled to his feet, limped over to Terran and grabbed Terran and helped him reach the window ledge, and almost jammed him through the open window. "Go! Go! Find someone to hide you."

"What about you?"

"I'll be okay."

"Don't move!" shouted Moshad. He was poised with his gun trained on Sanjur's back. Terran dropped to the inside of Hamid's office and lay against the wall below the window, listening, knowing their options were few. The only thing that was saving Sanjur was the fact that dozens of kids were watching from above, and even Moshad wouldn't kill an unarmed man in cold blood with an audience of children.

"Turn around with your hands in the air," Moshad ordered. Navid stood up and rubbed his jaw, spitting on the ground as he walked behind Moshad. Moshad had Sanjur cornered, and slowly walked towards him. A few seconds later, Josid appeared from around the corner, limping with a grin on his face.

"Sir, give me the honor of killing this man," Josid said, "with my bare hands."

Sanjur raised his index finger. "If I may, Sir, um, this man has been a true hero for your team. His skills are tremendous, and if not for his small brain, he would undoubtedly be the greatest warrior of all time—"

"Silence!" Josid shouted. "Please, Sir, let me kill him."

Terran wondered why Sanjur was making Josid angrier. Had he given up hope?

Moshad glanced up at the students who were watching. There were some teachers as well, but none of them posed a threat. "Terran, where is he?"

"I haven't seen him…"

"He's inside there. He went in through the broken window," Navid said, pointing to the window.

"Terran, show yourself or I will shoot this man now," Moshad shouted.

Terran raised his head over the window ledge and looked out. Sanjur's back was only a few feet away. Terran could see Moshad moving a little closer, his gun trained on Sanjur.

"I will give you one chance and only one chance. Come back out here, or I kill this traitor."

"Actually, I'm not a traitor," Sanjur interjected. "You see, I was never with you."

"Shut up, or I'll let Josid loose on you."

"Really?" Sanjur said. "That man with the tiny brain, and matching balls?"

Josid almost pawed his way past Moshad, but his training intervened, and he managed to compose himself, though his eyes were bristling with anger.

"I have a solution," Sanjur offered. "I will fight this small-brained animal you call Josid, and if I win, you leave Terran and me in peace. If I lose… well… I'm dead, and Terran will promise to come out and return to your village… or tents… or whatever the hell you live in. Is my offer acceptable?"

Josid looked eagerly to Moshad, nodding his head. "Please, Sir."

Moshad looked Josid over from head to toe. "You're fit?"

Josid smirked. "Fit enough for that gangly bag of bones."

The men laughed, and Moshad saw a way to keep the whole affair contained and heavily in their favor, and as a bonus, even entertaining. "Okay, we agree." Moshad nodded.

"Terran, do you agree to this?" Moshad asked.

Terran raised his head a little higher and nodded, not knowing why, but it seemed that if Sanjur wanted it this way, then it was proper to agree with him.

Sanjur turned around and placed his hands on the window frame, pretending to stretch his legs, and then mouthed a handful of words with great precision. "Do not watch this. When it starts, run and find help."

Terran nodded that he understood, and spoke like a ventriloquist so that Sanjur could hear, but no one else. "I trust you. I am with you."

"Let's go!" Moshad ordered.

Sanjur removed his shirt, as slowly as possible, and wound it carefully around his right hand and forearm like a shield. His physique, unfortunately, was not impressive in the least to Josid, and did little but draw chuckles from the onlookers.

As if to make clear his superiority, Josid removed his shirt as well, and for the first time, Sanjur could see why there were warriors, and *then there were warriors*. The baggy shirt had hidden all of the intricate, well-defined musculature. It was almost mesmerizing to see his torso gleaming in the morning sun.

A loose-knit circle of men formed at Moshad's direction, and then he motioned Sanjur to step inside the circle that was about thirty feet in diameter. Josid was chuckling to himself, eager to begin what to his mind was justifiable carnage in the name of revenge.

Sanjur, sensing that Moshad was ready to begin the fight, spoke up. "And what are the rules?"

"Rules?" Josid asked.

"Well, for example," Sanjur said, "do I win if I choose to simply withdraw after I have clearly rendered this monkey unable to fight?"

There were snickers among the Baluch who were watching, even Moshad smiled in disbelief. *This was either a very brave man, or one who had entirely lost his mind.*

"It is a fight to the death," Moshad answered. "Those are the rules."

"Yes, but let's say I feel sorry for this monkey, after all he's been beaten by a twelve-year-old boy, and very soon, an old man. I want the option to spare his life, but if I do so, I want assurance that I will still win. Do I still win?"

Moshad waved his hand dismissively. "Yes, yes, if you are in that position, and you spare Josid's life, we will still honor you as the victor. Now, are you ready to fight?"

Sanjur shook his head. "We haven't talked about weapons…"

"No weapons," Moshad answered reflexively.

"Nor are any required." Josid laughed, flexing his arms and cracking his knuckles.

"Only to be clear, we're defining weapons as guns and knives, is that correct?"

"Yes!" Moshad said, frustrated with all of the questions.

"So if I use my—"

"Enough!" Moshad shouted. "Now fight!"

The two men immediately began to circle in a crouching position. The Baluch men were chanting in unison as their beloved warrior Josid was about to slay an insignificant Turkmen. Josid was wounded, certainly not in ideal condition, but then neither was Sanjur. Both men were wounded, and wore their blood proudly on their bodies and clothes.

Josid growled. "I will begin by crushing your chest, something I started that I want to finish."

Josid then lunged at Sanjur with lightning speed. Sanjur was unable to take any evasive action, and ended up on his back with Josid's arms wrapped around him. Josid quickly stood up, and pulled Sanjur off the ground and threw him in the air ten feet. Sanjur landed hard, and the Baluch men let out a strange sound, somewhere between a moan and a cry of delight. Sanjur almost lost consciousness, but he struggled and found it, feeling like a crippled mouse between the paws of a cat.

Sanjur put out his hand. "Give me a moment to catch my breath, monkey."

Josid stopped and laughed. "Take as much time as you need. I want to savor your journey to hell. I want to hear the crunch of your bones, and the agony in your cries of pain."

Sanjur steadied himself as he found the vertical realms, and then looked dizzily at Josid. "You see I am only allowing you this promising start to build your confidence. Soon, I will swoop down on you, and you will wish you had run from this place."

Josid's irritation spiked, and he walked up to the Sanjur and stuck his hand out and gripped his throat with his right hand, and lifted him from the ground a few inches. Sanjur struggled to loosen his grip, but it was futile. His windpipe was being crushed, and then Josid, as if out of boredom, tossed him sideways to the ground and walked away.

Sanjur coughed blood, grabbing his throat hoping to find air. He could feel a blackness crowding him, but he fought it off with all his power.

"I am ready to finish you off old man. Your fighting is imaginary. You speak like a fighter, and you fight like a baby girl. You are pathetic." Josid spat on the ground and wiped his mouth with his forearm.

"One moment…" Sanjur managed to get to his feet, his voice raspy and uneven. He staggered a little bit.

One of the men encouraged Josid to deliver the death blow. Another agreed.

Josid put his arms out, and spun around. "Patience, brothers. This is *my* fight."

Josid leveled a powerful kick at Sanjur's side, and Sanjur crumpled on the spot in agony, gasping for breath. He felt a rib break, and knew he couldn't take another round. He gathered himself to the best of his ability, and looked up at his tormentor. "You are a strong monkey, but you are still a monkey."

Josid laughed. "You're still throwing out insults instead of punches or kicks."

In between gasps of exhaustion and pain, Sanjur managed to spit some blood and muttered. "Oh, believe me... if I had wanted... to punch you, you... you would have been crying in misery."

If not for his state of exhaustion, even Sanjur would have chuckled at the absurdity of his statement. The Baluch laughed heartily, they had never witnessed such a verbal lashing coming from a man who was being ripped to shreds.

"Give me your best punch, old man. I promise I won't even try to block it."

"You better cover your nuts," shouted one of the men.

Josid looked at Sanjur as he staggered over to him. "Above the belt, or I will make your passing unbearable."

Sanjur nodded. "I had no intention of hitting you below the belt; I couldn't possibly hit such a small target."

The men erupted again in laughter, and Josid, in a reflex of indignation, delivered a powerful jab to Sanjur's cheek, pushing him backwards about three paces where he fell to the ground. The blackness, when he opened his eyes, was nearly everywhere. He could see a small tunnel of reality, but it was only the diameter of a thread and he was afraid to close his eyes or even blink for fear it would all be gone. He willed himself to stand somehow, and then he found his speech was gone. He tried to say something, but his mouth was too slurred. He had to make his move now, or it would be too late.

He staggered to Josid's position and formed a fist with his left hand.

"Go ahead. Make it count, because it will be your last," Josid said, smiling down on the exhausted Sanjur.

Sanjur moved his tunnel of vision to a place on Josid's neck, and lifted his left hand, and then he summoned from some depth where he had never before gone, and called on some reserve that had been placed there when he was a child. He brought his right hand zipping across Josid's neck, precisely where his jugular vein lay, and he cried out in a Turkmen expression his father had taught him when he was only five.

Sanjur's fingernail was his weapon. He had been taught how to kill a man with this technique, though he'd never, in his fifty-three years, tried. The trick was to possess a loose arm, and whip the wrist at the last second. He had tightened his shirt around the fingers of his right hand so they were straight and reinforced. The shirt also added a little extra weight to the percussive blow.

After his strike, Sanjur watched the expression of Josid as if he didn't see or feel a thing. He even smiled at Sanjur, as if to say, that's the best you got? But then Josid felt the warm liquid pouring out of his neck. He touched it with his hand in amazement, and saw that it was spurting out. While his instinct was to crush Sanjur, he knew in that moment that he was a dead man. Josid dropped to his knees and Moshad rushed over to him in a panic, unclear about what or how it had happened.

A hush fell over the Baluch fighters. Sanjur staggered backwards, toward the school, toward Hamid's office. He prayed that Moshad would honor his agreement, but had little faith that he would, especially now that he'd killed his most valuable asset.

CHAPTER 30

Aftermath

Terran had peeked through the window and watched. He knew he should run for help, as Sanjur had asked, but he also knew that there was no help that could be pitted against Moshad and his men, and he did not want to be the person to lead lambs to their slaughter. From the time Sanjur had removed his shirt, and wrapped it around his right hand, Terran had become riveted on the fight. Sanjur had a plan, and he followed it to perfection, even if the result deposited him on death's door. He was alive. A fight to the death against a fighter of Josid's caliber—being alive, was enough. It was, in fact, a miracle.

When Sanjur made his strike, it was easily the most unexpected event that Terran had ever seen in his life, and for his victim—to the extent Josid could be called a victim—he, too, was undoubtedly astonished by the blow.

When Sanjur fell back against the outside wall of Hamid's office, Terran had jumped up and climbed back through the window, and dropped to the ground to comfort his protector, who lay limp on the ground.

Moshad was shouting orders to his men to apply pressure to Josid's neck wound. He then came over to Terran and Sanjur. "Where's the closest doctor?"

Terran knew of only one doctor, three blocks away. "You'll never make it in time."

"Tell me!"

Terran gave him directions.

Moshad ordered the men to lift him and run to the doctor. Four men pulled Josid up, while a fifth man kept a steady pressure on his neck. Collectively the small group ran at a surprisingly fast clip in the direction of the doctor's office. Moshad gave the directions to one of his scouts and told him to run full speed to the doctor's location and find him.

"Is there a sign on the building?" Moshad shouted to Terran.

"It's right on the corner, left side, it looks like nothing's there, but go in the very back. If he's there, that's where he'll be."

Moshad nodded to Shaheen, who then ran off like a sprinter.

Moshad motioned to Javad, and the two walked over to Terran's position, looking down at an unconscious Sanjur with shock in their eyes.

"He has more talents than we thought," Moshad said. "But I have to kill him."

"No!" Terran shouted. "No more killing. Tend to your man and make good on your promise." Terran turned to his teacher with pleading eyes. "Javad, please help…"

Javad slowly shook his head.

"Why do you care for this Turkmen?" Moshad asked. "He put you in danger. You could have been killed as a result of your running away—"

"At your hand, maybe, but this man has done nothing but protect me since I escaped your custody," Terran argued. "Your word is binding. Have you forgotten this?"

"He tricked us—"

"He did not. He did what he had to do to win."

Moshad looked disgustingly at Sanjur, whose head was resting on Terran's leg. He was beat up badly, his face was already bloated from the bruises and his ribs were mostly a bluish-purple tone. Blood was spattered across his body, intertwined with dirt and blades of grass.

"I will make a new deal," Moshad said, crouching down. "I will let you go in that school, and you leave this man to me."

Terran shook his head defiantly. "No."

Moshad turned to Javad. "Talk some sense into this boy, or I will take matters into my own hands." Moshad stood up and walked away, putting about twenty feet between himself and Terran.

Javad crouched down, and brushed some dirt off of Terran's forehead. "You know what you have to do. Come home with us. Stop this rebelliousness. How has it served you? Josid? Sanjur? Parto? Are any of them better for it? Please, you must come with us."

"No! Moshad gave his word. We all heard it."

Javad looked back at Moshad. "What if I could convince him to spare Sanjur if you would come home?"

"No. The deal was made…"

Suddenly, Terran heard footsteps, and saw children walking out on the schoolyard, tentatively coming in their direction. At first, there were ten or twelve, then dozens, and then a hundred, then two hundred or more. They came like a small army, cautious, awkward, curious, whispering among themselves. Terran smiled at the one who was the apparent leader, a young boy about his age, maybe a little older.

"That was amazing. Is he okay?" the boy asked, looking at Terran, and then Sanjur.

The group continued to stream out onto the side yard, and Moshad's annoyance turned swiftly into a muttering of some choice Baluchian obscenities.

Terran's vocabulary in English was not extensive, but he knew what they were asking, and he nodded. "Thank you, Sanjur… lives, he lives."

It wasn't perfect English, but the children understood, and they continued to gather closer. Javad watched as they poured into the yard and crowded around them like a sea of white cloth and black hair.

Moshad tapped Javad on the shoulder. "Let's go, we'll look in on Josid, and see if his spirit has decided to stay. There's nothing more to do here."

Moshad looked down at Terran, and pointed his finger at him harshly. "Do not think you have won this or that I am granting you release. I'll come back, and when I do… these children will not protect you."

Moshad looked to his side as Nouri Abbasi walked up to Terran, and crouched next to him. He was carrying a first aid kit. He glanced at Moshad while he examined Sanjur's wounds. "Leave. You've brought enough trouble to this place. Leave, and don't pretend to tell Terran what he should do. You have shown yourself to him, and proven to him that his decision was the right one. Go!"

Moshad started towards Nouri, but Javad grabbed his shirt and pulled him away. "Another time, Moshad. Another time. Let's go."

The two men walked away in silence. The children parted to make a path, and when they had gone by, a cheer was released by the children. Hamid had been in the background, watching them. It had been impossible to keep the students from going out. He had tried to contain them at first, but the children had defused a bomb, and he was glad now that he'd relented and let them go.

Nouri cleaned the wounds first, and tenderly applied bandages. Terran stayed still with Sanjur's limp head resting on his legs.

"Let's rest his head on the ground, okay?" Nouri asked.

Nouri gently put Sanjur's head on the ground.

Terran stood to his feet. He was exhausted, too. His energy suddenly left him, but he had been inspired by Sanjur, and refused to give in to it. He turned to Nouri. "I will go to the doctor, and bring him here."

"No, you certainly will not," Nouri said. "You need to worry about yourself. Your hands are cut, you haven't eaten… I'm sure you're dehydrated."

Nouri said something in English, and a group of students stepped forward and took Terran by the arm, and helped him walk to the school's entrance, past the stone bench he had laid on only a week before. A sudden flash of Parto and Dorri passed through his consciousness like a vision that descends in the cloak of a memory, beckoning from the future. He saw them, in a place of another time, a cipher for his new world. He smiled in the grip of his vision. He didn't notice the steps or the dazed guards that stood aside as he passed in his clutch of fellow students.

He entered the cool hallway of thick stone, that timeless archetype of birth, and he knew the inscrutable mystery that beckoned him would never let him die before its elusive course was known to him.

CHAPTER 31

Achilles

Captain Carson Brunel was tall, with sandy-colored hair that poked out from under his helmet. He wore military fatigues that looked well-worn, and perhaps even a bit shabby. Threadbare would be a kinder way of saying it, but semantics aside, he was rough in his appearance. He was thirty-nine and in good shape, though not a specimen of perfection by any means, as he had a slight limp from a bum knee that persisted from his days of playing football at Louisiana State University and his mid-section was beginning the bloom of middle age.

He arrived at the Preserve about thirty minutes after the fight had ended between Josid and Sanjur. Many of the students were still in the schoolyard, on its south side, as Carson Brunel drove up in his Humvee M1114 with two additional security personnel. Hamid noticed them immediately and walked to them with his hand outstretched.

"You must be Captain Brunel," Hamid said, as he approached, speaking his best English. "Did you have any trouble finding us?"

"No trouble at all, but just call me Carson, even my reports call me that—sometimes worse." He chuckled to himself. "I assume you're Hamid Mokri?"

"Yes."

The two men shook hands. "I speak pretty good Persian, if you'd prefer..." Carson offered.

"No, English is fine."

Carson looked around at the students outside, milling around, most of them now focused on him. "Did I miss something...? I thought you were under some kind of attack. I expected everyone would be inside waiting for the Cavalry—us." Carson chuckled again, relief showing on his face that he hadn't entered a war zone as he had been warned it might be.

"It's very complicated," Hamid said, smiling shyly with his eyes. He put his hand on Carson's shoulder. "Why don't we meet in my office… perhaps you could station your men out here. The troublemakers might return soon."

"Sure." Carson pointed to his two men. "One stays on the front entrance, the other circles the grounds, and keep in communication. Rotate. Understood?"

"Yes, Sir," they answered in unison.

They turned to walk up the stairs when a gunshot rang out, and one of Carson's men fell to the ground and didn't move. All the students fell to the ground, too. Hamid spun around as Carson and he crouched behind a concrete wall that acted like a railing for the stairs.

"Now why would they go and do that?" Carson asked, mostly to himself. "Frank, is he bad?"

Frank was one of his security team, huddled behind a tree, about fifteen feet from the fallen soldier. "Shit, he's not moving."

"Frank, every one of these kids speaks English, keep it clean. Okay?"

Frank shot a glare in Carson's direction. "I think he's dead."

"Any sense of where the shot came from?" Carson asked.

Frank, a strong looking man with coal-black hair, and a grizzly beard, pointed with his index finger to a building across the street. "I'd say over there."

Just then another shot rang out, and the rear tire on the passenger side blew out.

"Shit, they just took out our tire," Frank said.

Carson turned to Hamid. "Why don't you get all the students in? I'm going to open fire, and let them know we don't have pea shooters. They'll have their heads down, so I'll give you about thirty seconds to clear the school yard. Tell them… now."

Hamid looked into Carson's eyes for a moment, wondering if he should take orders from him, but he seemed to be his only hope, and securing the safety of the children seemed like the right move.

Hamid cupped his hands around his mouth and shouted as loudly as he could. "All students get inside as soon as the gun fire starts. Run as fast and as orderly as you can."

Carson checked his 30-round magazines and set his MP5SD on

3-round bursts.

Carson looked at Frank. "Let me start, when I empty my first clip, take over. Okay?"

Just then another gunshot took out another tire. "Okay, now they're really pissing me off. Ready?"

"Ready..." Frank said.

Carson took a quick glance behind him to Hamid. "Wish me luck."

He stood up and started firing almost immediately in the general direction of where the gunshots had come. He got to the Humvee just as his clip ran out of bullets. The students were running, and there was a two-second pause as Frank came from behind the tree and began emptying rounds from his M4 Carbine in the same general direction that Carson had been shooting. The students kept running up the stairs as Hamid encouraged them. While Frank was shooting, Carson slapped another magazine into his MP5, and watched for any movement across the street. Frank joined Carson at the Humvee as his own clip ran out.

"I'll fire one more clip," Carson said, "make sure all the kids are out of here when I'm done, okay?"

"Understood."

"And check on Joe," Carson said. "If he's dead, grab his gun and ammo. Got it?"

"Yes, Sir."

Carson stood up and began firing. Frank ran around to the side of the school yard and looked, but everyone was gone. He ran to Joe, and saw he had been shot through the head. He was dead. *Shit! I'm not getting paid enough to be shot at.* Frank grabbed Joe's gun and two rounds from his belt, and ran the short distance to the Humvee, and reported his news.

Carson replaced his clip. "Fuck! Joe was a good man. We have two choices, go in after these fuckers and clean them out, or retreat back to the school. I don't want to leave our Humvee unattended. I think they'll just continue to pick away at it. We can still drive it as it is, but she's my baby, and it pisses me off that they're shooting at it." Carson paused, and turned to Frank. "Do you think these fuckers could have RPGs?"

"It's possible, but wouldn't they have used 'em already if they did?"

"With the kids, maybe not. I'm not sure if it makes sense to stay here. If I was them, and I had an RPG, I'd use it, makes escape that much harder. If all they got is pea shooters, we can deal with that, and so can my little baby here." Carson paused and took a quick look inside the Humvee.

"Let's do this," Carson said. "I'm going to grab the rounds of ammo we have and the supply bag, and then retreat to the steps. You cover me. When I get to the stairs, I'll cover you, and you follow. Okay?"

"Yes, Sir."

"Let's go... now!"

Frank stood up and began firing. The building opposite the school was pockmarked from their gun fire, and the smell of gunpowder was thick in the streets. Carson grabbed their ammo and supply bags, and ran to the stairs, and then felt a sharp sting as he fell to the ground. What the hell was that? He looked down at his ankles and saw he was bleeding. A bullet had caught him in his right ankle. *Shit!*

"Frank!" Carson yelled. "Over there!"

Frank looked and followed his finger, and began firing indiscriminately in that direction, while at the same time retreating to Carson's position. Frank bent down and in one swoop, helped Carson to his feet, all the while firing his M4 in the direction of the phantoms that taunted them.

The stairs were no longer a sanctuary, a new angle of fire had opened up, and the men hobbled their way through the main door and fell just inside, shutting the heavy wood door with their legs.

"How bad?" Frank asked.

"Those fuckers got my ankle," Carson yelled, wincing in pain.

Frank looked up slowly to a hallway full of children, with Hamid, standing in front of them, his arms out as if telling the children to stay back.

Hamid smiled softly. "We're Iranians; we've heard swear words before."

Carson bent over and started to untie his right boot. "Well, good for them, they better cover their ears, because when I take this sucker off, I don't know what'll come out of my mouth. Maybe shoo them to their classrooms..."

Hamid turned to his students and motioned to some of his teachers who were among them. "Return to your classrooms and keep still."

One of the parent guards, an older, distinguished-looking man, stepped forward, speaking in Persian. "Hamid, I could help with the soldier. I'm pretty handy around wounds."

"Okay, Karim."

Carson turned around. "Where's the kid right now?"

"He's resting on the second floor."

"Is there any way to get to the second floor?"

Hamid shook his head. "No, except through the main staircase—"

"Any trees that're close to the building?"

Hamid shook his head gradually. "...No..."

"You don't sound too sure. I need absolute certainty."

"I'll need to check on one tree..."

"Do that," Carson said. "Anything else I need to know?"

Hamid cleared his throat, with his hand politely covering his mouth. "There was a man who helped him escape from the Baluch. He's here, too. His name is—"

"What's his status?"

"He's being tended to..."

"He's shot, too?"

"No, he was in a fight and was beaten up."

Carson turned to Frank. "I need you to keep an eye on the street." Carson looked back at Hamid. "How many adults do you have in here?"

Hamid looked around. "Maybe twenty..."

"I need ten down here as soon as you can get them—those who have experience with guns are most needed. The rest can stay with the children."

Hamid turned and walked briskly down the hall.

Frank cracked the door open and looked out. "I don't see anything."

"Good."

Carson finished untying his boot and looked back to the parent guard, Karim. "You said you could help?"

The man stepped forward, nodding. "Yes. Yes."

"In that bag," Carson nodded, speaking in Persian, "is a first aid kit. Grab it." He then spoke English. "Frank, you keep your eyes on the street. Anything that moves our way, carrying a gun, shoot it."

"Yes, Sir."

"I'm Karim."

"Hi, Karim, I'm Carson. You a doctor or something?"

"No, but I have a good way with wounds. After the Sunrot, people were dying from scratches on their finger. I lost a child that way; I learned how to treat wounds after that. A neighbor was a doctor. He taught me."

Karim opened the bag and started to look through its contents, selecting some things that seemed important to him. When he finished, he looked down at Carson's boot. "Do you want me to take it off, or you?"

"I'll take it off; I'm just building my mental energy. You ready?"

"I'm ready."

Carson struggled to get his boot off, wincing at the pain, but he managed to control his reaction without any major screams or expletives. Karim immediately looked at his left ankle, pulling down his sock, wiping the blood off the wound area with a sterile cloth he'd found from the first aid kit. "I've never seen a spray can of disinfectant before, I assume it stings—"

"Oh yah, it stings good," Carson said, laughing nervously. "Give it a go."

"I want to inspect the wound first," Karim said. He bent down to have a closer look. "It seems that the bullet went clean through, missed the bone. Mostly got the calf muscle, your Achilles tendon, is what got hit. It's a clean wound."

"Good news, right?"

"Yes, very good news," Karim said, smiling. "I'll make sure the wound area is clean, and bandage you up tight. You'll need to lie on your back with your leg up."

"That's the bad news… for how long?"

"I don't know, maybe a few hours at least," Karim said with a humble shrug.

"Shit…"

Hamid returned with reinforcements in the form of men, all looking uneasy. "I found the best men I could find, some of them have experience with shooting guns."

"Who's fired a rifle before?"

"I have…" a quiet-looking man said, raising his hand tentatively.

"See that rifle over there," Carson said in Persian, "it's an M4 Carbine, one of the most powerful weapons on the planet. It shoots three round bursts, has a 30-round clip, and can kill a man from two hundred meters. Only has a small recoil. Think you can handle it?"

The man nodded nervously.

"Grab it. I want you posted on any second floor window that has a good view of the street out front. I want you to bring two more with you, and those of you without guns are watchers. You watch for anything that moves. If it's carrying a gun, you let him know immediately, but you never take your eyes off the target. Got it?"

The man nodded.

Carson looked around to the assembled men. "Anyone else shoot a gun?"

"I have," a man said, raising his hand.

"Frank, give this man your gun," Carson said. "You'll use mine."

Carson winced as Karim began to disinfect his wound area. A loud expletive echoed in the hallway, and then he settled down and kept talking. "Okay, I have two handguns left. Who else can shoot?"

No one else raised their hand, and then one teacher stepped forward. "I have never used a gun, but I'm good with mechanical things."

"What, like, like cars?" Carson asked, mockingly. "These aren't cars."

"I was a mechanical engineer, I built reactor cores…"

"Really? And that qualifies you to shoot a gun? Well, hell, why not? Take it." Carson handed the man a Colt 1911. "That's a powerful weapon. I'll have Frank show you boys how to use these in a second. I need one more who thinks they can shoot a handgun. Any more mechanics out there?"

A middle-aged man stepped forward who was one of the parent guards. "I'll do it."

"Good, okay, we got our shooters. The rest of you are watchers. I want one shooter on the top floor—that's you with the M4. You, go!

Now, you, I want you and two watchers on that side, main floor. Pick a sightline that isn't blocked by trees. Go! You, I want on that side with two watchers. Hamid, is there a back entrance?"

"Yes, but it's always locked."

"Okay, I want you on the back entrance, with two watchers, one on either side. Go!"

Carson winced again as Karim bandaged his ankle tightly. "Hamid, I want to meet this boy. Can you arrange that?"

"I'll bring him here," Hamid replied, and then walked away.

"Frank, I want you to make the rounds, and show our shooters how to use their weapons. Don't take anything for granted. Okay?"

"Now, Sir?"

"Yes, start with the guy on the second floor who's watching the front entrance. Make sure the trees look okay; I'm nervous that these Baluchian assholes—who have a nasty reputation for sneakiness—will find a tree and use it as an access point. If you see such a tree, then make sure we have a shooter nearby and a watcher trained on that tree. Got it?"

"Yes, Sir."

"Take one last look out the front and make sure everything's clear. I haven't heard any other shots since we got inside… it makes me nervous, like why'd they suddenly go quiet… they run out of bullets or something?"

Frank looked outside, carefully surveying the street and buildings within range of their position. "All looks clear."

Carson looked at Karim. "I take it that your police avoid gunfights?"

Karim rubbed his fingers together with his thumb. "Unless there's payment, they don't get involved. Right now, with all these gunshots, the police are busy patrolling the neighborhoods of their wealthiest patrons, protecting their benefactors. That's all they do."

"What a bunch of worthless private security guards… Shit!"

Carson grabbed Frank's shirt. "Look, I want you to take my gun. I have a sidearm, and I'll cover the front. I want you to rotate. Keep a watch over everything. You have to be my eyes and ears. If anything smells wrong to you, you let me know. I'm not going anywhere."

Carson turned to Karim. "Can you be Frank's escort? Show him around... help him get his bearings?"

Karim nodded. "Yes, but you need to prop your leg up. I'll get you a cushion—"

"Just use the supply bag, it'll be fine."

Karim placed the supply bag in its most vertical position and carefully positioned Carson's leg on it. "Okay?"

"It's all good. Alright then, boys, get cracking."

Frank shut the front door. "You sure you'll be okay?"

"Hell, yes. Any Baluchian stupid enough to try and get through that door is going to be greeted by a Smith and Wesson 9-1-1."

Frank slapped Carson on his shoulder, and walked down the hallway with Karim leading the way. *All this for a little boy. It doesn't make any sense.*

CHAPTER 32

Impasse

Terran had finally eaten a full meal—the first in two days. He ate and drank until he felt his stomach would seize the last drop and expel it in a terrible reflex. Control. Hamid and Nouri had found him just in time, or he may have continued eating. Terran had wanted to look in on Sanjur, but was told he was sleeping, though, in an unconscious state, can one really be asleep? He had allowed their lie.

Terran had heard the gunfire earlier, but his hunger and thirst were his priority. He was well aware that help had arrived. He felt a certain type of comfort, despite the loud cacophony of guns. Some of the students who had remained in the schoolyard returned soon after the gunfire started and reported what had happened. "They have powerful machine guns, you will be safe now!" the students said. They knew his English vocabulary was small, so they showed him a pantomime. Terran understood perfectly.

Terran followed Hamid and Nouri down the central staircase to meet the Captain who would deliver Terran and Nouri to Delhi.

"Will Sanjur be okay?" Terran asked.

"I wish I could say 'yes' and be confident," Nouri answered, "but I don't really know. We're trying our best to get him to drink—"

"So he's conscious?"

"Yes, but he falls in and out of consciousness."

"What does he do when he's conscious?" Terran asked.

"He asks about you, where you are, where's Josid… things like that."

"When can I see him?"

"When we're finished meeting the Captain, I'll take you to him." Nouri glanced back at Terran. "Okay?"

"Okay, but I'm also reminding you that I won't leave before I see Parto and Dorri, too."

Nouri smiled, and nodded, as he glanced over his shoulder to meet eyes with Terran.

They walked down the stone hallway to the entrance, where Carson was lying on the floor, holding a gun, staring at the door.

Hamid made the introductions and then quickly excused himself.

Carson stumbled a little bit, trying to find a way to break the silence of Hamid's retreating footsteps. "Please, sit down and join me."

Nouri sat down and leaned against the wall, facing Carson perpendicularly. He patted the ground next to him, indicating that Terran should join him, which he did.

"You can speak English if that's easier for you," Nouri said.

"Persian's fine. I studied it for ten years for a reason; I like to use it when I can."

"You speak it well," Nouri observed.

"I assume the boy doesn't speak English—what about Persian?"

Nouri shook his head. "Terran doesn't speak either, but I can translate for him."

Carson adjusted his position, and put his hand up for a moment, indicating he needed to concentrate on something else. He grabbed his communicator microphone and swung it into position. "Then stay with the front shooter. Good job, Frank. Thanks. Over."

Carson pushed his communicator to the side, and returned his attention on Nouri and Terran. He looked at Terran carefully. There was nothing special that he could see, but when Terran looked at him, Carson suddenly saw Terran's eyes. "Where'd he get blue eyes?"

Terran spoke before Nouri could answer, and then Nouri relayed his comment. "He says that the color of his eyes is unimportant. He wants you to concentrate on the issue before us: how do we leave here so no one is injured or killed?"

Carson looked at the door, and chuckled to himself. "Well, as you can see, getting in was not so easy—I'm injured, and one of my men is dead. So I imagine leaving is going to be a lot harder. Those are my initial thoughts." Carson scratched the side of his face. His beard reminded him it'd been three days since he last shaved. He liked to be clean-shaven, as his beard's color was mostly red, and the men would always refer to him as Red Beard if he ever let his beard grow out. He hated the pirate reference. More specifically, he hated pirates, or so he told himself, but a psychologist, if one were ever consulted, might be more inclined to connect Carson's aversion to pirates to childhood associations of being a red head, and being teased for it.

"First things first. I need to understand what supplies you want to take with you… especially anything heavy."

Terran spoke again before Nouri could answer, and Nouri dutifully translated. "He says he wants to take Sanjur with us."

"Okay," Carson said, "I have a question. If he doesn't speak Persian or English, how is it that he answers my questions?"

"He's very clever, Captain Brunel, he hears a single word like 'take,' and in the context of our meeting, he understands the essence of your question. That's all."

"Humph," Carson muttered. "Who, or what, is Sanjur?"

"The man who saved him, and brought him here," Nouri replied.

"No…" Carson slowly shook his head. "No, my orders were to bring you, and only you two, back with me, no one else. Sorry, can't do. Won't do. Understood?"

Terran spoke passionately for a burst of ten seconds and then looked sternly at Carson.

Nouri couldn't hide his concern. "He says he refuses to leave without Sanjur. If Sanjur is left behind, Moshad will kill him. With Terran gone, Moshad will seek a revenge killing, and Sanjur will be his target… no doubt." Nouri turned to Terran, concerned at the potential impasse.

"Look, let's get something straight. I was hired by the Director of the Faculty. I take my orders from him. Not some twelve-year-old boy, and I don't give a shit how smart he is. I have experience in these situations, and his life—and yours—depends on your ability to listen to me and follow my instructions to the letter. You got that?"

Nouri flinched a little at the direct nature of Carson's words, and Terran could sense the anger in his tone, and spoke softly.

Nouri listened and then asked a question of Terran, and then turned to Carson, who, once again put up his hand and swung his communicator to his mouth. "Say again, Frank. Over."

Carson listened intently, and motioned to Nouri to open the door. "Open the door a crack, I want to see this."

CHAPTER 33

Our Problem

Javad was walking slowly across the street with both of his hands raised, and in his right hand he held a crude flag composed of a strip of a white shirt tied to a tree branch, which he waved faintly in the light breeze.

"Have everyone hold their fire," Carson directed into his communicator.

Carson turned to Nouri, and then Terran. "Who is this man?"

Nouri looked carefully, keeping Terran away from the door. "He was Terran's teacher, his name is Javad."

"Javad is here?" Terran instantly asked, trying to see from behind Nouri.

"Frank, I want you to come down here pronto, and give this man a good pat-down when I invite him in for a chat. You copy that?"

Carson was listening, and then turned to Nouri. "Any chance he'd be carrying a bomb?"

"None," Nouri shook his head.

"You sure?"

"Yes."

Carson spoke into his communicator. "Just get your butt down here. Over."

A muffled shout, in Persian, from Javad filtered through the thick, wooden door of the Preserve's entrance. "I am unarmed. I only want to speak to Terran and his representative... to see if we can find a peaceful solution to our problem."

"*Our* problem?" Carson muttered, and then turned to Nouri. "Tell him to come in."

Nouri opened the door about eighteen inches wide. "Javad, you can come in, but only you."

Javad nodded, and walked slowly to the front entrance, aware that several guns were pointed at him.

Frank and Hamid came into the front hallway, and watched as Javad walked through the door, bowing to Nouri and then Terran. Carson kept his handgun drawn on Javad, while Frank checked him for weapons.

"He's clean—figuratively speaking," Frank muttered, as he walked by Carson.

"Just to be clear, I trust you about as high as a snail can jump," Carson said, his tone threatening.

Javad stared at Carson like a strange apparition had suddenly appeared, and was only visible to him. "Who are you?"

"You asked to speak to the boy's representative… that's me. What's your proposition?"

"You're military?"

"You're Baluch, so what. Get to the point."

Javad sighed, his countenance confused by all the different people in the room. He turned briefly to Terran, and spoke in Baluch, but Carson interrupted.

"—No! No private chats until we have a deal."

Javad stopped, and then turned his full attention to Carson. "We want to return Terran to his home. He is very important to us. If you let him go with me, we will leave you peacefully and never return. You have our word." Javad bowed as he finished his statement.

"That's your proposed solution?" Carson chuckled. "Here's how I see it. One, the boy doesn't want to go back with you. That's pretty obvious. Two, you got nothing in the way of fire power, and if we're not back to our basecamp soon, there'll be more of my kind swarming around these grounds with big guns, and we'll exterminate you. Three, I have absolutely no trust in what a Baluch might say. So, you do the math, what you end up with is the following: you leave here, take your little gang, and get on your camels, and whip their behinds until you get back to your godforsaken patch of desert, and then you stay there. You do that, and I won't come after you. You have *my* goddamn word."

Javad looked to Nouri, and then Terran, as if he were suddenly deaf.

"His Persian is worse than mine, maybe he didn't understand. Hamid, can you tell him what I just said?"

Hamid took a small step forward, and put his hand up with his index finger extended, his eyes looked momentarily to the ceiling, and then he paused for a moment before speaking. "The Captain says that you're not in a position to take Terran by force, and because Terran does not want to return with you, then you must leave. The Captain will allow you to leave, and won't follow you to your home—if you leave peacefully. "

Hamid turned to Carson for confirmation that his translation was accurate.

"Spoken like a true diplomat," Carson said with a thin smile.

"You don't understand," Javad replied, "Terran is our hope for a better future. We see him as our spiritual leader, for all our people. We cannot let him go. We see this as a trial from Allah, to test our strength and resolve. Moshad and his men will not leave without Terran."

"Who is Moshad?" Carson asked.

"Our leader."

"And he's with you?"

"Yes, naturally, he's our leader."

"Why didn't he come instead of you?"

Javad hesitated for a moment. "He and Terran... they are not friendly."

Carson winced as he shifted his position. "Are any of your men injured?"

"We lost our best fighter a short time ago—"

"The man Sanjur fought," Nouri interrupted softly, nodding his head once.

"But none from the gunfire?"

Javad shook his head, but remained silent, not sure why Carson was asking him such questions.

"Well, I have a man, a good man, who was murdered by your spineless snipers, and I have a bullet hole in my ankle. Tell your leader—this Moshad—that if he wants to talk about restitutions, he can come and talk, otherwise, I'll wait until my army comes, and we can rid the streets of your mongrel gang. Oh, and one more thing—tell him if he takes one more shot at my Humvee out there, I'll make it my personal mission to find him. Did you understand all of that?"

Javad nodded slightly, but looked extremely uneasy. He glanced in Terran's direction, who was sitting with his eyes closed. Javad backed up slowly and found the door and walked out without another word.

Terran pulled on Nouri's shirt to get his attention. "Where's Dorri?"

CHAPTER 34

A Simple Touch

An eye, half-glazed from trauma, and tired from exhaustion, blinked in a spastic, uncontrolled quiver, and then slowly rolled in search of something familiar. A pair of blue spheres, glistening in their spaciousness, without shadows, without time, returned his wandering pursuit, meeting him in some bodiless middle-world formed from nothing but intention.

"Hi."

A voice tried to rise from some place, screamed out from the depths of his abyss, but vocal chords had been struck dumb, depleted to a mere croak. A whine, even a whisper was too much. He had so much to say, but he was like a word that had never been said in any language, waiting for its birth by a tongue yet to be inspired.

A hand edged toward the blue spheres. He hoped it was real, but the boundaries were uncertain. Ownership of muscle and bone, clenched and awkward, traveled the empty distance to find a warm, small hand that held something, a light, a pulse, an energy that entered him, and he suddenly felt his world saturate in clarity. It was not a revelation when that which was once a mystery is suddenly made clear. It was more a feeling; a sudden profusion of hope. The unsteady elements, so fine as to be invisible even to the invisible, became ordered in such a way that they could be seen and felt. They could reach out and fill the emptiness of retreat.

It was all in that touch. A transmission came his way. What had been shut down was suddenly open. What had been inflamed, redeemed by a cool rain.

His eye closed again. A deep darkness fell upon him as he knew he was finally able to sleep, and blend into the stillness of restoration.

But before he fell into oblivion a thought entered his mind that he vowed not to forget. *He is the Mahdi, and he doesn't even know it.*

CHAPTER 35

Passing

Carson was sitting in a wheelchair, which Nouri had arranged for him. His right leg was raised, resting on a pillow that was tied around the footrest. Carson, Terran and Nouri were in the school's health office, which was on the main floor in the back of the school, on the north side of the building. The health office consisted of two rooms, one in the back that possessed two cots, and an office area that had a small alcove with a single desk, and a large dresser filled with various bandages, a few herbal medicines, and books—mostly on first aid care. The school didn't have a fulltime nurse, but on every Wednesday morning, a nurse would come in and perform routine checks on the students.

Unfortunately, it was Thursday.

Carson leveled his eyes on Sanjur, who was sleeping on one of the cots, and then looked at Terran. "That's who you want to bring with us?"

Nouri glanced at Terran, and then back at Carson and nodded, as if the translation would only be redundant.

"He looks like a corpse. I'm no doctor, but even I can tell you that he can't travel—not the journey we have ahead of us. No way."

Nouri spoke to Terran, his face sober. He waited for Terran's response, and when it was received, he shook his head.

"Then we will stay. He's sorry you went to all this trouble to—"

"No, you don't understand," Carson interrupted, looking directly at Terran. "You don't get to say 'no.' The Director of the Faculty wants you, he's given me orders to take you to Delhi, and that's what I aim to do. If we bring this man—"

"His name is Sanjur," Nouri interrupted.

Carson controlled his voice and lowered it to an intense whisper. "If we bring Sanjur to Delhi, how long before he dies? How much more trouble do we bring to this mission? Look at me! I'm already trouble. We don't need more. I'm sorry, but this isn't a hospital, it's a goddamn convoy to Kandahar. No! He can't come."

Nouri translated, and as he spoke, Terran took a deep breath and held it, and then slowly exhaled, and at the end of his breath, said a few words.

Nouri's brow furrowed, but he remained silent.

"What did he say?" Carson asked.

"He says you are not God."

"What does that mean?"

Nouri looked at Carson with steady eyes. "It means he will follow his own way."

"Look, I came here to rescue you and take you to Delhi. I lost a man. I'm shot. You can't just dismiss us because you *changed your mind*. You're coming, and that's the end of it. This man's in bad shape. I have no way to care for him… you have to be reasonable."

When Nouri finished his translation, Terran looked soulfully in Carson's direction, and spoke quietly without pause for nearly a minute. Nouri turned to Carson when he stopped, and paused, as if he were contemplating the best way to translate what he had just heard.

Carson shook his head and muttered to himself. "Shit, I can't believe I'm arguing with a kid."

Nouri raised his brow and remained silent.

"Go ahead, tell me what he said. I can take it."

It was a sarcastic tone, and Nouri knew well that Terran's strong will was irritating Carson.

"He says that his mind is made up for reasons that he can't explain, or you can't accept… he's not sure which. But tomorrow it will be made clear. He suggests that we wait until tomorrow morning and make the decision then. If Sanjur is walking and talking, he wants your assurance that you will bring him. And if he is not, then we will leave him here as you wish."

Carson suddenly smiled, as the last sentence found his ears. "That's a reasonable solution. I accept."

Carson then put his hand in the air, and turned his communicator to his mouth. "What was that, Frank? Over."

Carson's expression changed from delight to concern in a matter of a second. "We have a developing situation. I need you to wheel me out to the entrance as fast as you can. Okay?"

Terran said something as Nouri jolted into action. "He wants to know what's happening."

"It sounds like our Baluchian messenger is back. This time with a young girl—maybe one of your students."

The instant Nouri finished his translation, Terran ran out the door, full speed in the direction of the front entrance. Carson shouted after him to stop, but Terran ran as if his life depended on it. When he got near the front door, Frank turned around as he heard the sound of wild running. "Whoa, hold up there, little man."

Frank blocked the door and held Terran in his arms, while Terran struggled. Down the hallway, shouts were coming from Carson, and Nouri was yelling: "Keep him inside!"

Frank Courtman was a large man, fairly average in height, but he had a thick, powerful build, and while Terran continued to struggle, it was futile against Frank's rhino-like physique.

Terran shouted at Nouri as the two men arrived. "They have Dorri!"

"How do you know that?" Nouri asked.

"How does that matter? We need to save her, and I'm the only one who can. They have to let me go."

Nouri made the translation, and Carson started to shake his head before he completed his words. "First, we see what they want. Open the door, so I can see them."

Frank disentangled himself from Terran and shuffled to the door and slowly opened it. There were two men and a small girl standing near the concrete bench just off the street. One of the men held a handgun.

"What do you want?" Carson yelled out.

The two men spoke to one another in hushed voices. "We have a proposition. We trade the girl for Terran. Very simple trade. Nothing complicated."

Carson yelled through the open door. "And if we don't?"

Terran squatted down so he could see between Frank's legs and survey the scene. It was Javad and Moshad, and Moshad held Dorri in one hand. Dorri was clearly afraid, but she was not crying. Her hair was all tousled, and her face had a bruise. The afternoon light was strong, as were the shadows from the nearby trees.

"We prefer not to say, but it will not be an easy night for the girl," Javad said. He was noticeably uncomfortable as a messenger.

Terran, in that instant knew he had to take action. He grabbed the sidearm from Frank's belt, and pushed Frank with all his might against the wall, and ran full speed into the street. Moshad and Javad instinctively stepped back, but when Moshad saw it was Terran, he held up his arm, signaling his men to hold fire.

Terran ran to within ten feet of their position, the whole time focused on Dorri. His gun was pointed at Moshad, who laughed when he saw it. "You're going to shoot me, now? You do that, and my men will fill you with bullets, and then this girl will join you. Put the gun down!"

Terran slowly dropped his gun to his side.

Carson was swearing, and told Frank to open the door wider so he had a shot. He ordered Frank to go upstairs to get a better sight angle, and to use single bursts. Frank ran off, pissed that a little kid surprised him like that.

"Have you lost all sense of honor that you would abduct an innocent girl?" Terran asked. "Let her go."

"Or what? Have you lost your sense of reality? *I* am the chief of police. *I* am the authority of Pirdah. You will not disobey me again."

Carson spoke into his communicator. "Frank, are you in position?"

He listened to Frank's report. "Do you have a clean shot?"

Hamid stepped up to Carson. "You have to do something. They'll take him!"

"Shit!" Carson said, as he watched Moshad pick the girl up and hold her like a shield, and then put his gun to the side of her head, and backed up slightly, moving to the far side of the Humvee for protection. "Last time. The girl for Terran." Shouted Javad.

Terran slowly raised his arm.

"Don't even think about it," Moshad ordered. "Put your gun down, or I will order my men to open fire."

"Javad, you were my teacher. Do you agree with this madman? Let the girl go. She's innocent. If you do that, I will negotiate—"

"There's nothing to negotiate," Moshad growled. "You come with us. You return to your home where you belong. You have ten seconds, and then I will give the order."

Terran looked at Dorri. Her eyes held trust. A single tear fell across her cheek, and Terran's arm fell with it, and he threw his gun down. "You win. I will go with you, on one condition."

Moshad couldn't mask his surprise. "What?"

"Javad returns Dorri safely to the school Director," Terran said. "When I see she is safely inside, I will leave with Javad."

Moshad turned to Javad. "Take the girl."

They were now on the other side of the Humvee, and Moshad set Dorri on the ground, feeling safe behind the armor of the metal beast.

Terran turned around to face the school. The gun was on the ground at the front of the Humvee, on his side, nearest the school entrance.

Javad yelled as he came around the corner of the vehicle with Dorri in hand. "I will walk her to the door and hand her off. Please, hold your fire."

Moshad looked through the glass windows at Terran. "Come over on this side."

"Not until I see she is safely delivered," Terran replied.

Terran took a step closer to the gun on the ground.

"Fine, then stay where I can see you," Moshad said.

Javad and Dorri climbed the steps, and Dorri rushed into the door.

"She's inside. Now get over here."

Javad skipped down the steps, walking briskly to Terran, hope written on his face. But it was short-lived, as Terran dove for the gun, and in one deft move rolled on his side and fired six shots in rapid succession underneath the Humvee. The first bullet grazed Moshad's ankle, but it was enough to get him on the ground. The second bullet missed, as did the third, fourth and fifth, but the sixth bullet found his thigh, and Moshad winced in sudden pain. Javad dove on Terran's side of the Humvee, as gunfire showered the street from both sides. It was like a hailstorm of metal spheres, hurtling their angry epithets like madmen.

In the pandemonium, Javad looked at Terran with terror-stricken eyes. *Had he just killed Moshad? Had he gone crazy?*

After a minute of chaos, the gunfire slowed to a trickle. Glass was everywhere. Clouds of smoke drifted through the streets like eerie ghosts, rising and falling in serpentine waves.

"Javad, get him." Moshad ordered, gasping in pain.

Javad put his arms out to Terran, who was still lying on the ground next to the front tire by the curb. "Come with me."

"Come with *me*," Terran said.

"You know I can't. This is what you must do. In two, maybe three years, your mission will begin—"

"Don't speak to me of prophecies, Javad. I know what they say, but I also know what I see. What I know. And I am not the person of those prophecies, no matter how much Pirdah wants this to be so." Terran paused and looked under the Humvee to check on Moshad, who was tearing off his shirt to wrap it around his upper leg. "How can you live among men who threaten innocent children? Come with me. You can join me."

"Are you alright, Terran?" Nouri called out from behind the main door.

"Yes, I'm fine," Terran shouted back.

Moshad grunted. "When Pirdah hears that you shot his chief of police—"

"—he will finally understand how committed I am to my path." Terran interrupted, completing Moshad's sentence. His voice was higher pitched, but the intensity was no less severe than Moshad's. "You are no victim here, so spare us your words."

Javad looked at Terran with admiration. He was in the presence of God, a warrior of God, the one who will unite all of humanity… and he had offered him a chance to go with him. Some impulse from deep inside Javad leapt to his mouth in the form of a whispered hope. "I will go with you."

Terran smiled, and looked to the entrance of the school. He could see Frank holding his gun, watching him with interest. Terran pointed to Javad and himself, and then pointed to the entrance. Frank nodded, and opened the door an inch or two wider, and looked around, and then backed up into the shadows. Terran could hear the faint murmur of voices. Seconds later, when Frank reappeared, he signaled a countdown with his fingers. Ten, nine, eight…

Then suddenly the Humvee shook, and Terran looked and saw that Moshad was struggling to get inside. Terran knew they had to run fast.

"Go!" Terran shouted.

Javad followed Terran up the stairs, and everyone was startled.

Not a single gunshot was fired, and Frank stayed inside the door as he was caught off guard and didn't want to block the entrance. *They left on the count of six?*

Moshad struggled to get into a position to have a shot. Through the Humvee's busted windows, he swung his handgun into firing position, but had no clear shot. Frustrated, he yelled his order to shoot, and instantly an eruption of gunfire fell on the entrance. Frank was pinned down. There was nothing he could do.

Terran and Javad dashed into the entrance, and Frank slammed it shut with a hard kick. Immediately the gunfire stopped. Terran turned around to check on Javad and he saw the crimson outlines of gunshots slowly forming on his shirt. Javad's eyes already looked deserted of their spirit as they looked into Terran's. He rushed over to hold his teacher, and in many ways, his father.

Javad slumped over, his eyes staring out unfocused. His mouth moved like a mouth possessed, it twisted, searching for words, and all Terran could do was to weep and tenderly stroke Javad's cheek. Finally, a relaxation came over Javad, and his mouth exhaled its final breath, and with it, seven simple words: "At least I died in your presence."

The room darkened in that instant, as if a shadow fell from a passing God. Terran felt a hand on his shoulder, and turned to see Dorri smiling at him. He heard her say something, but Terran was in some other reality that shock shelters from words, thoughts and anything that assays the three dimensions. In that space, usually empty of anything that can confound, he embraced Javad's spirit with the simplest of feelings: love.

CHAPTER 36

The Path

A span of life stretches unattended by demons and angels; even God seems perfectly absent. So often a life is ready for monumental transformation, but it must wait for courage to bloom. Sometimes it even prepares for the transformation for years and years, observing the glimmers of hope that pass overhead like searchlights from the heavens, but their beams illuminate the cage, not the graceful, single essence. That brilliant speck remains unillumined by any light. (Can a candle brighten the sun?)

The indescribable is the only path. If it can be spoken, given life by the mouth, it is illusory. It is a thing locked in cages where the clearest eyes never look. The heart, that innermost core of consciousness, is not inside a body. It is not inside a thing of dimensions. There is *nothing* that can hold it! That central core *is* the path. It seems a contradiction that the core—the indivisible part—is the scale of a universe unfolding to become the one that is all. Yet, it is the tiniest speck of consciousness in the very center that is the most powerful, for it holds the path, not as a container or cage, but as an aperture to that intelligence of all things: love's essence.

When one looks through this aperture, they see how to be. Does it make them perfect in the human sense? *No.* Do problems beset them? *Yes.* So what is gained? *Nothing.* Then what is lost? *Nothing.* Then why seek the path? *Don't. Be in your heart. Be in your core. Be in your path.* But why?! (A long silence, the kind that commands attention.) *Because you will be you.*

*　　　*　　　*　　　*

Terran woke suddenly to see Dorri watching him. He rubbed his eyes, and then forced a smile in Dorri's direction. He was momentarily confused as the voices still echoed inside him. She came over and hugged him. It was a long hug, and Terran sensed that she was afraid of something. It was dark; a single candle lit the room. He had slept near Sanjur, who remained resting.

As Terran sat on the side of his cot, he tried to clear his head and get his bearings. The reality of Javad's death whirled around him, and he bolted to his feet, and walked down the hallway with Dorri in tow. He could hear voices coming from Hamid's office, and decided to make it his destination.

"Where are your other men?" Hamid asked.

"I made that up," Carson admitted with a grin. "They're not coming. At least I don't have any plans that they will. Hell, maybe they will. They're probably wondering why we didn't make it back, assuming they noticed. The rest of my *men*, as you put it, are hired guns. Frank and Joe were from my unit in Kandahar... the rest... they were cobbled together from God knows where."

Hamid looked up. "Ah, Terran's awake."

"What time is it?" Terran asked, looking in Nouri's direction, his eyes still blurry. The smell of jasmine tea and freshly cut wood filled the office.

Nouri tapped his wrist with his index finger, looking at Carson.

"About ten," Carson said as he looked at his watch.

Nouri translated.

Hamid's office had been transformed into a war room. The entire wall facing the yard was boarded up. A brass floor lamp provided the only light, and on the opposite wall was a blackboard that had been taken from one of the classrooms. A chalk outline of what looked like a bird's eye view of the school and its bordering neighborhood stood out with dotted lines slicing through rooms and windows.

"I want to bury Javad," Terran announced.

Nouri translated to Carson, who then rolled his eyes.

"Look, I have a man who's lying face down outside the entrance. I want to bury him, too, but I'm not going to risk another life to do so. It's dark—pitch black is a better way of putting it. I can't send anyone out there. Besides, I'm trying to figure out a way out of here, which is a higher priority than burying people."

After Nouri translated to Terran, Terran turned to Hamid. "Do you have a shovel?"

When Nouri finished, Hamid nodded, but Carson threw up his arms. "Is it just me, or does this boy totally disregard my authority?"

Terran spoke for nearly a minute, and when he finished, he urged Nouri to speak with a nod of his head.

"He says," Nouri began, "that it is best to bury the body at night. When he digs the grave, it will attract the attention of Moshad and his men. He will bury Javad near the school. He suggests that we have two spotters, hidden behind windows, who watch the area while he digs. Moshad and his men will not shoot him. If any of them try to get close enough to take him, the spotters can fire a warning shot, and they'll retreat. While this is going on, you have a distraction that will allow you to drive away and get more soldiers. He believes this is the best plan. If you would like him to bury your soldier, he will do that, too. But first we need to retrieve his body, and the cover of darkness is the best time— before the moon rises."

Carson looked at Terran, and scratched the side of his stubble-filled chin. He took a quick glance at the blackboard, and then Hamid. "I liked everything except the idea of a warning shot. We went way past warning shots when they killed one of my men."

Nouri started to translate, and then abruptly stopped.

Carson waved his hand. "He's doesn't need to hear everything."

Nouri nodded. "But he can bury Javad?"

"Yes, he can, but I want a say in the selection of the burial site, because it needs to have certain characteristics. Tell him."

Terran listened attentively as Nouri delivered the news, and then Terran spoke with confident gestures.

Nouri looked to Carson with eyes that were smiling. "He says he appreciates your help, but he already has a burial site picked out—it will be the place that Sanjur delivered the deathblow to Josid. He also asks if you would like him to perform burial rites for your soldier?"

Carson waved his hand slightly. It was an expression of annoyance, but he doubted that anyone in the room would recognize it. "Fine... it's pointless to argue with him, he might as well be my wife."

Terran then turned to Hamid. "Can you take Dorri to get some food or something to drink?"

Nouri delivered the translation. Hamid nodded, then taking Dorri's hand they walked out of his office As they walked he promised her a treat before she went to bed.

When they had left, Terran turned to Nouri, and whispered. "How did they find Dorri?"

Nouri took a quick glance at Carson. "They abducted her from her uncle."

"Is the uncle okay?"

"Yes. According to Dorri, he didn't even know she'd been taken until it was too late."

"How did they know Parto had a child?"

"We don't know."

"Did they interrogate the uncle?"

"No."

"Is there any chance they could know where Parto is?"

"We don't think so. Even if they knew she was at a clinic, they don't know where anything is in this city. They're four or five clinics in Mashhad… they're on foot. It's not likely—"

"What if her uncle went to the clinic after they kidnapped Dorri? They could follow him. If they find out where Parto is, they will do the same thing they tried with Dorri. Moshad needs leverage. He can't wait us out indefinitely. He'll either make a move to storm the school, or he'll seek a hostage that is meaningful to me—to us. Parto is the only one… who's not here." Terran paused. "We need to bring her here. Tell the Captain that when he leaves to get his men. He must get Parto, and you'll need to go with him so he knows the way. Yes?"

Nouri nodded nervously. "When I left her at the clinic, early this morning, she was inconsolable. The doctor said he wanted to keep her for observation. What if they don't want to release her?"

"Let the Captain deal with that," Terran said, glancing in Carson's direction. "He'll know what to do, just make sure he understands that there's no option to leave her there—for any reason."

Terran looked at the chalkboard, and ran his hand through his hair. "This plan would have failed."

CHAPTER 37

Host

Terran could see his breath like funnels of clouds. It was a cool night. He was glad the digging kept him warm, because he had no coat. The sound of the shovel hitting the ground echoed in the still night. He noticed that a few homes across the side street had lanterns on. Most of the neighborhood, being shrouded in a heavy blackness, made the school grounds stand out even more. Hamid had turned on the outside lights, so Terran could attract more attention to himself.

There was little doubt that Moshad and his men were already moving in on him. He glanced at the windows of the school; they were black, but he knew that spotters were there, watching. He also knew that Carson and Nouri were waiting by the front entrance.

Before Hamid had turned on the outside lights, Frank had already snuck out and gotten Joe's body, and then Frank had helped Terran wrap Javad and Joe into clean bed sheets, and helped him hoist the bodies through a lower open window. Terran and Frank then dragged the bodies into place. Once that part of the operation was completed, Hamid had turned on the lights. Terran was left illuminated with a shovel and two bodies wrapped head to toe in white bed sheets, with string tied tightly around each body.

At times, Terran felt like a glass bottle moving over the sea in passage to a random shore. He knew nothing of what waited him, only that he needed to go. He knew his life was bound somehow to understanding the forces that affected the fragile intersection of humanity and earth. And even as he dug the graves, he could feel his movement in this direction. The currents were unalterable.

A subtle movement caught his eye. He tried not to look, and pretended to be so absorbed in his grave digging that he didn't notice. His first grave was nearing three feet in depth when he saw a figure move across the street to a tree about a hundred feet from his position.

Terran glanced at the dark windows, hoping that what he observed was also seen by the spotters.

Frank looked through the first-floor window, keeping far enough back to remain unobserved. He saw a grayish figure run across the street, then another. Two Baluch fighters had crossed the street. Then a third blur whisked across the street. They were hidden behind large tree trunks that provided them invisibility—for the moment. Between their hiding place and Terran, was a span of a hundred feet of open grass and dirt from which they could not hide. Frank tensed up, knowing the fighters were unpredictable. Three would make it hard to focus, especially if they all came at the same time, but he suspected they would stagger their attempts to grab Terran. One thing was certain, he had to take them out before they got too close to Terran, otherwise his abduction would be impossible to stop.

Carson was using Nouri as his crutch. His keys were in his left hand, clutched around Nouri's shoulder; his handgun in the other. They waited for the gunfire that would signal their dash to the Humvee. His plan was to back-up the Humvee at full speed to avoid the side yard where Terran was, and then jet down an obscure side street. The door was open just a crack, and only the side yard was illuminated, but their path to the Humvee had more light than he wanted.

A whispered update came over his communicator from Frank. "Three of them just crossed the street. Over."

"Are they together?" Caron whispered.

"They're behind two different trees... spread about twenty feet. Present positions are about a hundred feet from Terran. Get ready. Over."

There was a long, tense pause. "What are they waiting for?" Carson asked.

"Don't know. Maybe they're choosing straws to see who goes first."

"How far along is Terran?"

"Looks like one grave is done... he just put one of the bodies in. Over."

"So it takes about twenty minutes to dig a grave..."

"Is it possible they won't make a move until he finishes. Over." Frank asked.

"Hell if I know," Carson quipped.

Terran bent down, and slipped Javad carefully into his grave. There was a sudden hush, as if his ears were popping. He heard a whispered, indistinct voice, floating on the still air, but couldn't, as hard as he tried, understand any words. An unexpected force thrust down from above, and he was transfixed in a dome of deafening silence. *What's happening? Whose presence do I feel?*

Then he saw it. A spiraling of energy came down from the sky, and he was spellbound. The school yard suddenly went black, as a form approached him that was hewn from light and nothing more. It drifted to Terran, hovering six feet away, and yet, when this Light Being looked at him, he saw no eyes or any discernible features.

"What are you?" Terran asked. Fear flooded his mind for a moment as he realized that this was not a good time to lose his situational awareness, because there were men nearby who were keen to abduct him.

Terran didn't know how it was possible, but in the next moment, he heard a voice, powered by ancient currents.

"I am the fleeting spark that becomes the consuming fire. I am the small seed that becomes the towering tree."

Terran stood to his feet, but wondered if he was still a part of time— he felt the tiny shudders of an emotion he could not fathom or call by name. It danced through his body like electric currents in a divine flux of power and ease. "Why me, why now?"

"You... because you are ready. Now... because I am ready."

"Ready for what?" Terran asked, awestruck by the voice and manner in which it spoke. Arcane symbols of nimble gold flowed from the Light Being like a river directly into Terran's chest, and as they entered his body they were converted into sounds—words, peeled to an essence that, amazingly, he could understand.

"I am that thing you call a muse. I am that thing that activates you. I am that thing that motivates you. I am that thing that ushers you to a higher and wider perspective. I am that thing that opens you. I am that thing that draws you forward. I am that thing that humbles you. I am that thing that is the breath within your breath. I am that thing that understands you, and needs to be understood. You are ready to know me, and even as you bury the one who taught you as a boy—a physical being—you have birthed me, and I will teach you as a spirit."

"But why now?" Terran asked. "When I have so much to do, and I have men who seek to capture me? Why now?"

"I observe. I know when the precise moment has arrived. Chaos may rule in your outer reality, but if the time is right for both of us, it does not matter. I will step forward anyway, and if you are aware, you will see me. It cannot fail. Our meeting is not of your time, it is of *our* time."

Terran stared at the Being of golden light that faced him. A million tiny light particles churned inside the rough perimeter of a humanoid shape, subtle and mysterious, its depths indiscernible. Terran sighed. "Is this part of the prophecy?"

"No, you are not a prophecy. You are not an actor or machine. You are a vibrant host who has come to realize a role of your own choosing, and what that will be, remains unrecorded and unpredictable."

Terran reached out to touch the river of light that connected them, and as he did, he could see that there were actually thousands of light filaments that connected them. He was intertwined with this Light Being in a complex of light and energy that was drawn to him through some form of inner gravity. His astonishment quickened when he watched the Light Being move inside him, and slowly dissolved into him. The silence that he had heard before only deepened, and he wondered how it was possible that he could be in two worlds simultaneously. He knew there were enemies stalking him. He could sense their presence, but for some unknowable reason, he didn't care.

He was a Russian doll, a constellation of layers and connections. If this enormity should reappear he would ask it more questions. He would be prepared.

He brushed the dirt over the body of his former teacher with the shovel's blade, wondering how his life could possibly become more surreal. An exegesis of the soul had never been so tortured and tangled in a twelve-year-old body. He was certain of that, and yet, he knew something foreign—made in a far-off land—had entered him to the very edge and depths of his being. Whatever luminous and unhidden grace that was stored within him, it now had a guiding hand, so full of patience, as to unmask his soul.

The very thing he most feared.

CHAPTER 38

Meeting of Foes

Terran stood in a daze. His burial task was dwarfed by the experience of the Being of Light that had entered him. *Did it enter me or I enter it?* He was standing over the packed dirt, rounded like two brown bellies arched beneath a yellow light that buzzed in a tall tree some twenty feet away.

Suddenly, he heard a gunshot, and the light instantly disappeared. Shouting from the school caught his attention. He turned just as he felt a hand grab him. He was still in a daze. On one level he was aware of what was happening—in fact, he was hyper-aware of every movement, every sound, even the scent of the Baluchian men who grabbed his arms and pulled him away.

He heard the spinning of flat tires as the Humvee started up and instantly lurched in reverse, and then sped down a side street. He could hear more shouting and several more gunshots. Terran didn't resist his abductors. They dragged him, one abductor on either side of him and ran hurriedly to the other side of the street. His mind was not contained in his body. It was traveling in some far-off world, crystalline, vast, and embroidered to depths he could not fathom. He was caught in two very different worlds, and he could not control his body in order to resist his abductors.

In a few minutes he was ushered into a small room with a single candle. Terran recognized Moshad, as he was tossed onto a barren cement floor. "You cost me my best warrior. You shot me in the leg. You created this chaos, and now you will pay."

Terran strained to look into Moshad's eyes, but he couldn't see them. The light was too dim, and all he saw were sunken shadows like dark pools from a violent stream. Moshad's voice was toxic. It held a scorn he reserved for his most pitiful criminals. Terran knew that there was a very good probability that he would not live another hour. Moshad would make his death look like an accident, bring his body back to Pirdah like a hero who tried everything he could to save Terran from the treacherous clutches of the infidels, but in the end, they had shot him in Moshad's heroic attempt to rescue him. Terran could hear Moshad's words as if he were listening to a future recording.

In that warped, alternate reality, Terran's head began to clear. He sat up with his back against the wall, pulled his legs up and wrapped his arms around them, never once looking in Moshad's direction. He hated this man. Moshad was the source of chaos. It was he who was inflicting the deaths of those who had fallen, and yet he placed the blame on Terran. Anger began to rise in him as he considered how to respond. A voice inside whispered: *Breathe slowly. Agree with him. No resistance.*

Terran took a slow, measured breath, and decided to listen to the voice he heard. "You're right. If I hadn't left, none of this would have happened. I bear this responsibility, and will face the consequences as they come to me."

Moshad smirked in quiet surprise. "You mock me?"

Terran shook his head slowly. "No, I agree with you."

Moshad struggled to straighten his leg. He had a red sash tightened around his upper thigh, and even in the dull light of the room, Terran was aware of the red color that glistened on Moshad's right pant leg. "We'll return home, and I will give you to Pirdah and leave it to him to assign your punishment. If it were up to me, you'd be dead, but I know that Pirdah would hold me responsible, and his wrath, I do not need... with two men dead, it will be enough."

Terran reflexively glanced in Moshad's direction. "Two?"

"Shaheen was killed this afternoon in the gunfire."

A deep silence rested in the room as Terran let the words wash over him. Four dead, several wounded, hundreds of children at risk, for what? His desire to learn? His wild craving to help humanity? A wave of emotion rushed through him. He suddenly felt hopeless and hollow.

"So what do we do?" Terran asked, his voice composed, but dry.

Moshad adjusted his position, sitting against the far wall underneath a dark window of broken glass. He grimaced, as he cautiously moved his wounded leg. "After the doctor looks as me, we'll leave here. You'll be bound like a prisoner, until we put enough distance between us and this foul city. What Pirdah will do with you is his business, but I will not spare him the details of your actions… and their consequences to me and my men."

Terran nodded quietly. He knew his fate had turned in a new direction, nearing a personal extinction or enfeebled imprisonment, he wasn't sure, but he reasoned that now—in Pirdah's control—imprisonment seemed the most likely option.

Terran let out a long sigh, and pushed his sleeves up. "Why can't you let me go?"

"You know why." Moshad shot a quick glance in Terran's direction. "Why do you insist on running from your people?"

"My people…" Terran's voice drifted across the room in a dispassionate whisper. "I don't understand this concept. I am bound to none if not all. If there's one thing the Sunrot taught all of us, it's that we're one people—no fractions or ratios—*one* people, Moshad. The old ways of seeing through a lens that splits humanity, they're gone. Our leaders are slow to see this… too slow, seeing things in pieces, and in these pieces, to see opposition and differences, rather than a human totality."

Moshad exhaled loudly, making his annoyance unambiguous. "You're naïve! Do you truly think the infidels understand or care about our history—what came before Sunrot? Do you think that just because Sunrot passes over us that suddenly our history is forgotten? You're a child, and that's why you see things this way. I've seen both sides, I've lived in both times, and the old times can never be forgotten. The people of the West are heathens. They believe in money, and in the lesser Prophet, who, in weakness, has allowed them to destroy our planet."

"They didn't destroy our planet. The Heavens did that!" Terran pointed upwards for emphasis, but in the dark room it was a symbolic gesture and little more. "I have never met a Westerner; I have never met a Christian or a non-Muslim. I don't have any experience outside of our small world, but I know this, they are human like you and me, and that is enough."

"It's not enough!" Moshad fired back. "They desire control. They want us to be slaves to their culture. To grovel in front of the twisted idols they create out of thin air. They worship mirages, and they want us to do the same. Our entire tribe—every one of our people—are called Old Schoolers, a term meant to demean us. To make us seem unworthy of the life they seek. We will get the crumbs, the high deserts, the brackish waters, the life of hardship, and they will get all of the bounty. This is an injustice that has settled over our people for hundreds of years, and the irony, the *real* irony, is that our Holy men believe that you are the one who will repair this injustice."

Moshad laughed with a sneer curled inside. "I don't see it. I don't see how you, an ignorant child, could possibly repair what no man, or Prophet, for that matter, has ever been able to fix. You have only one quality that I can admire, and that is your stubbornness. Every other quality in you is tainted with the desire to be of *their* world. To learn *their* knowledge. To leave your people for the sake of having it, when it is this very knowledge that has caused the destruction of our world. Do you not see this?"

Terran shook his head slowly. "The knowledge is not owned by anyone. It is the intermediary between the worlds of survival and the worlds of meaning, and for me to access the higher dimension of the worlds of meaning, I must have this knowledge. If it is in the hands of infidels, then I must go to them and get it. I wouldn't have left, if we had possessed it. Javad was the closest to having possession of this knowledge, but he is one man, and he knew his limitations. I must do this, Moshad. It is the one truth I know with certainty."

"And do you know what's wrong with this knowledge?" Moshad asked.

"What?"

"It's Godless."

"No, it's not."

"There're no higher dimensions or worlds of meaning that this knowledge can lead you to, because it is *wrong!* It is Godless, it is like a headless body that can do nothing but take up space."

"With the knowledge I will be able to create things that—"

"What things?" Moshad interrupted. "Ways to make new idols that are even more seductive? Ways to make the infidels feel better with their empty lives?"

"No!" Terran nearly shouted, and then instantly regained his composure. "Ways to harness the weather instead of being subject to it."

"That's what this has been about? You want to control the weather? You want to make it rain in the deserts, to... to weaken storms before they rise with their full power? Is that it? You want to play God?"

"Moshad, another Sunrot will come. We need to defend ourselves from its destruction."

"God will defend us if we are in His care. If we follow His Prophet's teachings. If we adhere to the Quran. We need to put ourselves in His hands. That's all. This mission you are on is misguided, and it will fail. *It will surely fail.*"

A deep silence filled the room, as Terran resisted the temptation to argue. Gradually, muffled whispers and the shuffle of feet could be heard outside their room. A light knock and a hooded guard opened the creaking door. "The doctor is here."

Moshad nodded. "Good, show him in. Did you find more candles?"

"Yes."

"Bring them, too."

Terran looked at Moshad, knowing his time was short. "If I fail, it will be because you and Pirdah refused my freedom. And when the next Sunrot hits, you can blame the infidels, but the real reason will be you. As a prisoner, I can never realize my mission, whatever Pirdah believes it to be, I will never be a Mahdi while held against my will. As a captive I will resist, and even those of weak faith will notice that Allah has turned away. So the best you can hope for is a prisoner... who takes up space."

Terran stood to his feet, and waited for a response, but only a cruel laugh spurted from Moshad. The next moment the guard came in, and silently exchanged Terran for the doctor, whom he knew, but in the dim light Terran kept his head down, hoping there would be no recognition. No words passed between them, and Terran sensed that the doctor was agitated and nervous.

Terran was led to an adjoining room that was dark, and then pushed firmly to the floor, where he was bound with rope at both his ankles and wrists.

As the guard tied his wrists, Terran winced. "It's too tight."

The guard never responded, but Terran could feel him loosen the ropes around his small wrists. "What is your name?" Terran asked.

"Shaheen," the guard answered.

"You're Shaheen! I thought you were dead?"

The guard stopped. "You *can* see me?"

"Moshad told me, only minutes ago, that you had died in gunfire this very day. Why would Moshad lie to me?"

Shaheen shook his head. "I don't know. Perhaps you misheard."

"Did anyone else die in the gunfire this day?"

"No."

Terran paused. "Shaheen, you know me. Your family knew my family. Why do you bind me?"

Shaheen knelt closer. In the deep darkness of the room, only an occasional glint of his eyes could be seen. "I'm sorry," Shaheen whispered, "but I must do this. Is it still too tight?"

"It's better. Thank you," Terran replied. "I ask you, in the spirit of Allah, let me walk out of here, Shaheen."

"I can't do that. If I did, then I probably would be dead... by Moshad's hands."

"When I escaped last time, did any of the guards receive punishment?"

Shaheen shook his head. "That was different, Sanjur masterminded it. None of the guards helped."

"I will make it look like I overpowered you... do you have a knife?"

Shaheen nodded. "Yes... but—"

"Okay," Terran whispered, "give it to me, and I will cut your arm, only a little bit, and you can say that I grabbed your knife, and then your gun, while you were tying me up. You were surprised because it was dark and you couldn't see well—"

"I can't do that!" Shaheen exclaimed. "I can't let you walk out of here. I have to obey my orders. You shot Moshad. It's personal now."

A muffled gasp could be heard in the next room, a clear sign that the doctor had begun to work on Moshad's leg. Silence returned to the room.

"There are more men outside in the street," Shaheen continued. "They will see you and probably shoot you on sight. You can't get away."

"Let me try, Shaheen."

"No, I'm sorry."

While Terran had been talking he had freed one of his hands from the loosened rope.

"Then I have no choice," Terran said. "I'm sorry."

Terran deftly reached to the side of Shaheen where the Baluch warriors usually kept their knives. He found it, and in one quick slash, cut across Shaheen's arm. Then he grabbed for Shaheen's gun, but Shaheen was faster and drew it on Terran, staggering back against the wall.

"Stay where you are, don't make me shoot you."

"Shaheen, let me go. *I am the Mahdi*, and I must have my freedom if I'm to fulfill my destiny. You know this is true. Let me go, and Allah will reward you. *Let me go.*" His voice was commanding, and yet soft at the same time; even Terran was surprised at how it sounded.

Shaheen's arm slowly fell to his side, and he motioned with his gun barrel to the door. "Go, but be very careful when you step outside."

"Give me your gun. It will be your alibi."

Terran cut the binds from his ankles and then tucked the knife in his sash. He stood up, and took the gun handed him. "Thank you for this. Give me one minute, and then scream as loud as you can that you need help. Okay?"

Shaheen nodded.

"And let the doctor have a look at that cut. It may need stitches."

Shaheen grabbed Terran as he passed by. "If you are the Mahdi, please, give me your blessing…"

Terran hesitated for a moment, and then reached out to Shaheen's forehead and touched it with his index finger. "You are not this. You are the presence behind this, and really nothing more. This is where you are blessed. Do you understand?"

"…I think so."

Terran raised his index finger. "Good, remember, one minute."

"Yes, one minute." Shaheen bowed, and sank to the floor with a long sigh, trembling like one who had suddenly become part of a divine plan.

CHAPTER 39

Clinic

The Humvee's powerful engine groaned, though its flat tires flopped in a steady, staccato drone. The clinic was about four miles from the school, and Carson drove at a slow rate, keeping his lights off in order to make it hard to track their direction. When they were far enough away from the school, he turned on the lights and sped up slightly.

"Turn here… to the left." Nouri suddenly pointed.

"Give me a little more warning next time, partner. This thing doesn't handle too well right now with the tires being shot out."

They narrowly missed hitting a row of trash cans, where several older men were gathered, warming themselves on the sidewalk. They stared at the Humvee as if it were an extraterrestrial spaceship swooping down from the sky. Toothless grins of amazement, beneath grime-filled turbans, spread across their bearded faces.

"What the hell were they saying?"

"Food…" Nouri replied. "They wanted to know if we had food."

"You're sure this is the way?"

"Yes, we're almost there. Just stay on this road. We'll be taking a right in about three blocks."

When they arrived at the clinic, it was a small, discreet-looking, concrete building. An indistinguishable Iranian flag, tattered, and at permanent half-mast, was the only thing that set apart the otherwise crumbling building. The flicker of lantern light could be seen from the street through painted windows that created an eerie glow.

As they entered the empty waiting room, Nouri found a bell on the countertop, and rang it lightly, because it was near midnight. A minute later, a nervous-looking woman, in her late forties, wearing a simple nurse's uniform, marched down a semi-dark hallway. "We're closed. Please come back in the morning."

"We're here to see a woman that was admitted earlier for a gunshot wound, right here." Carson swept his finger across his forehead.

Nouri cleared his throat. "Her name is Parto Jafari."

"And what is your business with this woman?"

"We're friends."

The nurse gave Carson a long look, skeptical that such a man could be friends with Parto, but then extended her hand. "I am Dubria, the night nurse. I've looked after your friend since she came to us. She's doing better, but not talking yet. She's asleep, and shouldn't be disturbed now. Come back in the morning… please… I have to go."

As she turned to walk away, Carson grabbed her arm, and nearly spun her around. "We need to take her now," Carson whispered, as he leaned towards Dubria. "We have reason to believe the men who shot her will return."

Dubria stared into Carson's face for a moment, and then looked to Nouri, her eyes nervous. "Please, I need you to leave," she said, aggressively shaking her arm free of Carson's hold.

Carson took out his handgun, clenching it at his side. His instincts on high alert. "Are they here?" He whispered with a new intensity.

She nodded almost imperceptibly, her mouth trembling.

"How many?"

"Two," she whispered.

"Is there another way out?"

"There's a back alleyway, but the door is locked. Please, they said I had to get you out, or they would kill us."

Carson nodded and turned to Nouri, suddenly speaking in his normal voice. "We understand. We'll come back in the morning, then. Thank you for your help."

Carson put his gun back and motioned with his head to Nouri that they would leave. As they got out on the street, Carson put his finger to his lips and whispered, "Follow me… silently, and let me lean on you. I want to look injured."

"You *are* injured…" Nouri reminded.

They walked awkwardly as Carson, a much larger man, draped his arm around Nouri and limped a few hundred feet. When they got to the end of the block, they turned a corner and stopped, leaning against an abandoned building hidden from the clinic. He looked around the corner, grabbing his gun from his side holster. "I don't see anyone following us."

"We have to get Parto safely out of their hands!" Nouri pleaded.

"I know, I know, but our best chance is to ambush them once they're out of the clinic. Otherwise, we put everyone inside at risk." Carson ran his left hand through his tousled hair. "Parto's only value to them is to bring her to the school and try and exchange her for Terran. That has to be their plan."

"What about that?" Nouri pointed down the block to their Humvee. "Won't they notice it?"

"None of these Baluchian camel jockeys have seen me," Carson replied. "I'm not sure if they even know about the Humvee. These two may have been tracking Parto the whole time, and they've never been at the school. If that's the case, they have no idea who I am, or what the Humvee is."

Suddenly a sound caught them; it was the clinic's entrance door opening into the dead-quiet street, and they could see Parto being pushed in a wheelchair, with Dubria at the helm. There were two Baluchian warriors in ready position directly behind them, sweeping the streets with their heads, swiveling to see any movement or threat. They had guns drawn and made no secret that they were armed and dangerous.

Carson put his finger to his lips as Nouri started to say something, and immediately crouched down low, looking around the corner. When Carson stood up, he drew Nouri close to his face and whispered, as quietly as he could. "They're headed in the direction of the school. There's no way I can keep up with them on foot. I'm going to give you a gun, and you're going to follow them. Once you're out of range, I'll take the Humvee and try and get between them and the school. I'll signal you with a quick honk of my horn once I'm in position—"

"What if they take a different way?"

Carson handed Nouri his handgun with a thin, quick smile. "Then it's up to you."

Nouri looked down, his forehead furrowed, staring at the gun that

Carson had just handed him. "I'm a teacher. I've never fired a gun!"

"Look, there're no options here. You have to do this. If you can't, then we'll have to let them have Parto and Dubria, and I don't like those odds." Carson took another quick glance around the corner. "You need to go. Stay well back, but make sure you don't lose them. When you hear my signal, you'll know I'm in place. Be ready to close in, and only help if I need it. Otherwise, stay low. Got it?"

Nouri nodded hesitantly, his mind struggling with the shock of what stood before him. His heart beat fiercely beneath his chest, and suddenly, the overwhelming thought that he might have to use a gun—kill another human being—erupted like a volcano in his mind. He held out the gun to Carson. "I… I can't do this… I'm sorry, but I can't kill anyone—"

"I don't give a rat's ass what you think you can or can't do, just take the gun, and follow them. I might need your help, I might not, but if I do, you're going to have to rescue them. Be inventive. Do what you have to do." Carson reached down to the gun and unlocked the safety. "This baby is ready to fire, so stay away from the trigger until you need to pull it. It'll fire as often as you pull it. Only fire it at close range—we don't need any collateral damage. You can do this."

Carson's intensity was like a fire underneath Nouri, and he moved back a few feet and nodded his head, and then, to his own amazement, Nouri felt his legs take him around the corner in the direction of Parto and her captors.

CHAPTER 40

Interception

The night air was cool, but comfortable without the stir of wind. Nouri was trailing Parto by two blocks, locked in a one-way conversation with Allah—something he hadn't done in a very long time. Inwardly he kept repeating, *Give me strength and make me blameless.*

It was ten minutes since he had left Carson. He had heard the Humvee start-up in the distance, but never saw it. It was a phantom sound in an otherwise still night.

Dubria struggled as she pushed Parto in the wheelchair. The streets were cluttered with rubble and weeds. There was no talking as they made their way through the empty streets of Mashhad, and Nouri made sure to heed Carson's advice, staying well behind, careful in his silent shadowing.

Suddenly one of the Baluchian warriors—the taller of the two—began to argue with his comrade, and they quickly came to heated words. Nouri was too far away to make any sense of what they were saying, but after a minute of arguing they turned down a side street, and Nouri panicked as he lost sight of them. Nouri sped up, rushing against the sides of desolate buildings, careful not to kick a stone or trip on a crack. The moonlight was helpful, but his eyes had adjusted to the dim light, and he was surprised at how well he could see.

His senses were on high alert as he heard the telltale horn of the Humvee far in the distance. "No... no, it's not right!" Nouri exclaimed in a clenched whisper. The horn was too far to the west. Parto and her group were going easterly. Carson was off course. What Nouri had feared was descending upon him with a crushing weight that he could feel in his bones. He looked down at his gun, and shook his head. *Steady. Think. Move! Keep pace. Think! What do I do?*

When Nouri got to the side street, he took a quick glance around the corner. The group had slowed even more, suggesting they were lost, or perhaps Carson's horn had startled them. They started to turn left, and the Baluchian warriors began arguing again and then suddenly stopped. Nouri waited. In ten seconds the small group continued left up a narrow alley. Nouri suddenly had the glimmer of a vague idea, and ran up the road he was on. Intercepting them was his only option, but how? He couldn't shoot a gun, his hands were shaking, and as he ran he remembered Carson's warning: *no collateral damage.* It meant he had to get close. Very close.

He ran as quickly and as quietly as he could. He ran parallel to their direction, about two blocks further to the west. After he had run eight blocks, he stopped to catch his breath, his lungs burning in the cool night air.

"What, or who, are you running from?" It was a croaking voice, deep in the shadows of a building overhang.

"Who… are… you?" Nouri asked between gasps of air, squinting into the blackness from which the voice came. He was almost too tired to be worried about his new acquaintance.

"What does it matter? I'm a homeless man, isn't that enough?"

There was a touch of madness or drunkenness that accompanied the voice, Nouri wasn't sure which, but he backed away a little as the outline of a man came towards him from out of the shadows. He was built stocky, but looked gawky, with a long billowing beard that was mostly gray. He seemed to be in his late sixties, but he could have been younger.

"So why are you running at this hour?"

"None of your business," Nouri said.

"Look, I virtually own these streets, especially at night. You barged right into my living room—woke *me* up! I was having a good dream."

"Do you have anything to drink?"

"Of course I do, but I don't share it for free."

"I'll give you my shirt and jacket for yours, and a drink of whatever you're drinking, as long as it has alcohol in it."

The man reached out and touched Nouri's jacket in a way that blind people tentatively reach for something unseen. He felt it with probing fingers, first the sleeve and then the zipper. "You're either very thirsty or a very bad judge of clothes. But I accept your offer anyway."

"Can we do this quickly?"

"What color is your jacket?" the old man asked.

"Dark blue."

The old man smiled. "I like that color."

"Great, can we do this exchange now... I'm in a big hurry."

"What about the shirt?"

"It's white."

"Do you have an undershirt?"

"Yes, it's white, too."

"Haven't had any white clothes in a very long time," the old man remarked.

"Can we just exchange them?" Nouri said impatiently, handing his jacket and shirt to the old man, who appeared indifferent. Nouri dropped them to the ground.

The old man took off a tattered blanket he had wrapped around his shoulders, and then his undershirt. "I guess my days of being a "holey" man are over, at least for a while." He grunted a low laugh. The sharp sound of tearing ripped through the night as the old man took off his shirt. "A few of those holes just got larger... sorry about that."

Nouri donned the smelly clothes, first the ragged t-shirt that was more holes than cloth, and then a black blanket that held a stench so strong that as he put it on, his gag reflex pounced on him.

"It's been a while since I had a bath..." the old man offered apologetically, wagging his index finger, "...but it was your idea, I remind you."

"The turban, too. Give me your turban, please," Nouri said choking back the temptation to gag.

"Sure," the old man said, as he carefully lifted it off of his head. "I have to tell you that what I'm drinking right now... it's homemade, and it isn't tasty in the least, but it does the trick, praise Allah! A friend of mine makes it; just don't expect to wake up tomorrow feeling clear headed. Not gonna happen." He chuckled to himself as he shook his head.

Nouri nodded as he adjusted his new clothes, and fitted the turban over his head. "The drink?"

The old man, shirtless, shuffled his way back to his black corner like a spider and returned with a plastic bottle whose top had been cut off. "Drink up." He handed the bottle about two feet away from Nouri's position, and Nouri suddenly realized the old man was blind.

Nouri took the bottle, and then picked up his shirt and jacket, and handed them to the old man. "I didn't know you were blind."

The old man grabbed the clothes eagerly. "Like I tell my friends, I see better at night."

Nouri held the bottle under his nose, sensing its chemical potency. "Look, I'm going to take this with me—"

"No, just a drink. That was our agreement."

"I need it."

"No, give it back."

"You got the better deal," Nouri said, "and if I didn't need this I wouldn't take it, but I have no choice. I'm sorry."

With that, Nouri ran up the street, careful not to spill too much of the homemade brew. He heard the old man cursing at him, but a minute later he was once again in silence, and only the sound of his panting and footsteps filled the air.

Nouri made his way across a side street, and as he came to the alley, he stopped and turned cautiously around the corner. About three blocks down, he could hear the distinct scraping sound of the wheelchair. He took a deep breath and doused himself with the contents of the plastic bottle, sparing just enough to take one good swig, which he swirled in his mouth while he plugged his nose, and then forced a swallow, as hard as he'd ever done in his life. It was appalling, with the slightest taste of licorice!

What have I become? The depths of his descent were deeper than he thought possible, and yet, here he was, a stench-filled homeless man who was soon to be a murderer. In that moment, he knew exactly who he was—*whatever I need to be.*

The interception had begun, as he moved his feet in the direction of Parto and her captors. With each step he began to assume the role of his outward appearance. Nouri tucked the gun underneath his turban and tried to walk like a drunkard. His heart raced as he started to make out the outlines of the four people he would soon meet.

Though he had only taken one swallow of the foul-tasting brew, he was feeling its effects, and the notion of humming began to sound like a good idea, and so he hummed an old song he had learned in school. His right foot bumped into a can, and it knocked around noisily, but Nouri pretended he didn't have a care in the world, though nothing could be further from the truth.

As he got closer, he began to assume his new role with even greater nuance. Parto, Dubria, and their captors had stopped in their tracks, and all of them were now watching him. Nouri continued on his way, happy in his faux oblivion, closing the gap with each step. He heard some whispers, but ignored them. When Nouri got within ten feet of Parto's group, he suddenly stopped his humming and drunken stagger and pretended to notice them for the first time. He bowed his head purposely, knowing that his turban, and the gun inside, would fall into his waiting hands. He laughed as he caught the turban, and his right hand groped invisibly for the gun.

He completed his bow, to the snicker of one of the Baluchian warriors. "Peace be upon you. Beneath the eyes of Allah I go, and I greet you in His name." Nouri's Persian was slurred, and he staggered a little, trying his best to play the role of a righteous drunkard. Then he fell to the ground—turban in hand. His goal, to look as harmless as possible, seemed successful. While he was on the ground, he could hear a faint laugh from the Baluchian warriors who were amused by him, as if he were a circus sideshow. He now had a good grip on the handgun that was concealed inside his turban. His right hand clutched both the turban and gun—both pointing downward, as he slowly, awkwardly rose to his feet, bowing once again.

He did his best to avoid looking at Parto as he walked by, afraid she might recognize him. The Baluchian warriors wore grins of disgust when Nouri looked into their faces.

Shoot them! Where? You must kill them, or they will kill you. You must not kill anyone. Do it!

A thousand voices suddenly filled his mind, half angels, half demons, and the cacophony that played in his head grew louder and louder as he raised his right hand. Nouri's final act of drunkenness was suddenly replaced by a cold, crazed face, and he pointed the turban-covered-gun at the taller man, finger twitching from some black weight, and then a demon pulled his index finger towards him four times in rapid succession.

Time suddenly stopped, trickling through some dense filter of experience, and then the whole world sunk into a strange silence, surrounded by a rim of two-story buildings that watched with indifference, like cat's eyes. Two Baluchian warriors tottered, and then fell to the ground, their faces still wearing the look of surprise as they landed in a crumpled, vacant pose.

The two women faced him, trembling with fear. Nouri dropped the gun to the ground and knelt in front of Parto. His mouth opened, but no words came, as he could only find the poet's scream inside him.

Dubria slowly let go of the wheelchair, turned, carefully stepped over the dead bodies behind her, and ran down the alleyway in the direction they had come.

Parto stared into Nouri's eyes, and shook her head in fear. Her face contorted, horribly warped by the gunshots and violence. She pushed her arms at Nouri in an awkward gesture of *leave me alone*. Tears were streaming down her face, and Nouri panicked, not knowing how to get through to her that he was not a drunken murderer. "I'm Nouri. Look at me. I'm Nouri!"

He smoothed his hair back, untied the blanket around his shoulders, clasped his hands around Parto's face, and leaned in. "I'm Nouri. I love you!"

A small pale of hope crossed Parto's trembling face as she reached out to touch his cheek. "Nouri?"

"Yes, it's me."

"Nouri?"

"Yes, yes…" Nouri began to weep as Parto's hand reached his face. Her forehead was bandaged and there remained a shallow vacancy in her eyes, but behind that, Nouri could see something rising to the surface like an air bubble that glides fearlessly to the surface of a vast and open ocean. And then the smallest softening of her face, an avalanche of tiny changes brought her closer, and they embraced like two hands that come together in prayer.

CHAPTER 41

Between Worlds

Terran had no doubt of his assignation to the luminous spirit within him. He felt its presence, as if he were an asymmetrical being—the larger part of him unlimited—while his small body, a mere two-cubic feet, descended the dark stairs after his faux escape from Shaheen. At the bottom of the stairs he turned left, and went into a small room that faced the street outside. The Preserve, just across the street, was in total darkness, its front door closed like an eyelid.

Gun casings were strewn on the floor near the broken window, and as Terran crossed the room, they scattered, their metallic melody like wind chimes against the shards of glass in the silent night air. He waited, staring outside, mindful of any movement, but the darkness was as static as a black photograph.

A few seconds later he heard Shaheen crying out, "Help! I need help!" His voice, wavering from the weight of devised alarm, was faintly inauthentic. *He could be louder*, Terran thought.

Moshad's muffled voice came next: "What's wrong?"

"He's escaped!" Came the immediate response.

A second later the outside door swung open, and a darkened shape ran up the stairs like a wild animal. The glint of gun metal caught Terran's eye, but he stayed perfectly still. He glanced out the window. Shaheen had said that there were two guards outside, where was the other one?

He needed to get out before the other guard came down. He could hear panicked voices upstairs. Terran had seconds to decide. He ran to the door and opened it, and as he did, a bullet grazed the door, fired from behind him. He didn't hesitate a moment and hurtled through the door. He preferred the bushes, trees and buildings to the open street where he'd be vulnerable to a bullet. He was small, fast, and it was dark out. He wouldn't be an easy target, if he stayed away from open spaces.

Shaheen had been right that they would not hesitate to shoot him;

a fact that only slightly surprised Terran. As soon as he crossed an alleyway, he ducked behind a tree to assess his pursuers.

He heard whispered voices, but couldn't see anything. Terran slowly made his way to a group of bushes that covered the front of a dilapidated small home that provided better cover. He knew the Baluchian's were excellent trackers, but he also knew that in thick darkness there was little to track unless he made noise. He stayed perfectly still. Even his breath was measured and silent.

Terran gripped the gun he had taken from Shaheen, knowing that he had two options, stay silent and wait for an opportunity to dart across the street to the Preserve, or run away from the school into the streets and hide out somewhere until he could find a way to make it back safely to the Preserve.

He chose the ever-present third option: wait.

There is such a strange fusion of lucidity and confusion to the darkness when one is hiding from hands intent to kill. Terran focused all of his capacity to bring every atom of his being to the creation of an escape plan that could work. In the near distance, he heard voices inside the house he had just left—probably Moshad yelling at Shaheen. Then he heard the subtle scrape of a foot on pavement. It was close; maybe ten feet. Terran's senses went on an even higher alert as he held himself still, hoping his heartbeat would not betray him.

Terran held himself like a statue, frozen in place, afraid to even blink. The dark figure passed slowly in front of him. He could hear breathing as the Baluchian warrior came directly in front of him, only a few feet away. A minute later, Terran exhaled long and slow through pursed lips, unaware that he had been holding his breath. He shifted his position, and as he did, he brushed against some branches that scraped against the side of the house, and a sharp scraping sound filled the quiet yard. He immediately crouched down again. Suddenly, he heard approaching footsteps, and he knew he was vulnerable.

Maybe it was a pure instinct, but all the focus, all the planning, suddenly crumbled as Terran ran from the bushes and fled to the backyard, but as he darted away, a shadowy figure lurched in front of him. "Stop where you are!"

Terran froze, wincing at the prospect of being caught, his gun pointed at his captor instinctively.

"Back in the house," the voice ordered.

Terran squinted into the night, hoping to see something of his captor. "I can't do that."

"Then I have orders to shoot."

Terran swallowed hard, finding his voice. "I have a gun pointed at you, perhaps I will shoot first."

There was a long pause as the two shadowy figures stood facing each other, separated by a dozen feet and a mile of darkness.

"I'll slowly back away," Terran said, breaking the silence, "and disappear into the night. We can both live."

The Baluchian warrior shook his head. "You... you won't fire that gun. Look, I'm lowering my gun... I'm coming over to you slowly, and I'll take you by the arm back to Moshad. Neither of us needs to get hurt here."

The warrior tentatively stepped forward.

"I *will* shoot," Terran said. "Better to die than be a pawn in Moshad's game."

The Baluchian sighed, recognizing the impasse, and then slowly pointed his arm at Terran. "What is that?"

"What?" Terran asked, looking around with only his eyes, well aware that Moshad's men could be cunning, but this man's voice was sober and solemn.

"That!"

Terran looked around, but didn't see anything. "What do you see?"

"A light... it is a dêw... a demon... it's... it's not human—it rises in you. What's happening?"

Terran looked down at his body, searching for some clue as to what the Baluchian warrior saw, but everything was dimmed in the darkness of the night, and there was no light, at least to his eyes.

"Why does it touch me so?" the Baluchian warrior whispered like one who is entranced by a mirage.

"What? What is touching you?" Terran asked in disbelief.

A long silence ensued. Terran squinted, trying his best to understand what his adversary was seeing, but he felt nothing, saw nothing, and everywhere he looked there was only the thick blanket of darkness.

The Baluchian warrior began to back away in fear, dropping his gun to the ground, and then, with a sudden gasp, ran away like a madman possessed of an unwanted demon.

Terran spun around, trying to see something that would cause this fear in a Baluchian warrior—men who were known to be fearless—but there was nothing. He clutched his gun, ran his free hand through his hair, and stared into the black night, uncertain of his next steps.

As he glanced across the street, in the deep distance of the city, four gunshots rang out in staccato ferocity. Terran's heart bristled in panic, and he ran blindly to the other side of the street toward the Preserve, but stopped as he got to the curb. He began to cry. He couldn't suppress it. He fell to the ground on all fours, the murmurs of his weeping restrained, but Terran was crippled in an emotional vise that suddenly gripped him like a beam of judgment thrown from the heavens. He knew the bullets he heard were linked to him. *I have caused more death.* He laid on his back, and felt the tears drift across his temples to the ground below. It all suddenly came upon him as he stared through tear-filled eyes at the spiral arms of the Milky Way's starry shores.

His fight for freedom only condemned more to die. He should walk back to the house and give himself over to Moshad. Return to his home. Let Pirdah decide his fate. *Give up. Give up. Give up.* He repeated the words in hypnotic whispers that drifted from his mouth in vaporous puffs of air.

As if a strange curse suddenly possessed him, Terran's eyes stalked the corridors of the silver light above him. "Why? Why do I have this... this... this need to learn? I don't want it anymore. I don't want to learn if it kills. I don't want to live if others die for my life. Take me. You put me here, take me from here. I'm tired. I'm so tired. I give up."

Terran heard the words as they slipped past his lips. They were from a part of him that had long stepped from his heart's door. They were like the taunt muscles of weakened prey too far from home ever to return, and so he gave them his voice, but another part of him, steeled in the spread of wings, of seamless souls in the weight of eternity, knew he would never give up.

CHAPTER 42

My Daughter

When a great darkness threatens from every direction, there is an instinct to move inwards in retreat, into the imaginative denial that befriends the weary. But when pain is hidden too long, a truth is torn open, exposed beneath a leaden light. Any person who has seen this truth knows it is a messenger. Its message is seldom pleasant. Its story is never uttered. Being beyond comprehension, it is instead absorbed like an energy, seeping deep into your cells and atoms—the very structure upon which your body-mind is engineered. It pulls you in the blinking direction of hope, but directions are only preserved in time, and when the story is finally told, time is not in the equation. Nor hope.

*   *   *   *

Carson had heard the gunshots, sharp and metallic, and his stomach lurched in a throb of dread. It sounded like his handgun, but Carson feared the worst, knowing Nouri's incompetence with guns. He scrambled into the Humvee and drove cautiously in the direction of the gunfire, which had echoed from the northeast to his position. He drove warily without headlights, scanning the deserted streets. He suddenly glimpsed a subtle movement in the black shadows of a building overhang, and stopped the Humvee.

"You?" he called, his voice hushed and gathered in a loud whisper. "Have you seen anyone on these streets in the last ten minutes?"

"I'm blind; I haven't seen anyone in twelve years."

Carson paused. "Then have you heard anyone run by?"

"You're Persian… you're a stranger… driving a car. What do you want with this person?"

"Come out of the shadows so I can see you better," Carson instructed, his tone softening, but his hand gripped his gun a little tighter.

The old man shuffled out a few more feet, and stroked his beard. His long, silver hair, matted in peculiar directions, resisted gravity as though an electrical storm circulated directly overhead.

"That jacket is his... how'd you get it?" Carson demanded.

"What do you have to trade for that information?"

Carson cocked the trigger on his handgun. "Your life."

The blind man chuckled and slowly raised his arms, a mock gesture of surrender. "Be my guest. I'm too cowardly to do it myself, and the next life, such as it is, has to be better than this one. But then I doubt you have bullets."

Carson had no time to argue with a man so clearly indifferent to his plight, so he rummaged in the back of the Humvee, and found a carton of rations neatly bundled in a cellophane wrapper. He picked them up and tossed them on the street in front of the man. "There's enough food in that package to last you a week. Now tell me how you got the jacket?"

The blind man crouched down, ignoring, for the moment, Caron's question. His hands searched for the package that Carson had thrown on the street, and finding it, smiled and brought it to his nose. "It has no smell, are you sure it's food?"

"They're rations, they're carefully packaged. They don't have any smell unless you open them. Look, I'm in a hurry. Please, just tell me what—"

"Then you're military... *and* a foreigner... what's going on?"

"I don't have time—"

"These are *my* streets!" the blind man half-yelled, standing to his feet. He was not tall, but there was something imposing about him. Perhaps his total lack of fear was at the center of it, or the way his grizzled beard thrust down unevenly, covering his heart. "Tell me what's going on, or I won't tell you a thing. Besides, your friend is probably dead."

"Why do you say that?"

"If he drank the spirits he stole from me, he couldn't fire a weapon to save his life. That was pure, homemade arak. He'd be easy prey for anyone."

Carson sighed in frustration. "Look, old man, I don't know what's going on; all I know is that I heard four gunshots, and a friend of mine—

the man who gave you that jacket—"

"He didn't *give* it to me; we traded, like I said!"

"Whatever... that man's in danger. I'm just trying to find him. Help me!"

The blind man tucked the rations under his arm, and cocked his head slightly. "You a spy?"

"No!"

"You're American, a soldier, aren't you?"

"Yes."

"Don't you think I've heard the gunshots up by the Preserve? Everyone in this town has. And now they're in *my* neighborhood! What's happening? You tell me that, and I'll tell you what direction your friend went, but don't dismiss me with lies. I spent seventeen years in the Revolutionary Guard before Sunrot. I can smell the stench of deceit in you. *Now tell me!*"

Carson dropped his gun subconsciously, and looked around to make sure they were completely alone. "A boy from a Baluchian tribe is trying to go to school, some... unpleasant members of his tribe came here to bring him back—against his will—and I'm here to protect the boy. That's all. The man I'm looking for is the boy's teacher—"

"What's so special about this boy?"

"I don't know—"

"Yes you do, you're just not telling me." The blind man began to turn around as if he had given up on the conversation. "Your friend can die as far as I'm concerned. He stole my spirits—"

"Look, the boy is supposed to be some kind of a religious leader, I don't know the details, and that's the truth."

"Why would the teacher of a religious leader steal my spirits? Your words are twisted. I don't believe you. Go away."

"I don't have time to tell you everything. If you help me find my friend, I'll come back and... and reward you. I just don't have time now... he could be wounded..."

"...or dead." The blind man turned back to Carson, and scratched his neck, and let out a long sigh. "Your friend seemed in trouble, and in a big rush—"

"Please, where'd he go?" Carson asked.

The blind man pointed up the street. "Went that way, and turned right at the alley. If you find him, I'll be waiting here." The man quipped indignantly. "I expect a reward. A good one... a *real* good one..."

Carson drove off in the direction that the blind man had pointed. Despite the adrenalin that coursed through his body, he was tired. It had been a long day of dodging bullets. To make matters worse, the clutch pedal on the Humvee was irritating his injured foot. When he got to the alleyway, he turned off the engine, checked his weapons, and began to tune into his environment. He gingerly limped onto the street, mindful of the tops of the buildings—none of which looked inhabited. There was no movement or light. He surveyed his escape route options, and then, satisfied that he'd done everything he could to protect himself, he tuned his full powers to sound.

In the quiet of the night, a voice lilted down an unlit, narrow side street that jutted between brick buildings that had been pockmarked by the winds of Sunrot. Carson picked his way carefully, aware that his left foot was hyper-sensitive to any pressure.

"Nouri?" Carson called in a half-whisper, half-shout.

No response, but now he could hear two voices.

"Nouri?" He tentatively walked closer, his back scraping the wall as he went in the direction of the sound. Then he saw a strange figure emerge from around the corner of the alley, staggering in his direction, oblivious of his presence. Carson crouched down even further and remained still, watching. The figure was large, oddly shaped, and in the darkness, Carson could make out little more than its size and contour.

As the figure came closer, walking awkwardly like a wounded animal, Carson heard the murmuring of a female voice, and he instantly tensed up, squinting to see what eluded him. Then he heard a man's voice, and he suddenly realized it was a man carrying a woman. *Nouri and Parto!* Could it be?

Carson stood to his feet. "Nouri?"

The figure stopped. "Carson?"

"Are you okay?"

"Man, you startled me... yes, I have Parto. We're okay."

"And the nurse?"

"She ran… probably back to the clinic—"

"And the…"

"They're dead."

Caron relaxed. "You're sure?"

"Yes."

"My ride is back there," Carson said, gesturing behind him, "about twenty meters. Can you manage?"

"Yeah, she's light, and I'm floating on adrenalin."

Parto cleared her throat. "Who is he?"

Nouri explained in a whisper too faint for Carson to hear.

"Sir, can you take me to my daughter?" Parto asked.

"We need to leave here immediately," Carson replied. "They heard the shooting. They could be sending others. Let's go." Carson motioned with his right arm.

"My daughter?" Parto asked with a bitter edge to her tone.

"Yes, we'll do our best to get you to the school. Right now, it's surrounded by hostiles. I want to get reinforcements first. Let's hurry!"

They hobbled together to the waiting Humvee in silence, wary of making any sounds that could trigger a bullet. Like baby birds possessed of curious wings they walked awkwardly, avoiding the trash and debris that cluttered the alleyway. Parto was too tired to resist Carson's plan, even though it delayed her reunion with Dorri and Terran.

Being held in Nouri's arms, for the moment, was comforting enough.

CHAPTER 43

One Inch

Terran laid on the ground like a bandage of the sidewalk, imploring the emptiness above him—cluttered in silver light—to dissolve his destiny. Then, suddenly, he felt an inexplicable emotion, the kind you don't embrace, but rather expel. A deep frustration, yearning for equipoise, trembled within him. Holding nothing in, he screamed like a woman in childbirth; a piercingly loud shriek. The scream burrowed into the earth beneath him, and the veils of his forbearance tumbled into that hole, buried in its yawning depths, and like the final countenance of a death mask, stared up at him, but did not see. They had divided from him. All of the tethers to his culpability had fallen into that hole, and with it, his guilt. Terran was clear and pure.

The quiet of the streets returned, though muffled murmurs tended the scream's echo.

What am I conjuring with that scream? Terran wondered.

He felt something rub against his leg, and Terran sat up to see a cat with long, uneven fur, matted and splayed in every direction. It was not an attractive cat in the physical sense, but to Terran, it held a certain disheveled beauty, undone and uneasy. In the darkness he couldn't tell the color of the cat's fur, but its eyes glowed as if self-illumined. He picked it up and embraced it as he lay back down on the sidewalk. The cat perched on his chest like a skinny sphinx. The low rumble of its purring filled Terran's chest, and its front claws kneaded his shirt, cutting into his skin with ease, but Terran stayed calm and only bit his lip as the cat performed its acupuncture.

As he petted the cat, he could feel bones and little more. "Such a delicate skeleton," he mused. His voice cracked a bit, tired from the scream. He was about a hundred yards south of the school. Moshad's men would now find him. The scream was a beacon. His only surprise was that he still remained alone, but for the cat. In the silence of the night, the cat's purring was like a song of an ancient name, subtle in its modulation like the dim flicker of a candle flame when the wax was nearly gone.

"Didn't I scare you with that scream?" Terran whispered. "Instead, you came to me... you're a *strange* cat. I'll call you Mandana—she was the mother of the King of Persia. Her name means Eternal One."

The cat's head suddenly turned, her ears lurched forward, and Terran had his confirmation that Moshad's men were close by. He sat up with the cat in his lap, looking in every direction for approaching figures, but saw nothing in the pitch blackness. The gun Shaheen had given him remained on the ground. With one hand he unloaded its bullets and tossed them in his pocket. Within that scream was the vow that he would never use a gun. He reminded himself as he placed the worthless weapon underneath a bush behind him.

"Master, how is it that you lay there? Are you wounded?" It was Shaheen's whispered voice. "I heard your scream... what's wrong?"

Terran looked into the shadows of the night, squinting in an effort to make Shaheen visible, but only the dimmest of outlines could be seen. "Nothing. Nothing's wrong."

"Then why did you scream, Master?"

"Please, don't call me that," Terran said.

Shaheen bowed with his hands pressed together with his two thumbs pointed upwards. "I'm sorry; I only wanted to know if you were alright."

Terran paused, wondering how he could explain the unexplainable. "Sometimes things build up inside..."

"But Moshad can track you."

"I know."

"You wish to give up your freedom?"

Terran shook his head. "No."

"Then you must hide."

Terran paused for a moment, glancing up at the stars. "Was he hard on you?"

"He told me to find you or not come back," Shaheen said softly. "But you're the Mahdi. You will do as Allah wills—"

"Shaheen, I want to return to the school. Can you help me?"

Shaheen hesitated, his mind focused on the pivot he was living in. He was conflicted. Moshad was an enemy unlike any other. Shaheen had family. If he were caught assisting Terran, he would be banished from his village. His family would be cast out, too, and together they would perish in the desert within a week. But the Mahdi, in Shaheen's mind, was asking him a favor, and his heavenly reward would more than compensate for any material struggles. Shaheen's only reluctance was for his family's safety.

"If I help you, will you protect my family?"

"If you worry about your family's protection, then leave me now. I'll find my own way to the school—"

"I'm sorry, Master... Sir, I... if Moshad knows that I assisted you, I will be banished along with my family. I... I—"

"I understand, Shaheen. You've already risked a lot to help me. Go now. Tell them you found me, but that I escaped into the night, going south—away from the school. Can you do that?"

"Yes, I can do that."

An eerie call, cloaked as a bird, startled them. They both knew it was no bird.

"Go... or they'll suspect you're helping me." Terran whispered.

Shaheen bowed again. "I wish I could do more."

"I'll be okay."

"May Allah protect you."

"And you as well," Terran said.

A second later, Shaheen disappeared into the black void that surrounded Terran.

The night air was cool, and Mandana's warmth felt good next to Terran's chest and arms. He stood to his feet. Legs tired, he tottered for a moment and then gained his balance. He steered a course behind the buildings, picking his way cautiously, one deliberate step at a time.

Silence over speed.

Most of the buildings were deserted with boarded windows, and those that weren't held a pitch-black core that made it impossible to tell which were occupied and which were vacant. Gunfire was a rare sound in Mashhad—until yesterday. Without bullets to fuel guns, knives and swords were the weapons of choice. If people ever heard bullets at night, they knew serious trouble was afoot, and their lives went dark. No one used a candle. No fires. No movement. With pulled shades, they would lie on their mattresses, forming mute prayers that were jagged, like lightning, searching for a God to quash their fears.

After five minutes, Terran came to a clearing on the east side of the Preserve. Thirty yards separated him from the tangled clutter of bushes that he crouched behind, and the east wall of the school. His caution was extreme. Moshad's men had orders to shoot him, and his friends in the school—the ones with guns and bullets—could easily mistake him for a Baluchian warrior if he were to run towards the school and try to enter.

He could call out, but then he'd draw attention from one of Moshad's men who would undoubtedly be patrolling the school's perimeter. Terran studied the east wall, searching for any signs that someone was awake and tending one of the windows, but the black glass was absent any movement. He was distracted by Mandana's constant purring, so he set her down.

Terran bent down and stroked Mandana's head. "I have to do this on my own," he whispered. "I have to move at the pace of a tortoise and with the stealth of a serpent, and you, my friend, will be a distraction. Your eyes are too bright. Your purring, too loud."

Suddenly, Mandana stiffened and turned her head. The sound of a bird call filled the air. Its source was near, about fifty feet away in the direction of the street. Terran crouched down and squinted in the direction of the call, locked on to the amorphous target like a radar dish. Mandana slipped away in the direction of the sound, hopeful for a meal.

Far away, another call could be heard in response. Its distance and direction were harder to determine. Terran knew that the Baluchian were communicating. He could only hope that the calls were signaling that Shaheen had advised his comrades that he'd seen Terran escaping to the south, away from the school.

A few seconds later, he heard a loud, blood-curdling shriek from Mandana. Its intensity surprised him. It came from the same direction as the bird call, and Terran couldn't stop his legs from going there. As he arrived, he heard the sound of a gun's trigger cocking, and he dove behind a tree trunk.

"Terran, is it you?" It was a Baluchian warrior, but Terran didn't know which one. He remained silent, ignoring the question. He heard some movement, and then felt Mandana circling around his legs. He wished for a moment that he'd never met Mandana, but there was little he could do. She was oblivious to the danger he was in.

"I won't shoot if you come with me now. You have my word."

Terran remained still and quiet, wondering what to do.

"I know you can hear me," the voice continued. "You're right behind that tree. The darkness does not cover you. My eyes are not deceived."

His voice was calm, but commanding, barely more than a whisper. "If you run, I *will* shoot. Come with me, it's over. We can leave and no one gets hurt."

Terran cleared his throat. "I will not go with you."

"Maybe you think you have some of us fooled," the warrior said in a hushed tone, "I am not one of them. I know you are just a boy, a half-breed liar and a deserter of our people. You will not disobey us anymore. This is where it ends. Either you come with me, or you die. Those are the orders I have, and I *will* honor them." The voice became increasingly intense, and then paused. "Let's go. My patience is gone."

Terran's voice became louder. "I will not come with you. If you want to come here and shoot me, then come. I will not leave with you. I will resist you with all my strength. Those inside the school will fire down on you with a hundred bullets—"

"And you! Do you think they will not hit you as well?"

"I'm prepared to die," Terran said.

Terran thought he heard a Baluchian expletive, but it was too soft to make out.

Terran heard a subtle rustle, and his stomach winced. He knew that the warrior was coming for him, and there was little he could do. *Why isn't anyone watching at the windows? Are they all asleep?* He could hear the faintest footsteps as the warrior approached. Terran's heart quickened. He could still feel Mandana pressing against his ankles, and he bent down and picked her up, holding her close to him. "I'm sorry, girl."

He came from behind the tree trunk and faced the Baluchian who stood like a hulking black boulder that the earth bestows to shelter small animals.

Terran could feel the warrior's gun pointed at him, though he couldn't see its gun barrel in the blackness of the night.

"*Move!*" the voice commanded.

"Where?" Terran asked.

"Walk towards me. Do you have a gun… a weapon of any kind?"

"No."

Terran began to walk closer, but as he got within a few feet of the Baluchian, he stopped.

"I thought I kicked that cat to his next life, how is it that you're holding it?"

"She likes me—"

"Get rid of it. We have no need for a cat. *Now!*"

Terran took a slow breath, and in one fluid movement tossed Mandana directly into the face of his adversary, and ran as fast as he could to the front of the school. He knew Mandana's claws were as sharp as razors, and if this man had indeed kicked Mandana, her keratin revenge would be ample. From the string of Baluchian expletives that flooded into the night air, Mandana's claws had found tender skin.

Terran thought he heard the rifle fall to the ground. He was focused on running. Everything telescoped into a blur, except for one thing: the front door of the school. As he got to the school's portico, he dashed up the steps and pushed against the door, but it was locked. "I am Terran!" he said breathlessly, leaning with his back to the door, eyes watching for any signs of an attack. "Please… bring me in." He tried to speak in his best Persian, but he struggled to remember the right words. His fingers, coiled in a tight fist, pounded on the door lightly. He was afraid to make too much noise. He knew Moshad was across the street, and would probably relish pulling the trigger on his life.

"So the door is locked." Terran's adversary was back. A fiendish grin spread across his blood-smeared face. "Your cat is dead, and you're next." He lifted the gun to its firing position and pulled the trigger. A quiet, empty click filled the space between Terran and the warrior. He fired again with the same result. After the third time, he threw the gun down, and reached behind him and drew his knife, sweeping the sleeve of his shirt across his forehead to ease the blood flow into his eyes.

The warrior walked menacingly towards Terran. "You have no idea how badly I want to leave this place and go home. This is your last chance."

Terran's small fist was still pounding on the door like a subconscious call for help. Terran stayed with his back against the door, as the Baluchian warrior walked towards him.

"I will not go with you," Terran said, his voice stubborn, but for a slight quiver. His pounding intensified, as if his heartbeat was now directing his fist.

The Baluchian stopped two feet away, and grabbed Terran around his shoulder. "Will you come with me or not?" A twelve-inch blade of polished silver was placed against Terran's neck, its coolness felt good, but for the fact of its intent.

Terran struggled to speak, and tried to shake his head to leave no doubt that he would not go. *If I die now, it is God's will, and I will leave without regret.*

Then he felt it, the voice within him, like a meteor cast from his heart's core. It came out of him with unspeakable power, yet courageous in its restraint. "What proof do you desire that I am the Mahdi?"

The Baluchian lessened his stranglehold for a moment. "Proof? There is none! You are an imposter and nothing more!" He then resumed his piercing grip on Terran's shoulder, and leaned in within inches of Terran's face. "Your last chance or my knife will send you to hell."

Terran felt a vibration. The door behind him unlocked and he felt his body pushed forward slightly, and then a gun barrel slid through the one-inch crack in the door, and he knew that he must remain still. This was surgical. No room for error. His adversary seemed oblivious to the subtle movement, perhaps his vision was impaired, or he was too absorbed in his revenge on Terran to notice the small distance of one inch. The gunshot exploded behind Terran, and he felt the Baluchian hurtle backwards down the steps, while Terran was pulled in the opposite direction by powerful hands. In that moment he felt like a morsel of food engulfed by a giant mouth.

CHAPTER 44

Rescue

In mythologies we often find tales written about them. Mysteriously winged creatures of such intelligence and resource, as to make humans seem like mice. These creatures could clutch the hearts of their human quarry and carry them to God. The blessed human would never point downward again, and even those with unkissed mouths would know love in a way that the amorous would envy.

The winged creatures were thought to be a different order of existence; not human, not animal, not of this earth. They were never considered a part of the human timeline. As much as the ape was a part of our timeline's past, these creatures of divine destiny were never included in our timeline's future. Humans could never aspire to such powerful heights—their hearts were too dark and muddled. But what if these creatures *were* human? What if they were us—a future us—and they returned, albeit sparingly, to our time, as our benefactors?

Being masters of time, they would sometimes insert themselves in our world, speaking of our fabled future when our souls were unsheathed, and the scabbard of flesh was redeemed in transparency. Their solemn voices spoke of the convergence of humanity as one being. When this unity occurred, the darkest hearts would be cleansed, and all would be released to seek the greatest good for the greatest number, and that number would be *one*.

These creatures were not of a different order. They were of a different time. They were not simply winged creatures who had mastered time and space, and in doing so, were cloaked in a mysterious presence outside our perceptual world. They were also our creators… our makers. They became known as the WingMakers. The Ouroboros of time was not feeding on itself, it was *guiding* itself.

WingMakers were called by various names, contained in hushed voices, culled by reluctant theologians, despoiled by sinister forces who wanted them to appear fragile, vulnerable to the same emotions as us. This was not the invention of a myth. It was the manufacture of a lie. Humanity reached upwards, pulling the heavens down and infusing its considerable flaws into the creatures of the heavenly spheres. These stories were told so many times, in so many different ways, that soon, we believed the lie was a myth, and the myth was a lie.

Angels, it was written, were messengers of a hierarchy so far-reaching, so distantly regal, that it could only communicate with a human being through an angelic intercessor. There were good messengers, and lamentably, as it was written, there were bad. The bad were corrupt and corrupting. Lucifer was supposed to have been an angel. The fallen, when they fell, descended beneath human stature, living in the deep shadows of a subterranean world full of deception and painful revenge. But these are fictional accounts over brimming with deception for the purpose of wealth transfer and little more.

The myths of one world are but a grain of sand in the vast and infinite oceans of spacetime. They are the externalizations of a naïve fear and the patronage of a local universe fashioned of miles and measured in years. The true myths, the ones concerned with the soul and the soul's creator, these are post-human, imbued in the pre-human subconscious. They are founded not by humans as we think of them, but by the WingMakers. Our future selves. The field of the WingMakers is a span of spacetime that is un-measurable. Its arc traverses dimensions like a fractal that weaves its image across an ever-increasing scale until it finally disappears in sizes too vast to comprehend and too small to perceive.

The myth of soul is a fractal. Its scale is so far beyond the scope of the mind's eye, it is invisible in birth and destiny. The WingMakers set forth a method through which the human soul could be seen and experienced. It is a way of calibrating the fractal myth into the visible spectrum. It is a way of seeing beneath and above the material shells, bringing what is divine to the human senses. This method is known as The Grand Portal, and in it, there can be no denial of soul. The forces that have covered it up, swept it beneath the rugs of silence and distortion—the sterling imprint of science, they have met their match in this method, for it is based in science, and you are its emissary.

*   *   *   *

The words echoed away into a deep silence, and Terran shook his head, mystified as he suddenly realized he was awakening from a dream. There was a pale light coming through a cracked window. The room was cold. He figured it was early morning, perhaps 6 A.M. He had slept for three hours beneath a single scrawny blanket, but he'd been so exhausted that the cold air had no affect on him.

After he had been pulled through the front door by Frank, Terran had been given some water and a light meal. Frank had told him what he knew, as Hamid helped him find new clothes and drew him a bath. There still had been no word on Parto and Nouri, and he knew that Dorri was asleep in the girl's dormitory on the third floor. Before his bath, Terran had looked in on Sanjur, who was alive, but remained unconscious.

As his head cleared, Terran tried to remember the voice that had been speaking to him. Most of it was forgotten, except he recalled a strange word: "WingMakers." He remembered something about myths... and then angels. *The WingMakers were angels?*

It didn't make sense. *Why have such dreams, if I can't remember what I was told?* Terran shook his head again, as if it would clear his mind and restore what he had heard. *Who was speaking?* He tried his best to see a face or recognize a voice, but nothing would materialize inside the theater of his mind. The harder he tried to remember, the more obscure the dream became.

He took a few deep breaths and listened to his world. Beneath him, he could hear pots and pans clanking. Cooks were preparing breakfast. He could feel his stomach growling, but suddenly, all he could think about was Nouri and Parto. He knew the plan was for Carson and Nouri to find Parto, take her from the hospital and get reinforcements. They should be back by now.

Terran got out of bed and changed into his new clothes. Then quietly slipped into the hallway. He was on the second floor, in a private room that was reserved for guests of the school. It was right next to Hamid's room. As he entered the hallway, he noticed that Hamid's door was still closed.

At the very end of the hallway was a window, and a man was perched in front of it, silhouetted in the soft, pastel light. A gun propped against the corner of the hallway reminded Terran of the dangers that lurked outside. The guard looked tired, and barely summoned the interest to acknowledge Terran with a short bob of his head. "You're up early," he muttered.

Terran shook his head, pointed to his ears and then walked down the stairs, hoping to find some information about Nouri and Parto. He decided to walk to the front door where he knew Frank was stationed. With Carson gone and Hamid sleeping, Frank was the de facto leader. As he turned down the stone hallway that led to the front door, he noticed two men were sitting on the floor against the door, smoking cigarettes and chatting. The light was faint. Someone was sleeping on the floor next to them. As he got closer, he recognized one of the voices, and ran the length of the stone hallway to embrace Sanjur.

"You're okay!" Terran said.

Sanjur stood to his feet and hugged Terran gently. "I'm okay. A little sore around the ribs, arms, legs, face… well, just about everywhere, to be honest." Sanjur said with a playful grin. "But it feels good to be alive, I'll tell you that!"

Terran smiled. "It's good to see you alive *and* awake."

Sanjur pressed Terran away at arm's length, and looked down at him with questioning eyes. "And what about you? I heard you were out until two in the morning, stirring up trouble."

Terran nodded sheepishly. "It wasn't my intention."

"Never is," Sanjur quipped. "I know from experience. Life has a way of pulling you into trouble when you're important."

"Any word on Nouri and Parto?" Terran asked.

Sanjur looked down at the sleeping body, which suddenly began to snore. "I don't know this man, but Farid said he's in charge. So he might know something, but he was asleep when I got here about twenty minutes ago."

Terran was just about to poke Frank to wake him up, but changed his mind. He looked up at Sanjur. The morning light was starting to strengthen, and he could see the wild bruises on his face. Sanjur's lower lip was purple and twice its normal size. Under his eyes were bands of darkness that looked like strongholds of terror.

"I know, I know, I look terrible. I didn't know where to clean up so I came here." Sanjur stole a quick glance at the other man he'd been talking with before Terran arrived. "And Farid was kind enough to get me some bread and tea… and a cigarette—" Sanjur switched from Baluchian to Persian, "thank you." He nodded in Farid's direction.

"We need to get you a doctor," Terran said.

"I'm okay, really. I just need some time to heal and a place to properly clean up… maybe take a bath, change clothes, and I'll be my beautiful self again."

Terran took another look at his face, and Sanjur returned his smile. "I need to ask a favor."

"Anything… sit with me," Sanjur said, as he sat down and patted the ground.

Farid moved over to make room for Terran. Then, gathering up his things, excused himself by taking the teacups in his hands and left.

Terran crossed his legs, took a deep breath and pointed to the east. "A friend of mine is out there. She may be dead or injured… I need to see."

"A friend?"

"I met her last night… she's a cat."

"A cat?"

"Mandana… that's her name. She saved me last night. I need to see if she's alive."

Sanjur pursed his lips and exhaled a long breath. "You know that's dangerous," Sanjur said, glancing at Frank. "He'd never let you outside. I know if I so much as stuck my finger out that door, if they knew it was mine, bullets would fly. How do you—"

"I have a feeling that she's alive."

Sanjur looked into Terran's eyes. "Do you know where she is?"

"I think so."

"Could we see her from a window if we looked?"

"Maybe."

"Well, that sounds like a good place to start," Sanjur said, standing to his feet with a little wobble.

"Are you sure you should be out of bed?"

"If I'm sure about anything, I'm sure I should be helping you. So bed will have to wait for a while."

The two walked down the hallway slowly, Sanjur limping and Terran holding his right arm to support him like a human crutch. When they got to a window on the eastside of the school, Terran scanned the yard, and within seconds found what he was looking for—a small heap of fur.

"It looks dead," Sanjur remarked.

"Mandana is a girl."

"*She* looks dead."

Terran studied her for any signs of movement, but he had to agree with Sanjur's assessment. She looked dead.

"How'd you come to be friends with Mandana?"

"Sanjur, I need a distraction. I can open this window and grab her and be back in fifteen seconds—"

"And if they're out there waiting for you? It's light enough, there's nowhere to hide. That's open space. They'd see you for sure. And you'd risk that for what? She's dead. Nothing you can do now. We shouldn't even be near a window…"

They were in a classroom with desks neatly lined up in four rows, each with a computer terminal. The walls were peeling, their color a dull yellowish amber. Three windows looked out over the east yard, and the sun—still hidden like a mistrustful servant—would soon spread its light with zeal.

Terran began to unhook the latches on the window they were looking through. "I have to do this."

Sanjur tried to stop him. "Look, at least wait until the man in charge wakes up. He'd have some ideas on how we could do it. We could wait until nightfall—"

"It'd be too late. I have to go now!" Terran shook his hands free of Sanjur's arms, and stared at Sanjur. "I know you're trying to protect me, but I have a debt to pay, and Mandana may need me to pay that debt now… not tonight when it's useful to us. Crows could find her… a fox." He paused a few seconds. "Can you make a distraction for me?"

Sanjur looked up to the ceiling in frustration. "A distraction?

Like what, me going out the front door and offering myself for target practice?"

"There's a dead Baluchian at the bottom of our front steps," Terran whispered with new intensity. "Wave a white flag and tell them that they can collect the body, and we will hold our fire."

"And why would they believe us?"

"They won't, but in the time it'll take you to wave the white flag and yell to them with the offer, it's all I'll need to dash out and get Mandana. Okay?"

Sanjur stroked his scraggly beard, and sighed. "Okay, give me about five minutes. The moment you hear me, run, and *be very careful.*"

Terran nodded and raised his index finger to his lips. "And don't wake Frank to ask permission."

"Who's Frank?"

"The man sleeping by the front door."

"Ah, the man in charge… I'll pretend I didn't know that."

Sanjur flashed a grin and limped away.

Terran went back to unlatching the window locks as quietly as he could. He propped the window open slightly with a tooth-bitten pencil he had found on the ledge. The fresh air instantly brightened his mood. He stepped back and surveyed the east yard. It looked different than he had imagined it in the dark. He could see trees that he hadn't seen in the darkness. Slender evergreens that looked like phantasms with their arms raised in a netting of green plumage. Javad had taught him that they were Buxus sempervirens, but he preferred the term *evergreen.* There was a small garden near the back of the yard, and a stone pathway that was connected to the garden that wound between some tall conifers that stood likewise, conspicuous guardians.

Without a watch or clock, Terran was unsure when Sanjur's voice would finally break the silence. Five minutes was an abstraction, but it seemed to Terran that more than five minutes had passed since Sanjur had left. The sun continued its deliberate ascent, yet the light was still lingering in a diffuse glow unconnected to any source. Terran had his path to Mandana carefully scripted in his mind. Just as he was considering how he would carry Mandana, he noticed a small wicker basket sitting on a shelf in the back of the room. He grabbed it. A moment later, Sanjur's voice boomed outside in the front yard.

Terran opened the window and shot a glance across the yard. Stillness. Everywhere. Sanjur was explaining the offer, shouting it in Baluchian for any to hear. Terran slipped out the window, and ran fast to Mandana's body, which was a lifeless bundle of fur about sixty feet away from the east wall. As he got to her, he could see blood on the grass nearby, but he thought he saw her ears move as he got close. *She was alive!*

Terran squatted down and picked her up gently, placing her inside the woven basket he had brought. Her fur was matted in blood, and she looked weak, unable to hold her head up. "It's me, girl. You'll be okay now." Terran was crouched down and scanned the school's east wall. A gun barrel was pointing at him from a second floor window, but what was particularly odd was that there was an arrow stuck on the window frame right next to the gun barrel. *An arrow?* He heard voices near the street, but his mind was distracted. *Why is he pointing a gun at me?*

A gunshot rang out in the front, and Terran ran as fast as his legs could carry him to the east wall. Suddenly he felt a bullet whiz by his head. He could actually hear it pass by, feeling the change of air pressure, the sizzle of air skimming past his left ear. His heart swelled in that very instant to twice its normal size, and he could feel the injection of adrenalin in his bloodstream as he leapt to the wall and climbed through the window in blinding speed. Another shot rang out just as he fell into the room, and a shower of broken glass fell on the tile floor behind him. Terran lunged under a table and pulled the basket close to his chest. Mandana was still inside, her eyes closed, but trembling. Life, however tenuous, still persisted in her.

Terran was in a daze as he crawled across the floor of the schoolroom. As he reached the door, he stood up and ran down the hallway carrying the basket with Mandana inside. A dozen questions ran through his mind as fast as he ran through the school's corridors. Who was shooting? The man on the second floor or were there Baluchians he hadn't seen? Is Sanjur okay?

He rounded the corner of the stone hallway and saw a group of men standing around the front door. A white shirt tied to the end of a broomstick leaned against the corner. Bullet holes punctuated the makeshift flag.

Suddenly, Frank surged forward from out of the group, his face angrily contorted as he faced Terran who came to a puzzling stop.

"What have you done?" Frank demanded, looking down at Terran.

"Where's Sanjur?" Terran replied, not understanding Frank's question, but feeling the seriousness of his glare.

Frank pointed to the floor, where Sanjur was lying on his back. Terran immediately ran to his side, as the other men shuffled to give him room. "What's wrong? What happened?"

Sanjur turned his head to face Terran, wincing in pain. "You get the cat?"

"Yes."

"Good."

"What's wrong?"

"Just got a little too much excitement. Sort of passed out. I'm feeling better now." Sanjur, with Terran's help, managed to sit up, rubbing the back of his head. "That's all I needed, a good bump on the back of my head. Now it's complete…God, I feel terrible."

"You're not shot?"

"No," Sanjur pointed to the corner of the hallway next to the front door, "they got the flag though. Startled me. For some reason I wasn't expecting them to shoot at a white flag, but I think they heard my voice and that was probably enough for them to shoot, hoping they'd get lucky on a ricochet and end my life. Instead, I passed out."

Sanjur looked around at the assembled men in a daze. "Help me stand up, okay?"

Terran nodded and set his basket down. "Walk with me to the kitchen. I need your help."

"Kitchen sounds good. I think that's part of my problem. I need some food."

Terran handed the basket to Sanjur. "You hold this, I'll hold you."

Sanjur looked down at the basket. In the dim light, a few sparkling photons from Mandana's electric eyes escaped, and he thought he saw the willful glimmer of life. "She's alive?"

Terran nodded, and then turned to Frank. "Dorri?"

Frank pointed up, his face expressionless.

"Tell him to bring Dorri to the kitchen, okay?"

Sanjur looked at Frank and tried to smile. "Terran asks if you could please bring his sister, Dorri, to the kitchen." Sanjur bowed slightly when he had finished, and then limped down the hallway, leaning against Terran, who leaned against Sanjur like a counterweight.

Frank sighed, knowing that it was futile to argue. He pointed to one of the men behind him. "Guard this door with your life. I'll be back in a few minutes." He pointed to another man. "You, get some coffee or tea or whatever you can find and bring it here."

Frank went down the hallway, muttering under his breath a slew of English expletives that he hoped none of the Iranian men would understand. His body was stiff from sleeping on a stone floor, every bone in his body was infused with permafrost, and he had managed three hours of sleep over two days. A *fouler mood would be hard to conjure,* he thought, and then his attention shifted to another concern. *Where's Carson?*

CHAPTER 45

Briefing

Carson paced when he was nervous, but with his wounded ankle he was unable to pace—a fact that annoyed him, because he was definitely nervous. The extraction of Terran Khan was a lot more complicated and deadly than he had imagined, and that was just the part of collecting him. The journey was yet to come.

Earlier, when he had driven Nouri and Parto back to basecamp, Parto had fallen asleep in the Humvee. They had changed their plans and decided to catch a little sleep at basecamp, and then return to the Preserve at the first light. But that was before Farzad had informed Carson about the Boeing 777 that was coming to Mashhad at 0700 hours. That meant that they had only four hours to prepare to receive Peter Lucas, the new leader of the extraction project.

Terran Khan was of extreme interest to people in high places. Farzad, who was hired to run communications for the project, had spoken to a director of Helios, the man who ran the entire educational system of the planet. This was all the proof Carson needed that Terran was somehow an extraordinary asset.

Basecamp was a deserted building on the northern outskirts of Mashhad that consisted of an abandoned warehouse with a large, private backyard that accommodated their gear and vehicles. It was essentially a staging area where they could coordinate the extraction team, but the plans had changed. They were no longer extracting Terran to Kandahar and on to Delhi, now they were getting Terran on an airplane back to America.

Carson has a small inner circle that he had hand-picked for the job, and the moment he had arrived at basecamp, he called a meeting. He was missing Joe and Frank, but Omar Danson, Graham Onert and Farzad Ghorbani had remained behind at basecamp, and he had gathered them to explain their new situation. They were inside the warehouse, where they had a makeshift table assembled from cardboard boxes and a sheet of plywood. Carson sat on a folding chair with his bandaged leg propped on another chair—its bandage saturated with a purplish-red stain just below the ankle.

"Sorry about the sudden wake-up call," Carson began. "For what it's worth I haven't slept all night…I'm completely smoked." Carson rubbed his eyes. "Farzad tells me we've had a major change of plans, and I just finished looking over the project file… God, my head hurts." He let out a long sigh and looked among his men, as he ran his hands through his hair. "In about four hours we're to receive a flight inbound from Germany. It's a Boeing 777—didn't even know we had any flyers left, but that's a good bird. Any rate, onboard is a man by the name of Peter Lucas. Peter is the new project leader. I'll be reporting to him."

"Who is he?" Omar asked.

"Apparently, he's an expert at extractions… how the hell would I know. All I do know is that he's in charge of the project, and we're no longer going to Kandahar with the package—the boy."

"We still get paid?" Graham asked, leaning forward a bit.

"Yes, full compensation."

"Any bad news?" Omar asked.

"Joe's dead."

A chorus of expletives filled the room.

"What happened?" Omar asked.

"We got to the school and all hell broke loose. Remember we didn't think those desert hillbillies would have any bullets? We were wrong… in a big way. They shoot like there's an endless supply. They want this kid to stay. They made that point very clear.

Carson bit his lip and paused, staring unfocused for a moment. "Any rate, we buried Joe—"

"What about Frank?"

"Frank's in command of the school right now. I had to leave and get the boy's mother—"

"I thought he was an orphan," Omar said.

"Guardian," Carson corrected. "Any rate, she's here, asleep. She's been shot, too, but we had to get her out of the clinic, because we feared the Baluchians would capture her and hold her hostage, and we were right about that. So we have her in our custody. We also have the kid's teacher—"

"The other asset?" Omar asked.

"Yes," Carson nodded.

"He okay?"

"Yes."

"How many Baluchians are there?"

"Don't know. Maybe fifteen."

"Where's the boy?"

"Back at the school."

"So we need to get the boy and deliver him to the airport... in four hours?"

"Something like that," Carson said. He took a long sip of coffee from a Styrofoam cup. "We need to secure the boy. That's the most important objective right now. We can send a small team to meet the plane and secure it. The larger team will come with me, and we'll need to bring every weapon at our disposal. I want to be in position to frag those rags if we have to. Got it?"

The three men sat at the table, stunned at the turn of events, and nodded in unison. "Yes, Sir."

"Omar, I'm putting you in charge of the weapons and the shooters. I want them ready in one hour. Graham, I want you in charge of the vehicles. Make sure they're ready to go, gassed up and fully supplied. Farzad, you'll rendezvous with the bird. I need you to explain our situation to Peter, and make sure the airport's fully secured."

"Sir, what about the personnel?"

"What about them?"

"Some haven't shown up yet."

"We'll go with what we have. If they show up after we leave, there'll be nothing here. We'll split the wages saved. Fair?"

"Sure..."

"Okay, any other questions."

"They shot you, too?" Graham asked, pointing to Carson's leg.

"Fuckers got me in the ankle, about the same time they got Joe in the head. Like I said, these rags are nasty, and they want this boy back. When we ride into that school like the fucking cavalry, they're not going to sit back and watch. So be prepared."

"What about friendlies?"

"Yeah, thanks for reminding me. There're about five hundred students at this school. It's about the only thing that's kept those fuckers from going in there and shooting up the place."

"What weapons do they have?"

"Semi-automatic, but they know how to shoot them."

"Any RPGs?"

"No."

"Where're the police in this?" Graham asked.

"Good *fucking* question," Carson answered. "From what I'm told, they protect the wealthy pricks and leave the gun-slinging rags alone. They work for whoever pays them. Unfortunately, the school's not in a wealthy part of town… if there is such a place."

"What's all the interest about this boy?" Omar asked. "You met him?"

"He's a kid. Looks like he's eight. Smart though. Very smart. Something about him that doesn't make sense… if he came from these people, I don't trust him. All I know is that Helios wants him bad. That's enough for me… lines our pockets, so let's get this deal done, and we can be on our way in six hours. Anything else?"

"What's the range of our communicators?"

"Farzad?"

"Maybe two hundred meters if the batteries are good," Farzad replied.

"Frank's wired?" Omar asked.

"Yep."

"Is that range outside their perimeter?"

"We don't know. We don't know shit about their situation. We have no intel. Sorry men. We're blind in this mission, but we have superior fire power that much I know. Let's get ready, and keep asking questions as we go. I'm sure I'm forgetting some details, but I'm so smoked, I want to get an hour of sleep." Carson struggled to his feet and glanced at Farzad. "Wake me in an hour, okay?"

"Yes, Sir."

"Semper Gumby, men." Carson said as he limped off to a cot in the back of the room.

Farzad followed Carson to his cot. "Sir, I noticed one of our personnel was a medic. Arrived last night from Tehran. I can wake him to have a look at your foot."

Carson waved his hand obliquely. "Sure, in an hour. Must sleep now. Goodnight."

Farzad backed up and went to his communication's station isolated in the back of the warehouse. Communications, for missions of high priority, were always kept in private rooms. They were separated. Headphones were usually used. Encoded keypads, if possible, but in this case, Farzad entered his password, and opened the mission's project file, and clicked a link.

He adjusted the camera on his laptop, ran his hand through his close-cropped, curly, jet-black hair, and mentally rehearsed what he would say.

CHAPTER 46

Open Receiver

Dorri arrived in the kitchen, carried by Frank, still sleepy and rubbing her eyes. She lit up when she saw Terran, twisting out of Frank's arms and running to Terran. "You made it back!" she exclaimed.

Terran hugged her for a few seconds, and then picked up the basket and handed it to Dorri, who looked at Terran with wondering eyes. "Is it for me?"

Terran nodded, taking Dorri's free hand inside the basket so she could feel Mandana inside. She immediately placed the basket on the floor and dropped to her knees and looked inside, her face gripped with curiosity. "It's a cat... is it sick?"

Terran turned to Sanjur. "She asked if it was sick." Sanjur said quietly.

Terran moved a small bowl of goat's milk next to the basket and gently lifted Mandana out of the basket. "Tell her that she is wounded, not sick. She needs Dorri to heal. I would like her to heal her. Okay?"

Terran glanced at Dorri as he spoke, watching her touch Mandana.

Sanjur delivered the translation with a steady voice, and Dorri looked into Terran's eyes and smiled. "Of course I will. Does she have a name?"

"Her name is Mandana," Sanjur replied, and then, in Baluchian, turned to Terran. "She will take care of Mandana."

"Can I hold her?" Dorri asked.

Terran understood the question and nodded.

Dorri picked Mandana up like a child might pick up a newborn kitten, and brought her to her lap. "She's wet..."

"We washed some blood off her fur just before you arrived," Sanjur explained.

"Oh, she was bleeding..." Dorri reached into the bowl of milk and dipped her small fingers inside, and brought them to Mandana's nose. A pink tongue rolled out of her mouth like an awkward slug, slow, like something deeply caught up in the unexpected.

"It tickles," Dorri exclaimed with glee. She dipped her fingers in the milk again, and Mandana licked them.

Terran watched intently. "It's a good sign," he whispered.

The kitchen staff was watching, too. They were curious to know about Terran and his ways. Everyone at the school was well aware of the danger he had brought to them. Some were upset, but most were sympathetic.

There were many rumors as to why Terran was being sought by his tribe. Some believed that he must have dishonored his family by stealing something of value from his tribe, and they had sent their police to capture him. Terran was hiding out among children for protection. Others thought he was the son of his tribe's chief and had run away to avoid his training and future life of responsibility.

Hamid had done a good job of explaining the reality of Terran's appearance and situation, however, some of the parents were skeptical. They saw Terran as a threat to their own children's safety. So the rumors persisted—mostly among the parents who were now guards and protectors.

"What happened to her?" Dorri asked, looking to Terran.

Sanjur made a quick translation, and Terran reached out to pet Mandana.

"She protected me against a bully, and that bully hurt her."

After Sanjur delivered the translation, Dorri smiled. "Then Mandana is a very good and brave cat," Dorri announced. She turned to Sanjur for confirmation. "She's really mine?"

Sanjur nodded, his mouth occupied from eating some bread.

Frank bent down and tapped Terran on the shoulder and then pulled Sanjur by the sleeve, and the three drifted to a private corner of the kitchen where Hamid was standing as if he'd been waiting there all along. Dorri continued to feed Mandana.

"Okay, what just happened?" Frank asked, his whispered voice not hiding his anger.

Terran held his right arm up, signaling to Sanjur that he didn't need a translation. "Someone shot at me."

Sanjur's eyes widened. "Who? I thought they were shooting at me."

"I don't know, but I saw an arrow stuck on the window frame where one of our guards was stationed. When I was out in the yard, I saw his gun pointed at me, and then I noticed the arrow. Baluchians use arrows to deliver messages."

"Yes, but no one here can understand Baluchian other than you, me, and Nouri."

"Shaheen, one of their warriors, knows some Persian. His father was a very bright man and well-traveled by Baluchian standards. Shaheen could have written a note…"

"They're trying to get one of our guards to turn on you?" Sanjur raised his voice and then stopped suddenly.

"What's he saying?" Frank demanded.

"He saw an arrow stuck in a second floor window frame on the east wall. The Baluchians deliver their mail with arrows… especially against their enemies. They've perfected the art of bribery. Terran thinks they sent a note to one of our guards, and that guard tried to kill him this morning when he went to save Mandana."

Frank leaned back against the wall.

Hamid cleared his throat. "Because of an arrow, he thinks one of our own guards tried to kill him?"

"It'd be the perfect way to do it," Sanjur said. "Kill him in the yard; make it look like a Baluchian did it—"

"For what?" Hamid asked.

"The reward."

"These are desert rats," Frank said. "What reward could they provide—a camel?"

Sanjur shook his head. "Don't you understand that these *desert rats* have resources? Have you noticed the way they shoot their bullets? They've been stock-piling for generations. It could be gold, silver, jewels, anything… the point is that we need to investigate it, because we may have a murderous traitor in our midst, and that traitor is trying to kill Terran."

Frank stole a quick glance at Terran and then looked down at his boots. It was plausible. "Okay, we'll find the guards who've been on the east wall, and we'll have a little talk. Just a little talk. Okay?"

Sanjur translated for Terran, who nodded. "Tell him I want to be there… for the talk."

Frank started to shake his head as Sanjur spoke, and then stared at Terran, but remained silent. He walked away without another word, Hamid on his heels.

Sanjur took another bite from the loaf of bread he had been holding. "Do you know where they have a bathroom around here?"

Terran glanced at Dorri who seemed preoccupied with her new friend. One of the women who worked in the kitchen was watching her with kind eyes, and had offered her some breakfast.

"I'll show you a place where you can clean up," Terran said. He started to leave with Sanjur, assuming his human crutch role, when Dorri ran to them and looked up into Sanjur's eyes. "How do you say 'thank you' in Terran's language?"

Sanjur smiled. "Taee minnat vaaran."

Dorri repeated it to herself in a whisper, and then turned to Terran. "Tae minet varen." She smiled with her large eyes, so filled with the sparkle of life that Terran felt energized himself. Then her eyes became serious for a moment, and she turned to Sanjur. "Where is my mom?"

Terran spoke before Sanjur could translate. "She will be here soon. She and Nouri had to get some things for our trip. Very soon. You'll see. I have to help Sanjur now, and you have to help Mandana. I'll be back soon."

Terran bent down and kissed Dorri on the cheek. Then grabbed Sanjur by his arm, and the two walked out of the kitchen down the hallway. Dorri went back to Mandana, picked her up, and placed her in her lap. "That was my brother you saved. You did good."

CHAPTER 47

A Piece of String

As Terran and Sanjur shuffled down the main hallway together, they could see and hear the buzz of children awakening. The stairwell, from the upper level dormitories, was like a waterfall of children streaming down, its path diverting to the same destination: the cafeteria. Most students were in good moods, because their classes had been suspended. They had free time, with the caveats that they stayed away from windows and exterior doors.

Terran wore the standard-issue uniform for all boys: a white tunic with a bright burgundy-red sash. The girls wore the same uniform except their tunics were cut longer and had longer sleeves. Otherwise, it was hard to tell the difference.

Down the hallway, Terran watched a young boy, about eight years old, talking with a frustrated Hamid.

"Then where is it?" Hamid asked.

"I don't know. It was gone when I woke up."

"Where did you leave it?"

"Same place as always… under my bed, Sir, with my other clothes."

Hamid lightened his tone a little as Terran and Sanjur walked by. "I suggest you take another look and find it. We can't have missing clothes, now can we?"

The boy shook his head, and ran back up the stairs almost in tears.

"What was that about?" Terran whispered to Sanjur.

"Apparently he lost his sash."

Hamid came up behind them and cleared his throat very politely. "Two guards have been detained for questioning. Frank asked me to find you… follow me, please."

They walked slowly down a side hallway near Hamid's office, to a large converted school room that was the equivalent of a teacher's lounge, sparsely furnished with a nice view of the interior courtyard of the school. Two men sat in the middle of the room, looking disgruntled and impatient. Frank stood behind a small desk that had a coffee maker on it and an assortment of cups with handwritten labels on them. He was holding a handgun, and stopped speaking mid-sentence as they entered.

"And here they are now…" Frank said.

The two men twisted in their chairs to see what Frank had pointed to. Their faces filled with tension.

"Hamid, what is happening here—"

"Shut up!" Frank snapped, anger swelling in his eyes. Frank composed himself after a lengthy pause, while the two men fidgeted in their flimsy wooden chairs.

"Sanjur and Terran, this is Kourosh and Saeed, the two guards who were stationed at the second-floor post on the east wall—Kourosh this morning, and Saeed last night. Because Hamid knows these men best, we'll let him start with the questions. Go ahead, Hamid."

Frank walked to a corner of the room, and sat down. Hamid sat on the edge of a nearby desk, and folded his arms across his chest. "Gentlemen, I'm sorry to have to put you through this… this investigation—"

"Investigation of what?" Saeed asked, raising his arms up in frustration. "What did we do, Hamid?"

"Who was guarding the window this morning?"

"I was." Kourosh said, raising his hand slightly.

"And did you see Terran run out into the yard to rescue a cat?"

"Yes."

"And did you fire your gun at Terran as he ran back?"

Kourosh put his arms up and tilted his head. "Are you crazy? Of course not. Why are you making these accusations?"

"The boy saw a gun barrel pointed in his direction and heard a gunshot. You just admitted that you were stationed at the window at the time he went out into the east yard, did you not?""

"Well it wasn't from my gun. I heard gunshots, too."

Frank stepped forward. "Are you sure you didn't accidentally pull the trigger?"

"No! I mean, no, I didn't pull the trigger… yes, I'm sure."

"Are you sure you didn't mistake him for a Baluchian warrior?"

Kourosh pointed at Terran. "He's a small boy. How could I?"

Frank walked up to the two men, and pointed to the top of the table that they were sitting at. "Empty all your pockets and put everything you have on the table... now!"

"This is ridiculous and an outrage! What? Are we criminals now?" Saeed asked.

"Do it!" Frank shouted menacingly. His gun pointed conspicuously at Saeed and Kourosh.

Hamid stepped back, watching nervously as the two men emptied their pockets. "I'm sorry we have to put you through this, gentlemen. It's just a precaution."

After the men stepped back from the table, Frank pointed at their pants' pockets. "Show me they're empty."

Each man pulled their pockets outside their pants, and lifted their shirts up to prove that the inside of their pockets were clean, but for a few pieces of lint.

"Sit back down." Frank said.

A collection of small objects lay on the linoleum surface of the table. A piece of string, a safety pin, a rubber band, a smooth polished stone, but nothing that looked like a note, and certainly no object that looked like a bribe.

Terran examined the objects on the table with interest. He walked back to Sanjur, who had sat down in a chair behind the two men, and whispered in his ear. "I want to ask a question."

Sanjur waved his hand, catching Frank's attention. "Terran would like to ask a question or two, if that's okay."

Hamid and Frank were done examining the objects, and finding nothing that looked incriminating, nodded their heads.

Terran turned to Sanjur. "Do either of them have a child here at the school?"

Sanjur remained sitting, and the two men turned their chairs to face him, as he began the translation.

Kourosh shook his head. "I'm a teacher here. No kids... just students."

Saeed raised his hand. "Two. One boy, one girl."

"Ask them if they saw an arrow that had been shot into the

window frame."

Both men nodded when Sanjur asked the question.

"Ask them if they saw a note attached to the arrow."

Both men shook their head after Sanjur finished his translation, and replied, "no."

Terran paused for a moment. "Did either of them hear the arrow when it was first fired at the window?"

Both men shook their heads, but Kourosh offered an explanation. "I didn't hear it, but when I first noticed it was there, it was last evening, around seven o'clock."

"Why didn't you report it?" Frank asked.

"Compared to the gunfire, I wasn't worried about the arrow," Kourosh answered. "I only saw one. I didn't think it was important."

Terran turned to Sanjur. "Can we meet privately with Hamid?"

Sanjur stood to his feet slowly with a brief grimace, and caught Hamid's eyes. "Terran would like to speak with you... in private."

Frank sat down and put his feet up on another chair. "Make it quick."

The three walked into the hallway and huddled outside the closed door. Hamid looked irritated at the circumstances, and surveyed Terran with anxious eyes. "What?"

"Do you know Saeed well?"

Hamid nodded to Sanjur as he finished his translation. "Yes, he's one of our most loyal parents. His children are excellent students, and Saeed helps us around the school regularly. He's a very good man."

"What did Saeed do before Sunrot?" Terran asked.

Hamid grasped his beard and looked to the ceiling for a moment. "I believe he was a police officer in Tehran... if my memory is correct."

"Is he married?" Terran asked next.

"No, his wife died shortly after Sunrot. I don't believe he's ever remarried."

"How long has he worked at the school?"

"Almost four years I would say, but not fulltime... just helping out," Hamid answered. "What's the fascination with this man? He wasn't even at the post this morning when you heard the gun. How could it be him?"

Terran listened as Sanjur translated Hamid's question. "The piece of string on the table—it held the tension of a knot. The kind Baluchians use. It came from his pocket. If a note was attached, he would have burned it or hidden it somewhere. The string could be re-used. He kept it. I know he's lying by watching his eyes."

Hamid began to shake his head shortly after Sanjur began his translation. "No, you're wrong. Saeed is a good man!"

Terran raised his finger to his mouth. "I would like to speak to Saeed alone. Kourosh can go."

Sanjur put his hand on Hamid's shoulder. "Please. Let Terran talk with him. It's our best chance to get the truth."

Hamid took a deep breath and slowly exhaled. "Five minutes. If we don't get a confession in five minutes, we're done here, and we let him go. Okay?"

Sanjur delivered the message: Five minutes. Terran nodded, and then spoke for a few moments.

"He wants to know if Saeed's children are at the school now."

"Yes, they both are."

Terran said, "Thank you," in perfect Persian, opened the door and walked back into the teacher's lounge. Sanjur and Hamid looked at each for a moment, Sanjur shrugged his shoulders slightly and smiled, and the two men filed into the room.

"Kourosh, you can go, but keep our discussion private." Hamid announced. "Saeed, we'd like you to stay awhile so Terran can ask you a few more questions."

Almost instantly Kourosh stood, collected his few items from the table, and walked out the door, closing it behind him with a not-too-subtle thud.

Saeed sulked lower in his chair and folded his arms across his wide chest. He was a large man with a friendly face that seemed mostly hidden behind an unkempt beard that had long taken over nearly every available centimeter of his face and neck, save his eyes, nose, lips and forehead. Even the back of his hands were covered in a thick, black hair. He was tall, about six feet-three inches, and his bulky frame was similar to Frank's, though not quite as sculpted.

As Terran approached him, Sanjur followed, but lagged behind, as if giving Terran space to think. Frank was still sitting in the corner, mostly looking out at the inner courtyard, presumably, wishing he could be anywhere else.

Terran went over to the table and picked up the string. "Ask him how this string came into his possession."

Sanjur asked, and immediately an odd look spread across Saeed's face.

"Why do you ask such a question?" Saeed asked incredulously. "Don't we all have better things to do with our time?"

Saeed began to stand, and suddenly Frank stood in unison with his gun cocked, pointed directly at Saeed's chest. "Sit back down and stay there until I say otherwise."

Saeed sat back down very slowly, eyeing Frank with suspicion. "What are you trying to pin on me? That I tried to kill this boy? For what? Why would I do that? I'm guarding everyone inside this school. Why would I do that?"

"That's what we're here to find out," Sanjur said, and then glanced at Terran.

Terran still held the piece of string between his fingers. "Where is the note that was attached to this?"

Saeed fidgeted in his chair. "How would I know? Pieces of string, an arrow, a missing note, a little boy questioning me?" Saeed turned to Hamid. "Is this how you treat someone who has worked hard to bring order and peace to this school?"

Terran walked right up to Saeed, slowly, cautiously. Everyone in the room watched, especially Saeed, who looked uneasy at his approach. "This was used to tie a note to that arrow. That note was from the Baluchians, and they threatened to kill everyone, unless you first killed me. If you weren't successful, then they would burn the school down or attack it by some other means. Isn't that what the note said?"

Sanjur made the translation, his voice cracking at the import of what Terran said. Frank and Hamid were riveted on Saeed's reaction, who squirmed in his chair, his face tightened in the throes of panic. His lips began to quiver, as his gaze went to the floor.

Terran sat in the same chair that Kourosh had occupied, and touched

Saeed's arm. "I forgive you. I understand why you tried... it's okay, any of us would do the same thing under these circumstances. But there's one thing you should know about Baluchian warriors—they will not kill a child. They will threaten to do anything to achieve their end, but killing a child—they will never do that."

Sanjur translated one sentence at a time. When he finished, Saeed broke down and began to weep. "I wasn't trying to kill you... only wound you. I was trying to hit your legs, but you ran so fast... I couldn't do it... I couldn't. I thought if I wounded you, they would get you...and leave us alone. I'm very sorry. So very sorry."

Saeed wept for another minute, repeatedly apologizing to Terran, and Terran patted his back until Saeed was finally able to compose himself.

"Do you still have the note?" Terran asked quietly.

Saeed nodded, and reached down to his right ankle and pulled, from behind his sock, a piece of folded paper. He handed it to Terran, who unfolded it carefully and then passed it to Sanjur.

Sanjur looked it over, squinting at the words, trying to bring them into focus. He cleared his throat, and began to read the note aloud: "We are the army that surrounds your school. We are strong. More coming. We give you twenty-four hours and in that time, you give us Terran Kahn.

"You are a guard. You guard your children. What is one child when you have hundreds? We will kill them all unless you give us Terran Kahn. Their blood will be on your hands. You have twenty-four hours. Do not guard Terran Kahn. Give him to us and you and your children will be spared. It is the only way!"

Sanjur translated for Terran first and then re-read in Persian. The second time, Saeed started weeping again. Hamid offered him a cloth to wipe his eyes and nose, but Saeed refused, and instead looked at Terran with red, tear-filled eyes, pointing emphatically at the note in Sanjur's hands. "How can you be sure they will not do what they say in this note? How can you be sure?"

"Because, despite how they may appear, they are not barbarians. They are a cultured people, who care, above all other things, for their children. They will not attack this school. Their code of behavior will not allow it."

Sanjur translated, and Frank stood up and holstered his gun. "Maybe they wouldn't kill kids, but I don't have the same reason to doubt that they could sweep in here and kill every goddamned adult, especially if there's more coming. If they got this message to Saeed, they probably got it to other guards, too." Frank turned to Terran. "From now on, I want a bodyguard on you at all times. I don't trust anyone here."

Sanjur raised his hand. "I'm his bodyguard."

"Do you have a weapon?" Frank fired back.

"No."

"Can you run?"

"Not right now... in a day or two perhaps."

"Can you fight?"

"Well... not at the moment."

"Then you're not a bodyguard," Frank observed. "We need someone who can watch and react with mobility, and fire a weapon, if the need arises."

Saeed raised his hand. "I can do it, if he'd have me."

"Did you share the note with anyone?" Hamid asked, ignoring, for the moment, Saeed's offer.

"No," Saeed answered. "I was afraid I'd start a panic, and a mob would rise up."

"Are you aware of any other notes or arrows anywhere on the building?"

Saeed shook his head. He looked sad and tired.

Sanjur translated a bit of the conversation for Terran's benefit.

"I accept Saeed's offer to be my bodyguard," Terran announced.

"Okay, then it's settled," Frank said. "Saeed is off the hook, and for the time being, he'll shadow Terran as his bodyguard. I'll do a personal review of the building and see if there're any additional arrows. I'll update you after I finish my reconnaissance. But even if we don't find any evidence of arrows or notes, I would caution you to keep your guard up. Beware of anything that looks or feels unusual—that goes especially for you three." Frank pointed his finger at Terran, Sanjur and Saeed.

"What about the other guards?" Hamid asked.

"What about them?"

"Shouldn't we tell them what we know?"

"I don't have time, if you want to do that, be my guest."

Saeed raised his hand. "If I'm a bodyguard, can I have my gun back?"

Frank pulled a handgun out from behind his back and handed it to Saeed. "Anything else?"

There was a long silence in the room. Frank half-heartedly saluted and walked out in a rush. Those remaining looked at one another and treaded awkwardly to the door. Terran was Sanjur's human crutch, and they limped behind, while Saeed already seemed to be patrolling the hallways, as one does when they're a bodyguard.

An army can sometimes be more powerful as a vapor than a solid thing. The Baluchians were vaporous, seeping underneath locked doors, infecting with their threats of punishing violence. Even though Terran had dismissed their threats as only words, the words held a power over the minds of those four men in ways that they couldn't quite pronounce. They knew something was lost in that room. To step trustingly in the school was now a more difficult proposition. Now they saw a single piece of string as something sinister—fibers that held screams as well as knots—this was the imputation of despair.

Amid this loss of innocence and trust, a boy forgave a nameless sin, and that spread more brightly among the men than anything lost.

CHAPTER 48

Runway

The landing strip was such an underrated part of human flight. It was always assumed to be of ample length and width, flat, straight and the pavement of the same consistency from start to finish, but in the case of Peter Lucas' flight, it was not a good assumption.

Peter was tired from the lull of the aircraft engine. He looked out the window and could see the Caspian Sea to his left. The day was dawning. A faint glow of light suffused the horizon to the east, and he knew Tehran would be visible on the right side of the aircraft, but he was too tired to get up and look. He was glad he had been able to convince the flight planners to take the risk and try to make it to Mashhad's airport, because the runways were supposed to be in better condition than Tehran's. Unfortunately, they had to base their decision on data that was nearly two years old.

The earthquakes that had shaken Iran had been massive; in western Iran especially. There were some reports that the two main landing strips in Tehran's airport were so uneven that the ground was as much as three feet out of alignment on the southernmost landing strip. Without the availability of airplanes, mechanics, parts, and fuel, the airports had become deserted in almost every city of the world. Those airports struck by earthquakes were now overgrown with vegetation, and their pavements pocked by weeds and tufts of grass.

Fuel for their airplane was being transported from Kandahar to Mashhad. That had been a favor called in by Trevor Stanton. The cover story was a difficult one to sell, but because it had come from Trevor Stanton, the questions were sparse and easily deflected as a "need to know" mission.

The real problem they had wasn't fuel—at least, not yet. As they were flying over the Black Sea thirty minutes ago, they had calculated that they would have sufficient fuel to reach Mashhad. The real issue was the condition of the landing strip in Mashhad. Their plan was to do a fly-over of the airport at an altitude of 2,500 feet, and evaluate the landing strips and determine which of the two was in better condition. They had special cameras that would take photos, and the flight crew would then make a quick analysis. The concern was that the back-up plan, if neither of the landing strips was safe, didn't exist. They lacked the fuel to return to Tehran or fly south to Kandahar. One of the landing strips had to work. It was that simple.

Peter's ground crew was as lean as its only member, Jamere Wilson, who had been hastily recruited to ensure that communications were established when they landed. Jamere was a gangly African American with a hairless head, soft manner, and affable nature. Peter liked him and was glad he was now part of the flight crew that had come in from Berlin. Thankfully, the German pilot, Martin Handro, spoke English, but the rest of the crew were too busy to even notice Peter or Jamere, who were mostly left to themselves.

They had been in the air for over twelve hours. Tailwinds were in their favor, and they were making good time and conserving fuel. All was good. It was the landing strip that taunted them.

About thirty minutes later, Martin's voice came over the intercom and announced, in his thick German accent, that they were within ten miles of the airport. Peter had felt the descent soon after they had flown over Tehran. The picture of the landscape between Tehran and Mashhad reminded him of the desert southwest, but even more desolate. Sprigs of mountains would ripple to the surface, but nothing so high that they could sustain snow.

They came over the airport, low to the ground, at a speed of two hundred miles per hour in a steep bank that allowed the co-pilot to take pictures of the runways. From 2,500 feet, they looked overgrown with patches of grasses and weeds, and one of them looked like it was a refuge to the remnants of a plane's fuselage.

Peter stood up once the plane leveled off, and walked into the cockpit. "What's the verdict?"

Martin glanced back and smiled. "We'll do an analysis... and just circle now... we wait."

"Fuel?" Peter asked.

Martin glanced down at his instrumentation. "Enough… to stay in the air for about fifteen more minutes—at this speed."

One of co-pilots came into the cockpit with concern on his face. To Peter's surprise, he spoke near-perfect English. "The photograph shows some cracks at about the midway point for runway one—they're estimated to be between twelve and eighteen centimeters. However, at about fifteen hundred meters, the runway has a major crack…"

"How bad?" Martin asked.

"Two meters wide… maybe more."

"And runway two?"

"It's much worse… there's plane debris cluttering the runway."

"Shit," Martin mumbled under his breath. He shrugged his shoulders and looked into Peter's eyes with a sense of resignation. "You're in charge, what now?"

"How much runway do we need?"

"Twenty-three hundred meters is as tight as I can stop this thing… what's Mashhad's altitude here?"

"About a thousand meters," replied the co-pilot.

Martin turned to Peter. "Make it twenty-five hundred meters."

"What about a freeway?" Peter asked.

"Too narrow, light posts, billboards, have to be perfectly straight… I don't know…"

Peter walked deeper into the cockpit, looking down on the ground below. "What's that?"

The co-pilot looked at his radar display and then down at his map. "According to this, it's the Northern Bypass Freeway. It looks straight."

"What about lights or billboards?" Martin asked.

"What choice do we have?" Peter said. "We're down to ten minutes of fuel."

"I can't turn around on a freeway to take-off," Martin protested. "I need six thousand meters of straight road. Does it make sense to land if we can't take-off?"

"Does it make sense to fall out of the sky, because we ran out of fuel arguing about it?" Peter asked.

Martin adjusted his strap tighter. "I suggest you find a seat, and buckle up."

Peter went back to his seat in first class. In all of the conundrums he had endured, trying to rescue various dignitaries and political heavyweights after Sunrot, he had survived them all. Now, in the desolation of Iran, he suddenly felt a terror welling up inside him. *Not here.*

"Everything okay?" Jamere asked.

"Buckle up—this could be a bumpy landing."

"When you say bumpy, on a scale of one to ten, what're we talking about?"

Peter looked out his window, noticing their altitude was rapidly decreasing. "I wish I knew."

"That's not comforting, in case you thought it was."

It was about 7:10 A.M. local time and Peter wondered for a moment what his wife would be doing. Probably sleeping, he figured, as he made the mental calculations. He had only been married for six months, and it had been very hard to suddenly leave her. No explanation, she didn't even know where he was going or what his mission was. If she had any sense that he was a minute away from landing on some deserted highway north of Mashhad, Iran in a Boeing 777-X that originated from Berlin, he was quite sure she would dismiss it as impossible.

He remembered the days before Sunrot when smartphones ruled the pockets and purses of nearly everyone on the planet, now they had an intercom and nothing more. There was no tower from which the pilot could seek advice. There was no communication to the ground. Once in the air it was radio silence. It was a lonely feeling. He hated it.

He could see the ground now clearly. Scrub brush and tan-colored dirt everywhere. No light posts, so that was good. No billboards—promising. He didn't realize it, but he was holding his breath. He closed his eyes and remembered a quote of Rumi, the Persian mystic, that seemed appropriate somehow, in this place and time.

Be a spot on the ground where nothing is growing, where something might be planted, a seed, from God.

Peter prayed that he could be a seed.

CHAPTER 49

Bribery

Moshad Adali was the consummate warrior; strong, imposing, willful, and clever beyond any of his adversaries. The morning, however, had not gone as he had expected. Another of his men was lost. He was now down to only eight warriors. The whereabouts of two were unknown. The fact they were missing was not a good sign, and the actual number could be six, if they too, were dead.

He had sent two men to bring him the local police chief. He wanted to meet and discuss an alliance. Shaheen was the only one among his men who knew enough Persian to extend an invitation. While Moshad himself could speak adequate Persian, he was in no shape to walk the three miles to the police station. Had it not been for Shaheen's language skills, he probably would have perished at the hands of Moshad. Moshad no longer trusted him, and when that happened, more times than not, a warrior would turn up dead or missing.

It was still early in the morning when Moshad heard the footsteps of men marching up the stairs, and he readied his gun. A sharp knock and the creaking door opened slowly, revealing Shaheen and a stranger.

Shaheen extended his arm and made the introductions. "This is Officer Akhtar, and this is Moshad Adali."

Shaheen motioned to a wall and offered some water to their guest before he backed quietly out of the room, and closed the door.

"What is your first name?" Moshad asked.

"…Namvar," he announced, looking around the dilapidated room.

"I know it's not exactly a palace, but I'm the equivalent of royalty to my people. I hold the office of Director of Security. As you must know, those who secure a people's well-being and safety, are among its most prized possessions… are we not?"

Namvar nodded and smiled politely. He was middle-aged with gray hair overtaking his tightly curled black hair, and a bushy moustache that covered his upper lip. His nose was bulbous and unnaturally large, his skin pockmarked, but despite these imperfections, in the low light of the room or from an appropriate distance, he could still be considered handsome. "Your servant mentioned that you had a proposition for me. I am a very busy man, and would like to get down to business."

"Ah, you are one of those who doesn't like to waste time on social pleasantries. Another thing we have in common," Moshad intoned with a lively grin. "Before I get to my proposition, tell me, Namvar, how many men do you have at your disposal?"

"You want to hire our services?"

"How many would I be hiring?"

"What is the service?"

"One of our own, a young boy, is being held against his will at the Helios school. We need your help to get him back."

"And why can't *you* get him back?"

"As I said, he's being held against his will, and the men holding him there seem intent on murder."

"They've kidnapped him?"

Moshad nodded. "Because he is in a school with hundreds of young children around, we don't want to poke around too much and cause harm to the children."

"We've heard the gunfire," Namvar said, "Obviously, you've met a lot of resistance. Not the kind we see in these parts, especially when a child is the issue. Why is this boy being protected by the military?"

"Did I say he was?"

"Indirectly. The sound of bullets speaks to us. Who else has that kind of weaponry? Who else drives armored Humvees?"

"Ah, so you've seen these men before?"

Namvar shook his head. "We have eyes all over this city. We know something's going on, Moshad. What we didn't know was that a little boy was at the center of it. Who is he?"

Moshad moved his leg and winced loudly, hoping to buy some time to sort out his story. It was going in the wrong direction. Namvar was better informed and more intelligent than he'd expected. He pointed to his bandaged leg. "A casualty of our boy's captors I'm afraid…"

Namvar nodded, but remained silent.

Moshad finally found a comfortable posture. Without chairs he couldn't find relief for more than a few minutes at a time. Dr. Najafi, who had tended to his bullet wound the previous night, had been detained indefinitely, and was now a captive held in the basement—three stories under Moshad's lair.

"The boy..." Moshad began, "he's been selected to be one of our religious leaders. He's very important to us, and Helios knows this and wants to take him from us."

"Why?"

"They want to weaken us. As you know, my people have not joined the Greater Nation. We withhold our support on religious and moral grounds. They do everything in their power to punish us for our resistance. The taking of one of our religious leaders, though he is yet a boy, is one form of their twisted punishment."

Namvar nodded almost imperceptibly. "And what did you need the Police for? If the military is behind this, we can't intervene."

"Ah, well, you are making an assumption that this is the military. What if it's just a group of militia or ex-military who plan to sell our boy to the GN?"

"And how do you know this?"

"It's a small team from what we've seen. Only three, but they're well-armed."

"Have you tried to meet with them?"

Moshad motioned to the far wall. "Go to that window, the one on the right, but be careful." Namvar stood up and cautiously walked over the window, and looked over its bottom edge. "Do you see the body of that man who lies in front of the school door?"

Namvar nodded. "I do."

"That was the messenger I sent. He's dead, as you can plainly see. There's no reason for me to talk with those devils."

Namvar, hunched over at the waist, walked back to his previous post and sat back down on the floor. "What're you proposing we do? They might shoot us just as they shot your man."

"You're the local power. They might listen to you, and if they don't, then I would ask that you help us free our boy—by force, if necessary."

"So now the question rises… why would we want to put our lives at risk to help you?"

"Ah, well, that's a reasonable question, and one I'm prepared to answer, once I know how many men you have at your control."

Namvar sighed. "And I can't give you a number until I know how much you're willing to pay."

Moshad repositioned his leg again, wincing several times as he moved it to a more comfortable angle. "What do these men make in a typical day?"

"It depends on the day. One that puts their life at risk, they want twenty mesghals of gold. If they have to fight a military operation, they'll want thirty."

"Each man?"

"Each man."

"And what about you? Do you also require thirty mesghals?"

Namvar smiled coyly. "No, you simply give me all of the money, and I'll take my cut and distribute the rest to the men."

Moshad smiled knowingly. "I see… so let's say I agree to twenty—"

"—Thirty mesghals."

"Thirty mesghals per man, how many men are at your disposal?"

"I can find at least twenty."

"And you provide your own bullets?" Moshad asked.

"For thirty mesghals we do."

"Then we have a deal. I would need twenty men, all armed, good shooters, and strong in courage. I will also need an escape… a car, truck; I don't really care, as long as it's fast and reliable."

"That can be arranged, but it will cost extra."

"How much?"

"For how long would you use it?"

"I only need to get to our basecamp in the southern part of the city. Maybe fifteen kilometers away."

"So you need a fast car and a driver… that'd be one hundred mesghals."

"Okay, now for payment," Moshad said. "I propose two hundred now, and the balance when you take us to our camp with the boy in hand."

Namvar shook his head and smiled. "Three hundred and fifty now, and the balance when we deliver you to your destination."

"And how fast can you be ready?" Moshad asked.

"If you agree to my payment terms, I can have my men here in one hour."

In the quiet of the morning, far in the distance, the sound of an engine broke the stillness of the morning.

"What is that?" Moshad asked.

Namvar's head tilted upwards, and a look of astonishment rose on his face. "It's an airplane!"

"I thought they were all—"

"They're coming for this boy..." Namvar whispered to himself. The sound grew louder and louder like a roaring of engines that no one in that part of world had heard for at least twelve years. Namvar went to the north-facing windows and looked up at the sky. Through the trees, he glimpsed it, a huge jet, white and silver with a red tail. It was the biggest thing he's seen in the sky for as long as he could remember. "It's not military... so strange."

The building began to shudder. As the plane came closer, they could feel its force reverberate through the floorboards that rattled in sympathy to the powerful engines overhead.

"They want that boy bad." Namvar said, his voice almost shouting over the sound of the engines. He returned to his seat and crossed his legs, eyeing Moshad who looked irritated.

"Who is this boy?" Namvar asked with a new intensity.

"I told you, he's—"

"Don't try," Namvar interrupted. "Don't try to feed me your prepared stories. I want the truth or our deal is off. I won't put twenty of my best men against the forces of the GN. So, you need to tell me the absolute truth or I walk."

Moshad listened to the engines as they drifted into a relative quiet, and contemplated how to tell the absolute truth. "Are you a religious man, Namvar?"

"Once... a long time ago."

"Ah, like everyone else. Sunrot took away our God. It killed the faith. In our world, we knew this would happen. We didn't know how exactly, we only knew there would be a purging of humanity, and faith would be purged as well. Our prophets told us that the day this began— the purging, one would be born to lead humanity to a new calling. We named this person, *Mahdi*.

"The boy I'm referring to is this person. He was born on June twelfth—the very first day we felt the storms rise up. He was not like other children. He… he is bright beyond any man. He understands at once. His mind absorbs and never rejects. It's like an endless sponge that can soak up the oceans. He is our hope."

"Whose hope?"

"Everyone's."

"Did they really kidnap him?"

"Yes. That part is true."

"What do they want him for?"

"They plan to kill him."

"You know this for sure?"

"It is our prophecy."

"I don't believe in prophecy," Namvar said. "And I don't believe that the GN would send an airplane and a military escort unless this boy was something more than a prophecy. If all they wanted to do was to kill him, he'd be dead. They're a secular society. They don't care about religion. They don't give a shit about Baluchian culture or prophecy. And you know it."

Moshad remained silent; listening to the engines as their roar began to build again, signaling that the plane was circling above the city. Even before Sunrot, he'd never heard engines before. He saw airplanes gliding in the sky with their white tails, but they always displayed themselves in the blue robe of silence.

Moshad stared down at the floor, his voice introspective for the first time. "If they take him, our culture, religion, everything will change. It won't happen immediately, in four years it will be subtle… in forty, our religion will be a thing only the zealots believe. In four hundred years it will be gone from this planet. Even the Quran!

"You can sit there and tell me you don't believe in prophecy or the importance of our culture to the GN, but our prophecy stands tall. It foresaw Sunrot and it foresaw the birth of the Mahdi. He's now twelve years old. Our Holiest man has trained him since he was an infant. I really don't know why the GN would go to this trouble to take him, if the prophecy wasn't accurate. You tell me... why are they here to take a child that is *ours?* A resource that is *ours?* A Holy child that we developed over countless generations of time in the cradle of humanity. *Why?*"

Namvar shook his head in disbelief as the engines roared louder, and again the floorboards began to vibrate. He waited until the engines quieted down, wondering what he should do. To fight against the GN was tantamount to career suicide, and possibly death. Something big was happening. Moshad didn't know or wasn't telling, and Namvar couldn't tell which it was.

"They can't possibly land at the airport... not a plane that size." Namvar's eyes were glazed over as he stared in deep thought. "They're north... they're going to land on the highway. They'd have to refuel. They'd need a ground team. You said they only had three operatives?"

Moshad nodded, admiring Namvar's insights. "You think they're landing on the highway to the north?"

"Are you sure he's inside the school?" Namvar asked, ignoring Moshad's question.

"Yes, we saw him only an hour ago. We know he's there. I have three men patrolling the school's perimeter. There's no way they could get him out without us knowing."

"How did the boy end up here?"

"His teacher told him about this city, he came here and took some tests. The GN identified him. They knew he was the Mahdi. That's when they seized him. They killed his teacher, too. I need your help, Namvar." Moshad pointed to his wounded leg. "Please, you can see that I'm nearly worthless here. We can't let them take our best hope. What do they know about our culture? They want one culture, and ours, it will be blended into theirs until its values, its power, is sucked out and lost. Help us, I beg you, help us."

Namvar kneaded the back of his neck with his right hand and then stood to his feet. "Okay, I'll need more resources. If my men and yours are going up against the GN, I need enough mesghals to quit my job and move."

"How much?" Moshad asked, hope returning to his voice.

"Instead of seven hundred, I'll need two thousand."

"I don't have that much with me," Moshad replied, his arms raised in protest.

"How much do you have?"

"Half that amount."

"Could you raise the rest within a week?"

"Yes, of course."

"What about collateral?"

Moshad squinted and shook his head. "What?"

"Do you have anything that would be valuable that you could leave behind as a reserve payment… in case you didn't come back to pay the rest of your debt."

"Ah, well, I have camels… at least three that I could leave behind. Each of those is worth at least five hundred mesghals, but my people always pay our debts, so put your doubts to rest."

Namvar started pacing in the room. "Okay, I'll send a team to recon the airplane. The rest of my men will come here, and we'll meet in this very room in one hour. Then we'll set our plans to rescue your… Mahdi."

Moshad leaned forward, wincing as he did. "You have to take down that plane. If that plane is allowed to leave…"

"We have hand grenades, but if I use them, I'll need to charge you extra."

Moshad waved his hand. "The goal is to get the boy, not to save money."

Namvar smiled at Moshad's response. He may have found his golden ticket.

He bowed and quickly walked down the stairs, collecting his two men who had accompanied him. They jogged through the back alleyways to their station. Namvar answered their questions about the airplane, and explained how they were going to keep it from ever flying again.

CHAPTER 50

Agreement

Amid emptiness, the smallest object becomes the centerpiece of attraction. Gleaming in the black solitude, it tells stories of creation and purpose. Its creator seems strangely present in the spacious space. If the object were a soul, flicking its light into the black solitude, it would cause all manner of curiosity, for the object would not be of three dimensions. The soul—that rarest of all forms that treads above death's surface, that never succumbs to time—is so seldom seen in the world of dimension and form that humans have become uncertain of its very existence.

They are anxious to know it, but must see it first or at least its effects. It is not enough that it remains the subject of words. Billions of people have been lost to its shadows and echoes as they searched for it, hoping that this book or that teacher would finally expose the truth of its existence. Perhaps, if they were pure enough, it would reveal their own soul. Yet soul remains the smallest object; invisible to all instruments that pursue it.

The object remains a subject, consigned to words of every language. Artists have tried to capture it in symbols, but like broken flowers that wilt when the root is gone; the symbols advertise themselves, blind to their source. The smallest object denies our greatest creators, taunting them to deliver what they cannot touch. Even if they step out of the house where they know all things of glitter and substance, where all is measured in time, the soul will only expand into another distance. It will cite the differences between mind and body and between the heart and the soul. It will lessen the linkages and make clear the distinctions.

When the soul is under the eye, and the beholder can open the final, semi-transparent lid, and witness its supernal glory, that is the day of humanity's birth. All previous marks of time, tethered to their earthen moorings, will promptly vanish, and the destinies of the smallest object and the largest project meet for the first time in human clay.

*   *   *   *

Parto blinked her eyes, unsure if the voice she heard was outside or inside her head. Nouri's face was pressed close to her. "It's time to get up."

"How long was I sleeping?" Parto asked, rubbing her eyes.

"About three hours."

Parto sat up immediately, feeling dizziness spread over her body. Out of instinct, her hand went to her head. "We need to go!"

"There's a lot going on outside. It looks like they're moving their operations. Carson asked to talk with us, so I came to wake you."

"You've been up?"

"I got up an hour ago… too much noise."

"What's happening?"

Nouri kissed her on the cheek. "Let's go talk with Carson and find out."

"You smell…"

"…normal," Nouri said, completing her sentence with a mischievous smile. "I washed up. You're welcome." He smiled with a sparkle in his eyes, and helped her out of the small bunk bed she had slept in. They had slept in one of the trucks that had been brought to take Terran and Nouri to Kandahar.

"Can I wash up, too?" Parto asked. "It'll only take a minute."

"Sure, can you manage by yourself?"

"I think so."

The truck was a military ambush vehicle, originally the property of Special Forces, with only six ever commissioned, and as far as Carson knew, it was the only one that had survived Sunrot intact. It had accommodations for eighteen service personnel, weapons cache, bulletproof windows, MRAP-style shell, and two remote weapons stations called CROWS, one in the back and one in the front. It was not luxury by any standards, but the purpose of the vehicle was to withstand any assault short of a Tomahawk missile.

After Parto had washed up, she and Nouri walked to the abandoned warehouse and met up with Carson and Farzad. There were at least a dozen men either carrying, checking or loading supplies onto various vehicles. Basecamp was a beehive of activity, and sunrise was just beginning to swell.

"We have coffee... it's not very good, but it wakes you up," Carson offered. He looked up at Nouri and Parto as they approached his improvised war room, replete with plywood table and cardboard boxes. "How're you feeling?"

"I'm okay," Parto replied. "A little dizzy, but mostly anxious to get back to the school. When will we be able to go?"

They both sat down to the chairs offered them by Farzad, who introduced himself.

"Farzad's my communications guy," Carson said. "Yesterday, he received a communiqué from Helios. They made a change of plans." Carson closed a folder he'd been reviewing, and looked at Nouri. "They're deploying a plane to pick you and Terran up, and fly you back to Denver or whatever the hell they're calling it these days."

"A plane? I didn't think anything was flying..."

"Apparently, Helios has a few under their command."

"When does it arrive?"

Carson looked at his wristwatch. "About twenty minutes. We're going to separate into two teams: one goes to the airport, one goes to the school."

Nouri reached out and took Parto's hand. "I want Parto and Dorri to come, too. It's a big plane, yes?"

Carson leaned back, smiled briefly, and then turned serious. "Look, I'm not the one to make that decision. A new man, Peter Lucas, is the project leader. You'll have to talk with him."

"Is he here?" Nouri asked.

"He's on the plane."

Parto looked slightly embarrassed by Nouri's sudden avowal, but couldn't hold back a subtle smile. "Do you know anything about the school and the conditions there?"

"There's been no communication between us and the school." Carson picked up a communicator. "We get a maximum range of two hundred meters with these suckers, so until we get that close, we won't know anything."

"When will we leave?" Nouri asked.

"About ten minutes. Just waiting to get gassed up and final supplies onboard the MRAPs."

"MRAPs?" Nouri echoed.

"Mine-Resistant Ambush Protected vehicles," Carson replied. "Gas mileage sucks, but they get the job done."

"Do you hear that?" Carson suddenly stopped talking, and turned to Farzad. He got up from this chair and motioned to Farzad to run out and get a look. "It's gotta be them. Check it out!"

Outside, the clear and distinct sound of jet engines could be heard in the distance. It grew louder by the second. The men stopped working and watched the skies. Even Carson limped to the closest window to have a look.

Nouri and Parto remained sitting at the table.

"Nothing's landed at the airport in twelve years," Nouri whispered to Parto. "I don't know how they're going to land there."

"You really want us to come with you?" Parto asked.

Nouri nodded. "I do."

"I'm scared... I don't know anything about Denver or what we'd do there. Dorri and I... we have our family here. My father... I don't know... I need to think—"

"What do you feel? What do you think Dorri will feel?"

Parto brushed her hair back away from her eyes and looked into Nouri's face. "I don't know what I feel. All of this has happened so suddenly. I don't know what to do, Nouri. I have strong feelings for you and Terran both, and so does Dorri, but... this is... it's a step... it's a step into the unknown. I feel like I'm wading into an ocean and I can't swim. That's how it feels."

Nouri listened and nodded, but only sighed and said something so softly that it was lost.

The plane's engines continued to grow louder. Carson exclaimed it was "a huge fucking bird" and laughed with abandon. He hobbled back to the table. "Well, unless they're bringing a small battalion, I think there'd be plenty of room on that bird."

"Nouri, what do you know about the airport here?"

"It's been abandoned since Sunrot. I don't know how they'd land there."

"They must have some intelligence about it—they wouldn't fly here without a plan. That's probably one of the most important assets Helios has... they gotta have a plan."

Farzad yelled from outside through an open window: "It's circling around again."

"Is it going to the airport?" Carson shouted.

Farzad watched for a full minute with binoculars before he answered. Their basecamp afforded a good view of the city to the south. "I don't think so. It's probably trying to assess the runaways. Well, I'll be damned—they're coming our way... north, and dropping altitude. They're not going to the airport, that's in the southeast quadrant."

Carson turned to Nouri. "What the hell is up north where they could land a plane that big?"

Nouri shrugged. "The freeway—the Northern Bypass, that's all I can think of."

"Farzad, are you sure it's dropping altitude?"

"I'm sure. It's coming in for a landing and it's going to be close to our location."

"How far are we from the Northern Bypass freeway?" Carson asked, turning back to Nouri.

Nouri paused for a moment. "I... I don't know where we are..."

Carson threw down a map of Mashhad and pointed to their location. Nouri and Parto leaned forward and examined the map, and then Parto pointed. "It's here. Right there."

Carson circled the spot that Parto had pointed to. "Farzad, get in here, now!"

The sound of the jet continued to grow louder, as Farzad ran in. "What?"

Carson pointed to the map on the table. "They'll probably land it right here... it's the straightest part of the freeway, so that puts 'em four clicks away. Let's get our security team there now! Are they ready? Where's Graham? Shit! Can you get him here?"

Farzad ran out the door and yelled at the top of his lungs. "Graham!"

just as the plane went overhead. Its roar was almost deafening.

Graham sprinted into the war room in an excited mood. "That's one big bird! Everyone in this town just got a wake-up call they'll never forget. Holy shit!"

Graham nodded to Parto and Nouri, and started to apologize for his choice of words, but Carson clapped his hands to focus everyone's attention.

"Yeah, well that includes the bad guys," Carson shouted, "so we need to get over there yesterday! You and Farzad are in charge of securing that plane. No one, and I mean no one, gets within a football field of that plane. Understood?"

"Yes, Sir."

"Okay, Farzad knows the way. I'll get the boy, and return to the plane. If I'm not back by 0900 hours, send one of the MRAPs to the school. We might need help. Any questions on mission protocols?"

Both Farzad and Graham shook their heads.

"Good... Farzad, stay here for a moment. Graham I want you on the road in two minutes."

Parto waved her hand. "We need to get Dorri, too. You said 'get the boy.' We need to get Dorri, too!"

"Just a figure of speech. Of course, we'll get your daughter, too." Carson sat back down, cursing at the pain in his ankle. "I want you both to go with Farzad. It'll be safer at the plane than at the school—"

"No... no," Parto shook her head vehemently. "I have to go with you."

"We can't risk it—"

"I am coming with you. I've lived through Sunrot, I lived through more hell than most men can imagine, so don't try to protect me. *I have to be there.* I know this in my heart." She turned to Nouri, looking for support.

"I want to come as well," Nouri said, firmly. "We'll be no problem to you or your men. We promise. Besides, you might need a translator." He looked at Parto who nodded her agreement, and the two sat resolute in their chairs like royal portraits hung in a great hall.

Carson glanced at Farzad, who shrugged his shoulders. "I'll let you come under the following conditions... one, you stay in the MRAP. You don't get out for any reason." Carson held up his hand as Parto began to speak, silencing her before she could start. "And two, you don't ask any questions—you don't argue. You comply with my orders." Carson leveled his eyes, his face expressionless.

Nouri and Parto looked at one another, and then turned in unison to Carson and nodded their agreement.

CHAPTER 51

Second Arrow

The second arrow was distressing. Frank found it on the west wall overlooking the yard where Sanjur had fought Josid and won. Where Javad and Josid were buried. It was a place of withdrawal that had once been where children played. The second arrow was missing its note, too, a fact that particularly unsettled Frank. He had taken the arrow down, breaking it off in one rapid motion, careful to be quick. It was the only other arrow he had found that morning.

He had asked the guard about it, but the guard claimed that he didn't know how or when the arrow got there, or anything about an attached note. Frank had his suspicions, and had asked the guard to empty his pockets, but there had been nothing on him that looked incriminating—not even a piece of string.

Frank was on his way to Hamid's office when he thought he heard something like a shaft of sound breach the walls of the school. He began to run.

Saeed was outside Hamid's closed door, and nodded as Frank came down the hall, pointing to the sky. "Is it an airplane?" Saeed's face looked disbelieving.

"I don't know... but I found another arrow." Frank held it up for Saeed to see.

"Any note?"

"None that the guard would admit to."

Frank opened the door and closed it behind him.

Terran and Sanjur were eating some fruit and bread, while Hamid smoked a cigarette, nervously eyeing Frank's right hand that held an arrow. "You found another?"

"Yes, on the west wall, second floor."

"Do you hear that?" Hamid pointed behind him. "It's an airplane, isn't it?"

Frank stood in silence, listening. "It's a *jet* airplane, flying low, and it's coming this way."

"Why?" Hamid asked. "We don't have a working airport... it's been closed since Sunrot began. Where would they land a jet, and more importantly, *who* would land the jet?"

Frank set the arrow down on the desk, and ran his hands through his bushy hair. He hadn't shaved for weeks, his hair was nearly down to his shoulders, and he felt like a barbarian. Part of him wanted to scream at what he'd become, at what the sound of that airplane reminded him of, when he first entered the Air Force Academy; hair neatly trimmed to a one-inch buzz cut; uniforms pressed and clean; polished boots of ebony; and no facial hair whatsoever. If he could, he would cry at the contrast of fifteen years.

Now, he was a vigilante, not much better than the man he killed last night on the steps. One good thing about Sunrot: few people used mirrors any more, and he was one of them.

"They have to be ours..." Frank said. "No one else has a jet... let alone pilots, mechanics, parts, fuel... it has to be ours."

"But why?"

Frank flashed a look at Terran who was eating unperturbed by the sound. "Man, they want him bad," he whispered mostly to himself. Frank glanced back to Hamid. "I hate these fucking boards over the windows. Yesterday you mentioned there was a way to get to the roof from the inside."

Hamid nodded. "Yes, but it's dangerous."

"Show me."

"Now?"

"Now!"

Hamid stood up and carefully rubbed the tip of his cigarette on a saucer like a woodcarver on a lathe, licked his fingers and lightly squeezed them around the tip of his cigarette, and then set it carefully back inside his plastic bag. Already, Frank was at the door, instructing Saeed to keep an eye out for any trouble.

The two men then bolted up the three flights of stairs. The whole time, they heard parents and teachers shouting to the children to stay away from the windows. They knew an airplane was flying overhead and few had ever seen one, and the temptation to look was too seductive. The older kids crawled to the windows on the south side and looked up, hoping to spy the jet.

When Frank and Hamid got to the third floor, Hamid motioned to a door and unlocked it from a wad of keys he always carried with him. Frank, out of training, took his gun out as Hamid sorted through his many keys. The door started to rattle as the engine's roar became deafening. Hamid opened it, stood on a small stool, and unlatched a trapdoor on the ceiling above him, pulling down a ladder.

"Let me go first," Frank said.

Hamid stepped aside, catching his breath and watching Frank's large frame squeeze through the trap door.

"It's an attic, but how do I get to the roof?"

"Do you see the window on the far side?"

"Yes."

"Open it, and you can pull yourself up onto the roof."

"I said from the inside," Frank complained. "I'll be a target if I do that."

"I said it was dangerous…"

Frank walked gingerly on creaking floorboards that curved beneath his weight. Hamid had climbed the ladder just far enough to poke his head up like a periscope.

"You sure this floor is solid?"

"I think so."

Frank got to the window, which was covered in dirt and dust and unlatched as quietly as he could. "When's the last time you did this?"

"Never."

"Then how do you know it's dangerous?"

"I know it's dangerous to fall three stories, but I've never done it."

"Three stories… more like four." Frank muttered to himself. He looked over the edge of the window and could see the north yard. "It sounds like the plane is leaving now. Maybe it's not worth the trouble. Where's your airport?"

"It's to the southeast of town, about ten miles away."

Frank made a calculation in his head. "Probably looking at the landing strips."

"Hamid, I'm going up on the roof anyway. I should check it out since I'm here. Be back in a few minutes."

"May Allah protect you," Hamid intoned, too quietly for Frank to hear.

Frank opened the window, put his leg on the window's ledge and pulled himself through the window frame. It was a tight fit. He was well concealed by the trees. The fresh air felt good in his lungs, especially after being in a sealed attic. He gripped the roof's edge and jumped up enough to see over the ledge. The roof consisted mostly of white gravel, dead leaves, and bird droppings.

The sound of the airplane began to get louder. *They were circling.*

Frank hoisted himself up on the roof by putting his left leg on a drainpipe, and then snapping his right leg over the roof's ledge and rolling onto it. The blue sky had a rosy tint from the sunrise, and he lay on his back for a few seconds while he soaked it all in. The plane's persistent and escalating rumble got him to sit up and for the first time he caught a glimpse of that silver bird. It was beautiful. He immediately knew it was a Boeing 777-X, a quarter-billion-dollar hotrod of the skies, at least for civilians. "God, I miss those birds!" He smiled, as he watched it streak across the sky. It was coming closer at a low altitude, and Frank began to wonder what was happening. It was descending. Its landing gear was deployed, and they were nowhere near the airport if Hamid was right, and why wouldn't he be?

Then it hit him. They're going to land on a freeway.

CHAPTER 52

Chute

The Northern Bypass Freeway on the northern part of Mashhad—from either 2,500 feet altitude or a map—looks perfectly straight in several sections, until you drop down to a few hundred feet and you begin to see the organic nature of its gently winding length. It's by no means a serpent's trail, but it gently undulates in both axes. Martin Handro, the plane's pilot, was happy to see that the freeway's condition, apart from the occasional scrub brush, was intact. Large cracks made landing a real hazard. If they were large enough, cracks could destabilize the plane. Given the width of this crude, improvised runway, a few feet the wrong way, the plane could fall off the road and tip a wing into the dirt. Then it would never be able to get back on the freeway for a take off. It would become a landmark of Helios' hubris; a legacy that Martin wanted no part of.

He certainly didn't want to make Mashhad his new home.

At altitude 600 feet Martin began to wish he had started his descent earlier. A car was on the freeway—a lone car. It was driving toward the plane some two miles out. "Shit, I didn't expect to see any cars out here." Martin exclaimed to his co-pilot, Fritz Garven. "It'll just have to move."

"Where is it?"

"See it, that little silver speck coming in our direction. If he wants to play chicken with me, he'll lose." Martin smiled, as he shot a glance at Fritz. "How're the flaps?"

"Forty."

"Wind speed?"

"Negligible."

"Checklist complete?"

"Complete."

"Approaching minimums," said an automated voice.

"Continue," Martin replied.

"Five hundred," intoned the onboard computer voice.

"Smart driver, he's pulling off the road. I hope he's not high or drunk." Martin chuckled, trying to lighten the mood of the cockpit.

"One hundred," the computer reminded.

They were the equivalent altitude of a nine-story building, and now they could see the real conditions of the terrain.

"Let's keep it as gradual as we can make it. We have plenty of runway."

The computer's voice counted down the altitude. "Fifty, Thirty, Twenty, Ten."

There was a long paused after ten.

"Steady..." Martin said.

"One hundred twenty knots and holding..."

The plane touched down, and Martin held the tiller with expert hands, making the smallest corrections as the plane began to twist a little on the uneven pavement.

"Eighty knots," Fritz half-shouted.

"TRs on... auto braking on one." Both of Martin's hands tightened their grip on the tiller, as the thrust reversers turned on. "Steady..."

There was a nervous wobble for about three seconds as the plane settled into its landing like a wild horse broken of its flare.

"Release brakes," Martin said. "We'll drift to stop."

The cockpit swayed slightly as Martin tweaked the tiller, but he already felt confident that the landing was a success, and opened a com-channel to the cabin. "Glad to report we've landed safely, all systems go. Thank you for flying Helios Air. We'll be stopping shortly, and we'll deploy the emergency exits for deplaning. Stand by."

Peter and Jamere let out a whoop of joy, and high-fived each other.

"I can hardly wait for take-off," Jamere said, chuckling nervously. "I hear it's even better than the landing."

Peter laughed, unbuckled his seat belt, and shuffled to the cockpit. "Nice job!"

"Thanks," Martin nodded. "We have about ten feet on either side of our wheels before we touch dirt or sand or whatever the hell that is." He looked out the window as the plane finally drifted to a complete stop. "Take-off is going to be a real bitch."

"Why?"

"Because this isn't a runway and I can tell it's soft underneath. It wasn't built to withstand this kind of weight," Martin said, pointing down the freeway that lay ahead. "We'll go down that way, but I want to survey the road first. I'd rather have virgin road than to back-up and take-off on what we just landed on."

"You could back this thing up?"

"It's not easy, but, yes, I could do it. I just don't like the odds."

"Is it straight enough up ahead?"

"I think so, but I want to survey it before we decide."

An SUV honked its horn as it drove by slowly off to the shoulder. Several of the Iranians were half out of their windows, excitedly waving their arms. Martin waved politely in return, and then turned to Peter. "It'd be nice to have the use of their SUV to survey the road up ahead. I could do it a lot faster."

"I'll see what I can do. Jamere knows some Persian, so we'll put his resume to test."

One of Martin's staff was already deploying the chute from the front-most emergency exit. The smell of jet fuel entered the cabin, and Peter grabbed Jamere and showed him their new welcoming party. "When we get down there, I need you to ask them if we could use their SUV."

"Do we know them?"

"Not yet."

"They could be drug dealers for all we know, and want to commandeer this plane and slit our throats. What makes you think they'd let us use their SUV?"

"To them, we're rock stars," Peter quipped. "Act cocky and they'll do whatever they can to please you. Don't worry. If they have an SUV with gas in it, they must be important."

"Exactly... like drug dealers."

They walked to the open door and surveyed the barren landscape that stretched before them. The sun was just starting to cast its slanted rays across the plains, turning the golden sand into rust.

"You first," Jamere said, pointing to the chute with his arm extended like a carnival barker.

Peter took a long look at the SUV that had parked just beyond the end of the chute, and waved back at the four young men who were waving at him. They looked affable and eager to meet their new friends.

"I think they call this an encounter of the fourth kind," Jamere said in a half-whisper.

Peter smiled at the reference. *It's not too far off,* he thought as he slid down the chute like an infant down a birth canal into a new homeland ineffably foreign and strange.

He waited for his first breath. On arrival.

CHAPTER 53

Trade

Inwardness is the way he grew. Even as a young child his gaze seemed internal. He would journey to the object that interested him with such earnestness that his guardians would wonder if he would return, and how he would be different if he did. His differences were never fully understood by those who watched him. He would gladly hide in darkness for hours at a time, and no one understood his behavior, for children were supposed to be afraid of the dark. He shunned the streets where people strode in hurried postures, their eyes, drooping from the weight of their God's indifference.

Born on the first day of Sunrot. Born like a spark from a terrible fire. They looked at him as a deformed child that God had sent to taunt them. "No wonder he turns inward," some would whisper. "He's embarrassed to show himself when his father has punished us and those we love. He feels our anger though we don't bare our teeth or wag our tongues for fear of more retribution. He knows our spitefulness will find him."

They were right.

He was hunted by some as a symbol of Sunrot's inflection towards the base, the sediment, the absolute ground where hell cannot be named. Yet, there were those of great power who protected him. They knew the prophecy: a child would be born on the day of destruction that would lift humanity into the brave memory stored within each person—a human rainbow. The prophets had written that his inwardness would be the mark that would distinguish him, and once the prophecy was his cloth, the whole world would know him.

The prophets knew that this boy would be persecuted. He would be so different as to attract death even in his first year of life. Death would seek him with a relentless reach, and he would need protection from those who had lost their faith and did not want it rekindled. They wanted desolation, for that, at least, could be understood in the aftermath of Sunrot.

Hope had begun to whither across all nations just as he was struggling to speak his first word. When he was five years old, and could speak words that others could understand, they sensed he was using their language in a new way. He had found a new well from which to draw the words that would be visited by angels. His guardians listened and wondered how it was possible that they were so blessed to be in his presence. They felt the prophets within him, and they were sure of his mantle.

*   *   *   *

Saeed heard the hum of a mob before he saw them. Hamid and Frank had left to see the plane from the school's roof. Terran and Sanjur were still inside Hamid's office eating breakfast. A group of men marched down the hallway, their eyes locked on Saeed. One of the men in the front, Amir Banai, appeared to be the leader. He walked up with his gun drawn, waving it as he spoke.

"You protect him now? Don't you know what they'll do to our children if we protect him?"

"I know what they *threaten* to do, but they're empty threats," Saeed replied. He had his gun out as well, pointed to the floor, trying his best to act composed and confident.

"You would believe him?" one of the other men asked spitefully.

"He brought all of this risk to our school," said another.

"He's the one who's endangered our children and our teachers. I say… if they want him so much that they're willing to threaten the lives of our children, then we give him to his people!"

Saeed raised his hands as the men began to shout their support. "I've seen what this boy is—with my own eyes. You know me. I have children here like you, but I will not give this boy to those murderers. I'll protect him with my life, if necessary."

Amir was an older man in his late fifties, with a booming voice despite his average size. He turned to his group of eight men. "Saeed has become blinded. Perhaps this Terran Kahn practices magic— you've seen his eyes. Maybe he's turned our friend Saeed into a slave of some kind, but I will not stand and let our children become pawns of a Baluchian dispute. This is *their* problem, and we should not make it ours, especially if our children pay the costs."

The men behind him nodded and mumbled their support. Amir softened his voice, "All we want to do is to take him across the street and hand him over. That's all. No one gets hurt."

Saeed looked into Amir's eyes and each of those behind him. "How would you even begin to take Terran to them? You saw what they did when Sanjur waved a white flag this morning—"

"They heard his voice," Amir said. "They were shooting at *him*. They want their revenge."

"Revenge for what? Our children watched his fight. He fought honorably."

"It doesn't matter, we have a plan," the Amir exclaimed. "Now, move aside."

Saeed moved forward half a step. "I won't let you take him. I don't believe their threats. You should go now… before someone gets hurt." Saeed's voice cracked a bit, but his intensity was strong.

Amir leaned back slightly and squinted in quiet rage. The sound of the airplane returned. The hallway filled with silence and a distant engine's roar. "And this…" Amir said, pointing to the ceiling. "This is a coincidence? What if the Greater Nation is sending an army, and our children are caught in the crossfire and destruction? We can't take that chance, Saeed."

"I will not let you take him. When Frank gets back, we can discuss another plan. Wait here with me. He should be back soon."

"That man is not one of us. He has no children here. He's little more than a mercenary. You know that. He gets paid to deliver Terran to whoever the hell wants him. Now, step aside, Saeed."

"No!" Saeed said with quiet force.

Amir's face turned red with frustration. He looked behind him to his followers, as if he were going to address them, and then, with incredible speed, slashed the butt of his handgun across the side of Saeed's head, knocking him to the ground. Two men broke from the group and subdued Saeed, taking his gun. Saeed sat dizzily on the floor, staring up at four gun barrels all converging on his head. "You… you don't know what you're doing…"

"Watch him," the Amir said, opening the door.

Sanjur was standing in front of Terran when the men came into Hamid's office. He looked fragile and frightening at the same time. Baggy clothes hid his sharp skeleton, but his bruised face—coupled with the fact that his fight against Josid had conferred legendary stature to his six-foot, four-inch frame—made him an intimidating foe. Still, Sanjur was without any weapon, and his health wobbled like a cheap, dime-store pendulum. His options to protect Terran were limited to words and little more.

"We don't want any problems…" Sanjur said nervously, as five angry men crowded into Hamid's office.

Amir smirked, his gun pointed at Sanjur's chest. "We don't want any problems either, but you've brought them to us anyway. We'll escort you to the street. Follow us."

"You do know that they'll kill me, and probably him?"

"That's their business."

"Instead of protectors you'll become murderers. Is that what you want?" Sanjur asked.

Terran pushed himself free of Sanjur's frame and spoke. Sanjur translated. "He says he will go, but it should only be him, because he's the only one they want."

"They want you, too," Amir said, looking into Sanjur's eyes. "And if we exclude you, they may still come for you."

Terran spoke again.

"He says they'll forget about me when they have him."

The sound of the plane was more distinct in Hamid's office than in the hallway, and Amir glanced up, wondering why it was so loud. "Do you know anything about this plane?"

Sanjur shook his head.

The sound of the plane seemed to make Amir panicky. "Okay, you can stay here. We'll take the boy."

"Where he goes, I go," Sanjur said defiantly.

"You just said you wanted to stay."

Sanjur pointed to Terran. "That's what he said, I was just translating. If he goes to the street, I go to the street."

"Whatever you want," Amir said, and stood to the side, motioning with his gun to Sanjur and Terran to leave the office.

As they walked out, Terran stopped for a moment by Saeed, putting his hand on his shoulder. A trickle of blood seeped out of Saeed's temple.

"Thank you." Terran squeezed his shoulder lightly.

Saeed hung his head down in shame. He had failed to protect him.

Terran and Sanjur walked side-by-side slowly, Terran the human crutch, Sanjur the intermediary between worlds. Sanjur's body ached as he walked the hallway, surrounded by a small throng of fathers trying to act in the best interests of their children, but doubt sprang from their eyes, as they all walked the hallway to the front door.

"Pick-up the pace," Amir chortled, feeling the need to hurry in order to assuage the guilt he and his men were already feeling. A wounded hero and a small boy who limped together—guilt was difficult to sidestep. A few children had gathered to watch from the stairs, and suddenly, a girl's voice filled the hall, accompanied with the sound of running footsteps. "Terran! Terran, wait!"

It was Dorri shouting, and Terran and Sanjur stopped in their tracks, waiting for her to catch up. There was little that Amir could do. A child as innocent and beautiful as Dorri leaves wide gazes in their wake. The men made room for her as she ran to Terran, who waited with a smile.

"Are you leaving?" Dorri asked.

Terran nodded before Sanjur could translate.

"Why? Can Mandana and me come with you?"

Sanjur began the translation, and Terran replied to him, "Tell her we'll be back soon."

Sanjur wiped his eyes, and told Dorri what Terran had said.

"I want to go with you."

"You can't," Sanjur said. "We're just going for a little meeting. We'll be back as soon as we can. Besides, you have to take care of Mandana."

Dorri motioned for Sanjur to lean down, and when he strained to lower his head to her level, she whispered in his ear. "Tell him that I want to be with him, these men, they seem mean. I can protect him. I'm a little girl." As Sanjur lifted his head back up, he caught Dorri's eyes, and they twinkled in a knowing way like someone shouting from the Heavens.

Dorri looked expectantly at Terran.

"She says she wants to stay with you. She says these men are mean, and she thinks she can protect you, because she's a little girl, and these men will not harm you if she's with you." Sanjur paused, and winked. "I think she's right."

"Tell her that I trust her."

"Enough talk," Amir said. "Let's move!"

Sanjur resumed his position with his head down, but this time, whispered in Dorri's ear. "Terran says to stay with us, and that he trusts you."

Dorri barely nodded, while a smile slowly spread across her face. She turned to Amir. "I will not leave him. He's my brother."

Amir paused, his face totally blank for a moment. He then turned to one of his men. "Take her to the staircase!"

Dorri screamed in a high pitch wail that could only be compared to the sound of a dog whistle, only an octave lower and three times louder. The man, who had stepped forward to grab her, lurched back and put his arms back down awkwardly by his sides.

"I said, take her," Amir repeated.

Dorri screamed so loudly that the man reversed his course again, looking at Amir with apologetic eyes. "I'm sorry... I can't do it."

A large man who had been standing to the side with an annoyed look on his grizzled face, stepped forward. "I'll take her. I'm deaf in this ear anyway."

Sanjur stepped between Dorri and the man, locking eyes. "Lay one hand on her and—"

"And what? You'll slit my throat with your fingernail?" The man glared at Sanjur. "You can barely walk, old man, move aside."

Snickering filled the hallway, but Sanjur stood his ground, tucking Dorri behind him. As the man tried to brush Sanjur aside, Sanjur's right arm thrust with explosive speed, his two knuckles meeting the man's eyes. It was a quick jab, but the man keeled over instantly with a loud moan. Sanjur looked around to see if anyone else was bold enough to challenge him, but the men seemed intent to stand back with their guns, like magnets, pointing at him.

Amir snarled. "You said you'd go to the street with us, and now you're hiding behind a little girl. If she wants to go with you, then let her, but move, now!"

Sanjur put his arms out. "Not to be overly precise, but to say we agreed to go to the street with you is absurd. You forced us. As for hiding behind this girl, she offered to protect us. Her courage is more than any of you, because you're hiding behind your guns. I'm a wounded old man, and I will fight any of you if you care to settle this matter here and now." Sanjur paused and looked into the eyes of every man. "Do I have any takers, or will you remain behind your guns?"

A woman, dressed in an apron, came down the hallway carrying Mandana. "What are you doing?"

Amir sighed. "Go away. This isn't your concern."

"It is my concern. I work here. These are my children. What are you doing? Why is this girl screaming?"

Amir's frustration was building. "Take her and get out of here."

"I want to stay with my brother," Dorri cried.

The woman was young, perhaps twenty-five. She had a scar on her left cheek, and her hair was tied behind her head in a long ponytail. She looked half-Indian, half-Arab. Her Persian, a bit stilted, held the telltale inflections of stress. "I don't know what you intend to do with your guns pointed at an old man, a boy, and a little girl, but you should be protecting our school—"

"We are! We're returning them to the Baluchian, where they belong. She came into this on her own, please, take her."

"Does Mister Mokri know you are doing this?" the woman asked.

Amir went over to the woman who was standing ten feet away and lowered his voice to a whisper, but in the stone hallway, most of his words were audible. "Mister Mokri… he wants, above anything else, to protect his students, which is exactly what we're doing."

"Does he know?"

"We don't know where he is. We believe he's entertaining the mercenary from Kandahar. The Baluchians have communicated that they will leave us alone if we turn over this boy—the one who ran away from their tribe. If we don't, they'll storm our school, some of our children may die—perhaps some of us, too." Amir stopped for a moment, noticing more children had accumulated on the grand staircase, having finished their breakfasts.

Dorri's scream had found a curious, if not sympathetic, audience. She stepped from behind Sanjur and walked to the woman. Everyone's eye, even the man who kneeled on the floor after Sanjur's jab, watched as Dorri came up to Amir and the woman, holding out her arms. The woman handed her Mandana very carefully, and Mandana, like a boneless pile of fur slipped into Dorri's grasp.

"I was taken by those men," Dorri said. "They are mean. My brother ran from them for a reason, and he saved me from them, just as he saved this cat and gave her to me." Dorri turned directly to Amir. "You want to give my brother to these men? Why?"

Amir looked at the woman, then Dorri, the children on the stairs behind them, and finally his men. He shook his head. "Let's just go... this is too complicated."

Amir shuffled away, dejected and lost. His men looked equally lost, and like any mob that turns to reflection, they abruptly disbanded like mourners after a funeral prayer rings in silence.

CHAPTER 54

MRAP

The MRAP was close to the school. Only an occasional view of a person, looking furtively out a window, gave proof to the fact that Mashhad had not been abandoned. The streets remained desolate. Danger was in the air. Carson was in the navigator seat trying to get a channel open so he could talk with Frank. Their route was on the northern or back side of the school, and they were about three blocks away. "Frank, this is Carson, do you read me?"

Static was all he heard in response. "We need to get a little closer. We have to be within two hundred meters."

"Maybe the map's wrong," LB said. LB was driving, and in the last few minutes was literally driving two miles per hour, while Carson tried to hail Frank on the communicator. LB had worked with Carson for three years in Kandahar, mostly as a supply manager who knew how to stretch resources and inventories to the maximum. Atkins was a master at making things last, and was well known for his cunning, but he was not a warrior. In fact, he had never fired a gun in combat, preferring the desk to the grave, as he put it. Among his peers, LB was considered a bean counter, which was why Carson had nicknamed him LB, for Left Brain.

"Nouri, can you come here for a minute?" Carson said.

Nouri walked up to the front, and sat behind Carson. "Are you lost?"

"No, I'm trying to get close enough so I can get Frank on the Communicator. Do you know where we are right now?"

Nouri looked out the window and pointed. "The school's about three blocks in that direction."

"That's what I thought, but I can't get through. That's gotta be less than two hundred meters… right?"

"It's about that."

"LB, we need to get closer. I think we're just out of range. Pull up to that corner and stop… I'll try it again."

LB drove another twenty meters and slipped the MRAP into neutral.

"Frank, this is Carson, do you read me?"

In the ensuing static, a voice came through indistinctly. "Carson? This is Frank, you're breaking up. Where are you?"

"About three blocks north of the school. Copy?"

"Copy that. We've been waiting for you. Thought you might have gone to Base to shoot pool, and left me to deal with these fuckers. Over."

Carson smiled broadly. "That would be too smart. It's over my pay-grade to think like that. What's your situation? Over."

"Everyone is here. Had some issues, but all is normal again. The hostiles are trying to create a panic among the parents. Sending notes tied to arrows. One tried to kill Terran last night, but I got him first. He's sprawled on the steps, only a few feet from where they bagged Joe. You got firepower? Over."

"Copy that. Terran's okay?"

"Yes, he's here. Over."

"Frank, we have a change of plans. That plane you heard… it's ours, courtesy of Helios. It's here to take Terran and Nouri to Denver. We have a team on its way to the freeway where it landed. We'll secure it, but we need to get Terran into the MRAP—"

"And Dorri," Nouri interrupted, tapping Carson's shoulder. "Don't forget."

"We'll take Dorri, too. Over."

"Copy that," Frank said. "What about Sanjur? Over."

"He's alive?"

"Yes. Over."

"Shit… can he walk?" Carson asked.

"Yes. All things considered, he's a walking miracle. Over."

"The plane has room, but I'm not the project leader anymore. It's not my decision. Over."

"Copy that. The boy will resist. Those two are joined at the hip. Over."

"As long as he doesn't slow us up, we'll take him to the plane. He's on his own from that point. Any signs of the hostiles? Over."

"Yes, they shot at Sanjur this morning at 0620. Nothing since. Over."

"Copy that. Why did they shoot at him? Over."

"Long story. Over."

"Based on your intel, what's the best way to smuggle them out unseen?"

"Not sure. We don't know how many there are, but I'd guess eight, maybe nine, based on what Sanjur and Terran have said. We think their base of operations is on the other side of the street, one block to the east. That's according to Terran. If we staged a conflict in the front, we could smuggle out the back. There's a back door, never used, but we could open it. Over."

"Copy that. Any sense of their perimeter? Do the hostiles have guards on the north end? Over."

"Haven't seen any, but we think they're out there. How far and how many, I can't say. Over."

"Okay, I'll take a small team, and we'll come in the back. Open that door and guard it well. We'll be there in ten minutes. Over"

"Copy that. Ten minutes, back door. We'll be ready. Over."

"Frank, have Terran, Dorri, and Sanjur ready to go—packed light. Over."

"Copy that. See you soon."

"Over."

Carson pushed the boom mic to the side of his face and looked at LB. "Time to roll. You stay here with Charlie, he'll operate the CROW. Nouri and Parto will stay in the back. I'll radio you as we head into the school, if we don't see hostiles, you come in closer." Carson paused, and pointed to the map he was holding. "Maybe here. We'll exit off this street, and then take a left here. This connects up to the Northern Bypass Freeway. Okay?"

LB nodded. "Sounds good. How long do I wait?"

"Until we get back."

Carson stood up and addressed his team of three soldiers, who were sitting in foldout side chairs with M4 carbine assault rifles, Kevlar body armor, and backpacks supplied with extra clips and hand grenades. "We're going to the school now. We'll go in the back entrance on the north side. We'll take this street down one block and turn right. We'll use the alley from that point on. If you see anyone that has a gun, consider them hostile, and engage, but do everything you can to take them out silently. The moment we fire our weapons, we lose our stealth advantage. Keep an eye on windows of homes nearby. They could have snipers inside. We don't know what their perimeter is or how strong it is, so make no assumptions.

"Because of my bum leg, I'll take up the rear. Do *not* go at my pace. Move as quickly as it's safe. Frank will meet you at the back door. Keep com channels open at all times, and remember to use your name designations, so we know who's talking. Any final questions?"

The men shook their heads in unison. "No, Sir."

Carson looked to the back of the vehicle. "Charlie, any movement out there?"

"No, Sir," Charlie replied. "All's quiet."

"Remember," Carson continued, "a quick extraction of three people. If you get there, and there's no resistance, take Frank and the three packages and move back to the MRAP. Don't wait for me to get there. I want this to go as quick and quiet as possible. Good luck!"

Parto and Nouri were watching, concern and anxiety seemed to build on their faces with each passing moment, and Carson saw it. The men filed out the side door that LB opened, and then Carson limped to the door and looked at Parto. "Don't worry, we'll get her back as fast as we can."

Parto's eyes were tear-filled, her face quivered from the stress. "Please, be careful."

Carson nodded, took a quick look at LB, patted the side of the MRAP, and said, "Lock it up." He disappeared as the doors closed and a sudden, eerie hush consumed the vehicle and its four occupants.

CHAPTER 55

Prayer

Eleanor Sinclair heard the computer calling her, waking her from a deep sleep. She struggled out of bed, put on her slippers and robe, and walked the twenty feet to her desk. Her room was austere; blushing in the haze of her monitor's dancing light. The instant she moved her mouse, the computer signaled the caller, and the video pop-up appeared.

"You're an early-to-bed girl. I'm surprised to see the sandman in your eyes at one A.M."

"Ha ha," Eleanor replied, managing a sarcastic grin. "Is this karma or something?"

"Isn't everything?" Josh replied matter-of-factly.

"So, what's the news flash?"

"Our man on the ground… Farzad Ghorbani just called before they left their basecamp in Mashhad—"

"Did they get him out of the school?" Eleanor asked, leaning forward in her wooden chair.

Josh looked tired, and let out a long sigh. "Unfortunately, no. The good news is that we've got confirmation that the plane made it to Mashhad. The bad news is that Carson is injured, one fatality reported and the Baluchians have proven themselves to be good fighters. Apparently Carson and his team met considerable resistance at the school, but the school itself isn't compromised."

"And Terran?"

"He remains at the school. Farzad said they were deploying two teams—one to the plane to secure it, and one to the school to extract Terran and his teacher… um…"

"Nouri Abbasi," Eleanor reminded.

"Yes… anyway, that's the latest." Josh looked down at a folder on his desk. "What about Hamid Mokri? Have you spoken with him in the past twenty-four hours?"

"Yesterday... briefly. He said the school's surrounded—tantamount to a siege, and they were waiting for Carson to bring reinforcements and kick butt on the Baluchian assholes—my words. Hamid's fighting force is mostly parents and teachers. Not exactly what you'd wish for. He did say that Terran was there, but that they had two dead, and one of them was Terran's old teacher."

"A Baluchian?"

"Yes."

"How'd he die?"

"Shot in the back by his own, because he was trying to defect and join Terran. I don't know the details."

Eleanor paused and looked at a sheet of paper she had next to the computer. "You said that our friends in Tehran could transport jet fuel to Mashhad. Did they?"

"They said they could get the fuel there, but they didn't know where to deliver it."

"The airport—"

"The airport's condemned, Eleanor. They claim we couldn't land a jet on those runways." Josh looked down for a moment. "I kept that info from Peter."

"Why?"

"He wouldn't have gone. The whole mission would depend on a dubious overland journey through Pakistan. I didn't like those odds. I took the risk."

"And Stanton doesn't know?"

Josh shook his head.

"But you said that Farzad had told you that the plane—"

"They *heard* the plane, but he had to pack up his com unit before it landed. They believed it was going to land on a freeway."

"How much fuel would they have left?"

"They'd have to land in Mashhad," Josh said with finality.

"Shit! What can we do?"

"Absolutely nothing."

"*Shit!*" Eleanor slammed her fist down on the table. "So our best option is the convoy to Kandahar… at least Carson is equipped for that. Right?"

"I haven't lost hope in the plane. I told our contact in Tehran to bring the fuel to Mashhad anyway. It shouldn't be that hard to find a jet on a highway near Mashhad. From Farzad's observations it was going to land somewhere north of the city, and I've forwarded the general coordinates to Tehran."

"Okay… but do you think we lost the plane?"

"Peter's resourceful. If there's a way, he'll find it. A freeway could work."

"But it's a Boeing 777!" Eleanor groaned, putting her hands to her forehead, as if she had a sudden headache. "It's a big plane on a little highway. Who knows what condition their freeway system is in? If it's anything like ours, it's worthless. Shit!"

Josh shifted in his chair and leaned forward. "If we did lose the plane, I might be looking for a new job… somewhere in South America, I'd imagine." He flashed Eleanor a sheepish grin.

"They could land on a freeway, you know, it's possible." Eleanor offered, rolling the idea around in her mind. "With their terrain, freeways would be pretty straight… not a lot of billboards… sure, it's possible."

"Well, let's hope so. I don't relish the prospect of going into Trevor's office tomorrow and announcing that we lost our best plane in the Helios fleet, because of a simple miscalculation."

"You mean *omission*, don't you?" Eleanor added.

"That's between you and me. To everyone else, it's a miscalculation." Josh flashed his best boyish grin.

"If there's anything we can do on this end, let me know. Okay?"

"Thanks, Sis."

"When do you expect to hear from Farzad next?"

Josh glanced at his watch. "It's about seven thirty in the morning there now. I'm hoping that they can secure the plane, and reestablish communications within the next few hours. Jennings tells me that we have our KH-100 satellite in position at three-twenty Eastern Time, so Farzad should be able to connect then. I'll call you as soon as I know something. Okay?"

After Sunrot, only eleven satellites survived. Their fated nighttime orbits had positioned them on the far side of earth where they were spared the initial solar surges of Sunrot. Of those, twelve years later, three remained in viable condition. Just like its dwindling fleet of airplanes, Helios held onto their remaining satellites like a child coveting their favorite toy.

"Josh?"

"Yeah?"

"Do you ever pray?" Eleanor asked.

Josh swept his hands through his hair, stalling to collect his thoughts. "Not really. I did when Mom died, but that wasn't so much a prayer, as it was a pissed-off son wagging his finger at God and telling him to get lost... like he wasn't already." Josh laughed a bit. "Why?"

"Just curious," Eleanor answered. "I don't know anyone who does. I thought maybe you still did... that's all."

"I've thought about it," Josh said, "but whenever I got the urge, Dad popped into my head. He of all people had the capacity to forgive, but before he took his life, he told me that God had died. A lifetime of prayers, and five years of deafening silence. It wore on him more than he let on. He came to me one day—right after Mom died—and said that he couldn't see God anymore. Every detail he'd invented about how God looked and behaved, they had all faded. He couldn't see it anymore. He saw it as sign."

"Of what?"

"That his whole life was built on sand. Those were his words."

"You think Dad committed suicide because of *that*? I... I thought it was because of Mom."

Josh shook his head and stared soberly into the camera, a smile flickered on his face, but it was forced. "Well, Mom dying was a factor for sure, but God dying was even more of a shock to him, I think that was the main reason."

There was a long pause, as Eleanor absorbed Josh's observation. It was something they had never talked about before, and somehow it stumbled out through a computer, strangely imprinted with pixels and brazen silicon, and stood there in its heaviness, pulling her down, as if she were caught in a whirlpool.

"I miss them," Eleanor whispered, her eyes inward. "So much change. So much change."

"Resilience, my dear sister. Resilience," Josh repeated, trying his best to sound upbeat. "Do you pray?"

"I don't think about it too much," Eleanor confessed. "I'm surrounded by people who have these enormous intellects so crowded with information, I think the notion of prayer has been pushed off to the tiniest portions of their brains, and it's this part that withers. I mean they... they seem fine, they go about their jobs, but there's something hopeless about it all... like... like the mind isn't enough. I think we're missing something. A connection. Maybe it's just the feeling that someone up there cares... but it doesn't seem like anyone's up there... so why pray..."

"Are you okay, El?"

"Yeah, I know, I sound a little morose. There used to be a pill for that or a bottle, and now it's all on me." Eleanor took a deep breath and straightened her posture and closed her robe tighter around her neck. "I just want this boy to get here and begin to help us. We need his intellect. There's so much we can't repair... so much."

"It'll take time, be patient."

"Don't stay up," Eleanor mumbled.

"What?"

"For Farzad's call. Don't stay up. Get some sleep, you look tired."

"Sure. I'll let you get back to bed, too."

"Okay, love you."

"Love you, too, El. Goodnight."

"Goodnight."

The glow in the room changed as the pop-up video started to disappear, and Eleanor quickly hit the Control and F keys, which had the effect of freezing the screen. Her brother Josh was half ghost, half human, reaching for something she couldn't see. His whole body smeared in light, four inches in height. All her life, he was always above her: more mature, wiser, smarter, faster, kinder, and she—practiced in his shadows—hoped that time would transpose her into something more like him.

Envy was such a strange expression. Eleanor hid it as well as she could, but it was bright in its wretchedness. Envy was a blind beggar whose hand was out, and in that palm, money never fell. Fingers closed, the palm was hidden beneath, and a fist was formed and thrown to the sky. She had thrown her fist so many times, she wondered if her prayers were deceitful. Perhaps she cursed as she prayed, and didn't know it. Every time she would pray, her mouth would form words like *why?* And she knew the silence—taut, willful, and lifting like a hammer—mocked her.

Eleanor reached her hand to the screen, and whispered, "I don't believe you."

CHAPTER 56

Vertical Light

Dorri and Terran walked down the hall to the back door, trying to keep up with Frank and Hamid. Sanjur was assisted by Saeed who followed behind them. Dorri clung to Terran with one arm, and held the basket that contained Mandana in the other. Terran looked over his shoulders periodically to check on Sanjur. *Saeed is a much better crutch than I am,* he thought.

The back door was always locked, because the school cafeteria stored its food in the back of the school in several large, windowless storerooms. In Mashhad, food was more valuable than just about anything else. So it had to be kept in a secure location. In most countries, food was the reason that the majority of students came to school, and Helios knew that they had to make food available to their Preserves or many children would work as scavengers, panhandlers or cheap laborers, instead of getting an education.

Similar to the front door, the back door was accessible through a stone corridor with arched ceilings. It was always cool, according to Hamid, who opened the inner door to the stone corridor. It was nearly pitch dark in the passageway, but for the light behind them. Frank took out his flashlight and surveyed the remaining distance to the back door. The corridor was about forty feet long. It had a stone floor that was mostly flat. The back entrance was a large wooden door, easily ten feet tall, cut in two halves, each with its own handle. A tiny—almost imperceptible—vertical strip of light in the middle was the only hint that the door led to the outside.

It was just before eight in the morning. As they got to the door, Frank held up one of his hands and flipped his communicator to his mouth. "Say again. Over." He listened for about five seconds. "How many?"

In the stillness of the stone corridor, the voice on the other end, though faint, sounded animated, perhaps even horrified.

"Stay where you are, everyone load up, make sure all positions are covered, especially the street side. I'm on my way."

Frank turned to Hamid and handed him his flashlight. "You stay here with them. We have visitors, with guns—lots of them. It could be that the police are simply investigating... or it could be that the Baluchians bribed the police to do their bidding. I'm not sure, but I've no choice, I have to check it out. I'll radio Carson and tell him that when his men come to the back door, they knock five times. If you hear that, open the door, and from that point, they're in charge of getting these guys to safety. Got that?"

Hamid nodded his head slowly, his face wearing a shocked expression. "The police... wouldn't be here... unless they were being paid... handsomely." His words felt wounded in the manner he spoke them—slow, stilted. Hamid stared at him, knowing Frank's importance to all of them, and solemnly said, "Be careful."

Frank nodded and jogged off, nodding at each of the others as he passed. "Good luck."

The mood suddenly shifted. Sanjur started to walk to the door, but Saeed stayed.

"I need to go with Frank. I'm sorry." With that, Saeed turned and ran down the long corridor.

Hamid turned to face those that remained. "I really don't like how this is going."

Terran turned to Sanjur with anticipative eyes, and Sanjur translated all that he had heard the past two minutes. Terran sat down against the corridor's wall, and Dorri and Sanjur followed suit. Hamid paced nervously near the door, waiting for the five knocks, hoping they would be distinct. A minute passed. The thin strip of light began to undulate. Hamid held his fingers to his lips and turned to Sanjur and the children. He waited.

A subtle tug at the door alarmed him, and he stepped back, his arms waving behind him to Sanjur, as if saying "get Terran and Dorri out of here," but the three of them fixated on the door's thin strip of light, and the shadows that danced in its midst.

Then some voices, muffled, indistinct. Urgency in their tone. It felt like animals were trying to claw inside, but there were no knocks. Certainly nothing that could be interpreted as five knocks. Hamid stepped back again, and motioned to Sanjur, Terran, and Dorri to follow him down the corridor. "Let's go back to the second door. I don't think these are our rescuers. They were supposed to knock five times."

The four of them walked backwards cautiously watching the back door.

"How thick is it?" Sanjur whispered.

"What?"

"The door, how thick is it?"

Hamid tilted his head a bit, and spread his fingers apart about four inches.

Sanjur nodded. "Good. Wait here."

Sanjur stepped gingerly, favoring his right leg, but made his way to the back door, staying on the left side. He could hear some kind of jangling sound, as if someone on the other side were trying to pick the lock. Suddenly, he bellowed into his cupped hands, as loudly as he could, "We have guns pointed at you. Identify yourselves, or we will shoot you down like animals!"

The motion ceased, the sound stopped, and there was a long pause that filled the air, as if all sound and motion had collapsed inward. Into a void.

"We are the Police." The voice was modest in its volume and clearly not Baluchian, because it spoke perfect Persian.

"And why are the Police trying to break into the Helios Preserve?" Sanjur demanded, knowing that his choice of words would aggravate them.

Another equally long pause.

"We are investigating the death of the man who is on your front steps. Please open this door."

"Prove to us that you're the Police, and we may do that," Sanjur shouted, and then added, "But our fingers are impatient!"

Sanjur turned around to his team, and flashed a quick smile.

There was more movement in the vertical light beam, and then silence. The silver beam that had pulsed between the two halves of the door was now static.

"They're gone," Sanjur whispered.

Hamid stepped forward tentatively. "The problem is that our rescue team won't be able to come in as long as the Police are here. I need to go to the front door and see what's happening. If you hear five knocks while I'm gone, here's the key." Hamid took off a key from a ring of keys he had been holding, and handed it to Sanjur.

"We'll stay here. Good luck, Hamid."

"That was brave," Hamid said to Sanjur. "Thanks."

Sanjur bowed slightly. "Sometimes I do things that even I can't understand. That was one of them."

Hamid smiled, and then walked briskly, by his standards, to the front door.

CHAPTER 57

Conversation

When Frank looked out the window, he was surprised at what he saw. Twelve men, all armed with guns, dressed in civilian clothes were rummaging around the dead Baluchian warrior that sprawled across the bottom steps of the school's entrance. They would glance in the direction of the school, but seemed afraid to look too long. Something wasn't right. Why would the Police suddenly take an interest in the school and a dead Baluchian?

"Are there any Baluchians with them?" Frank asked Saeed.

"I don't think so; they don't like to wear civilian clothes. These men are bullies… they use what little power they have as Policemen, to get money from the people. Saeed suddenly pointed. "I know that man. He's been to the school before, trying to get payments to protect us." Saeed shook his head. "These are not good men."

There was a loud knock on the door, and a voice shouted. "This is the Police, open your doors, or we will be forced to break them down. We will not wait forever!"

Frank turned to Saeed. "Do you see any alternative to talking with these men?"

"They heard the plane… they smell money. Do you have money?"

Frank shook his head. "Probably not enough."

"Then I think you should talk with them and see what they want. They have eyes and ears all over town. I know one thing: they don't care about the dead Baluchian. That's not why they're here."

Frank stood up and stayed out of sight. One of the guards behind him caught his attention. "You, you're supposed to be on the back wall. Why're you here?"

"I was told to come to the front," he blurted out.

"Return to your station, and keep an eye out." Frank grabbed his transmitter and positioned it over his mouth and turned it on. "Carson, are you there? Over."

"I'm here. My men are watching from a safe distance. We see you have company. What's your status? Over."

"Our visitors claim to be Police. One of the guards here believes they're basically planning a shake-down. They heard the plane, probably figure something important is going on here, and they want some money to escort us to the plane, or something like that." Frank moved further back into the interior of the room and lowered his voice. "I assume we don't have any money with us, do we? Over."

"Gold? Hell no, not that I'd give them!"

"Copy that." Frank said. "I need to talk with them and see what they want… otherwise they're threatening to break down the door. Over."

"Do what you have to do," Carson said. "We'll stay back, until we hear gunfire, or you call us out. Over."

"Frank, this is Winston. Over."

"Hey, Winston. What's up? Over."

"I saw a small group of men huddled around the back door. It looked like they were trying to get in. Over."

"Shit. Are they still there?" Frank asked, motioning to Saeed.

"No, about a minute ago they walked away toward the front. We assume they're not ours. Over."

"Anyone outside is not one of ours. Over."

"Copy that. Just wanted to check. Over."

"Stay back until I get a chance to talk with these supposed Police, and see what they want. I'll leave my transmitter on so you can hear the conversation. Feel free to advise if you want. Over."

"This is Carson, Frank. Make sure you have sufficient firepower when you talk with these guys. We'll patrol the back and sides so you can focus your men up front. Over."

"Copy that. Thanks. Stand by."

Frank tapped his communicator to idle. "Saeed, I need you to go check on Terran and Sanjur. Some of these guys were prowling around the back entrance. Make sure they're okay."

Saeed nodded and ran down the hallway. He hadn't gotten far when he passed Hamid. "Where are they?"

"Sanjur's with them. He has the key to the back door. Please stay with them, Saeed. Okay?"

"I will."

"Where's Frank?"

"He's going to the front entrance to talk with the Police, and find out what they want."

"They tried to break into the back. Sanjur scared them off. Where's Carson?"

"In the back somewhere. Just waiting."

"Okay," Hamid said. "Stay safe."

"You, too," Saeed said, and then ran off.

Hamid made a beeline to the front door. But on his way, by the main stairs, he whispered to several of the teachers to take the kids back to their dorms, away from windows, and pull all the curtains. They were to read and stay quiet. No one steps on the first or second floors. The teachers nodded and immediately rolled into action.

As Hamid got to the front door, he saw Frank was conferring with five guards. He looked like a quarterback in a huddle.

Frank looked at him as he walked up. "Glad you're here. The Police insist on talking." Frank used air quotes when he said the word, *Police*. "Because you're the Director, you should be the one to let them know what our situation is. I want to be more focused on watching their body language and what they seem to be interested in. Beside, you're more fluent in Persian than I am."

Hamid nodded. "So what's the plan?"

"I'll invite the Police in, but I'm going to limit them to three. We'll talk right here. We'll have these five to protect us, plus I'll be watching for anything that looks suspicious. I'll keep my transmitter on, and I'll jump into the conversation if I feel I have anything to add. You ready?"

Hamid nodded nervously.

Frank leaned in towards Hamid and whispered. "How much money do you have on the premises?"

Hamid whispered in Frank's ear. "There's about six-hundred Mesghals in our safe."

Frank nodded, and readied his weapon. All the guards brought their weapons up, too.

Frank yelled through the door. Unlike the back door, the front door was battered with gunfire, its wood chipped and broken, but none of the bullets had broken through its four-inch thickness. "I'll open this door, but only three of you can come in. Understood?"

"I'm agreeable to that. We just want to talk."

Frank unlocked the door and opened it slowly. There were seven or eight men waiting on the steps. "Three of you can come in, no more," Frank said.

The leader, the one who had been shouting, stepped forward. "I am Namvar Akhtar, and you are?"

"You can call me Lieutenant Wolfe. This is the Preserves' Director, Mister Mokri. Come inside."

Frank backed up with Hamid. Namvar and two of his men followed them into the stone vestibule. Frank kicked the door closed and locked the latch with his elbow, keeping his gun pointed menacingly at the visitors.

"In our country," Namvar said, "it is polite to put your guns down when you invite guests inside, especially when those guests are Police." Namvar frowned in a subtle protestation.

Frank and his guards remained unmoved by Namvar's comment.

"There is a dead man on your steps," Namvar continued. "A Baluchian, I believe. Can you tell me what the circumstances were that led to his death?"

Hamid cleared his throat. "Yes, he attacked one of our students with a knife, and we had no choice but to shoot him. We would have given him a proper burial, but his friends remain somewhere out there, and as you can see by the condition of our door, they seem to have an endless supply of bullets. They've killed two others, both of whom we've buried."

"And why are the Baluchians so interested in this school and its students?"

Hamid stole a quick glance at Frank. "One of their children walked across the desert to come to our school and learn. Intellectually, this student is very gifted, and wants to learn. The Baluchians have tried to kidnap him and return him to his village, against his will."

Namvar smiled. "Mister Mokri, isn't it an odd twist of logic to say they are kidnapping this boy, when the boy is one of their own?"

"I can understand how you could see it that way, but the boy has his own will, and he desires to learn."

Namvar crossed his arms over his chest. "Isn't it possible that the best solution to this problem is the simplest—to give the boy back to his people? I'm sure they would leave our city, and everyone can get on with their lives as before. Isn't that a logical solution?"

"Except for one fact," Frank said. "The boy doesn't want to go back."

"And in your country, Lieutenant Wolfe... do children always get their way?"

Frank stared at Namvar for a few seconds. "They do when they're as smart as he is."

"And what is your role? You're obviously from Helios. Why does Helios send military personnel to guard this school?"

Carson's voice, compressed into digital frequencies, burst into Frank's earpiece. "Tell him it's none of his goddamn business!"

Frank paused to hear Carson's input. "It's the business of Helios to protect its schools and its students no matter where that school is."

"Do the Baluchians have more than one student here?"

Hamid shook his head. "No..."

Namvar put his hands behind his back, and a puzzled expression crossed his face. "This boy must be worth his weight in gold, if Helios sends a military team to escort him out of our country. Isn't that really the definition of kidnapping?"

Carson again burst into Frank's earpiece. "Don't answer that!"

Hamid began to answer, but Frank cut him off. "What do you want?"

"You said the Baluchians remain outside with guns. You obviously want to take this boy to the airplane you landed north of our city. We could provide you with safe passage, if Helios is willing to compensate us for the risks we would be taking."

"And how much would that compensation be?" Frank asked.

Namvar looked up to the arched stone ceiling for a few moments, as if making a spontaneous calculation. "The Baluchians are very cunning. They have, as you said, plenty of bullets. My men's lives will be at risk even after you fly away never to be seen again. I think five thousand mesghals would be sufficient compensation."

Hamid glanced at Frank, whose head was shaking. "In my country, we call that a nonstarter." As he spoke he could hear expletives from Carson in his earpiece, a few of which—under different circumstances— would have made Frank chuckle, but he was too angry. Five thousand mesghals was nearly double what their entire operational budget was.

"If you have a different number in mind, I'm willing to listen," Namvar said calmly, as if he negotiated these kinds of services several times a day.

Carson's voice was intense in Frank's earpiece. "Tell him five hundred... no more."

"Our number is five hundred and no higher."

"Is your proposed number a result of your current holdings, or is that all this boy is worth to Helios?"

"What difference does it make?" Frank asked. "It's all we've got."

"The difference is that if Helios wants this boy, five thousand mesghals is nothing. I would extend credit to Helios for forty-five hundred mesghals for a reasonable time." Namvar looked around the hallway, his eyes exploring the interior of the vestibule. "If your payment isn't made in the agreed time, it's quite possible that this school could fall under harm's way... a fire perhaps..."

Namvar's henchmen smiled unrestrained, while Hamid flinched, and turned to Frank with an open mouth. He was speechless.

"Give me a minute." Frank held up one finger to Namvar, who nodded, and then he walked down the corridor and turned left at the intersecting hallway. "Carson, this is Frank. Over."

"I heard."

"Here's the deal," Frank said, "these guys look like professional extortionists. If they've been talking with Moshad, they already have a deal. Probably why they're here. I think he's just trying to negotiate a better arrangement, because he heard the damn airplane, and that shouts how important this whole operation is to Helios. The question is, would Helios pay both of us? Would they even believe us? Over."

"You hit the nail on the head, man. We can't negotiate that kind of money without talking to Helios, and the only way I can do that is to go back to the plane and hope Farzad can find a link-up. Under these conditions, I'm not going to leave. I think we can take these assholes and shoot our way out. I prefer those odds. Men, what do you say? Over."

"This is Omar speaking. I'm in. These guys look poorly armed. They're packing basic handguns, and who knows if they even have bullets. We're armed with superior weapons and training. We can take them... I sure don't wanna give 'em any of my money. Over."

One by one, the men voted and it was unanimous. They would fight.

Finally, it was Frank's turn. "I'm in, too, but what do I tell him, Carson? Over."

"Tell him we'll do four thousand max. Not one mesghal more. We'll need twenty minutes to get the five hundred to him, and he should come back. That should buy us enough time. Over."

"What if he wants to keep negotiating? Over."

"Go as high as forty five hundred, but resist. Make it seem real... like it's your own money. Over."

"Copy that. What about his threat to the school?"

"He's bullshitting. If we get Terran to Helios, and he's what they thought he was, Helios will pay whatever they need to hunt these bastards down and install a new Police force, if necessary. Iran's part of the Great Nation. There's no place they can hide unless they want to hang with the Baluchians in the deep desert. We're just gonna let him think we're going to play ball with him. Over."

Frank walked in a haze, back down the stone corridor that in many ways had become his new home the past twenty-four hours. Namvar and his men were debating the weather as he approached.

"I can do four thousand," Frank said, as he came to a stop ten feet away, his gun, for the first time, pointed to the ground.

Namvar looked down, disappointment written on his face. "It took you that long to decide on an insult? I'm disappointed." He wagged his finger back and forth while he talked. "I'm asking my men to put their lives at risk... not just for today, but tomorrow, a month from now, even a year from now. The Baluchians are ruthless hunters with long memories. Without our help, I doubt very much that you will ever make it to your plane. *You need us.*" Namvar paused, and looked at his men. "I have to pay these men. I have fifteen here. It's very dangerous work. I don't know... maybe I'd go as low as fourth-eight hundred..."

This time it was Frank's turn to shake his head and look disappointed. "Can't do it. Forty three hundred, and that's final. Give me twenty minutes and I'll have the five hundred. The balance we'll get to you within a week. Do we have a deal?"

"Do you have the five hundred here?"

"Come back in twenty minutes, and I'll have that ready."

"You understand the consequences, if you don't pay the balance?"

Frank nodded. "You'll get your money."

"I have one condition," Namvar said. "If I accept your proposal, I will need to speak with the boy."

"Why?" Frank asked.

"It is my condition. I want to meet this boy who is worth so much to Helios that they would dispatch an airplane to take him from my country. I want to be able to tell my men that this boy exists, and that they're not smuggling some contraband."

"No!" Carson said emphatically. "Don't let him!"

"No," Frank said.

"Then your deal is unacceptable, and I would wish you a safe journey to the airport, but I now know better." Namvar turned towards the front door, put his hands behind his back and sighed impatiently for the door to be opened. His men joined him.

Frank glanced at Hamid who looked completely unnerved. In a strange way, Frank was alone. He heard Carson telling him what to do next, but he couldn't really understand the ranting voice. Somewhere in his head, he heard another voice. Frank believed it was his own, but he wasn't sure. He clicked his earpiece off. "What are your conditions to meet this boy?"

Namvar continued facing the front door. "He only speaks Baluchian, I presume."

"Yes."

"Then I need a translator, and ten minutes alone with the boy. No one else. No weapons. Just a conversation. Those are my only conditions."

"When?"

"Now."

"Forty-three hundred and a ten-minute conversation. That's the deal?" Frank asked.

Namvar turned slowly towards Frank as he spoke. "And five hundred mesghals now, and thirty-eight hundred within one week... and one final detail, *collateral*."

"Collateral?"

"I need something to hold until I get the balance," Namvar said. "Your Humvee, for example."

Frank was glad he had turned off his transmitter. He could easily imagine Carson's response, but Frank was too deep to back out now. The deception was already complex, what was one more lie?

"It's pretty shot-up..."

"We know it still runs. It will do."

"Okay," Frank said, extending his arm. The two men shook.

Frank stole a quick glance at Hamid, who looked back at him as though shock had taken over his body and he was merely an empty shell.

"Bring Terran and Sanjur to the courtyard." Frank waited for some kind of confirmation from Hamid, but he simply stared. "Hamid, do you understand?"

"To the courtyard?" Hamid looked perplexed.

"Lots of windows. I'll be watching their conversation—"

"I said just the boy, his translator and me."

"I won't be listening, just watching. His translator is old, badly injured and can barely walk. I want to have an eye on you and the boy at all times."

"Lieutenant Wolfe, you think I want to harm this boy? Nothing could be further from the truth—"

"That may be. I'm here to safeguard the boy. I'm doing my job."

Namvar scratched his nose and smiled. "Okay... I'll accept this condition."

Frank, for the first time in fifteen minutes, relaxed a tiny bit, yet he knew that eventually he'd have to turn on his tactical headset, and explain what he'd done. That was not a conversation he was looking forward to having with his Captain.

CHAPTER 58

Black Hole

The courtyard was quiet. It was small, about the size of a classroom, used mostly by the teachers as an outdoor eating place. There certainly wasn't any privacy in the courtyard, but its tranquility and sense of intimacy made up for the fact that it felt a little like being in a fishbowl. Hamid had arranged to have Sanjur and Terran brought to the courtyard, while Frank escorted Namvar.

Just outside the courtyard, in the teacher's lounge, Frank tapped Namvar on his shoulder. "I need you to lean against that door and spread your legs."

"You're going to pat me down?" Namvar asked indignantly.

Frank's face was the definition of implacable, and as he stared into Namvar's eyes, Namvar slowly turned in resignation, and placed his arms against the door's aluminum frame. Through the glass door Namvar could see a tall, brittle-looking man whose face was badly bruised, and a young boy who looked about nine years old. They were both sitting quietly in the courtyard, as if they were waiting for a train.

Frank held up a pocketknife. "I'll hold onto this until you're done."

Namvar nodded absentmindedly, his attention was already riveted on Terran. *He's really the Mahdi? So young. So small.*

"I'm sorry, what was your surname again?" Frank asked, as he opened the door into the courtyard.

"Akhtar."

"Okay, I'll make introductions, and then let you have your talk."

Frank brought Namvar over to the table where Sanjur and Terran sat. "Sanjur, this is Mister Akhtar, the Chief of Police in Mashhad. He's asked to meet Terran in order to verify that he's the student we're escorting to the plane. He's requested a ten-minute conversation. Any questions?"

Sanjur shook his head, trying to look comfortable, but it was clear that he wasn't. Like any self-respecting interloper of a post-Sunrot society, Sanjur had a deep fear of the Police, especially if they were at the top of the food chain.

"I'll be watching from there." Frank pointed to the teacher's lounge. He checked his watch, nodding to Terran who sat on a concrete bench with curious eyes. Sanjur translated what Frank had just said, and Terran nodded.

"Okay, you have ten minutes," Frank said.

Namvar was instantly caught up in the eyes of Terran. He heard the door close, and not wanting to waste any time, turned to Sanjur. "Ask him if he knows who I am?"

Sanjur smiled politely. "I already told him."

"No, I mean ask him if he knows who I am beneath this flesh."

Puzzled, Sanjur went ahead and asked. Terran nodded at the question and responded in a burst of Baluchian. Namvar had one confirmation: Terran was Baluchian.

Sanjur cleared his throat. "He says that you're a collection of atoms and space... like a galaxy. Inside this galaxy, at its very center, is a black hole, and in this black hole is hidden your soul. It hides, because you have hidden it in shame."

Namvar swallowed hard, his eyes watering. *This is not a boy.* "Ask him who I was?"

Terran nodded and smiled after Sanjur's translation. "You were a Mawlawi—a scholar. You were a bright teacher, but you lost your faith, as so many have in these times. You taught at a madrassa. You had a very special understanding of the Quran. You were a teacher of soul."

As Sanjur relayed Terran's words, he tried his best not to stare. The man who stood before him could not be the same man that Terran described, and yet this man began to tremble almost imperceptibly, as one does when they try to hold back a flood of emotion.

Namvar asked Sanjur another question. This time, his voice, quivering with an edge of anxiety, seemed even more intense.

Sanjur turned to Terran. "He wants to know why he is so lost."

"Tell him that his heart feels the neglect that his soul feels. It's covered in shame, and it no longer guides him. He seeks conquest and control, and because he once knew about the worlds of soul, he feels lost.

Before Sunrot, this man was a servant of all. After Sunrot, he became a servant of himself. He sees no hope, and in this hopelessness, he's become lost in his own interests."

Sanjur translated to Namvar, who then sat down, and remained quiet for a few seconds, collecting his thoughts. Heaviness like a deep river flowed over him. "Ask him what he thinks I should do next."

Terran listened to Sanjur's translation and responded calmly. "Tell him that his view of the world has narrowed to what can only be touched. What is inside him will come out again. Rumi said the cure for pain is in the pain. He must clear his heart. That is all he needs to do."

After Sanjur translated, Namvar looked into Terran's eyes and spoke one word, "How?"

Terran spoke with a young voice, but his words writhed up from some depth that few men could find. "The heart is where your experiences can be spiritualized. Where what has caused pain can be seen as the universe nurturing you, preparing you for something yet to come."

Terran paused for a moment and softly pounded his chest five times with his right hand. "Look here, breathe here, feel here, see here, bring your past to this place and burn it. Light it on fire and it will light your way."

Namvar listened as Sanjur translated. He closed his eyes, and tears sped down his cheeks on both sides of his face. "Can you *really* see me? I'm so ugly. I'm a murderer. I'm a cheat. I'm a liar. I'm selfish. I have no map or compass. I have not prayed in ten years. *Ten Years!* I am… worthless. Every day I imagine my destruction. I see it, and I know it's well deserved, and if I didn't fear the judgment that awaits me so much, I would've killed myself a thousand times these past twelve years."

Namvar paused, as he struggled to keep his composure. Sanjur translated. When he finished, Terran remained quiet, waiting.

"You're the Mahdi," Namvar continued. "You're the chosen one who will unite our world. I'm… I'm like a locust who feeds on our world. Please, help me to change. All of those sins, those weaknesses… they are not me. They are not me. I swear to you, on the heart of Allah, they're not me!"

Terran stood to his feet and walked to Namvar even before Sanjur finished his translation. Namvar looked up as he heard the footsteps, apprehensive at the power of this boy who approached him. *Perhaps, he will judge me.*

Terran took Namvar's hand in his. Terran's voice was barely a whisper. "Your self-judgment is with words and thoughts that live in the past, but the clear heart is not of these things. It's of love. Love is the action of appreciation, humility, forgiveness, understanding, courage, and compassion *in the present.*"

Terran paused to allow Sanjur to translate. When he finished, Terran continued. "You rise and fall, you breathe in and breathe out, you gather and release. You are bad and you are good. You are all of these things, but there is a part of you that remains pure and faithful to your creator, and that part of you is what you've wandered away from."

Terran glanced at Sanjur, signaling him to translate. When he finished, Terran placed his right palm on Namvar's forehead. "Forgive yourself for wandering. Come home. Your heart is clear at some level. You must find this level. Seek it. And when you find it, you will see that heaven is open everywhere and to everyone. It has no gates or borders. No one to protect it. It only waits for *you* to claim it as your own."

Namvar closed his eyes when Terran placed his hand on his head. He was well aware that Sanjur and Frank watched him. He knew that he looked weak. But this was the Mahdi; a legendary being that touched him through the hand of a small boy. There was no way to shun his nearness. There was nowhere to hide from his sight. He could feel his faith returning. If only he could stay with this boy, everything would be okay. Everything he had done that was bad would be forgiven.

Sometimes, in the presence of one we believe to be divine, they *become* divine, and in their divinity we are healed. Life enlarges to such an extent that we transform in that moment. Our past is circled in red and a diagonal line is slashed through it, and we step out of that circle and it simply vanishes. All of the fears that forced our compliance have fallen into a wondrous thing: the memory of soul.

CHAPTER 59

Defection

A distant look can mean different things. In some people, it can mean that they're self-absorbed, drilled into the tight, inner windings of their world. In others, it can mean that they're revising their past with the grace of a new memory. In Namvar's case, he was deciding his future. His conversation with Terran had changed him. Something irrevocable had happened, but the crossroads he stood upon were dangerous. He had to sort them out before he returned to his men.

When Frank had interrupted their conversation after ten minutes, Namvar asked for one more talk—this time, with Frank. The four sat in the courtyard. Frank was curious about what had happened. He has seen Namvar weep, and it looked genuine. He knew a change had occurred. What that change was, however, remained a mystery.

"I need to tell you something…" Namvar said slowly. "I met with the Baluchian leader called Moshad before I came here. I was hired to take Terran from this school and return him to Moshad."

At the admission, Frank's right hand clutched his gun a little tighter. The silence in the courtyard was immense.

Sanjur began to speak, but Namvar held up his hand. "Please, no translations. Let me speak and get it all out before I change my mind."

Sanjur nodded in confusion.

"I know this boy seems like a boy, but he's not," Namvar began. "There's a presence inside him, one that I've witnessed, and it confirms his standing as the Mahdi. This is what Moshad told me, and I now know that it's true. The Mahdi is not someone to thwart. He must be supported. What he wants, I want.

"The problem is that I understand what he is, but none of my men will believe me, and we have eight Baluchians who will fight to their death to prevent him from getting on that plane."

"Are you saying you want to help us?" Frank asked.

"Yes, but I'm one man. I can't control my men... unless I give them money."

Sanjur leaned forward a little. "It'd be better if you didn't say that you're with us. If you go back to your men and Moshad, let them believe you're even more convinced, having met Terran, that he needs to be returned to them. Gain their trust."

Sanjur turned to Frank. "Do we have money?"

Frank nodded. "A little. We'll give you the five hundred mesghals as promised. You take it with you, and tell Moshad that we hired you to escort us to the plane. Tell him we'll go out the west yard, and that your men should be focused there. We'll go out the east side, and no one has to know that you helped us."

Terran tapped Sanjur on his forearm, and Sanjur updated him on the conversation. Terran listened intently, and then said, "They will know that he deceived them if we leave in the opposite direction that he said we would go. Moshad will kill him."

"Are you sure?" Sanjur asked.

Terran nodded. "Tell him to speak only with his own men—not Moshad." Terran pointed to Namvar. "He will give the money to his men and he will stay with us. His men will protect the school from Moshad. We'll go out the back. Whatever they require to protect the school, we must pay it. That's all he needs to learn from his men. Find a number that will guarantee their loyalty and protection, and then agree to pay it. Helios will approve those terms and fight for us."

When Sanjur finished his translation there was a long silence. Frank rubbed his neck. "I don't know... if your men get greedy—"

Namvar looked hopeful for the first time. "I can deal with my men. It's a good plan."

"Okay," Frank said. "Let me check in with my captain and make sure he's onboard. Give me a second."

Frank walked out of the courtyard and into the teacher's lounge to speak privately with Carson. He swung his transmitter over his mouth, and was just about to turn it on, when suddenly two gunshots erupted in rapid succession, somewhere within the school. He bolted to the door, ran down the hallway, and could hear men shouting by the front entrance. The smell of gunpowder hung in the air as he got closer to the front door. A body was slumped on the ground. It was one of Namvar's men. The other one was hunched over the body, leering at the guards whose guns were all pointed at him.

"What happened?" Frank yelled as he ran up.

Saeed pointed at the dead man with his rifle. "He was boasting that if they weren't paid... our children... that... that they would be killed if we didn't pay. We started to argue and then... then one of us accidentally pulled the trigger. It was an accident..."

"Who pulled the trigger?"

Before Saeed could answer, a loud pounding on the door interrupted him. "Namvar, what just happened in there? Is everyone okay?"

Frank ran his hand through his hair, not sure how to respond. Namvar's associate looked at Frank. "I can tell him."

Frank nodded, but pointed his gun at him.

"Parshan, this is Raji. We had an accident... Shamil's dead." Raji yelled through the door, but kept his eyes on the guns that were pointed at him. He stood slowly to his feet.

"I heard two shots," Parshan shouted through the door. "How's that an accident?"

"We were just arguing... one of their guards accidentally fired his rifle."

"Where's Namvar?"

Raji looked at Frank, and put his arms out, palms up.

Frank whispered. "Tell him that Namvar will be here soon. That he was talking with the boy."

Raji nervously yelled to his comrade on the other side of the thick, wooden door. "He went to speak with the boy, he'll be back soon."

As if on cue, Namvar walked briskly down the hallway. "I'm here. What happened?"

Raji was a slender man, with the wiry build of a long-distance runner. "Shamil was arguing, and..." Raji pointed to one of the guards. "...and his gun fired. He said it was an accident. But Shamil's dead..." Raji spoke, as if he was in shock, and couldn't believe it had happened.

"This will complicate things." Namvar said, glancing in Frank's direction.

Again a pounding on the door, and several of the guards flinched. "I want to speak with Namvar, now!" Parshan demanded.

"I'm here," Namvar shouted. "I'm here... give us a second." Namvar glanced at Frank again, who stepped over the body of Shamil, in order to open the door. As soon as it cracked open, three men pushed against it, with guns poised to shoot. "Put your guns down, we don't need any more accidents."

The men followed Namvar's orders.

Frank looked at his own men and nodded, as if the instructions were applicable to them as well, and each of them did the same.

"Pick him up and take him outside," Namvar said. "Parshan, stay with me, so we can talk. The rest of you wait outside."

Parshan nodded, while two others picked up Shamil's body and carried it out the door. Frank closed the door and locked it.

Namvar turned to Frank. "

"Is there a room we could sit and talk?"

Hamid cleared his throat. "Yes, my office... follow me."

Frank pointed to Parshan, and shook his head. "No guns. Leave it there. Saeed, pat him down."

Parshan glanced at Namvar, who nodded.

When the four men arrived at Hamid's office, Hamid went straight for his half used cigarette. "I'm sorry, but I have to smoke this... I'd share, but I'm afraid I have a very limited supply."

Namvar put his hand up and looked down. "It's fine."

"Please, sit," Hamid said, as he lit his cigarette.

"The death of one of my men changes the price," Namvar said.

Frank sighed. "It was an accident and nothing more. These men are teachers and parents... they don't know how to fire a semiautomatic. You can't hold us responsible for that."

"Regardless of the reason, I have to support Shamil's family. The new price is sixty-five hundred mesghals. So you pay five hundred now, six thousand within a week. All of the other terms stand—including the collateral."

Frank sighed and reluctantly nodded. He understood that Namvar was acting. Parshan was his messenger and he had brought him along so he would tell his men that Namvar had negotiated an even better deal. It would add to his credibility.

"Do you have the money?" Namvar asked.

Hamid put his cigarette down for a moment. "Yes, the five hundred… we have that. I just need to retrieve it from the safe."

"Good, then perhaps you could do that now, and I could speak privately with Parshan."

Hamid glanced at Frank who was nodding. "Okay…"

After Frank and Hamid left to get the payment, Namvar shifted his chair to face Parshan. "I'll stay here with the boy and make sure he gets on the plane safely. You take the money. I want you to tell the men that our plans have changed. We now work for Helios, not the Baluchians—"

"Why not both, Namvar? We can take both monies… I know we can do it."

"I'm convinced that Helios will pay the balance, more than I'm convinced the Baluchians will. We have a much safer deal with Helios, and three times the money. I'd rather be aligned to them, anyway." He paused, and lowered his voice. "I need you to meet with Moshad and tell him that our deal is off."

"He'll try to kill me."

"I know. Take your men with you. He won't do anything in close quarters, if you have armed men with you."

"But as soon as we leave, they'll open fire on us."

"Then fight. Be prepared."

"He'll want his money back."

"Give it to him."

Parshan narrowed his eyes, as he mentally rehearsed what he was being asked to do. "What's in it for me?"

"You can have an extra share."

Parshan slowly nodded. "Okay…"

"There's one problem," Namvar said. "I sent Kazem and four other men to sabotage the plane. I need you to send Raji to the plane. He can use the jeep—do it before you go to Moshad. Raji needs to stop them.

This is the number one priority. Understood?"

"So, we're really trying to help them take this boy from here?" Parshan asked.

"Yes, and if we don't save that plane, Helios will have no reason to pay us." Namvar said emphatically.

A light knock on the door and Hamid and Frank entered. Hamid carried a small cloth bag that looked heavy, and handed it to Namvar, who then gave it to Parshan.

"Five hundred," Hamid declared, sucking the last residues from his dwindling cigarette.

"Are the plans clear?" Frank asked.

"My men will tell Moshad our deal is off. I have to send one of my men to the plane—"

"Why?" Frank interrupted.

"Earlier this morning I had sent a small team to try and prevent the plane from being able to take off." Namvar averted the glare from Frank.

"When did your men leave for the plane?"

"About seven-thirty."

"Shit."

"You must have some protection there, right?"

"Yes, but I don't know if they'll get there before your men… okay, look, you do what you can to stop your men. We have our own team out back who will get us to the plane. I want your men to stay here and protect the school. That's all they need to do. They do that, then Helios pays them."

Parshan looked uneasy. "So… you don't need us to escort you to the plane?"

"No," Frank said. "I need you to protect the school from the Baluchians, and once they know you're on our side, they'll make a move. So, as soon as you leave Moshad, come back to the school and protect it."

Parshan glanced at Namvar for confirmation, who nodded his agreement. "Do what he says," Namvar said, "and we'll all be wealthy in a few days. Now let's go."

The four men walked swiftly down the hallway to the front door.

Hamid trailed by himself, unable to keep up with the brisk pace. He was uneasy at the turn of events. Every direction seemed to put his students, teachers, and him at risk, and now the Baluchian threat seemed all the more real, because of the deception Namvar and his men were soon to spring on Moshad.

CHAPTER 60

Escape

Frank took off his tactical headset with a tremor of frustration, and swept his hands through his hair. What he wouldn't do for a hot shower, a sirloin steak, and a cold beer. His chat with Carson had been painful. Carson couldn't believe that the payment had escalated to sixty-five hundred mesghals, and that his beloved Humvee was being used as collateral. After the initial verbal battle had time to simmer, Carson, to his credit, came around, and decided that the plan was "tolerable."

Namvar, Saeed and Hamid were standing in one group, while Terran, Dorri and Sanjur sat on the ground near the back door. Parshan had left only five minutes earlier, and now it was time for Frank to say goodbye to the school. He walked by the stairwell, and waved at some of the faces he recognized. They were teachers, guards, parents, cooks, and helpers. In a way, each of them were supporting Terran's journey, even to the extent that their school's money was now in the hands of mercenaries who called themselves Police. These were the men who would safeguard the school and its occupants after Carson's team had completed their extraction.

Frank swore under his breath that he would make sure Helios paid up. These good people and the students deserved it.

When Frank got to the back door, he was all business, barely acknowledging the others, as he talked into his headset. "Carson, it's Frank, do you copy? Over."

"Yes—loud and clear. What's your status? Over."

"We're ready to open the back door. Over."

"Copy that. We're ready on our end, too. Omar is on the lead. He's about thirty meters straight out the back door. We've swept everything in the back, and there's nothing out here. Over."

"Copy that. We'll leave in about two minutes. We'll go altogether.

Omar, bring in two spotters with you, and we'll wait until you get here. Over"

"Copy that," Carson said. "Omar, take your time getting there, but once you have everyone, signal us, and run as fast as the slowest person can move. Frank, I want you to guard Terran, and Omar, you take the girl. Over."

"Copy that." Frank and Omar responded in unison.

"Frank?"

"Yes?"

"Thank Hamid for me. He was a big help in this whole thing, and tell him I'll make sure our contacts at Helios know that. Okay? Over."

Frank smiled. "Copy that, and I couldn't agree more. I'll tell him. Over."

"Gentlemen, this is Carson. Two-minute countdown commences *now*. Keep your eyes peeled, your butts down, your head up, and let's get this boy and his entourage safely out of here. Go!"

Frank motioned to Hamid to unlock the door. As he was struggling with the key, Frank leaned in. "Carson said he'll make sure our contacts know how much you helped us. We'll get that payment made to Namvar's men, don't worry. Okay?"

"In all of this," Hamid replied, "I've had one belief, and that belief was in that boy." Hamid glanced in Terran's direction. Terran was in the midst of helping Sanjur to his feet, and caught Hamid's eyes and smiled. "Take good care of him."

The door unlocked, and Frank pulled up the latch and slowly opened it. The creaking of the door was louder than he had expected, accentuated by the acoustics of the stone vestibule. Omar was already visible from across the yard. Two other men—the spotters—followed him. They moved cautiously through the yard, stopping at every tree trunk to survey and assess their situation.

Omar was close, perhaps five meters away from the back door, his two spotters another five meters behind him. Omar nodded to his spotters, and dashed the short distance to the back door. He was a relatively stout man in his late thirties, with very bright eyes and a thick mustache. He wore a gray, faded t-shirt and khaki pants. As he came in, he embraced Frank quickly. "Damn good to see you, Sir."

"It's mutual," Frank replied.

"That the kid?" Omar said, taking a quick glance at Terran.

"Yep."

Omar looked around. "Okay, so who's going?"

"Everyone, but him." Frank pointed to Hamid, who then nodded politely at Omar.

Omar, looked back to his other two spotters, and waved to them to come to the door. The men moved backwards towards the door, scouting for any movement. Suddenly, gunshots rang out in the distance. The shots sounded like they were two or three blocks away, but the ferocity of the gun battle was enough to get everyone instantly agitated.

"Come on, let's go everyone!" Frank yelled. He ran to Dorri, and picked her up. She was holding the wicker basket that held Mandana, and he handed her to Omar. "Take her," Frank said. "Dorri, this is Omar. You grab his shirt, and don't let go."

Next, Frank grabbed Terran by the hand, and stared into the eyes of the men he was about to lead out to the back yard. "We don't have much time. You can hear the gun battle. I'm guessing Parshan delivered the bad news, and Moshad didn't like what he heard. Run as fast as you can, and follow me. Ready?"

Saeed, Sanjur, Namvar nodded, their eyes electric.

"Let's go!" Frank said. He ran out first with Terran, and then Omar and Dorri followed. The other men followed them. Sanjur limped, hanging onto Saeed. Namvar brought up the rear, and then the two spotters followed him, mostly backing up, watching the surrounding tree trunks for any movements.

Hamid watched through the half-closed door. His heart sunk in the sound of the gunfire, and the all-too-sudden departure of his new friends. He shut the heavy wooden doors and locked them, closing the final latch to punctuate his separation. He had wanted to say his goodbyes with more time, more peace, but the gun battle had smothered that hope. He walked as quickly as his aging legs would carry him, amid his sorrowing mood. His school was now without money, Baluchian thugs remained to torture their already fragile sense of security, and the swath of a new light, contained in a young boy, was now gone.

CHAPTER 61

Deflating

It was already warm, though it was barely 7:30 A.M. and the sun was just cresting over the eastern foothills. Peter Lucas, having slid down the emergency slide of the Boeing 777, found himself face to face with four Iranian men who appeared to be in their early twenties. They smiled broadly, as he walked up to them, their heads pivoting between the airplane and Peter's comparatively unimpressive scale and presence. If awe had a face, all four men wore it unabashedly.

Jamere came up behind Peter. "So you don't speak *any* Persian?"

"Nope."

"Now, I see why I got this assignment."

"It was one of the reasons." Peter quipped.

"Salaam," came the chorus from the group.

"Salaam," Peter and Jamere replied, smiling.

A chorus of questions suddenly erupted from the young men. "Who are you? How did you get here? Why did you land here? Where are you from? Why did you come to Mashhad?"

Jamere did a quick translation, and held up his arms as if he were a conductor, asking for more pianissimo from the strings. It was a universal gesture, and the men followed the invisible baton. Quiet resumed on the expansive high desert.

Jamere took a long pause, composed his response and opened his mouth, hoping that Persian, of the comprehensible kind, spilled out. "Gentlemen... we are from Helios. We are here to... receive a group of... people... and take them back to Helios. Our airplane... driver... um... he needs to use your..." Jamere pointed to their jeep, not knowing the Persian word for car or truck, "so he can look at the road. Can we do that?"

What it lacked in elegance, it seemed to work as communication, because the four men stepped aside and nodded enthusiastically.

"You're going to take off on this highway?" one of them asked.

Jamere nodded, squinting into the sun as it broke over the foothills like a searchlight.

"Do you know how to drive a stick-shift?" one of them asked.

Jamere turned around and motioned to Martin, the pilot, to join them on the ground. "Do you know how to drive a stick-shift?" Jamere yelled up to Martin.

"Yes." Martin nodded, and slid down the chute like a professional stunt man.

Peter saw something out of the corner of his eye, several miles to the east. It was a small plume of smoke rising from a fast traveling vehicle. It was closing on their position fast.

"What's that?"

All of the men turned to follow his pointed arm, another universal gesture.

"The Police are coming to check you out." The men started to jump in their jeep. They looked longingly at the plane. "Sorry, we can't stay. We're not on good terms with the local Police. Good luck to you. We apologize for our poor hospitality."

With that, the jeep lurched into first gear and drove off as fast as it could.

"Let's get back inside the plane," Peter said, slowly backing up. "What I read in the project brief didn't speak too kindly about the Police. Basically a bunch of extortionists."

The approaching Police vehicle was still two miles away, but closing fast. They probably had less than two minutes to climb the chute and close the door.

Martin reached the chute first. "Follow what I do. One at a time."

"Couldn't they be our men?" Jamere asked, as they watched Martin scramble up the chute.

"It's possible. I just don't want to take the chance. Protocols."

Fritz, the co-pilot was standing at the door with a pair of binoculars. "They have guns whoever they are."

Martin took Fritz's hand and climbed up and motioned for the next. "Let's see, you went first last time, so I suppose it's my turn?" Jamere said with a chuckle.

"Go ahead," Peter said, pulling a handgun from behind his back. "Just be quick about it."

Jamere went up the slide like a jaguar, just as a bullet danced in front of Peter, ricocheting off the pavement. "Are they actually shooting at us?" Jamere yelled as he struggled up the chute.

Another bullet glanced off the fuselage, and Peter tucked himself behind one of the 52-inch tires, waiting for Jamere to complete his climb.

"They stopped," Martin yelled. He reached down and offered his hand to Jamere and then pulled him up to the doorway and he ducked inside.

Suddenly, a distant gunshot and then the sound of hissing air.

"The bastards hit the chute. Fuck!" Peter said to himself.

The chute was deflating. Rapidly.

"Come on, Peter. Hurry before it deflates." Martin was pumping his arm. Peter tucked his gun behind his back and started to clutch the plastic of the chute, which was starting to assume a more vertical angle to the door as the air escaped. Another bullet hit, and the chute began to deflate even faster.

"Come on, just climb with your hands. Hurry!"

Peter did the best he could, but the chute was quickly becoming a ragdoll of indifference. His handholds were slipping before he could propel himself upwards. Peter decided it was futile, and chose to let go and slid the ten feet to the ground. "I'm going to stay down here. Send down a rifle and extra clips."

Ten seconds later Martin slid a high-powered rifle and four extra clips down the broken chute. "We'll figure another way to get you up, don't worry."

"I'm not worried. I'm going to let them know we have weapons, and probably a hell of a lot better than the ones they're using. I'll try to push them back."

Another bullet whizzed by Peter. It was a close call, as it ricocheted off the shock absorber of one of the tires he was standing behind. Peter steadied his M4 Carbine and aimed it at the Police vehicle that was racing their way. He let go of the safety and pulled the trigger. Nearly twenty rounds fired off before he let go of the trigger. The vehicle came to a sudden stop, and instantly began to back-up. Peter stood up slowly, watching the SUV retreat to a safer distance. He had another ten rounds and took aim at the vehicle and pulled the trigger. He could see the puffs of white impact smoke as the bullets hit their marks. One of which looked like it hit the vehicle. The dusty SUV backed up even further.

"Tires okay?" Martin yelled down.

"I think so," Peter said.

"They're hard to penetrate with low caliber guns, but if they have anything like yours, and get close enough, it might be another story," Martin said. "Are you ready to try climbing again? From that range I don't think they can do anything."

"What's that in the distance?" Peter asked.

Martin brought the binoculars to his eyes and focused the lens. "It's a military vehicle of some kind."

"Why do you think it's military?"

"It's camouflaged."

"Could be ours, then."

"Or another one of theirs," Jamere added. "Maybe you should get back up here while you have a chance."

"Thanks, but I'd rather take my chances down here. At least down here, I can shoot in any direction. With this rifle's range, it won't be easy to approach us without seeing them.

"Two men are getting out of the vehicle. They're walking this way."

"Which vehicle?" Peter asked.

"The first one... the one that was shooting at us a few minutes ago."

Martin put the binoculars down for a second. "They're splitting up. They're each carrying something, but I can't make out what it is."

"What's the other vehicle doing?" Peter asked.

"I don't know... they've stopped. About a hundred meters from the SUV."

"What's the status on the two walkers?"

Martin turned his binoculars back to the previous spot, but saw nothing but scrub brush. "I don't know... I'm not seeing them right now... hold on. Shit, where'd they go?"

"You lost them?" Peter asked.

"They disappeared."

"What distance would you estimate they were when you lost them?"

Martin squinted in the direction of the SUV, and slowly shook his head. "Maybe a mile... maybe a little more."

"Point in the direction you last saw them," Peter directed.

"About there," Martin said, "but they split up and I can only assume they're crawling now. If they were walking I'd see them. Give me a second I'll look on the other side."

Martin left the doorway, and Jamere poked his head out. "The second vehicle just started moving again... in the direction of the Police."

Suddenly a series of gunshots rang out in rapid succession. The SUV tried to get away, but it was hit hard by gunfire, and flames started to shoot from its interior.

"It's on fire... holy shit," Jamere said excitedly. "That's got to be our team. Give it to 'em boys!"

Jamere turned around, and then yelled down to Peter. "Martin says he still doesn't see any movement out there. He says they might have retreated out of sight, now that the cavalry is here."

Peter stood up and looked out to the scrub brush terrain. If they were crawling, it would be hard to see them, until they got close. "What's the status of the second vehicle?"

"It's coming our way, slowly."

Peter walked in the direction of the military truck. As it got closer he could see the camouflage paint and the wide body stance of an IVECO M65. "It's an Italian armored vehicle. Could be ours..."

"All I know is that the enemy of our enemy is our friend. Right?"

The vehicle approached cautiously, and Peter kept his M4 pointed down. When the vehicle got within a hundred meters... it slowed to stop, and a latch opened up and a man poked his head out waving his hands over his head. "We're Helios. I'm Farzad Ghorbani."

In the stillness of the high desert, Peter could make out his name clearly. Relief returned to his mind. He motioned them in, and shouted, "I'm Peter Lucas. I was hoping it was you."

The vehicle drove up behind the plane slowly, and parked almost directly under the tail. Peter walked swiftly over to the vehicle and as it opened its doors, Peter dashed in. "Close the doors. Stay inside the vehicle."

"Why?"

"Two men from that Police SUV are unaccounted for, and are assumed to be trying to get to the plane. What's going on?" Peter looked around the inside of the vehicle. "Where's the boy?"

CHAPTER 62

The Return

Sometimes we live at the very edge of our lives. We pray that evil sleeps, hoping that it will pass into a dream so powerful, that when it awakens, it would not remember its nature. Sometimes, when we look behind our heart, in that carved out, non-human place, where the spirit shines like a wondrous light, humble and forgiving; we sense that our next step may outlive our body. That it could go out like a reverberation that enters a thing quietly, signaling it to vibrate, and when it does, we live there, too. We become imperishable, not because we did some great thing, but because we took the next step, even when we were surrounded by distances so vast that the next step seemed meaningless.

*　　　*　　　*　　　*

Terran was the first to be thrust inside the MRAP, and Parto was eager to embrace him. Dorri came next, and Parto held her tight, and then Dorri pushed back a bit and showed her Mandana. "We can keep her, right?"

Parto was overcome with joy, and could barely speak, but managed to nod. Her hands, like butterflies, caressed Dorri.

Nouri hugged Terran, and then pulled Parto and Dorri deeper inside to give room to the others who rushed in. Sanjur struggled up the steps. It was obvious that the run had been tough on his body. Saeed helped Sanjur to a seat and then joined him, both men panting. Frank and Omar stayed outside the door, with their guns at the ready.

Parto looked at Sanjur and whispered to Nouri. "I know that man, he was the drunkard. He worked with them. Why is—"

"He's here, because Terran chose him. He's the one who saved Terran."

"What about the others?" Parto asked.

"I know him," Nouri said, pointing to Saeed. "He's a parent at our school." Nouri nodded at Saeed. "Greetings, Saeed."

Saeed nodded his head. "Salaam."

"The other one, I don't know who he is," Nouri said.

Namvar nodded. "I'm Namvar. I'm with him." He glanced at Terran.

The spotters came in with Carson, who seemed to be in great pain as he sat down in the front seat. Then Omar came in, and finally Frank, but not before he surveyed the streets, and seemed satisfied that they'd made their escape unseen.

"Close the door," Carson said to LB, as Frank got inside.

"Good work, man." The two leaders slapped hands in a high-five. Frank made introductions to Carson, and then set his rifle down and looked at Carson. "I think we're ready."

"Sir?" Saeed asked.

Frank turned around. "What, Saeed?"

"I need to go back. I know I promised to protect Terran, but he's safe here." Saeed looked around with a sense of awe at the military prowess of their MRAP. "I have my own children. I know there's a gun battle out on the street in front of the school. I need to go back."

"I don't know..." LB started to say.

Carson looked at Frank. "Do you think we should help them?"

Frank nodded. "We could stay in here. Their peashooters aren't going to do anything against this beast. We have two CROWS with .50-caliber rifles. We could drive up to Moshad's hideaway and blow it to smithereens. It'd only take a few minutes. What do you think?"

Carson slowly began to nod his head. "Okay, let's do it, but only long enough to get your friend back in the school."

Frank turned around. "Saeed, we're going to blast Moshad's bunker, and when we do that, you run to the school. When we start shooting, the Baluchians will hunker down or run. Okay?"

Saeed nodded with a nervous smile. "Thank you."

LB started up the MRAP, and backed up a block, turned south and went slowly down a side street.

"Namvar, show us the building Moshad was in," Frank said.

The MRAP was three blocks east of the school on a side street, waiting to turn left. There was a pause in the gun battle. Only an occasional shot was fired on either side.

Namvar stood up to see better through the high windows. "It's down one block, second building on the right."

"How many stories?" Carson asked.

Namvar looked puzzled.

"Levels," Frank said, using his arms to explain.

Namvar nodded. "Two levels, but a basement would make it three."

"Okay, here's what we'll do," Carson said. "We'll use thermals, and lay down a spray of bullets targeting Moshad's men. If we see any engagement coming from that building or anywhere near it, target it immediately—use the lasers. If not, keep the focus on Moshad's building, and only that building. We'll stagger the CROWS. Omar, you take the CROW system up front, and work the top floor. Start with the M2, and then switch to the .50-caliber. Charlie, you take the back CROW and work the ground floor. If you see any body heat signatures and they're in that building, use the MK-19 and take them out. Understood?"

"Yes, Sir," Omar and Charlie responded in unison.

Sanjur was watching the whole situation unfold, and Terran grabbed his sleeve, a signal that he wanted a translation. Sanjur explained what he had just heard, and Terran became silent and closed his eyes. Sanjur watched him for a while and wondered what he had said that had caused him to shut down.

The MRAP started to turn, and Terran stood to his feet and looked at Sanjur with his intense blue eyes. "Tell them to stop!"

Sanjur immediately sat up straight. "Frank, Terran said to stop!" Sanjur shouted.

Frank held up his hand. "LB, hold up a second." He turned around to Sanjur and Terran. "What's wrong?"

Terran began to talk, as LB brought the MRAP to a halt.

Sanjur listened and then looked in Frank's eyes. "He says the doctor is in that building."

"What doctor?"

Terran spoke again, short and to the point.

"He says we need to save Dr. Najafi."

"Shit!" Carson exclaimed. "It's happening again."

CHAPTER 63

Thermals

Terran described his experience after he had been abducted the second time by Moshad's men. He explained that they had kidnapped Dr. Najafi to treat Moshad's gunshot wound. Given Moshad's importance, they would keep Dr. Najafi close, so he could continue to treat Moshad and prevent infection. Terran said they would most likely hold the doctor prisoner in the basement in an interior room.

After Sanjur's translation, Frank leaned forward. "We could just use the .50-calibers on anyone that engages. Wait for them to shoot, use the lasers to track them, and then take them out. That'd keep collaterals out of the equation." Frank said.

Sanjur interjected a short translation from Terran. "He reminds us that it doesn't save Dr. Najafi."

Carson finished a swig of water, and then cleared his throat. "First of all, we don't know for sure that they have this doctor as a prisoner—"

"Terran's logic makes sense," Frank said. He then leaned over and whispered into Carson's ear. "Trust me... he has a sixth *and* seventh sense."

"So what does he want, a search team dispatched to Moshad's bunker?" Carson asked rhetorically. "We could lose men doing that. I'm too banged up to help. So what the hell does he suggest?"

Sanjur translated, and Terran spoke to Carson. "Is it true that you can see body signatures with your technology?"

Sanjur translated, and both Frank and Carson nodded.

"Two men leave here," Terran said, gesturing with his arms, "and travel along the back ally, while we monitor the body signatures. We'll know if anyone sees them by watching Moshad's men. We can warn our team if they're spotted. Once our team is in position, we'll start shooting, but only to get their attention, not to kill anyone. While this is going on, our team will break into the basement and free the doctor, and then return here."

Sanjur took a long breath, and began his translation. Carson squirmed in his seat as he listened.

"Look, this could work, but it could also cost us two men, and a lot of time. We've already blown ten minutes. If the doctor's in the basement like you think, then we won't shoot low. Only high. But we need to take these bastards out. I don't like the idea of not killing anyone when that's the entire point."

Frank nodded. "I have to agree with Carson. The Baluchians are a threat to the school and everyone inside. They'll take their revenge out on them. If we leave the Baluchians unharmed, and we're gone, what then? I don't know if Namvar's men can hold them off, or if they'd even continue to try tomorrow or the day after that."

Terran nodded after Sanjur finished the translation. "When you've dropped us off at the plane, you'll return and protect the school. Namvar's men will not be needed. Anyway, Moshad will lose interest as soon as he hears the airplane take off."

Carson rolled his eyes at the suggestion that they would return to protect the school. "Look, we're getting paid to deliver you to Helios. Once you're on that plane, our job is completed. A few minutes ago, we were willing to take the Baluchians out to spare the school. Now you've complicated it, and for what, to save some Baluchian thugs who threaten children?"

Carson paused to allow Sanjur to translate, and then continued when Sanjur finished. "I don't know this doctor, and I understand we want to save him if we can. However, if we knock out all of these thugs, we can walk into that building and release him. Why isn't that a better solution?"

"Because these are my people," Terran said, "and one of them saved my life yesterday. If we kill them all, that is when the Baluchians will seek revenge. If we spare them, they will leave. They will give up."

There was a deep silence inside the MRAP as Sanjur delivered the translation. Carson stood to his feet, hanging onto a support pole. He turned to face everyone. "Omar, I want you and Frank to do this, but only if you volunteer. I'm not going to force anyone under my command to take these kinds of risks for a project detour. What do you say?"

"I'm in," Frank said, turning to Omar, who hesitated.

"I don't know... I can operate the CROW..."

Saeed stood. "I'm the reason we're even discussing this issue. I need to get back to the school. So let me go with Frank. I can help."

Carson shook his head. "No, I need trained operatives. This isn't—"

"I spent ten years with the National Police in Tehran. I'm trained... and motivated. Dr. Najafi has saved many lives at our school. It would be an honor to help him. Please, let me go with Frank."

Carson glanced at Frank. "You okay with that?"

"Let's go," Frank said, turning to Saeed.

The two men stood up and checked their weapons. "Let them have your packs, men. They might need extra clips. Saeed, take this rifle instead. You ever saw one like this?"

Saeed shook his head. "Safety's here. Auto control's here. Keep it in this position for auto. Has thirty rounds. There're four extra clips in the pack. Any questions?"

"No."

"Okay," Frank said, "We'll go up the back alley and stay in communication. Give Saeed a headset, too."

Omar grabbed an extra headset and handed it to Saeed while Frank kept talking.

"Once we're in position, I'll let you know. Just be sure to keep your fire high. We'll do our best to stay low. We'll enter and exit on the east side. I assume you'll come down the block nice and slow to keep pace with our progress. Once we've got the doctor, we'll rendezvous back here. Sound good?" Franks looked around at the faces and ended on Carson's.

"Okay, let's do it, and do it safely," Carson added, slapping his hands together once.

Namvar raised his hand tentatively. "What about my men? They might see this... this vehicle as a threat to them."

"When they see our CROWS pointed at Moshad, they won't," Frank said.

Carson waved at the two CROWS operators. "Make sure you're honed in on Moshad's building."

The two operators sat down at their consoles, fastened their seat belts out of habit, and adjusted their trackballs to lock their weapons' systems on Moshad's building.

"Okay, we're in ambush mode until I say otherwise. LB?"

LB clicked a few switches and the interior lights dimmed, as the windows darkened. A palpable tension spread through the cabin interior as LB opened the front door at Carson's command. Frank and Omar shuttled out silently, and the doors closed behind them. Everyone, other than the CROWS operators, looked around not sure what to do.

"For what's it worth, our MRAP can take everything the Baluchians can throw at us. You'll hear bullets, but they can't penetrate this thing, and that includes the windows, gas tank, everything. But more importantly, as soon as someone fires on us, our weapons will lock in on them, and we'll remind them of our superiority with a blast of gunfire… over their head." Carson turned to Terran as he spoke. "So I don't expect we'll catch many bullets."

Carson looked over Omar's shoulder. "That's them?"

Two thermal images were moving, clearly hunched over, keeping a low profile.

"Yep, that's them."

"LB, let's inch forward at two mph," Carson ordered, and then turned back to Omar. "Do you see anything else?"

"There're no other thermals that I see. These buildings are all abandoned… wait a second, maybe I spoke too soon. There's one right there. I think he's watching us. He's on the top floor of that building." Omar pointed across the street.

"Frank, you copy? Over."

"Yes, we hear you loud and clear. Over" Frank whispered back.

"There's a thermal in the front of the building you're passing behind. It's watching us, but we don't see any evidence of a gun. Could be a citizen, could be a Baluchian. Just pass by quietly, we'll let you know if they move in your direction. Over."

Thermal images of humans bear an eerie resemblance to apparitions, the kind painted from nightmares. They move like people, but they reminded Carson of ghosts. Even friendlies looked less friendly as a thermal. Carson didn't like them.

They continued to drive at the pace of a leisurely walk. Whoever was watching them seemed to be an interested observer and little more. If they were Baluchian, they would have been firing their gun in the last gun battle, and the heat would have registered on the thermal.

"Frank, I think we have a citizen and nothing more. It's just one person, on the top floor watching us. Doubt they've ever seen anything like this before. Over."

Carson was right about one thing, a double MRAP, the size of a small city bus, with two CROWS and a carrying capacity of twenty-four people, was not a standard issue vehicle. It had been the coveted property of Special Forces, and was one of the vehicles that had been preserved and maintained throughout the reign of Sunrot. The U.S. base in Kandahar had several underground bunkers that had housed some of the military's best kept secrets in tactical warfare.

Carson had seen some of the most advanced technologies in personnel cloaking and biorhythm jamming. All of these were lost when Sunrot hit, not because the technologies were damaged, but because the people who knew how to use them, maintain them, and repair them had died, or left in despair. Some simply gave up and wandered away from the bases in deep shock, without a destination or goal, other than to die. The degree of apathy was what startled Carson the most in the first six months. When people knew they were never getting home, that home was probably gone, that the presence of death was everywhere, they gave up. Apathy... God, he hated it.

Carson had proven himself to be a fighter, but for him it had come easy. He didn't have any attachments at home, no wife or children. He had one brother, who was a peacenik, so Carson and he weren't close. When Carson's friends died all around him, with each new death, he used it as a spur to drive on. His commanding officer died five months into Sunrot, and gave Carson the reins to the base. It was informal. No one at that time cared about hierarchies or command-and-control systems, but Carson, over time, rebuilt that sense of order.

Eventually, communications came back on, and when they did, Carson was at the top of the food chain. He was the default base commander, but what made him different was his sense of action. He never wanted to be inside, behind a desk, staring into a computer. He was a warrior. Warriors want the rush of the wind in their face; the heat of the sun on their back; the smell of gunpowder in the air. They like the muscle ache that reminds them of yesterday's victory. They live for that sense of triumph when they have conquered a piece of fear that lives inside them. Carson was nearly fearless, at least on the battlefield. His only fear was of other commanders that shared his sense of conquest, and Moshad was one such person.

"We have a sightline to Moshad's building," Omar announced.

Carson dipped low to see the monitor better. "How many thermals?"

"I count six... no, seven."

"Looks like all of them have guns," Carson observed.

"This one has to be Moshad. He's sitting on the floor. Three thermals are in that room."

"Okay, get a lock on that one," Carson ordered, pointing to a thermal that was looking through binoculars, directly at them. "I have a feeling he's the eyes of Moshad. Probably his right arm."

"Yes, Sir." Omar replied, as he moved a square, blinking cursor over the thermal, and pushed his trackball's control button. The thermal image instantly had an orange rectangular outline around it with the number "1" above it. Omar confirmed coordinates. "Thermal One is laser ID'd at eight-two point six meters away."

"What's Frank's position in relation?"

Omar clicked a button and reported, "Frank's seventy-one meters from thermal one."

"LB, increase speed to four MPH."

"Yes, Sir," LB intoned.

"Frank?"

"I'm here. Over."

"We see seven thermals in the building. Three on the top floor, four on the ground floor. Over."

"Copy that. All armed, I presume?"

Carson tapped Omar on the shoulder. "All armed, correct?"

Omar zoomed in on the thermals in seven separate windows that neatly auto-stacked, each had tracking numbers above their heads, and each was bounded in a rectangular box. "Thermal Five, the one on the ground doesn't. All the others do.

"That's strange... the weapon IDs seem to be SIG 510s."

"They probably stole them," Carson said.

"Still, those have good range."

"Can you tell if they're scoped?"

"No scopes from what I can see here, but scopes don't conduct heat well, so they may not show up."

"Frank, they're using SIG 510s, no scopes. Over."

"Copy that. We're about to cross the street. One building after that. Do you see anyone on the east side of the building? Over."

"Negative. They're all on the south side watching us. Over."

"Copy that... we're crossing now. Over."

The thermals for Frank and Saeed could be seen running across the street and then ducking behind the building closest to the street. "We're across. Over," Frank said.

"Okay, you can proceed—"

Charlie half-yelled from the back of the MRAP. "I'm seeing activity on the first floor. Someone looks like they're going outside... in the back."

Omar pointed to his screen, and Carson saw it, too. "Frank. Lay low. Over."

"Copy that. What's happening?"

"One of the men is going outside. For all we know he's just taking a piss, but keep down and make sure he doesn't see you. Over."

"Copy that," Frank whispered. "What's he doing now? Over."

"I think I called it. He's taking a piss. You can relax. Over."

"He's going back inside. Wait until I signal you. Over."

"Any signs of the doctor?" Frank asked.

"No. He must be in the basement... if he's there. Okay, he's resumed his post on the south wall, east corner on the first floor. Can you see any windows into the basement? Over."

"No windows. I think we may have to go in the backdoor and then downstairs. I don't see any other option. Over."

"Shit!" Carson said under his breath. "What about a cellar door in the back? Over."

There was a long pause. "No, I don't see anything unless it's on the west side. Over."

Carson grimaced. "Copy that. Stay east. Look, I think we're going to have to draw their fire so you can run in the back. Let me know when you're in position. If we fire off a few rounds, I'm sure they'll focus on us. Frank, you to go in alone, Saeed stays where he is. Okay? Over."

"Copy that."

There was a pause. "I'm ready when you are. Over," Frank said.

Carson tapped Omar. "Hit them with a few rounds from the fifty, and let's see what they do. Keep your aim high. Three-round bursts, wait a few seconds, and then another burst. Do that until I say stop. Okay?"

Omar nodded. "Yes, Sir."

"Charlie, you lay low on this one."

"Yes, Sir."

"Frank, we're going to lay down some cover in ten seconds… five, four, three, two, one… *go.*"

Frank stood up with his gun in the ready position. The .50-caliber bursts were incredibly loud, echoing in the streets, and Frank could hear the carnage in the building of ripping plaster and debris falling. He opened the backdoor, and for a moment froze, as his eyes adjusted to the dark interior. He saw an interior door and opened it, it was an empty closet—probably a pantry. *Shit!* To his right was a kitchen. Another round erupted overhead, and he could hear the men shouting in Baluchian.

He looked to his left and grabbed the only other door, and immediately sensed the cool updraft of a basement and the dark interior swallowed him. Suddenly, quiet returned to the building, and he gingerly closed the door behind him with a slight creak. Utter darkness was all he could see. Frank gripped the handrail with his left hand and started to walk down the stairs, praying that the steps would hold his weight.

"Frank… you in? Over," Carson asked.

"Yes. I'm going down the stairs… in the pitch dark," he whispered.

"You got matches, take a look around. Over."

Above him he could hear the sound of men talking and restless pacing.

The building was like a beehive that had been bludgeoned by a stick, and the bees, or in this case, the Baluchians, were riled up and angry.

He fumbled in his shirt pocket for matches. Finding them, he noticed his hands were shaking slightly, as he tried to light one. On the second strike his match ignited. The light revealed that he was halfway down a steep staircase, whose next step was completely missing. At the base, the starting step looked like someone had smashed it with a sledgehammer. *Someone went nuts in this place.*

Frank stepped over the missing step and quickly got down to the floor level just before his match started to burn his thumb and index finger. He lit another match immediately.

He was in a large open room with old, faded mattresses leaning against the walls. There was a chalky smell with a faint odor of urine. He saw three doors to his right, and opened the first one, just as his match went out again. He shut the door and struck another match. It was an empty room, but he thought he saw an old desk and several lamps piled against a far corner.

"Frank, report. Over." There was more static than he liked. His headset was definitely having problems in the basement.

"Sorry… I… I'm exploring the basement, trying to find the doctor. I'm trying the second door. Hold on."

Frank lit another match and then opened the door. There was a man slumped over unconscious, tied to a support beam, in the middle of the room, which looked like it had once been used as a bathroom, but all of the fixtures had been taken out. "I found him, Carson, but I'm not sure he's alive. Over."

Frank rushed over and felt for a pulse. "He has a pulse." Frank slapped his cheeks several times. "Wake up. Wake up! We've got to go!"

The man stirred, trying to open his eyes, but was too groggy to sustain consciousness. "Carson, I don't know how I'm going to get this guy out unless he wakes up."

"Give… some water," Carson ordered. "Do whatever … but… him up." Every other word was missing, but Frank understood what he needed to do.

Frank opened his canteen and took a long sip, and then blew it hard into the man's face. He stirred again. "What?" He put his hands out in front of him wildly. Frank set the water down and grabbed another match and lit it. "Listen, I'm Lieutenant Frank Wolfe. I'm a friend of Terran. He's sent me to rescue you. Are you Dr. Najafi?"

"Water?" the man croaked.

Frank held his canteen up and let him drink, spilling most of it over his shirt.

"Can you walk?" Frank asked.

The man spit out some of the water and began to cough. He was a distinguished looking man, with wire-rimmed glasses, but his hair was disheveled and his beard scruffy. The whole room smelled of urine.

"Please... take me... from... from here."

"Are you Dr. Najafi?"

"I... I am."

Frank took out his knife and cut the ropes around Dr. Najafi's wrists and ankles. "Can you hold still?" Frank asked.

"It's not... something... I... I can... can control."

Frank grabbed Dr. Najafi's wrist with his left hand and cut the ropes with his right. Once he had freed him from the ropes, he lit another match. "Okay, I need you to stand up. Can you manage if I help you?"

"I'll try."

The two men stood up together. Frank, still holding the match in his right hand.

"Carson, he's standing. I'll try walking with him. Over."

Dr. Najafi eyed Frank. "You're... military?"

Frank nodded. "Yes."

They walked out of the room. Frank, half-carrying Dr. Najafi. "We have a staircase coming up. It's in rough shape. I'm not sure we can both be on the same step at the same time. There's a handrail on the right, do you think you can climb the stairs?"

"I'm feeling... better now. I... I think so."

"Carson, can you give me a status report? Over."

"The thermals are huddling in an interior room in the second floor. We think Thermal Five is Moshad, because he's on the floor. We assume he's called a meeting of sorts. Over."

"Did they fire any shots at you?" Frank asked.

"Negative. Over."

"We're going to try and make it up the staircase. Dr. Najafi's in bad shape. We aren't going to be able to run, let alone walk fast. I'll need Saeed to help me. Saeed, do you copy that?"

"I'll help you," Saeed replied. "Just let me know when you need me. Over."

"Okay, when I get to the top of the stairs, I'll signal Carson to start the bursts again. As soon as you hear the first shot, Saeed, you run to the back door. Over."

"Copy that," Saeed said.

"Carson, I need you to bring the MRAP to the side street—the one we crossed. Meet us there. I don't think we'll be able to make it to our rendezvous. So after you fire your rounds, back up to the side street, and head north. Over."

"Copy that, Frank. Standing by. Over."

Frank lit another match. "Okay, Doc, you hang onto this handrail and step carefully. Take as much time as you need to be safe. I'll be right behind you, and if you feel like you're going to lose your balance, just let me know. Okay?"

Dr. Najafi stepped over the starting step "Okay." He pulled on the handrail and made it to the second step, and paused.

"Okay, you're doing great. Keep going… just like that. Halfway up, there's a step that's missing. I'll light another match when we get that far."

The house was completely still. A thin, horizontal beam of light identified the door above them, and now that Frank's eyes had adjusted to the darkness, he could see the vague outline of the steps and handrail even without matches.

Suddenly, Dr. Najafi's right leg went through a rotted step, and the dull cracking sound jolted Frank. Both men clutched the handrail, and Dr. Najafi lost his balance and fell back on Frank, who caught him, and held him up, but the pressure of two men pulling on the handrail was too much for it, and it popped out from the wall, and the men tumbled down the stairs. The handrail and its now loose hardware, jangling loudly to the floor.

Frank could hear the footsteps above them. He could also hear Carson's muffled voice raging in his headset somewhere on the floor. He knew he was in a delicate position, but his first concern was Dr. Najafi. "Are you okay?"

"I'm sorry... my leg went through... I lost my balance... do you think they heard?"

Frank reached in the direction of Carson's voice, and found it in a wild stretch and put it on. "...coming! Frank, do you read me?"

"We fell down the stairs—"

"Three thermals are running down the stairs to your position. You have to hide!"

Frank reached for his M4, and scrambled to pull Dr. Najafi behind the stairs, out of sightlines from the basement door. "You said three?"

"Copy that. Three."

Frank could hear footsteps, and he knew he was trapped. No windows. One exit. He glanced around the corner to look up the stairs. He could see movement in the beam of light, on the other side of the door. The door knob turned. *No killing...* he could almost hear Terran's voice. He reached for his handgun and aimed high on the door. "Carson, I'm going to squeeze off a few rounds just to let these guys know I'm armed."

"Copy that."

As the door opened a crack, Frank fired off three times at the top of the door, which instantly closed, and the beam of light was now complemented with three semi-round holes, almost in a triangular pattern.

Frank crouched down, and turned to Dr. Najafi. Is there any other way out of here?"

"Not... not that I know of."

Frank handed him his Canteen. "Drink some more water. We might be here a while."

Frank stood up. "Carson, any ideas?"

"Have you searched the basement? Over."

"Most of it, but not all."

"We see the thermals are to the left of the door, huddling. Another is coming down. Saeed, you should retreat to a position where there're no sight lines from Moshad's building. Saeed?"

"Copy that," Saeed whispered.

"Frank, if I were them, I'd be thinking that there are more of us in the neighborhood, and I'd send someone out to check. As for you, assuming there's no other way out, I'd create a barrier, or if I really wanted the doctor, I'd smoke you out, but that's dangerous. Either way, I'd make sure I had an escape route open, and I'm betting that's what they're about to do. Thermal Two and Four are going out the back door. Saeed, are you repositioned? Over."

"Copy that, I'm tucked behind the building to the east. They can't see me. Over."

"I copy that. Stay there for now. Over."

"Carson, I'm going to do a quick search of the basement. Damn, I wish we had flashlights."

Frank could hear Carson chuckling, as he struck another match. He walked to the third door and opened it. It looked like storage for more desks. No windows. No other doors.

Across the hallway was one door. He lit another match and then opened it. It was a cellar for food storage. Round jars were everywhere, empty and dusty. Some broken on the floor, but again, no windows and no doors.

"Carson, there's nothing here. No exits. We're trapped. I bet they know that. Over."

"Give me some time, and I'll confer with everyone here and see what plan we can come up with. We'll get you out of there, don't worry. Over."

"Frank, they're on the move. Over."

"What do you mean?"

"Thermal Five is being helped down the stairs. That's Moshad. I think they're leaving. The building's too hot. Shit, the thermals look like they're moving something to the back. Can't see what it is…"

"I can hear something being dragged across the floor. Over."

"Something just lit up, Frank. I think they're going to smoke you out. Do you have any water left?"

"Shit. I don't know. The doctor was dehydrated."

"Then stamp it out. Do you have anything down there you could smother it with?"

The basement door suddenly opened and a jar with something was quickly tossed down the stairs, followed by a torch of tree branches. It instantly flared up in flames, and began to engulf the staircase. Frank ran to Dr. Najafi, grabbed the canteen, and pulled him up and together, they stumbled down the hallway. He could hear something like a heavy table leaned against the door.

"Carson, the basement's on fire. They've blocked the doorway. We're dead, if you can't get here in two minutes. Over."

Maybe it was the fire. Maybe the batteries on his headset finally gave up, but whatever the cause, the loss of Carson's voice left a deep hole in Frank's hope. He had known Carson like a brother for six long years. They were as close as "lips and teeth," a phrase that Carson used once when he introduced him to a visiting comrade of arms.

Their situation was dire by any standards. They went into the third room, and closed the door, and Frank took off his shirt and stuffed it under the door. Then he took his under shirt off and ripped in into two halves, pouring water over the cloth, and handed one to Dr. Najafi.

"Thank you for trying," Dr. Najafi said, as he took the damp cloth.

"We're not dead yet," Frank quipped. "I know someone who'll do anything in his power to save us, and his power is considerable."

"I hope you're not talking about God," Dr. Najafi said, sitting down on the ground. "Because I've tried that someone, and he seems too busy for me."

CHAPTER 64

Fire

Carson was so distracted that he started to pace before he remembered the stinging pain in his ankle. "Ouch! Damn!" He sat down, cursing his leg. "LB, I want you to position us on the east wall, now!"

"Yes, Sir." LB swung the MRAP to his right and drove over the curb, a hedge and smashed down a fence between the buildings.

"Omar, get the nineteen ready. I want an opening on that wall big enough to crawl through. Got it?"

"Yes, Sir."

The CROWS included an MK-19 grenade launcher and these were imprecise when compared to the other weapons systems, but Carson had no time to worry about precision. He could already see smoke coming out of the first floor windows.

"They're leaving out the back in a westerly direction." Charlie shouted. "Do you want me to take them out?"

Carson glanced at Terran, and shook his head. "No, let'em go."

"Yes, Sir."

Omar, aim low, at the very base of the wall. Ready?"

"Ready, Sir."

"Fire."

Omar made one delicate, down-stroke movement with his right index finger, and a moment later an explosion erupted twenty feet from the front of the MRAP, which rocked from the shockwaves. Smoke came billowing out.

"Charlie, status on the seven thermals?" Carson yelled.

A short pause, then, "They're seventy meters plus heading westerly."

"Saeed, you still there? Over."

"Yes."

"I need you to come to our position and search the hole we just blasted in the side of this building."

"I'm on my way."

A few seconds later, Saeed came running up to the hole that was billowing smoke, and tried to get close enough to see inside, but it was too strong, and he had no choice but to back up.

Terran went to the front and stood facing the door, beating his hand against it. "Let me go."

Carson narrowed his eyes, and turned to Sanjur.

"He wants to go," Sanjur said.

Terran kept beating on the door, looking at Carson while he did.

Carson shrugged and nodded at LB. "Open it."

Terran ran to the hole, his shirtsleeve held over his face. He squinted into the black space with billowing gray smoke coming out. He took off his shirt and wrapped it around his face.

"What's he going to do?" Sanjur asked.

"He can't be thinking he can go down there. *Shit*, I wish we had a fucking fire extinguisher."

"We'd need more than a fire extinguisher against that thing," Omar said.

Terran ran inside again, and immediately began talking excitedly. Sanjur translated. "He says we should crash the MRAP against the wall, and bring it down all across its width. He says the wall is dry and brittle—it'll come down easily. If we widen the hole, maybe we can find a way down, or they can find a way up."

Carson limped over to LB. "You heard the man. Let's bring this wall down."

LB backed up the MRAP, and in a succession of impacts began taking the wall down, starting with the existing hole, and then expanding the hole on either side. In two minutes the wall was nearly demolished and the smoke was mostly billowing out of the back side. Terran went to the front section of the wall, nearest the street, and Namvar followed him. "I'll go down," Namvar said, pointing to his own chest, and then pointing down.

Terran nodded, and ran back to the MRAP and stuck his head in. "Ropes?"

Sanjur explained. Omar grabbed a rope and ran with Terran to where Namvar was crawling down the side of the basement wall. It was a tight fit, the hole was less than three feet high with splintered wood beams, nails and adobe bricks. Saeed was there, too, and went down next. The fire was still in the back near the stairway. It was growing vertically more than it was spreading out towards the front of the building, but it was still chokingly thick.

"Charlie, I need a status on the seven thermals," Carson shouted.

"They're still heading in a westerly direction. The laser IDs them at one-hundred seventy meters… wait a minute…" Charlie's voice suddenly became distant, as he began clicking his trackball. "There's only six… I'm missing one…"

"What do you mean you're *missing* one?" Carson went to Omar's station and looked at the screen. He did a quick calculation and confirmed that the group of thermals was six in number. "It's Thermal Three that's missing. Find it."

"Working on it… okay, I found it. Thermal Three is at forty-eight meters. I think it's dead or dying. It's on the ground."

"They shot their own. We didn't hit anyone. Confirm."

"No, Sir, there were no hits on our rounds."

"You're sure Thermal Three is down and not moving?"

"I just did a regression track, and it's not moved for three minutes and twenty seconds."

"Okay, keep an eye on it. I know there's a lot going on, but I need you to focus on those thermals."

"Yes, Sir."

When Namvar hit the ground he could barely see, not because of the smoke being so thick, but because his eyes stung from the smoke and he could barely keep them open long enough to see his way. He saw several doors and opened the first one he saw, burning his hand in the process. He screamed, but no one was there. Saeed caught up with him, and they both went to the next door and opened it. The room was reasonably smoke-free, and Frank was conscious, but the doctor was not.

"Frank, can you walk?" Namvar asked.

"I think so," he said, coughing nonstop.

"Go straight out the door and to the right. You'll see a rope. Climb out. Saeed and I will carry the doctor."

Frank stood up, still coughing and rushed out the door.

"Grab his feet, Saeed. Let's go."

The two men pulled the doctor out the room just as a large beam over the stairs fell, and a huge pile of debris dropped down from the first floor. It had the effect of temporarily dampening the fire, but the fire was displaced horizontally and caught some of Namvar's clothing, which caught fire. He dropped Dr. Najafi, and stood ablaze. Saeed tackled Namvar, beat the flames off of him, and rolled him on the ground. Then the fire started to build again, this time with greater ferocity.

"We have to get out of here now!" Saeed yelled.

Namvar was in pain, and with intense pain, it's almost always accompanied by shock. He looked at Saeed as if he were a stranger.

Saeed knew that Namvar wouldn't be able to help him. Saeed was alone. He pulled Namvar to the rope. Frank was just putting his leg over the edge. He made it. Saeed took some satisfaction from that. He grabbed the doctor next and pulled him over to the rope and yelled up. "I need help!"

Omar scrambled down. Without saying anything, he took the doctor on his back and shimmied up the side of the wall. It was as if Omar had held his breath and dove into a pool. Saeed instantly saw what he needed to do with Namvar, and followed Omar's example, but he was too weak. The smoke was affecting him. He was having trouble focusing. Saeed collapsed under Namvar's weight. Suddenly, another explosion of debris fell down, and this one shot sparks into Saeed's hair and face that he could feel it burn deep. He closed his eyes and surrendered. He could feel his body darkening, and some part of him broke free of his body, wanting to visit his children who were just across the street.

Then he felt a pair of hands on him. Powerful hands like those of a giant. They picked him up as if he were a ragdoll and pulled him out. He coughed at the fresh air, the bright light. Was he alive? Was he really alive?

Chapter 65

Two Words

When the one who is the Mahdi merges with the boy, the miraculous one that is thirsted for walks unhidden in his shadows no more. The eye of the Holy One is upon all, and the claims of ownership fall mute and dumb. The Mahdi does not live in the body of the boy. It is the boy who lives in the Mahdi. When this reordering occurs, when the night becomes day, when the resistance within the boy is overcome, he will walk without his own bearings. His map and compass will be folded away, and the unsayable will be finally said. The undoable will be done.

*   *   *   *

Saeed shook his head. His lips moved. "I'm alive? I'm alive?"

His vision was murky. Objects were swimming around him. The solid state of a world of objects seemed more like a kaleidoscope of colors destined to confuse and distract, rather than to elucidate the normal. He saw a fleshy face over him, looking into his eyes. He spoke to those eyes, which seemed, for a tiny instant to be his father's, but his father had died a long time ago. *How could it be?*

In the next moment, Saeed began to feel a pain throughout his body like needles pricking him. He wondered from where this pain issued. Surely his father would not torture him in this way. He tried to open his eyes wider: to see more clearly. He willed his eyes and mind to see the face above him, and slowly, a boy's face appeared. "You're alive, Saeed," said the smiling face. He could then feel a hand touching him, so gently that he was sure it was his wife, but she, too, was dead. *I'm delirious or dead. Which is it?*

The pain that wracked him subsided. His vision slowly came to a clearer stability, and the reality of muffled sights and sounds settled under a pale blue sky with Terran's face looking down on him. Saeed heard his voice, but didn't understand the words. However, he felt the tone of his voice, and it brought him to an even sharper focus. He sat up and looked around. He was about thirty feet from the front wall. Many men were standing around on the street—Namvar's men, he reasoned. The MRAP was behind him. Smoke continued to billow out of the wall, and the building's heat was enormous, but for some reason, Saeed was not alarmed.

"Carson says to get everyone inside the MRAP," Omar said. "Let's go."

"I'm alive?" Saeed said like a robot that had been programmed to speak only two words. He had wanted to say something else, but only those words could be found in his mind. Someone helped him to his feet. He saw the doctor who was already walking, though he was coughing badly. Frank was talking with some of the men by the street, naked from the waist up, with black marks all over his torso. Terran was under his right arm, helping to guide him to the MRAP.

It was all like a dream. Simple words and thoughts dawned on him. Time was different. Slower. There was a crush of thoughts like water rushing against a dam, piling up. Their weight he could feel, but he was getting more comfortable with the reality that he was indeed alive. Then, two new words, found their way to his mouth as he turned to Terran. "My children?"

CHAPTER 66

One Last Meeting

The clock said 8:07 on the MRAP's console. Terran noted it as he walked by. Carson sat on the navigator's chair, and swiveled around with a tunneled gaze to Charlie.

"Status on thermals, please," Carson said.

"It looks like they found a new building," Charlie announced. "Laser IDs them at just over two hundred meters... haven't moved in about five minutes."

"And Thermal Three?"

"If I didn't have the laser ID, I'm not sure I'd see it," Charlie replied. "It hasn't moved. Thermals down to 18 percent of its original level, which says it's barely hanging on, or it's dead and these are just residual readings. I'm guessing it's dead."

Terran's pull on Sanjur's sleeve was all he needed. Sanjur explained the latest info to Terran, who then stood up and walked to the door.

Sanjur started to translate, and Carson held up his arm. "No one's leaving the MRAP right now. We need to stay focused on getting out of here. Frank and Namvar are working out how to get Saeed back in the school. Just because Moshad moved a few hundred meters further up the street, doesn't mean we can move around at will."

Carson took a long breath and released it slowly. "What does he want?"

"He wants to go and see if Thermal Three needs help."

"He doesn't even know where it is."

"He knows."

"How?"

Sanjur shrugged. "Let Omar go with him. It'd only take a few minutes."

Carson scratched his scruffy beard. "Omar's busy."

Nouri cleared his throat. "I know you didn't want us to ask to go out of the vehicle, but I can go with him."

"And do what?" Carson asked. "If a hostile came at you, what would you do?"

Nouri looked around sheepishly. "I think I'm the only one here who can say they've killed two Baluchians."

Terran knocked on the door.

Carson smiled at Nouri's comment, grabbed his handgun and handed it to Nouri. "Remember how to use this?"

"Yes," Nouri replied.

"Okay, then put this on," Carson said, as he tossed a headset to Nouri, "and we'll tell you when you need to return."

Nouri put the headset on. Carson double-checked to make sure it was on, and then glanced at Sanjur. "Are you sure he knows where to go?"

Sanjur shrugged, and looked away, his arms folded across his chest.

"LB, open it up," Carson ordered.

"Yes, Sir."

"Five minutes... so I suggest you run." Carson said.

The door slid open and the two ran out.

"Omar, how's the doc doing?"

Omar was hunched over Dr. Najafi, wrapping his left arm with a gauze bandage. "He's still unconscious. To be honest, I don't know what more to do. I'm treating the burns... mostly second-degree, so that's not his problem. He's probably dehydrated and in shock. Plus he looks like he's pretty old. That was tough down there... like a piece of hell."

"Saeed, how're you doing?" Carson asked.

"Groggy... a few burns, but I don't really know what happened," he said putting down a canteen of water. "Can anyone explain it to me? I mean... I was dead. I got hit by a spray of embers... I mean... I could feel my body burning... and... and I look at my body... and it's like it never happened. Could I have imagined it?"

"We don't know how it happened. Terran was the only one there who could have helped, and..." Carson shook his head slowly, "I don't think so. He may be bright, but brawn isn't his thing. Just be glad you made it."

"Oh, I'm glad; don't worry about that, I... I just don't know who to thank."

Dorri looked up at Saeed, holding Mandana on her lap. "My uncle says when you don't know who to thank, thank yourself, because you probably did something to deserve it."

Saeed nodded with a smile.

"The mind can play tricks on you in life and death situations," Carson said.

"Yeah, maybe you're right," Saeed said. "Can I go now? Back to the school?"

"That's what Frank and Namvar are working out right now. Be patient."

"What about Dr. Najafi? What will you do with him?" Saeed asked.

"I'm not sure. For now, we'll take him with us. We'll be back after we drop Terran off at the plane. Hopefully, the Doc'll be feeling better by then. The school is probably the safest place."

"You'll stay?"

"We'll stay." Carson nodded and then looked at the screen. "Omar, can you laser-ID them? I'm not sure if I remember how..."

Omar sat down at the CROWS console and started clicking immediately. "They do seem to know where it's at. They're taking a straight path."

"All I know is that kid is *not* normal!" Carson blurted out.

Parto and Dorri both looked up and smiled. "Do you have any milk?" Dorri asked, looking at Carson.

"Milk? No milk, sorry." Carson turned to Omar. "Are you locked?"

"Yep."

"Distance to target?"

"They're within ten meters," Omar replied.

Terran could see the body lying in an alley, next to some tall trees and a garage structure that looked dilapidated and near collapse. He ran over and knelt down next to the body, which was face down on the ground. "Help me roll him over."

Nouri knelt down, too, and together they carefully rolled the body over. A knife wound near the chest was bleeding profusely. "It's Shaheen..."

"He's still breathing," Nouri said in amazement.

Terran bent down with his lips near Shaheen's left ear. "It's Terran. I came to tell you something. Can you hear me?"

Shaheen's hand twitched and his eyes strained to open, but seemed unable to do so. His head nodded slightly.

Terran grabbed his right hand. "Were you stabbed because Moshad knew you had helped me?"

Shaheen struggled again to open his eyes, but was only able to nod.

Terran moved even closer to Shaheen's ear. "I will talk with Moshad and convince him not to harm your family. You have my word. Do you understand me?"

Shaheen suddenly began weeping as he nodded. His eyes opened up briefly, and he glanced at Terran, and then his eyes looked up, just one second more, of blue sky and air. Then, a single, drawn-out breath, released like a pledge of finality.

Nouri stood up slowly, and watched while Terran arranged Shaheen's arms so they lay over his chest.

"Nouri, I need a status." Nouri's headset jarred him into a different reality, as Carson spoke.

"Shaheen is dead. We'll be coming back now."

"Good, be as quick as you can. Over."

Nouri continued to watch as Terran whispered something into Shaheen's ear, and then kissed his forehead. Terran's eyes were tear-filled when he looked at Nouri. "I need to speak with Carson." He turned and ran toward the MRAP. Nouri followed, trying his best to keep up.

When they arrived some thirty seconds later, Terran ran in and looked at Sanjur with eyes that got his attention, and he immediately sat up straight. "What's wrong?"

"Tell him I want to speak with Moshad."

Sanjur turned to Carson, blinked his eyes several times, paused, and then put his index finger up in the air, as if he were about to make an important point. "He wants to speak with Moshad."

Carson immediately started to shake his head. He limped out of the MRAP, and waved to Frank. "I need your help in here..."

Frank and Namvar had been talking with Parshan and a few of his men, watching the fire, and making plans to get Saeed returned to the school, since they weren't sure if Saeed could walk the distance.

"What's up?" Frank asked, as he came inside the MRAP.

"Can you talk some sense into this kid? He wants to have a friendly chat with Moshad."

"What the hell for?"

Carson folded his arms and lowered his gaze on Sanjur, who shrugged his shoulders. "I don't know."

"Find out."

Sanjur asked Terran to explain his desire to meet with Moshad.

"I need to get his word that he will not harm or endanger Shaheen's family. Once I have that, we can go."

"And what if he won't grant it?" Sanjur asked.

"He will," Terran said stubbornly.

Sanjur translated, and Frank put his arm on Terran's shoulder. "Look, I know you mean to do good here, and help Shaheen and all, but Moshad isn't going to honor anything, even if he agrees with you. It's out of your hands. We can't change his nature."

Terran listened to Sanjur's translation. "We will drive up to his building. I will shout my desire to meet. If he wants to meet, he will do so, and I will have my meeting in private... his men will clear the building. With your technology they cannot cheat. It will only take five minutes. Please? I promised Shaheen I would do this. We're this far anyway. I promise it will be the last meeting, and then we can go to the plane."

Sanjur translated, and Frank turned to Carson and whispered. "He's right, we could do this. I doubt Moshad's men would leave anyway. Let him try."

Sanjur started to translate, but Frank turned around and shot him a look that said: "That was private," and Sanjur stopped in mid-sentence.

Carson rubbed his stubbled chin for a few moments and then looked down, shaking his head as one does in self-wonderment. "I don't know why I agree to do these things... I'm either getting senile or just plain stupid, but fine, we'll drive over there and he can try to meet."

Frank spun around and looked at Sanjur, and then nodded.

"LB, pull back on the street. We'll mosey down the block two hundred meters."

"Yes, Sir."

Carson glanced at Frank. "Have Parshan and his men walk with us to the school. The MRAP can protect them. We'll drop Saeed off on the way. Sound good?"

"Let me tell them. LB, crack a window."

LB pushed a button on his console, and the window powered open. Frank told Parshan their plan, and the three men filed up alongside the MRAP as it slowly made its way down the block, closer to the school and closer to Moshad.

CHAPTER 67

Deal

When chaos looms in the wake of His appearance, the time will come when men will resume their evil ways to govern what is not theirs. Men of power will rise up with their new machines to harness nature once again, their memories shortened by greed and power. They will even do this with the Mahdi. They will try to harness Him, and when they cannot, they will seek to copy Him, but they will fail. There is no machine that can make a Mahdi.

*   *   *   *

Saeed stood to his feet as the MRAP came to a complete stop. He hobbled over to Terran and glanced at Sanjur. "Can you give him my thanks for what he's done for me?"

Sanjur nodded and passed on the sentiments to Terran, who smiled, and then clasped his hands together and bowed.

Saeed walked out of the MRAP, favoring his right leg, knowing that something had happened between him and Terran that was not meant or even possible, to be spoken. Parshan guided Saeed by the arm, as the MRAP backed up to the school door, with the four men hidden behind the metal beast. When they'd gone far enough, Parshan knocked on the door, and it opened to let them in.

The MRAP pulled away, heading further down the street, and then came to a stop about seventy meters past the school.

"Six thermals accounted for?" Carson asked Omar, as he walked over to the main console.

"Yes, they're all up on the second floor. One is watching us, the others seem to be eating or talking amongst themselves."

Carson eyed Terran, who was sitting with his eyes closed. "Terran?"

Terran opened his eyes.

"Tell him that we're here, and he can make his appeal to Moshad by talking into this device." Caron held a PA microphone.

Sanjur explained, and Terran stood up, taking the microphone in his hand.

"Push here to talk," Carson instructed.

Terran took a deep breath and slowly exhaled. He brought the microphone to his mouth. "Moshad, this is Terran speaking to you from the vehicle in the street. We can see you, we can track you, we can shoot you. If we wanted to kill you, you would be dead in a matter of seconds. I didn't know that technology like this existed, but I have seen it with my own eyes, and it is astonishing.

"I know that you killed Shaheen, and it's because of this that I want to meet with you. But this meeting must be only between you and me—no one else. If you agree to this meeting and my terms, then have your five men leave the building, and go to the backyard of the building next door. Once they have left, I will come in the front of your building and meet with you. If you are willing to do this, I will see that your lives are spared. If you are not willing, then I will let the leader of this vehicle kill all of you, and you will meet your judge.

"When I see your men leave, I will know you have chosen to live. If they stay with you for more than one minute after I finish speaking, I will know that you have chosen death and the judgment that waits you."

Terran released the talk button and handed the microphone back to Carson.

"What'd he say?" Carson's head pivoted between Sanjur and Nouri.

Sanjur remained silent. Nouri squirmed in his seat. "He basically said that they have one-minute to move everyone other than Moshad out of that building or we would kill them all."

Carson, Frank and Omar all stared at Terran. "Now he's talking," Carson said. "One minute! You heard him, Omar. What're they doing?"

"They're all talking among themselves. Some sitting, some standing."

Frank and Carson were huddled behind Omar, watching the monitor. Several of the thermals were animated. It looked like an argument was ensuing. Frank pointed at Thermal One. "He's pissed."

"It's amazing how much info you can get from these ghosts,"

Carson whispered.

"Did he just plunge his knife into the floor?" Omar asked, pointing to Thermal Five.

"I don't know, but it looks like they're leaving," Frank said. "Walking down the stairs… okay, Thermal Five is staying on the first floor. The rest… yes, they're leaving."

Frank turned to Sanjur. "Tell him that Moshad is waiting for him on the first floor. The others have left, and are moving to the back of the building on the north side."

After Sanjur finished his translation, Terran stood up and went to the door. Frank came up behind him and held out a handgun, but Terran shook his head. Both Frank and Carson knew it was pointless to argue, so Frank set the gun down.

LB opened the door, and Terran walked out without a word or a look. His focus was elsewhere. The building was about half the distance of a football field away, and Terran walked like a person on a mission. The building that Moshad was in was a two-story that looked pitted by a century's worth of sand. It was an old adobe building with high, narrow windows. It had a small porch and a front door that was half-open and mostly unhinged.

As Terran came to the porch, he stopped. "Moshad, can you hear me?"

"Yes, I can hear you."

"I'll get straight to the point. You murdered Shaheen and this is your mistake."

"If it was my mistake, then you wouldn't be here lecturing me. He assisted you, and I knew it. It was no mistake!"

"Call it what you choose, it was your mistake to murder him, and now you will try to cover this up with Pirdah. You will try to exile Shaheen's family, adding to your offense, but in your eyes, justifying the murder because you will paint Shaheen to be a traitor. Shaheen was only doing what I asked him to do. If there's a traitor, it's me."

"And what is it that you want—to confuse me?" Moshad said. "You did say you would get straight to the point."

Omar pointed at the monitor. "He's moving. Thermal One is moving."

"Maybe he's just taking a piss," Carson offered.

"He's moving closer… to Terran."

"I want a weapons lock on Thermal One now," Carson said.

Omar clicked his mouse. "Weapons locked on."

"Nouri, come here," Carson said, grabbing the PA microphone and holding it out to Nouri. "We're going to shoot one warning round, and I want you to tell this thermal that it's his last warning. Got it?"

Nouri nodded. "…His last warning."

Carson put his hand on Omar's shoulder. "As close as you can to hitting him… without hitting him. Okay?"

Omar drew a small box on the side of the building about five feet in front of Thermal One, who was slowly inching forward, and then Omar clicked it. It immediately turned red. He waited until the thermal was two feet away from the red box, and clicked his cursor over the word "Single Round—manual." Instantly a single shot fired. And the thermal imprint of a .50-caliber bullet gash replaced the red box.

Carson immediately motioned to Nouri to press the talk button. "This is your final warning shot." Nouri spoke in a stilted voice.

"He probably took a piss now," Carson said as he grabbed the microphone from Nouri.

Frank and Omar chuckled, and watched Thermal One retreat with great speed to the backyard with his four comrades who crouched down, their thermals changed from the stress-induced threat.

"Why are you shooting at my men?" Moshad yelled.

"Your men were warned. Twice," Terran replied. "Let's hope a third time isn't required." Terran paused. "What I want is for you to repair the damage you made by murdering Shaheen."

"And why would I agree to that?" Moshad asked.

"Because I will spare you."

There was a long pause, while Moshad dragged himself to the door so he could see Terran, who remained standing by the front steps. "You will spare me? Who do you think you are?"

"I am the one who can call that machine to destroy you and your men."

Moshad looked at the menacing MRAP with its CROWS pointed in his direction. "You wouldn't dare kill us. If you *are* the Mahdi, you cannot kill."

"It wouldn't be me that did the killing. It would be me who did nothing to prevent it. These are two different acts."

Moshad leaned against the door jam, positioning his leg straight. "You stole my doctor—"

"He wasn't your doctor."

Moshad sighed. "Let's say that you leave here... you go to your new world of brilliant teachers and technologies that you so love that you would forsake your own people. You're on the other side of the earth. How would you know what I did with Shaheen's family, and moreover, how could you punish us even if you did know? You see, there's nothing you can do either to prevent it or to punish the act. The only way is for you to stay. It is the only way you can protect them."

"Then you have made your decision to die," Terran said. He began to turn around and walk back to the MRAP.

"Wait! Wait! I was only speaking in theory," Moshad professed. "Come back, maybe there's another arrangement."

Terran stopped and returned. He walked up the stairs within a few feet of Moshad, squatted down, and stared fearlessly into his eyes. "Do you not understand that if you do anything against Shaheen's family, I will know? What will I do with this knowledge? It will be like a curse that hangs over you, and you will never know the time or the place when my wrath will fall, but it will surely fall. The only path for you is to repair the murder of Shaheen by placing his family in good standing within our tribe. Shaheen's death is a hero's death. Do you agree to this?"

Terran could feel a power issuing through him as surely as lightning issues from a terrible dark cloud. He did not know its source, but he knew it traveled through him with a ferocity and power that was not his.

Moshad turned away for an instant. "You talk like one who has been given authority over all, but you are still a boy—"

"If I am still a boy, then why have you let me shoot you, out maneuver you, place you in the crosshairs of death's bullets? If I am still a boy, then what are you, Moshad? What are you?"

Terran stood to his feet, looking down on Moshad with penetrating eyes. "I need only to hear you say that you will grant Shaheen the status of a hero to our people, the same as you would Josid. If you do that, I will forgive your other sins, and let you live."

Terran looked back to the MRAP and took a deep breath, waiting for Moshad to respond, but he remained silent. "Moshad?"

"What?"

"Your decision..."

Moshad chuckled softly. "I don't know what to think of you. Part of me wants to strangle you with my bare hands. Part of me wants to worship you. I don't know what to do, which voice to listen to. Prove to me that you're the Mahdi! Prove it, and I will honor your request."

Terran walked down the stairs and turned around to face Moshad. "Doubt is standing in two boats, with one foot in each. Eventually, if you want to get to shore, you have to choose one boat... one belief. What other proof do you need, Moshad, than the reality you are in at this very moment? What more do you need, a trumpet to sound in the air? A light to overtake you and render you blind?"

"Can you heal me?" It was said almost in the tone of a child's whisper.

Terran could finally see a crack in the shell. He looked inside Moshad for a split second, and could see the child within, and in that very moment, he could feel the pain that had wrought his personality—that has sealed his fate as a punisher of men.

Terran could feel something slip from the bounds of his body and reach out to Moshad. There was nothing he did, but to allow this thing, this inexact love that was poised to heal after every evil deed. There was no conjuring of this spirit, it lurched forward of its own will, and all Terran could do was to watch.

Moshad took a long gasp of breath as it entered him. His mouth remained open, his eyes immediately turned inward as though some powerful temptation had suddenly let him go, and some essence remained by which alone the invisible was made visible for the first time. His face relaxed, and he suddenly looked like one who had experienced an ecstasy, the kind only summoned by a pure heart. His eyes fluttered, and when they opened, they looked confused.

Moshad grabbed his leg and winced in pain. "I thought that you healed me."

"The healing was deeper, the proof more subtle," Terran replied. "The leg is easy to heal. Your body knows the way, but what was dark in you, had remained dark for forty years, and you had no way of knowing how to heal it, because you never saw it as something that needed to be healed."

"Then you healed the wrong thing..." Moshad said, shaking his head slowly. "What... are you trying to make me a virtuous man? Good luck with that. I am anything but virtuous, and that has kept me alive all of these years. If I was anything but hard and conniving, I'd be dead long ago. So, if you took that from me—healed me, then you have effectively killed me. How am I to live, now?"

"Be your new self before you believe it is the death of you. That is all I can say. Do we have a deal?"

Moshad took a deep breath, holding it for a while, and then released it like a flood of air into the stillness of the morning. He stared straight ahead into the crooked door that hung like a mockery of purpose. "We have a deal, but not because of what I felt a minute ago, because I know that will fade. I will do it, because you came to me like a man and begged me to make Shaheen a hero. You, the Mahdi, begging before me... Moshad, a simple man..." Moshad chuckled to himself, and then started coughing. "That's why..." He turned to face Terran, but Terran had already gathered his presence, and was walking back to the MRAP.

The small figure, walking away from him, draped in a school uniform of a student was magnetic. Moshad knew he was anything but a student. He was the Mahdi, the *Ancient Presence*. He had no doubts at that exact moment—watching him walk away. It was the solidifying moment for Moshad. It was precisely what he needed to convince him. Sometimes it is the accumulation, and not the event, and when the final piece enters the frame, the picture is whole, and there is no more room for even a particle of doubt.

CHAPTER 68

Desert Rats

The high desert that surrounded Mashhad, Iran held a primeval quality that was cast in every shade of brown imaginable. It was spacious and light giving. It reminded anyone who looked that the world was a big place. Peter remained inside the MRAP that held Farzad and his small crew. Their MRAP was more of a standard-issue version, much less sophisticated, and about one-third the size of the MRAP that Carson commanded.

Peter had explained that there were two missing policemen that seemed to have disappeared in the shrub terrain, and their motives, while not entirely clear, were definitely hostile.

"Why would the police be shooting at the plane?" Farzad asked.

"I have to assume they're trying to prevent us from leaving," Peter said. "We need to find them before they do any damage to the plane."

"Graham, we're going on a little search and destroy mission," Farzad said, as he tapped the shoulder of the driver, and then turned back to Peter. "Do you know the last whereabouts?"

"The SUV you shot up… they got out of that about a minute before you arrived. They were coming up from that direction—from the south—and then we got distracted and lost them. They could be almost anywhere."

"Were they armed?" Graham asked.

"I'm not sure, it looked like they were carrying something, but we couldn't ID it. Too far away."

"We have an automated weapons system," Farzad said, "unfortunately, the thermal detection system is busted, and the laser targeting was cannibalized for parts to make sure the main vehicle was operational back and front. So, we have to rely on our eyes. The good news is that the .50-caliber gun works like a charm."

"Do you have headsets?" Peter asked.

Farzad nodded and reached over to a drawer underneath the CROWS console. "Did you bring extra batteries?"

"There's a box of a hundred and twenty-eight inside the plane," Peter said.

"Great, here you go… it's switched on and ready to go."

"Thanks. Give me another one. I want to toss one of these up to the pilot." Peter put the headset on in one deft movement. "I'll be a pair of eyes under the plane. Martin, our pilot, will be watching from inside the plane. You circle around the plane at an ever-increasing distance. Keep in radio contact at all times—no one leaves the vehicle. If you see anything move bigger than a rabbit, fire a warning shot. If they don't surrender, shoot at will."

"These are Police, right?" Farzad asked.

"We don't know that. You saw that they opened fire on you. Why would Police do that?" Peter knocked on the door. "Open up."

Graham released the door locks, and Peter scurried to his previous position by the airplane's back tires. Farzad and his team backed up, and started circling the plane in a spiral formation.

Peter took a good 360-degree view of the surrounding environment. He yelled over to Martin. "Any sign of them?"

"Nothing. Either they're lying low or they're gone."

"I have a headset I'm going to toss up to you. Be ready to catch it. When you have it, put it on. Okay?"

"Understood," Martin shouted down.

Peter took one last look around, and then ran under the fuselage, and tossed the headset up to Martin. The first try fell short, but the second one made it. "Okay, this is Peter, checking in. Martin, do you copy?"

"This is Martin, I can hear you fine, over," Martin replied.

"Farzad, can you hear us?"

"Copy that. Loud and clear. Over."

"Farzad, Martin is our pilot… Martin, Farzad is our communications expert. Expand your circle, Farzad. Maybe go out another hundred feet or so. Over."

"Copy that," Farzad said. "Once you get off the highway platform, this is pretty soft sand. It wouldn't be hard to bury yourself in this sand

and hide. Over."

"Copy that," Peter said. "Martin. Keep sweeping with your binoculars and report if you see anything that looks suspicious. Take note of what Farzad said. They could be half-buried in the sand. Over."

"Understood," Martin replied. "I'll let you know if I see anything. Over."

Peter saw a glint of metal in the far distance. "Martin, could you check out the vehicle coming from the east? Report."

"Hold one second… it's our tank truck. Right on time."

"Awesome. Best news of the day so far," Peter said. "Farzad, go meet the tanker. I want you to escort it in. Okay? And keep your guns pointed to the desert."

"Copy that, on our way." The MRAP made a beeline toward the truck, which was still several miles out on the freeway, but closing fast. It was a large tank truck, with a rusted tank, but enough aluminum remained that it gleamed in the sun.

"Peter, this is Martin. I see something that looks round, black and spherical and it seems to be moving slightly… but I can't hold my arms still enough to make sure it's not me that's moving. Over."

"Copy that," Peter said. "Can you give me general coordinates and range? Over."

"It's definitely moving… I see him. Yes, he's moving towards us from the southeast. He's crawling pretty fast—"

"What's his range!" Peter interrupted.

"Um, sorry about that… about eighty meters. Over."

"Farzad, I need you to return and zero in on those coordinates. Take this guy out. Over."

"Copy that," Farzad said. "Martin, if you can keep an eye on this guy, just direct us to his position. Over."

"Take a southeasterly track. I'll direct you once you get in range. Over."

"Martin, no distractions." Peter instructed.

"I think he sees you're coming back… he's digging in. He'll be hard to spot…"

"Martin, do not take your eyes off him, even if he becomes a pile of sand. Over."

"Copy that." Martin's voice sounded distant.

The MRAP slowed up some as it got within about fifty meters of the plane in the southeasterly area. "Martin, can you direct us in? Over."

"Go further to the east... he's about twenty meters from your position."

Farzad was looking at his monitor and couldn't see anything that resembled a human head or hand or any other body part. "Martin, do you still see him? Over."

"I don't see him, but I'm viewing the area where I last saw him, and he's literally ten-to-twelve meters to your four-o'clock position. You're very close. Over."

"Peter, we can lay down some rounds where we think he is, and ask questions later... or we can do the warning shot. What's your preference? Over."

"Copy that. Lay down a few rounds in the sand and see what he does. Martin, keep a sharp eye out. Over."

A few seconds later, Peter heard three gun shots in thundering succession. From his position, underneath the fuselage some eighty meter away, the sand spray was still clearly visible.

"He's throwing something... it could be a hand grenade!" Martin shouted.

"Farzad, move!" Peter yelled.

"He's throwing another... shit!"

The MRAP suddenly jumped in the air and rolled over on its side. Smoke billowed from its undercarriage, but no fire was visible. Seconds later another explosion erupted, and then silence swept across the desert. The tanker pulled to a complete stop about a half-mile away from the plane, accentuating the stillness.

"Farzad, report!" Peter demanded.

Silence.

"Martin, what do you see?"

"The man who threw the grenade is pointing a handgun at Farzad's truck, and circling it cautiously." A gunshot rang out. "He just fired it... I think he tried to break the window."

Peter ran towards the scene at full speed. He climbed a small embankment of sand and flung his body in a firing position. His M4 was equipped with a scope, and he looked through it with minimum magnification, locating the policeman on the far side of the MRAP. Peter didn't have a good shot.

Another gunshot resounded in the desert, echoing like ripples of terror. Peter had been trained in all combat situations, but his sharp shooting wasn't his strongest skill, nor was the M4 the best choice for long-range shooting. He calibrated his scope and zoomed in, placing the man in his crosshairs.

"He's trying to break the glass," Martin repeated. "Do you have a shot?"

Suddenly the tanker's horn blasted, and Peter instinctively looked. Running across the desert was a second man at full sprint. He was running towards the tanker, carrying what Peter could only assume was a knapsack full of hand grenades. Peter's hand was already shaking lightly, but now his heart beat frantically, because he knew that if the tanker was blown up, their mission was effectively over.

He steadied his gun against his chest. The sprinter was a good hundred and fifty meters away, well within range of his M4, but luck would have to play a role if he were to be able to stop him. He pulled the trigger once. It was a practice shot. He missed by ten feet. He compensated and fired again, a little higher. It was closer, but still a miss. The runner kept getting closer to the tanker. With a strong arm, he was only five seconds from launching a grenade and erasing their mission.

Peter pulled the trigger and held it down while twenty-two rounds exploded out of the nine-inch barrel. The man fell down in a dramatic roll. One of his bullets must have hit. A millisecond later, a puff of sand exploded to Peter's right, about three feet away. He was now under fire from the first policeman, who, ironically enough, had taken refuge behind the MRAP.

Peter hugged the ground, and scrambled down the slight embankment he was on.

"Martin, report!"

"He's behind the vehicle. I can't see him. Over."

"Can you see any movement inside the MRAP?"

"The truck?"

"Yes, the truck... it's called an MRAP... any movement?"

There was a pause. Peter looked through his scope to check the runner he'd just shot, but couldn't find him. *Shit!*

"Peter, he's got a bag. I think he has more hand grenades. He's stepping back from the... the MRAP."

Peter lurched up the sand embankment and steadied his gun, concentrating with all his power on the image in the scope. He exhaled, and let all of his training take hold of him. He knew he only had three rounds left, and the other clips were back at the tires. Peter watched as the man carefully stepped back, fumbling a bit on the loose sand. He needed him to go far enough back so he would have a head shot, which at that distance was no easy task, especially for Peter.

"I see movement inside the MRAP," Martin said.

"Farzad, can you hear me?" Peter asked.

"I'm... okay. What happened?"

"You have a hostile right outside your MRAP. He has a bag of hand grenades and a handgun. Hold still... I'm going to shoot... him... just a little bit more..."

Peter pulled the trigger once. His bullet hit him, and he fell. Through the scope, it looked like it hit his left shoulder, but that would be an incapacitative wound from an M4. "Farzad, can you get out?"

"I think so... Graham, are you okay? Graham's still unconscious. I'll need to open the door myself. Hold on..."

"Farzad, can you see the hostile?"

"No."

"I'm coming in," Peter said with a new urgency. He stood to his feet, staring at the place where the second runner had been taken down. He could see nothing. The truck started up, and began to back up slowly, probably as a precaution, Peter assumed.

Peter held his gun in combat mode, running toward the MRAP as fast as the sand and his legs would allow. It was difficult running, but he managed to keep on his feet and close the distance. He was not a great athlete. The word *adequate* described him well, at least in comparison to his fellow officers in training at the Naval Academy.

As he came within ten meters of the MRAP he pulled up. The policeman was lying on his back, bleeding from his left shoulder, just below the scapula. In his right hand he held a hand grenade in a threatening gesture. Peter could see the pin was still attached.

"Drop it!" Peter shouted, motioning with his gun to the ground. He didn't know any Persian, other than a few pleasantries.

The policeman was clearly in pain, and like any wounded animal, humans can be unpredictable when they're in severe pain and cornered under a gun barrel. He took the hand grenade to his mouth, and bit the pin.

"Stop!" Peter yelled at the top of his lungs. For a split second, the policeman paused, but there was something in his eyes that looked hopeless like someone who had already passed through terror, and now desires only to surge into his own shadowy world.

Peter watched in slow motion as the policeman bit the pin and tossed it inside the knapsack. The policeman's eyes stayed on him the whole time. Peter counted the ten second countdown for the grenade, as he staggered backwards. He heard Farzad beating on the glass door to his left, but everything telescoped out of time. The policeman grabbed the bag and began to swing it over his head, and Peter's finger twitched subconsciously, his first shot missed, but the second one found its target and the bag fell down. Peter jumped as far away as he could, and then an explosion, so loud, that his first thought was that his ears had exploded.

CHAPTER 69

Oath

Moshad watched the MRAP move down the street, past his building. Its weapons aimed ominously on his position. He remained sitting in the threshold of the front door, nodding to the MRAP as it passed by. Moshad thought is looked vaguely reminiscent of a mechanical dragon, and he felt like a knight who had only his bare hands to slay it.

The instant it passed, he yelled to his men. "Come back."

In a few seconds, the sound of footsteps coming through the back door resounded in the empty, first floor room.

"Careful, there's a broken floorboard there." Moshad pointed it out. "Sit."

He took a deep breath as his five remaining men sat down. He had one left at their basecamp, but half of his men were dead or presumed dead. Moshad kept his view on the street, while his men sat inside in a semi-circle. "I have one last card to play, but it will require that we have camels."

"What's our plan?" The men asked in a broken chorus.

We'll go to the airplane. We'll shoot it down, we'll shoot out its tires, we'll shoot its gas tank, we'll do everything in our power to make sure it never leaves the ground. But to do that, we need our camels."

"We're giving up on the school?"

"Terran's gone. The school is emptied of our interest."

"Do we know how to find the plane?

"Of course, that monstrous vehicle just left. We simply follow its tracks."

"But their technology—that truck... against our camels... how do we defeat it?"

Moshad glared at the man who spoke, and then softened his tone. "Every battlefield and every commander has a weakness. When we see the battlefield, we'll see a weakness. And we'll exploit it."

"What about your leg?"

"My leg is fine. I can certainly ride a camel… Jalil, you and Navid are my fastest runners. You get to the camels and bring them here. Tell Afshin to come, too. There's no need to protect our basecamp."

"And the other camels?" Jalil asked.

"We'll pick them up on the way home."

"What about the Police… they still patrol the school. Their numbers are strong."

"They won't come knocking on our door," Moshad said. "They'll sit back and collect their money. These are lazy body-wasters."

Moshad grunted, as he moved his leg so he could address his men eye to eye. "One last thing… Shaheen's death is my concern. None of you will speak of him again, unless it reflects on him kindly. When we return home, I'll speak well of him for the sake of his family—"

"But he's a traitor, Sir, how can we speak well of him? You said it yourself, he assisted Terran to escape. He lied to us. How can we speak kindly of a traitor?"

Moshad's face turned red with anger, and he beat his fist on the ground several times. "All you need to do is to say *nothing* if that's the best you can do. If I hear one word about Shaheen that isn't generous, I will cut your heart out."

Moshad rubbed his fist with his other hand and paused, his color returning to a less volatile shade of red. "I am asking you to support my example. Shaheen is a fallen comrade, and no one can know otherwise. If you can't support this, tell me now, but do not disappoint me later."

Moshad put each man, one at a time, to the test, asking for their word, their solemn oath of loyalty to Moshad.

Everyone agreed.

CHAPTER 70

Gorgin

Peter felt the shaking, but couldn't make sense of anything. It was much worse than being woken from a dream in the middle of the night. Which world is real? Someone was shaking him, he could feel the pressure on his shoulder, he could sense the movement of his body, but something was wrong. *The silence.* Why is there no sound? More shaking. Everything was jumbled. No words, no sounds, nothing. He opened his eyes, and saw a blinding light. The next feeling was excruciating pain. He reached his hand to his right ear, and felt the viscous liquid he feared. He smeared his hands on his trousers and tried to stand up, but it was impossible.

He felt like a drunkard who has stepped into hell, a place where sound was absent. Only the infernal lights shone, and people shoving on you. He wanted to strike back, but his strength, what little he had, was preoccupied in the notion of understanding who or what was pushing on his shoulder. He kept thinking it was just a nightmare; everything will come back to normal. Be patient, but the soundlessness was too much of a shock for him to bear. He wanted to lose consciousness. He prayed that the confused world he was in would go away.

There was more shaking of his shoulder. Someone slapped his face, not hard, but over and over. Something deep inside him began to upsurge, anger so dark that he could feel it taking over his mind. He opened his eyes and shouted at the person as loudly as he could fathom to yell. "What do you want?!"

But he couldn't even hear his own voice. It felt a million miles away, muted in some underworld heaviness, toiling against a gravity that swallowed his every word. A face began to come into focus. His eyes were blurry from tears, *why am I crying?* Everything was confused and abnormal. From out of that face came the realization he was in Iran. It was not a familiar face. He looked around. He was in a desert.

Where is the sound?

He turned to the man who was talking to him, his lips moving in some strange order that he'd never seen. His face was dark with close-cropped jet-black hair, wild eyebrows, and wide eyes that clearly signaled alarm. Peter grabbed his shirt. "Who are you?"

Again his voice was so distant. He could hear the words as a vibration and a ghostly thought, but not as sound. If his mind hadn't thought of the words, he would not know that he had spoken them. *I'm deaf!*

The thought was a kick to Peter's gut. *I'm deaf in the middle of Iran.* Then his nose caught the scent of something burning. He could feel himself being dragged away by strong hands. He suddenly realized that the smell was burned flesh, and then the whole scene came into sharp focus. He remembered what had happened.

"Farzad? Where is Farzad?" His dry mouth mumbled.

Peter looked back at the stranger who was pulling him. "Where is Farzad? We have to save him!"

Suddenly, a new face thrust itself in front of him. He recognized Jamere, who was panting and completely out of breath. He said something to him, but only one word was sensible to Peter's lip-reading eyes, "Hurry."

Jamere ran away, and Peter suddenly lost consciousness.

The MRAP was burning, and Jamere tried to get close enough to help whoever he could, but it was too late. A dark, billowing smoke rose from the vehicle like blood oozing from a deep cut. A clip of ammunition suddenly exploded inside the MRAP, and Jamere ran back to Raji and Peter.

"Can you help me get him in your Jeep?" Jamere asked.

"Sure…"

The two men hoisted Peter's limp body onto the back of the Jeep, and the two jumped in and drove in the direction of the plane.

"Who are you?" Jamere asked, holding onto the top of the roof to stop from falling out the side of the Jeep.

"I'm Raji. I was sent to stop my brothers from trying to sabotage your plane. I'm with the Mashhad Police."

"You're one of them?"

"It's very complicated," Raji said. "We changed our alliance. These four didn't know that. I got here too late."

"That's an understatement," Jamere whispered under his breath.

When they got to the airplane, Peter was yelling something unintelligible, but at least he was conscious.

"Martin, throw me down a water bottle," Jamere said.

As soon as he had the bottle in hand, he ran it over to Peter who was trying to claw himself upright in the Jeep's backseat. He looked terrible. His face was covered in blood, and the front of his light gray shirt was soaked in blood.

"I'm sending down the First Aid Kit, on a rope. Grab it!" Martin yelled.

Jamere handed the water bottle to Raji. "See if he'll drink any of this."

Jamere ran to the First Aid Kit dangling in the air, untied it and ran back to the Jeep. "Look, we need to see where this blood is coming from. Let's get his shirt off."

Peter flayed his arms around as they tried to take his shirt off. He was speaking, but they couldn't understand him.

"What the hell are you saying?" Jamere asked.

Peter pointed to the spot where the second runner had been shot. "Yours neet to chet hem ouy. Gos!"

"You speak English?" Jamere asked, turning to Raji.

"Yes..."

"Maybe it's just me, but do you understand anything he's saying?"

Raji shook his head.

Peter passed out again, as though his battery had run out.

Raji helped Jamere unbutton his shirt and opened it up carefully. "It looked like he saw a ghost?" Raji said. "What was he pointing to?"

"About ten minutes ago, a tanker pulled up to refuel this jet, and a man with a bag full of hand grenades ran at it, and Peter, well, he shot 'em down before he got close enough. Maybe he was asking us to go check him out. Make sure he's dead."

Raji looked around. "Where's the tanker?"

"It backed up. Probably didn't like the idea of grenades being tossed its way."

Raji looked in the direction that Peter had pointed. "If you help me lift him out, we can lay him on the ground. I can see if I can find him. Maybe he's dead, maybe he's not, but if he's alive, I can tell him that you're not the bad guys anymore."

Jamere stepped back so he could see the emergency exit where Martin was standing. "Martin, this is Raji, he's with the Police, but he's on our side. He's going to have a look at the guy with the hand grenades."

Martin nodded. "I'd rather he chase down the tanker and get him to come back. We're sitting ducks until we get refueled."

"Okay, I'll tell him."

After Jamere explained, Raji reluctantly agreed to find the tanker, but first he would check and see if his associate was still alive. Jamere gave him the coordinates as best he could, and then Raji drove off. Jamere cleaned the blood off Peter's face, neck, chest, and arms. Shrapnel was evident in his upper chest and right arm, but the worst of the blood was from his right ear and the left side of his chest, where he had a large gash from an object that was still sticking out of his skin, buried an inch deep, and Jamere had no idea what to do about it.

"Martin?"

"How bad is it?"

"I have no fucking idea! All I know is we need to get a doctor... is anyone in your crew handy with First Aid Kits?"

"Peter told us to not leave the airplane under any circumstance. I had to swear to him that I would do that."

"Did any *circumstance* include his death?" Jamere asked in a mocking tone.

Martin paused, and pulled back inside the cabin. A minute later he returned.

"I'm sending Fritz down... he can help you."

Jamere continued working on cleaning various wounds with an antiseptic. Peter remained unconscious.

Raji slowly drove up to the general coordinates and stood up in the Jeep as he drove. "It's Raji, are you there?" he shouted. "We have new orders. Do you hear me?"

Raji was driving about two hundred feet off the freeway when he suddenly saw a dark shape, mostly hidden behind a four-foot scrub tree.

He recognized Gorgin, and ran to him. "How bad?"

"Where am I?" Gorgin's eyes fluttered, not able to keep a focus on Raji's face.

"Don't give up, brother... I think the bullets went clean through," Raji said, inspecting the wounds. "We just need to bandage you. You'll be okay." He grabbed Gorgin's hand and placed it over the wound on his side. "Press down hard, and hold it there for as long as you can. I'll be right back."

Raji ran to the Jeep and rummaged through the back for a First Aid Kit or anything else he could find that could be used to patch Gorgin up. He couldn't find anything other than empty oil cans. He jumped in the Jeep, and drove up to Gorgin's position within a few feet, got out, and with great effort, managed to heave Gorgin inside the Jeep. Raji drove off, heading back to the plane.

"Now, why is he coming back here?" Fritz asked. "I thought he was going to get the tanker."

"Must've found his friend," Jamere said.

Raji drove up right next to where Jamere and Fritz were working on Peter. "Can you give me a hand?"

Jamere stood up and grabbed Gorgin's ankles, while Raji pulled his arms and body up, and together they placed him next to Peter. Gorgin was a strong looking man with thick legs and stout body. No fat, all muscle, and noticeably proportioned like a Greco-Roman wrestler. Jamere tore open his trousers to expose the gunshot wound on his lower thigh. "Looks like it went clean through, because there's both entrance and exit wounds."

"Yeah," Raji nodded, "I think the same thing about his side."

Raji looked at Fritz who was trying to remove some shrapnel from Peter's chest. "Can he suture?"

Fritz looked up. "I'm Fritz, I can suture. How big is the wound... in centimeters?"

"They both look about two centimeters in diameter..."

"Okay, take this, and clean the wounds about four centimeters beyond the actual bullet hole. Have him lay on his good side.... keep the pressure on after you clean the wound... clean whatever you use to apply the pressure. I'll be two minutes before I can look at him."

Fritz was impressive. Jamere felt like a nurse in an operating room in the middle of an abandoned freeway, underneath a plane's fuselage. It was surreal, but then most of his life the past twelve years qualified as surreal. He looked at two men, lying on the surrogate tarmac, who were hunter and prey ten minutes earlier, and were now both patients of a German pilot in the middle of an Iranian highway.

How did I get here? Jamere scratched the back of his head out of some primal instinct. *And how am I going to get out?*

CHAPTER 71

It

"In the aftermath of idols, when glamour is torn down, and all are once again equal in circumstance and hardship, the Mahdi is born. He is born into this specific time to bring a new light to the old darkness. This light is not of scripture, but of science. As a boy, the Mahdi will need a teacher of greatness, and so he shall find it. The teacher is not human. We cannot say their name or even describe them, for we lack the words. We can only say that God is ineffable, and so is this teacher."

Pirdah turned the page of *The Book of Prophecy*, and paused for a moment as he considered the words he had just read. The prophets were writing in the middle ages, when technology was a blacksmith pounding out swords or an aqueduct that channeled water. Surely, they couldn't imagine what kind of teacher the Mahdi would require. Javad was an excellent teacher, selected by Pirdah himself.

The one word that had always troubled Pirdah in that paragraph was the word "it." Why did they use the word *it* instead of *him*? What possible reason would the prophets choose that word to signify a teacher? It seemed a very odd word, because even God was clearly a *He*, not an *It*. Besides, even if the reference was meant to be God, why would they not use a capital "I"?

The prophets made it clear that they had seen the future. They had written the details of their vision in *The Book of Prophecy*, and no one had yet found an error in their writing. But this one word, small as it was, troubled Pirdah greatly. The sentence that followed the word also bothered him, though most scholars considered the reference to mean an angel, but even angels were still described in terms of gender. Pronouns were not provisional terms subject to whim. They were fixed, carved in granite. The prophets knew this.

The graver consequence to that simple word was in the reality that nothing called *it* could be good, and certainly not great. It was devoid of human reality. Therefore, it was neither good nor evil. It was bland. It was neutral. It was nothing. So how could *it* be the great teacher for the Mahdi?

Pirdah had pondered this question for fifty-three years since that one little word revealed itself to him. Every permutation of the word had been methodically considered. Now, thinking about it in his tent, it remained the pebble in his shoe.

Pirdah had not heard anything yet from Moshad, and the fact that they had not returned, was a clear sign they had met resistance. He felt it in his heart, too. Something was wrong. He had said he would wait a day before deciding to send reinforcements, but that simple little word had him agitated again. He called his guard in waiting, and told him to assemble the leaders of his army and police force. That it was time to reclaim their Mahdi, and they would ride out that very night.

CHAPTER 72

Stay

The black smoke on the horizon was the first thing Omar noticed when their MRAP left the city limits, and headed onto the Northern Bypass Freeway. Its skyward trail was twisted and fraying, telltale signs that it had happened earlier, perhaps as much as an hour. Carson saw it too. "A plane that size would have a hell of lot larger smoke trail… it's not the plane."

"Yeah, but they had no fuel left, so—"

"Look, it's not the plane," Carson insisted. "LB, can you go any faster?"

"Optimal speed and gas conservation is forty-five mph. If you want to go faster, I will, but we'll burn gas faster, too."

"Burn it. I don't care. Get us to that plane as fast as you can."

"Yes, Sir."

The MRAP began to speed up. The freeway was bumpy and full of plants, and even the occasional small bush, which made it a little tricky to dodge holes and bushes, but LB was an expert driver and handled the challenge. As they got closer to the high desert plateau that the plane had landed on, they could see two smoke trails. The first one was closer and fainter, originating from an SUV that was gutted.

"Namvar, is that one of yours?" Frank asked.

Namvar stepped forward to have a look at the burning vehicle. "It could be… yes, I think it's ours."

"How many did you send?"

"Only one."

"That means that one is ours…" Carson said, pointing to the second vehicle in the distance. "*Shit!* LB, you got to give me more speed. Let's go! Come on!"

"Yes, Sir, I'll try."

"That's one big plane, and it looks intact." Frank was looking through his binoculars. "No damage that I can see, though their emergency chute looks deflated."

Namvar pointed to his truck as they passed by. "What if there were casualties, shouldn't we stop and check?"

"No time. We're guarding the plane. That's job one," Carson said. "Omar, sweep for thermals by the SUV."

"No active thermals," Omar reported almost instantly. "But there's a Jeep under the fuselage, and there're five thermals there." Omar said. "Two of the thermals are grounded."

"Wounded?"

"Probably... one of them has a weak reading."

"Shit."

"Omar, what about the other vehicle, are we in range to get any thermals?"

"We're in range, sir, but I don't see anything active. The heat coming from the MRAP could be hiding them though."

"Excuse me, but you said you saw a Jeep?" Namvar asked.

Omar nodded.

"That's Raji. He's the one I sent to warn our men to pull back."

"From the looks of it, he got here too late..." Carson said.

"What kind of weapons did your men have, anyway?" Frank asked Namvar.

"They were going to use hand grenades to blow up the plane."

"How many grenades did they have?"

"Twenty—there were two backpacks, ten in each."

"Shit." Carson said under his breath.

As they came up on the plane, one of the men waved his arms, and motioned them closer. He was a bald African, with a bloody shirt.

"Never seen him before, he's not one of yours, I take it?" Carson asked.

"No... just Raji..." Namvar said, "I think I recognize Gorgin on the ground there, the big one, with the bandage on his leg."

The MRAP finally came to a full stop. LB opened the doors, and Carson turned around to address everyone. "Only Frank and I will go out, the rest of you stay inside. If we feel it's safe, we'll let you know, but be patient." Carson glanced at Omar, and nodded for emphasis. "Stay alert."

Carson limped out the door with Frank steadying him for support. He did his best to walk toward the waiting men with his hand out without grimacing from the pain. "I'm Captain Carson Brunel, project lead for the Terran Kahn extraction project. This is my second in command, Lieutenant Frank Wolfe."

"I'm Jamere Wilson, and this is Raji and Fritz."

"Where's Peter Lucas?" Carson asked.

Jamere backed up a few steps, and pointed to a shirtless man bandaged and unconscious on the ground. "He's been unconscious for a while now," Jamere said quietly. "He caught some grenade shrapnel…"

"How bad is he?"

"We don't know… Fritz is a pilot, but he's pretty handy with a First Aid Kit, and stitched these guys up. We did the best we could."

"Fritz, can you take off?" Carson asked.

"Yes, Sir, but we need fuel."

Carson pulled his sunglasses down, and looked around the desert. "Any sign of the truck?"

Jamere pulled his hands out of his pants pockets. "It came about forty minutes ago, but then that guy ran for it with a bag of grenades, and that guy shot him down. Since then the truck is missing."

"What do you do, Jamere?"

"I'm communications."

"What happened to our MRAP, and where's its crew?" Frank asked.

"An associate of that guy dropped a bunch of hand grenades on it. No survivors. Sorry. Peter did everything he could to save them, but by the time I could climb down from the plane and run over there, it was over, man." Jamere looked to the ground and shook his head. "Tough scene, very tough scene."

"Excuse us for a second," Carson said, and then turned and limped back towards the MRAP, pulling Frank with him. "Look," he whispered, "I don't know anything that's a higher priority right now; we have to get that fuel. The fastest vehicle here is that Jeep. I think you and Charlie take the Jeep, find the fuel truck and get it back here on the double. I'll stay here and get the passengers on the plane, and see if the doctor can do anything more for Peter."

"Keep an eye on Namvar," Frank said. "I don't trust him. His thugs killed our men, and almost took down this plane. I'll get that truck back here as soon as I can. Also, make sure Omar stays on the CROWS. Moshad knows where we're going; I don't put anything past him…"

"I hear you." Carson nodded.

"Okay, well, good luck."

"You, too."

Carson turned back to the other men, while Frank went back to the MRAP. "I'll send two of my men to get the truck. I assume it went that way?"

Jamere nodded, pointing to the north. "It had to back up, so it couldn't go very fast… for all we know it's just over that hill."

"Let's hope you're right. We'll take the Jeep, you okay with that?"

Raji shrugged. "It's not mine."

Omar and Frank filed past Carson, and jumped into the Jeep, and started it up. "It went north. In reverse. Couldn't have gotten too far away." Carson put his hand on Frank's arm. "Frank, keep your eye on the gas gauge, don't get too far out. You're no good to me stranded out there. Okay?"

"I've got about half a tank of gas… in a Jeep that should get me at least a hundred and fifty miles. I'll turn back after sixty if I haven't caught up with the truck by then."

Carson shook his head. "No more than fifty, I want you in fifth gear the whole way doing eighty minimum, unless that road is a lot rougher than it is here."

"Once you get over that hill," Raji pointed. "You'll be able to see the highway for about thirty kilometers. About five kilometers down, there's a place where a big truck could turn around."

"Thanks for the info," Frank said, and then shifted in first gear, and lurched off, quickly building speed.

Slowly, Carson got everyone out of the MRAP. Other than Omar, Terran and Dorri, everyone else was in some kind of pain or had a mobility issue.

"This is the thing I hate most about Sunrot," Carson said, "no, goddamn pain killers. Doc, can you help Peter—the white guy on the ground over there with his shirt off?"

Dr. Najafi nodded, walked over gingerly, and slowly bent down to have a look at Peter. Carson waved at Martin who was watching from the exit door. "Who are you?"

"I'm the pilot."

"We have two pilots?"

"Fritz is my co-pilot."

"Oh, you're the main man, then. Cool. How do I get my passengers up there?"

"I've been asking that same question… some of you look like you're in pretty rough shape."

"We're not all going, but thanks for that observation," Carson said wryly. "Do you have another chute?"

"Yes, in the back, but it's not easy to get up if you're injured. They were designed for a quick exit."

"Got that, but I need you and whoever else you have up there, to think about it and get a solution in play." Carson had barely finished his sentence when a new voice starting talking loud, and caught his attention. It was Peter.

"Go and check… he might not be dead… who *are* you?" Peter was holding the shirt of Dr. Najafi, and then turned to see Carson who was walking as fast as he could in his direction. "Who are you people?"

"Peter Lucas, I'm Captain Carson Brunel. The man's shirt you're holding is Dr. Najafi."

Peter loosened his grip on Dr. Najafi's shirt, his head pivoting between the two men. "There's a man out there, who has a backpack full of hand grenades, I shot him… I think… but he's possibly still there… and…"

Carson had knelt down and was pointing to Gorgin as Peter was talking. Gorgin was sleeping just behind Peter.

"That man?" Carson asked.

Peter craned his head to see Gorgin, who was, at that time, snoring quite loudly. "That's the man I shot?"

"Bullet wounds and all," Carson said with a smile. "How are you feeling?"

"I can hear you… that's all that matters right now." Peter winced as he moved his body to sit up and look around. "That's him?"

Carson glanced at Terran who was playing tag with Dorri under the tires. "Terran Kahn, in person."

"Looks like a normal kid," Peter said.

"I've said it many times the past few days, there's nothing normal about that kid."

Peter squinted in the sun, and tilted his head like a swimmer whose ears were plugged with water. "I feel like my ears are at about 30 percent capacity. I hate this feeling." He feigned a yawn several times trying to clear his ears, but finally gave up.

"How's your chest wound?" Dr. Najafi asked.

"Until you asked, I didn't feel a thing... now it hurts like hell... Martin..."

"Yes?"

"Throw down the blue box in the overhead compartment... above my seat."

A moment later, Martin tossed down a blue box about the size of a shoebox. Omar retrieved it and brought it to Peter, who immediately opened it. "Looks like everyone here has some medical condition... bullet wounds, cuts, burns, good team we make." Peter chuckled, and then winced again.

"I brought codeine. Who wants some?" Peter was suddenly transformed from a patient to a pharmacist, and several hands thrust forward at his offer.

"Only two at a time," Dr. Najafi urged.

Nouri told Parto, but she shook her head. "I'm okay."

"Can we talk?" Nouri asked.

They walked hand in hand away from the plane, directly underneath the tail section.

"Have you decided?" Nouri asked.

Parto looked at Terran and Dorri, who were trying to get Mandana to drink some water. "I have only one fear..."

"What?"

"The world you're going to... will it be for us?"

"What do you mean?" Nouri asked.

"I have no doubt that Terran will be embraced by them. Initially, you'll be embraced, too, because they need you to communicate with him. But what happens to us? And what happens to you once he learns English? How long will that take him? A week, maybe two? Then what?"

Parto swept a strand of hair from her eyes. "I love you, but I want to live here. This is my home. Come back to me, when he's learned English."

Nouri's eyes flooded with tears as he listened. "I can't leave without you. I *won't* leave without you. If you want to stay… if that's truly what you want, then I will stay. But what about, Dorri? You know how she loves Terran—"

"Dorri's young. She bends to the wind like the tall grasses. She'll be fine. She starts school next year… your school. I want her to go there." Parto paused, and leaned to kiss Nouri on his cheek. "You're a good man, Nouri, I know this. If you told me that you had a destiny that was… that was wrapped up in this boy, I would understand. Terran is like a meteorite that fell in my backyard… a piece of the stars, and I know he will change the world. I have no doubt."

Parto took a deep breath, looking deep into Nouri's eyes. "You, on the other hand… I want you to change *my* life, *our* life. I don't need you to change the world. I want your destiny to be here, with me and Dorri."

Nouri was quiet. His eyes looked down, focused on the curved lines of his hands. He couldn't believe that he was even considering the possibility of not getting on that airplane. "I haven't thought about what would happen to me when he knows English better than me. That day is probably two weeks away, and you're right, when that day comes, what purpose do I serve?"

"The thing about Terran," Parto said, "is that he has a destiny that will eclipse everything around him. He will attract the attention of the most powerful of this planet, and they will want to control him, for their own purposes. If you are to go with him, then you would need to be a protector more than a translator or teacher. Are you really that person?"

Nouri shook his head slowly. She was right. How had he not seen these things? Perhaps he'd been too caught up in the allure of a new world filled with the smartest minds and the best resources. He was a simple teacher who had found love, the one thing he had thought impossible when his first wife had died in his arms. It was the kind of love that filled to overflowing; the kind that blooms amid chaos. It wasn't anything that he had done. It was all her. Quiet and composed, she had made it all happen by a single act of care. Suddenly he realized what he had known in that moment in the alley when he, still in the aftershock of killing two men, blurted out the simple words of his heart. That love was not a convenience or a thing controlled by the mind. It was a tapestry of lives that branched into a hundred lives, and then a thousand, and then a million and never really ended or stopped. He saw this at that very moment.

Nouri turned to Parto. "Then I will stay."

CHAPTER 73

Reinforcements

Carson hated the idea of asking for his help, however, Martin and his team had produced only lame ideas for bringing the wounded up the emergency chute. Terran was leaning against one of the tires, sitting next to Dorri who was trying to feed some rations to Mandana. Terran looked up, as Carson and Sanjur limped over.

"When will we be able to get on the plane?" Terran asked.

"Soon," Carson replied, "but first, we need to get people onboard who are weak… like Parto, Peter and this Goliath slayer, Sanjur." Carson smiled, while Sanjur made the translation. Both Sanjur and Carson sat down with some effort, though their pain was made more tolerable with their recent dose of codeine. "Any ideas?"

Terran began to ask questions. How many people were inside the plane? How strong were they? Did they have ropes? Were there other chutes? Carson answered and Sanjur translated. Terran considered the deflated chute that hung vertically from the exit door. "We could take the chute that's deflated and place it on top of the good chute. We could tie a person to the deflated chute and the men inside could pull the deflated chute up. That should work."

Sanjur translated and Carson nodded his head when Sanjur finished. "Okay, that makes sense." Carson stood to his feet and limped over to the exit door, and yelled. "Martin?"

A few moments later Martin appeared. "What?"

"We have a plan. Can you roll this chute up?"

Martin looked down at the ungainly chute, and shrugged. "I think so."

"Okay, then deploy a new chute, and once you have this one rolled up, place it on top of the new one. We're going to hoist the injured up on the deflated chute. Oh, and we'll also need some rope, so drop some rope down, too. Okay?"

Martin stood silent for a moment, computing the plan in his head, and then nodded. "Okay…"

About a minute later a new exit door opened towards the back of the plane, behind the wings. A new chute deployed, with a vibrant swoosh of compressed air. Martin and one of his crew members pulled the deflated chute inside the cabin, and in about ten minutes had rolled it up and dropped it over the new chute.

Terran watched as they got everything in position, and walked over to Sanjur. "Remind them about the ropes."

"Yes, we haven't forgotten," Marin replied, after Sanjur relayed the message.

Suddenly Omar ran out of the MRAP and shouted to Carson. "I need to see you inside, we have a situation."

Carson limped hurriedly to the MRAP, swearing under his breath the whole way—partly out of the pain from his ankle, but mostly out of his fatigue, hunger and constant anxiety about how to get Terran and Nouri on that Plane and in the sky. Only then could he finally relax.

Inside the MRAP, Omar stood by his console to let Carson sit. He pointed to the screen. "See them?"

Carson got closer to the monitor and squinted. "Camels? Really, they're going to storm us with camels?"

"Nine camels, eight men, by my count," Omar said.

"Where'd the two extra men come from?"

Omar shrugged. "Maybe where they were hiding their camels?"

Carson studied the screen. "They're at four thousand plus meters right now. Remind me, what's the range of our MK-19?"

"About half that."

"If they get within three thousand meters, they're in range to take potshots if they have any good rifles. They could hit something, as big as the airplane is. Can we get a make on their weapons?"

Omar dialed a virtual zoom nob with his trackball, and then typed a few commands on his keyboard. "They have Russian made AKMs and AK-103s… hold a second… the effective range is around four to five hundred meters for either."

"I don't give a shit what the effective range is… they have an airplane to shoot at. Just give me the maximum."

"Twelve hundred meters, sir."

"If we want to take them out with MK-19, what's our effective range for an accurate strike?"

"About fifteen hundred meters is where I'd like to be."

"Assuming they come that close, and I suspect they will, drop a hundred rounds on them."

"A hundred?"

"What do we have?"

"We have that, but not much more… there're only eight men…"

LB was sitting in the driver's seat, and swiveled his chair to face Carson. "We could drop twenty rounds, assess damages, and if necessary, drop ten more. I doubt more than thirty rounds would be necessary for only eight men."

"The problem with that plan," Carson said, "is that they'll scatter like cockroaches after the first round, and then we've lost our advantage. No, we'll drop everything we have at fifteen hundred meters. I mean everything."

"And if they split-up before fifteen-hundred meters?"

"Let me know," Carson said, standing to his feet. He walked to the door, and turned around like he forgot something. "Call me when they get to two-thousand meters."

"Yes, Sir."

When Carson returned to the emergency chute, it was with a new sense of urgency. "Everyone, listen up!" He shouted. "Moshad and his men are about five miles away. The good news is that they're on camels. If they come close I will shoot to kill. I spared them before, I won't do it again."

Sanjur delivered the news. Terran nodded and remained silent for a while. He, along with everyone else, looked out to the horizon, shielding their eyes from the sun.

"I don't see them," Terran said.

"They have special technology that can see them," Sanjur explained.

"We must fire only warning shots. They're defenseless against Carson's technology. We can't simply slaughter them. It isn't right,

Sanjur. You must convince them to fire only warnings—"

Sanjur put his hands on Terran's shoulders. "I don't think anyone can convince Carson to hold back, and I don't really blame him. Moshad's persistence and character, even in the short time I've known him, is clear. He will not be warned away. Sometimes, your opponent leaves you no choice. It's kill or be killed."

"He's a reasonable man," Terran said. "If he knows he's outgunned he'll stay away. He's not suicidal."

"And yet there he is…" Sanjur observed.

Carson watched as Sanjur and Terran talked, but then interrupted them. "Our plans to get people on the plane have been moved up. We have to move fast since the plane is more protected than staying down here, so we'll start with Parto and Dorri, and then Terran…"

Nouri raised his hand and stepped forward. "I'm sorry, but we're not going."

"Who exactly is *we?*" Carson asked.

"Parto, Dorri and myself. We're not going. We're staying."

Carson stepped forward and winced. "Look, I have orders, and my orders say that you and Terran are going on that plane. Now, it's a big plane, and I agreed that you could take Parto and Dorri with you…" Carson paused, and looked over at Peter who was sitting up, leaning against one of the tires. "Peter, do you have any problems letting Nouri bring his girlfriend and her daughter along?"

Peter shook his head. "It's a big plane; we have plenty of room and provisions." Carson put his arm out, as if to say "See?"

Nouri shook his head. "We're not going."

Peter half-shouted. "You're his teacher, right? You speak his language? You're critical to this mission. We need you."

Dorri started to whimper as she listened to the conversation. She had assumed they were all going together.

Terran could see something was going on, and went to Nouri. "You're not coming?"

"I love her," Nouri said, glancing at Parto. "She doesn't want to leave her home. I want to stay. Sanjur can perform my role. You don't need a teacher anyway. There'll be plenty of those where you're going." Nouri dropped to one knee and embraced Terran. "I'll be able to talk with you on the computer. I'll watch you from afar. I know you have great things ahead of you, but my path is with Parto and Dorri. I'm sorry."

Terran pulled back. "There's nothing to be sorry for. I'll be fine with Sanjur, but I will miss you." A single tear rested on his upper cheek, pausing before it fell to the dry pavement in wait. "I'll find a way to see you when I arrive. I promise."

Terran embraced him one more time. Parto walked over with Dorri and they all embraced Terran, and like a small group of embers that clutched a great wind, the four of them ignited in a common love and bitter parting.

Carson held up his arms and turned to Peter. His mouth mimed the words, "What the…"

Peter stood up, slowly, cautiously and walked over to the emergency chute where everyone had gathered. "I don't know any of you, so I'm admittedly out of touch with your various back stories and relationships, but I was sent here by the President of the Greater Nations, of which Iran is a member. Our agreement was to return with Terran Kahn *and* Nouri Abbasi. If Nouri declines to go, then my mission is compromised. So, before anyone decides not to go, they need to discuss it with me."

"This isn't about politics or the Greater Nation," Sanjur said. "This is about love. So, I would suggest you get over your issues with this, because this decision has been made, and it's the right one."

"And who are you?" Peter asked.

"My name is Sanjur, and I'm the one who will replace Nouri, since I can speak Terran's language and act as his translator."

"Then you're a teacher as well?"

"No. I'm a merchant."

"Then your vocabulary is reduced—"

"My vocabulary is adequate. Do you see other prospects around here?"

While Sanjur and Peter were talking, Terran asked Nouri to translate. When he'd finished, Terran spoke fervently to Nouri. "Tell him that plans change. Sanjur's right. He will be a good translator for me, until I learn English. We have bigger issues than to waste time arguing about who goes and who stays. I want Namvar and Sanjur to accompany me. We need to get everyone on the plane and ready to go."

Nouri translated, and Peter listened calmly.

"Who is Namvar?" Peter asked.

Namvar raised his hand. "I am."

"And what is your role in this?"

"I am the Chief of Police in Mashhad."

"Really? And why does Terran require your services?"

"You can ask him… he's right there."

Peter turned to Terran. "Why do you want Namvar to go with you?"

Nouri translated and Terran smiled. "Because he reminds me of my father."

After Nouri translated, Peter looked up to the sky and raked his hand through his hair. "I know you're an orphan, so don't play games with me. Why do you want to bring him?"

After Nouri translated, Terran folded his arms across his chest.

"He stands by his former statement," Nouri announced.

Peter turned back to Namvar. "And you want to go?"

"Yes. Very much."

"And why is that?"

Namvar glanced in Terran's direction. "I believe he is the Mahdi. I want to be close to him. To protect him." Namvar bowed his head slightly after he finished.

"Maybe I took too much codeine…" Peter whispered. "I feel kind of… faint…" Peter began to fall, and Carson grabbed him just in time, but because of Carson's injury, they both fell to the ground.

Nouri and Raji rushed to help them. Carson fought off any help, and stood up mostly on his own with a little support from Nouri, but Peter was groggy, and had difficulty regaining consciousness.

"We should get Peter on the plane," Terran said through Nouri.

Carson shook his head. "Let's try someone who's conscious first. Namvar, let's send you up first."

They worked quickly, wrapping Namvar in the bottom of the deflated chute and then tied it around him with rope. When they were done, they gave the signal to Martin and his team to pull, and within three minutes, they had retrieved Namvar and were leading him into the cabin. Sanjur was next, and he said his goodbyes to Nouri, Parto and Dorri, and then came to the chute, and got wrapped up and tied down. He looked at Carson, just as they finished prepping him. "Thanks for letting me go." Sanjur's eyes seemed a little loopy from the codeine.

"No problem, just take good care of him."

"You know one of the things I like about Sunrot… if there's anything to like, is that I'm about to go to America. Before Sunrot, I couldn't even get a passport. Kind of ironic isn't it?"

Carson smiled.

"I'll tell you one other thing… but it's a secret… Namvar has posters of me in his office. Isn't that funny?"

"You were a wanted criminal?" Carson asked, suddenly interested.

"Well, it was for something I didn't do, of course, but that's not the point. I'll be sitting next to him, and he doesn't even know it's me." Sanjur's voice became a whisper, as he put his finger to his thin lips.

"I doubt he cares anymore," Carson quipped, then nodded to Martin's team. "Pull him up."

Sanjur laughed as they pulled him up the chute.

Carson bent down to look at Peter. Dr. Najafi was already looking at him, checking his pulse and respiration.

"He's probably just reacting to the codeine," Dr. Najafi said. "Most of us have been off medication for so long, if we ever got some, its side effects are more intensely felt. The good news is that his pulse is strong."

"I want to get him up next. Do you think we can do that?"

"Sure."

"Raji, Jamere can you give me a hand?"

Raji and Jamere came over to Peter, lifting him onto the tarp-like chute. Then they wrapped him up in it, tying it around his body securely. Peter remained semi-unconscious the whole time, and then Carson signaled to Martin to pull Peter up the chute.

"Jamere, you might as well go up with him… just keep him perpendicular to the plane. You don't need to push."

Jamere nodded and followed Peter up the chute.

"Why is Namvar going?" Raji asked.

"There's something he's not telling. I don't know what it is, but that's no police chief. I'll tell you that."

"No, he *is* police chief," Raji refuted in stilted English. "He's been police chief for eight years. He's very smart man. Very cunning. I just don't know why he would go to America. He called it the devil's... playground. It doesn't make sense."

"Well, your guess is as good as mine," Carson said, as he walked away.

"Captain," Omar poked his head out of the MRAP, "they just passed two thousand meters."

"Still together?"

Omar nodded.

"I'll be right there."

"Can I see, too?" Raji asked.

"I need you to watch your comrade over there. Eventually he's going to wake up, and when he does, you're the person he needs to see first. Okay?"

"Yes, you're right. Okay, then." Raji bowed politely several times.

Carson looked at Terran who was sitting in a circle with Nouri, Parto and Dorri, talking and laughing.

"Terran, I need you up on the plane," Carson said.

After the translation, Terran held up five fingers, presumably meaning five minutes. Carson nodded, and then climbed into the MRAP. Omar was biting his fingernails, staring at the monitor. Carson sat down in the CROWS seat and grabbed a ration bar, a *chocolate-covered maggot*, as it was referred to by his men, but he was so hungry he didn't care.

"I'm surprised they're still together. Whoa, they just dropped off their camels. Looks like they plan to walk the rest of the way."

"Probably figured they were too much of a target that way," Omar said.

"How is it that Moshad can suddenly walk?" Carson asked.

"No way... something's wrong."

"Do any of our MAVs work?"

Omar opened up a locked side case and looked inside. "This one is solar... it might work."

Omar held a Micro Air Vehicle that looked remarkably similar to a large moth. It had a wingspan of three inches fitted with micro solar cells. It had been one of the most advanced surveillance weapons that Special Forces used regularly throughout the Middle East prior to Sunrot.

"How long before that thing is charged?"

"We'll find out... maybe a few minutes."

Omar stuck the device on top of the MRAP in direct sunlight. He fiddled with the trackball, and a picture opened up in a small pop-up window in the upper right of the screen. It was static video capture of the CROWS weapon's system.

"It's talking with our onboard OS, so we're halfway there. Battery is charging, when it gets to 70 percent, we should be good to go."

"I want you to do some fly overs and get pictures. Terran can ID these guys. Can you do a thermal read at this distance and compare with the previous six we had?"

Omar glanced down at his keyboard, and made a few clicks. Immediately the screen refreshed and the Baluchian men became thermals. He clicked a few more times on his trackball, and he had comparison scans. "Not enough resolution to get above 60 percent certainty and less than 60 percent is basically useless data."

Omar clicked off the thermal mode and returned to regular video feed. Then he drew a box around the eight Baluchian men on the monitor and clicked the word *Locked* onscreen.

"They just crossed eighteen-hundred meters," Carson said, pointing to the high resolution color monitor.

"Okay, our bug's ready." A bright green light was blinking on the pop-up overlay.

"Let's send her on her way."

Omar turned on the MAV with a bit of trepidation. It flew off controlled by a homing system that targeted the subject on the video screen. Omar could manually change the elevation, but the computer controlled the flight plan once the subject was selected. Omar clicked a button, and the MAV video was full screen.

"How fast can this bug go?"

"It's going about thirty mph right now, but I could crank it to forty."

"What kind of moth goes that fast? We have time. Keep it at thirty."

In less than a minute they had clear images of the eight men walking towards them. Each had assault rifles. One had a pair of binoculars. A yellow light started to blink, signaling the MAV was at target, and ready for manual override. Omar asked if he could sit down in front of the console. Carson gave up the CROWS seat, and stood behind Omar, his eyes fixed on the screen.

"Let's get a good view of their faces."

"I'll try..."

A second later, Omar had swooped down and grabbed a good frontal shot of the men's faces. They walked together, separated by about five feet on either side of each man. They had left their camels behind, loosely tied to shrub brush.

Carson tapped Omar on the shoulder. "Can you get Terran and Nouri in here?"

Omar got up, and placed the MAV in *Hover* mode. Thirty seconds later he returned with Terran and Nouri.

"Show the images we have," Carson ordered, and then turned to Nouri. "Ask him to identify these men."

"I know myself what Moshad looks like," Nouri said, "and he's not any of these men."

"Ask Terran who these men are."

Terran studied their faces and slowly turned to Nouri. "These men are soldiers. They are low rank... the lowest rank. I don't know any of them. None of them were with Moshad."

After Nouri translated, Carson and Omar looked at each other with open mouths.

"They must be reinforcements," Omar said.

Carson looked at Terran and then Nouri. "Why would Baluchian soldiers be approaching us?"

Nouri made a quick translation. "He wants to know if we can see further away. He believes there are more."

Carson tapped Omar on the shoulder. "Take our bug up and go south... in the direction these men came from, and crank its speed to forty."

The monitor showed a video stream of a spacious desert environment.

The altimeter displayed 2, 240 feet discreetly on the left side of the screen. An outcropping of rocks and a few scrub trees caught the attention of Omar. "This looks odd…"

Omar pointed to a bunch of dark shapes in the shadows of the rocks, and some were clearly moving.

"Get our bug down there," Carson ordered.

Nouri, Terran, Carson and LB were all straining to see what the MAV would reveal as it made its dive to the outcroppings some seven miles away from their position.

"Count them," Carson said.

Omar was pointing to the screen, and silently counting. "More than twenty, maybe twenty-five."

"Bring the bug closer; I want to see their faces."

Omar made some fine-tuned adjustments on his trackball, and flew the bug closer just as one of the men brought his binoculars down. He was an older man, with graying hair and beard, distinguished by the fact that he wore something that approximated a uniform. Terran exhaled a long jagged breath as he saw the face. "I know him. His name is Borzin Amirmoez. He is our General."

CHAPTER 74

Return

Frank was not prone to exaggeration, but he was so hungry that he had told Charlie that he was almost ready to stop the Jeep and grab some of the plants along the freeway and chow them down, to which Charlie had nervously laughed. They had gone forty, long, bumpy miles in pursuit of the truck. When they had arrived at the high point that Raji had mentioned, they had seen the truck some fifteen miles down the road ambling away from them—its speed impossible to predict, but both Frank and Charlie knew it would have to be significantly less than their speed, which hovered between 80-90 mph. They had five more miles in which to catch up, and if they weren't successful, they'd have no choice but to turn around.

"That last turn, I saw it, just for a second. I'd say we're only a few miles from it now."

Frank looked at his odometer and did a quick calculation. "We have a few more miles before we need to turn around or risk running out of gas. Do you think he saw us?"

"Probably."

"I could be wrong," Frank said, "but I think he's going faster. We're not gaining on him like we were earlier."

A few minutes later, Frank slammed his fist onto the wheel. "Okay, I'm going ninety, and he's got to be going eighty, and the only way he'd be going that fast is because he doesn't want us to catch up. What the hell!"

As they got closer, within a half mile, Frank sighed. "We passed the turnaround mark about a mile back. We're all in at this point, so we better hope we can stop this guy and hitch a ride, because this Jeep belongs to the freeway now."

Frank's hunger was now lost in his obsession to catch up with the truck and somehow bring it to a stop.

"Do you think he'd be packing any weapons?" Charlie asked.

"I'd be surprised if he wasn't, and I'd also be surprised if he didn't have a co-pilot."

"How do we signal to him that we're the good guys?"

"I have no idea… that's all I've been thinking since we got on the damn freeway."

They were within a few hundred feet of the back of the truck when they heard a gunshot whistle past their Jeep.

"I hate it when I'm right…" Frank yelled, as he swerved the Jeep toward the driver's side of the road. The road suddenly deteriorated into a bumpy mess, and the truck slammed on its brakes.

Frank yelled two words, "Hold on!" Instead of braking, he accelerated, and passed the truck in a second of total chaos. His front passenger side wheel hit a huge pothole that rocked the Jeep to the right, spinning it around, exposing its passenger side to the onrushing tanker. Charlie screamed for a full five seconds as the slow-motion scene from hell transpired. To Charlie, who could see it all, the look of terror on the faces of the two men in the truck's cab was mesmerizing. The sound of brakes squealing in a high-pitched frenzy filled the air, and Charlie finally closed his eyes, waiting for the crash.

Frank was too focused to scream. His foot was pumping the brakes, his hands controlling the steering wheel that seemed to have a mind of its own. When it was all over, the Jeep was at the end of black, squiggly tire tracks, approximately ten feet in front of the silver grill of a 1985 Peter built tanker truck. The Jeep's front passenger side wheel was slanted at a 45-degree angle. Steam was rising from its engine. Red lights flashed annoyingly on the console.

Everything was settling back to a new reality of calm and quiet. Frank managed to compose himself. He took off his seatbelt, put his arms up defensively and walked to the truck on the driver's side.

"I'm Lieutenant Frank Wolfe. I'm with the plane… we need you to return."

The man in the passenger seat leaned out the window and lowered his gun barrel at Frank. Frank looked him in the eyes. "I'm unarmed. We don't mean you any harm. This mission is of the highest priority. I'm authorized to double your fees."

The last part, Frank let slip, because he had a gun pointed at him. From his experience, it was always a smart thing to change the conversation from death to money. Charlie remained glued to his seat, his face still strained from the near crash, and eyes watering beneath the reflected glare of the chrome grill.

"Triple..." the driver said, glancing at his comrade.

To Frank, that single word couldn't have been spoken from an angel any more beautifully than the wretched truck driver that stared down at him. Frank was so programmed to barter that he almost countered with two-and-a-half, but thought better of it, and nodded instead. "Triple, if you let us ride back with you."

The driver came down from the cab, and shook hands with Frank as if they were old friends. "We have plenty of room. My name is Hafiz and my navigator is Arvin. Your Persian is quite good. I was once in the military too. Come on."

He motioned to Frank to climb up into the cab, and Charlie, still weak-kneed from the stress of the near accident, followed him slowly, as if he were still in a dream.

CHAPTER 75

The Battlefield

As the video streamed, Terran pointed to more faces that he recognized, some of them were Moshad's men, some were elders of his tribe, and one was Moshad himself, who was sitting on a camel next to General Amirmoez. The two men seemed to be talking to one another.

"Put our bug in hover mode above the General, and give Nouri the headphones so he can listen to their conversation," Carson instructed.

Omar held the headphones up without looking away from the screen. Nouri grabbed them and put them on. The audio was full of static. He closed his eyes to concentrate.

"… soon. Their guns probably have a kill range of a thousand meters."

"And how many?"

"We don't know…. Maybe six."

"And the fuel truck?"

"Either it's already fueled or it hasn't arrived yet. We don't know."

"There's a great deal that you don't know, Moshad. It concerns me."

There was a long pause. Nouri could hear some voices in the distance, too weak to stand out clearly against the static, but they sounded alarmed. Nouri pressed the headphones closer together.

"Then shoot it!"

"Can they see our bug?" Omar asked, looking more closely at the screen. "He's taking aim." Omar pointed to one of the men who pointed his gun directly at them, or more accurately, the MAV's video lens.

"Move it, now!" Carson said, but before Omar could move the MAV to safety, their video vanished, and the monitor screen was suddenly a dark gray. Omar clicked a button and deleted the video window. The eight men they had been tracking earlier reappeared. They were crouched down, probably because of the gunshot behind them, but their video was now full screen, and the *Distance to Target* showed 1,689 meters.

"Shit! How high was the bug?" Carson demanded.

"About two-twenty."

"Why so close?"

"Audio range is limited… we had to get that close to hear."

"Well, we know now they have some good marksman to shoot that bug down from two-hundred twenty feet. Shit!"

Carson glanced at Nouri. "What'd you hear?"

"They believe our kill range is a thousand meters. They don't know if we've already fueled the plane or not, they think we have six guns… I think that's all I heard."

"Any more MAVs that're solar-powered?" Carson asked.

Omar stood up and went over to the device drawer, opened it and rummaged around. He held up another device that looked similar in his hand. "An older version, but it might still work."

"Give it a go," Carson said. He walked over to his navigator chair and sat down. "So they have about thirty men, and a General who's commanding them. He's sending in these eight to find out what our range is… which they currently think is a thousand meters." Carson paused a moment. "Omar, what's our range to lock-in thermals?"

"In these conditions, out in the open… um, maybe thirteen hundred meters."

"Okay, let's save the nineteen's power. Let these guys get within thirteen hundred meters, lock-in, and then take them out. Okay?"

"Yes, Sir," Omar said.

Carson put his fingertips together and swiveled back and forth in his chair. "We'll save the nineteen's thunder for the General. I'm sure he'd appreciate it more in person anyway."

"This one'll take longer to get a charge," Omar reported, as he put the new MAV on the roof of the MRAP. "Probably a good ten minutes."

"Alright, Terran, we need to get you in the plane," Carson said, standing up.

Terran shook his head, and turned to Nouri. "Tell him that I should stay right here. I'll be more useful here than in the airplane."

Nouri relayed the message, and Carson started to shake his head almost immediately, and then sat back down in his chair. "Sure, why not."

Carson stretched his legs out. The constant emotional ups and downs, the lack of sleep, the pain in his ankle, and the hunger were all stacking up on him, and he could feel himself weighed down. "Where the hell is Frank? He should be back by now."

"Sir," LB said, "we could drive over to that highpoint where Raji said there was a thirty mile view. We'd be able to see where they were, if they were on their way back."

Carson took a deep breath. "How long do you think it'd take?"

"Five minutes tops to get there, a couple minutes to establish a sighting, and five minutes back."

"Omar, at the rate these guys are traveling how long before they get to thirteen hundred meters?"

"Fifteen to twenty minutes. The sand out there is deep and soft; it looks like they're walking in three feet of snow."

"LB, let's do it. Let's go have a look. Besides, it'll keep them off balance."

LB fired up the MRAP's engine. Omar grabbed the MAV from the roof and brought it inside. Parto and Dorri watched with surprise, and Carson shouted for them to get inside. Carson then shouted at Raji to hide behind the plane's tires until they returned in ten minutes, and to keep an eye on Gorgin.

As soon as Parto and Dorri stepped inside the MRAP, it lurched into gear and drove off around the plane, in between the north and south bound lanes, ducking under the wings, and then back onto the freeway.

"Go as fast as you can, LB. Parto, sit down and buckle up. Omar, keep those eight in sight at all times. Let me know if you see any changes."

"Yes, Sir," Omar said. "Right now, they stopped walking. They're just watching us pull away."

"Got them scratching their dusty little heads… good!"

Terran and Nouri sat down next to Parto and Dorri on the side seats, and buckled themselves in. In three minutes they had come to the highpoint, and it only took about ten seconds to spot the truck off in the distance. "Omar, use the other CROWS console and get a distance reading on the truck. Okay?"

Omar shuttled to the back of the MRAP, and within a minute had a reading. "They're traveling at a rate of seventy mph, and they're a little over ten minutes away, assuming they maintain that speed."

"Good, let's head back. Omar, back on the front console."

The MRAP backed up carefully, and quickly got into its former position near the back section of the plane.

"Distance of the soldiers?" Carson asked.

Omar paused a moment. "Hold on, I'm only seeing six right now…"

"Where're the other two?"

"I don't know…" Omar replied.

"When'd you lose them?"

"I… I don't know exactly. They were there two minutes ago."

"You sure?"

"I'm positive."

"What's their range?"

"Thirteen hundred forty meters."

"They moved pretty fast," Carson said. "Turn the thermals on, and find those other two."

"I did, I still don't get anything in the way of thermals… other than the six."

"Widen your range, maybe they went east or west. Hell, maybe they buried themselves in the sand. Find them."

A moment later a gunshot reverberated.

"Are you goddamn kidding me… they're firing from that range? Find out who fired that!"

Omar rewound the live video and flicked on thermal IDs to identify the point of discharge. "There, Sir."

"Lock it in and take the fucker out. Now!"

Omar clicked the trackball, and the subtle whirring sound of the weapons system could be heard as it dialed in ominously to its target, which appeared to be sand. The red box went from blinking to a solid red, and Omar pressed the trackball, and instantly the sound of a gunshot rang out.

"Again, fire," Carson ordered.

Omar clicked his trackball and again the loud gunshot resounded inside the cabin of the MRAP.

"Results?"

"He's done for," Omar said. "I think one was enough."

"I'm sure it was, I just want to send a signal that we're thorough and have plenty of ammo."

Carson stood up and took up a post behind Omar. "Okay, I want us to position the MRAP in front of the tires. LB, move it."

"Yes, Sir."

Just as the MRAP began to move, another gunshot rang out, and this time they felt the impact on their vehicle.

"Those aren't some old Russian rifles," Carson said. "They have something else. Take the shooter out, now! And make sure you get anyone who goes for the rifle afterwards."

About five seconds later, a gun blast sounded inside the cabin, and as before, Carson ordered a follow-up strike.

"Now… there *are* six," Carson said defiantly to no one in particular. "Time to make it zero." He turned to Omar. "You know what to do."

The video screen showed six thermals crouched down. The Distance to Target showed 1310 meters. "They're spreading out," Omar said. "You're locked in?"

Omar was busy clicking on his trackball and ignored Carson's question. "They're digging in… what are they pointing at?"

"Our fuel truck…" Carson whispered.

Carson limped to the front of the MRAP looking through the front windshield as the huge fuel truck, about a mile away, was bearing down on them.

Carson swiveled his head between the fuel truck and the video of the six remaining Baluchian soldiers. "Omar, can you take them out now? I'm not liking this situation with a fuel truck coming, and their rifles have a range beyond what our computer system thinks."

Omar clicked some buttons, all six thermals had a red square overlaid, and Omar clicked one button. The CROWS came alive, and twelve shots rang out in rapid succession.

The smell of gunpowder seeped into the cabin. Terran's eyes were closed, Dorri hugged her mom while she held onto Mandana's basket, and all of the adults looked between one another as if to say: "When will this end?"

"Check thermals." Carson rubbed the back of his neck as he stared at the fuel truck, which had slowed up considerably, since they had fired their rounds.

"All dead," Omar announced.

"Positive IDs?"

"I have positive IDs on eight thermals. All dead."

"Do a scan of the General's last whereabouts. See if you can see anything."

Carson reached forward to the console and opened the door. "LB, I want you to tell Martin to come down and supervise the re-fueling."

"Yes, Sir," LB said, running out the door.

"Anything, Omar?"

"I can only see the tops of that outcropping. Our visible horizon, at seven miles distance, is about eight meters. Even on camels... wait... oh, they're moving. Something is moving."

Carson came over to the CROWS console, and Omar immediately stood up to allow Carson to sit. Omar pointed to a black section of the video, at the very bottom of the horizon that looked like an amorphous blob, moving slowly and steadily in their direction. It was impossible to tell what it was even at maximum zoom as it was too far away, but Carson knew it was twenty men on camels galloping in their direction, armed with rifles, and intent on shooting the tanker.

Carson craned his head to Omar. "We're going to have to go meet them. We can't let them get close... not while we're refueling." He turned to Nouri. "You need to convince Terran to get on that plane now! I don't want any disagreements, discussion, or anything else. My decision is final. If I have to, I'll have him carried—"

Nouri raised his arm to Carson, and began translating to Terran, who slowly stood up just as LB rushed back into the cabin. Terran gave one more hug to Nouri, Parto and Dorri, and then looked at Carson, and in near perfect English said, "Thank you for your help." He then embraced Carson, and walked out of the MRAP without another look or word.

Carson glanced at LB. "Make sure he gets up the chute, and bring Charlie back with you. Frank can stay with Martin."

As LB left, Carson turned his attention to Omar. "What's their distance?"

"Six point two miles, just under ten-thousand meters, traveling at an average speed of seventeen mph."

"Have the computer plot an intercept course. What about our bug? Is it charged?"

Omar switched screens momentarily. "Close enough, I think."

"Then launch it, and stay in stealth mode."

Stealth mode, in the context of MAVs, meant two things: no hovering, and a minimum altitude of five hundred feet. If these two things were adhered to, the MAVs were impossible to see or detect. The software that ran them enabled stealth mode automatically, but it had to be selected by the controller.

Omar clicked his trackball and the video screen popped open. The MAV was already in the air, climbing to an altitude of 2,200 feet. This was the preferred altitude of an approaching MAV to allow a larger perspective on the target and its environment. Once the target area was achieved, in stealth mode, the MAV would drop down to five hundred feet and fly back and forth over the selected target area. If the target were moving, it would compensate for the speed and direction of the target, and remain in synchronous position to the target. The main problem was when the target was twenty men galloping on camels, and the watching as those camels split up going in different directions. At that point, manual override or new rules had to be programmed into the MAV or it would become confused, and in some cases, malfunction, to include the possibility of dropping from the sky.

LB rushed into the MRAP out of breath. "He's on the plane. Martin's working with the fuel guys, Frank's with Martin. Charlie's on his way."

"Okay, fire this beast up… stay in auto mode, and let's go." A moment later Charlie ran in, the door closed promptly behind him. The MRAP took off on a pre-programmed intercept course that Omar had plotted with the onboard computer.

"What's our maximum speed?"

LB glanced at his console. "It looks like thirty-five mph is what the detection system is suggesting, but that could change as we get further out. We'll see."

Carson turned to Nouri. "I know this is a scary experience for the three of you, but frankly, this is the safest place to be right now. They can't hurt us with their weapons because of their range limits and the way this thing is protected, so don't worry. We'll be fine."

Nouri and Parto nodded, yet anxiety remained on their faces.

"Any changes?" Carson asked, tapping Omar on the shoulder.

"None, they're still galloping at about fifteen mph. Still bunched up."

Carson looked at the screen's dashboard, and the *distance to target* was a fast moving number, but he saw 6,210 meters, and stuck with that. "When we get to four thousand meters, let's go to manual override and slow down. I want to find a good platform and then hunker down. We'll let them come to us."

"Yes, Sir," Omar and LB said in chorus.

Carson limped down to Charlie's station, and looked over his shoulder. "I want you on the M2, and I'll have Omar operating the MK-19. When these guys get in thermal range, ID them, and let me know when you're ready. Okay?"

"Yes, Sir."

"Good shooting."

Charlie nodded nervously.

Carson held onto the support straps positioned throughout the MRAP. It was a rough ride, and between his ankle injury and the swaying of the vehicle, walking the short distance from back to front was no easy task. On his way past the food cupboards, he grabbed a box of rations.

"Anyone want one?" Carson held up energy bars.

Everyone held up their arm, and Carson went around like Santa Claus passing out rations to everyone, including Dorri. "Are you sure you want one of these, they're not very good."

"I'll try one," Dorri said, "besides, Mandana might be hungry."

"Okay, here you go... enjoy, if you can."

"Four thousand meters... mark... now," Omar said.

The MRAP suddenly slowed down.

"Under manual override," LB announced. "Captain, that looks like a good place to defend from."

"We're not defending, we're the ones punishing, and don't forget it," Carson said with his Texan bravado on full tilt. "Okay, looks good, let's hunker down there and see what our General decides."

"Sir, they just stopped, too," Omar said.

"Put on the bug video."

The screen switched to the live feed from the MAV at five hundred feet altitude. Men on camels, loosely bunched up, carrying rifles, were suddenly forming a circle.

"It looks like they're having a little discussion," Omar said.

"They probably weren't planning on us coming out to meet them," Carson said, chewing on an energy bar.

"It looks like they're going to make it difficult on us… they're splitting into groups of three," Omar said. "They're spreading out wide… okay, I'm not sure where this group is going… they're staying right there."

"What's he got?"

"Do a weapon's assessment. I want to know what that is."

"I know what it is, it's an RPG-29," Charlie said. "It's Russian made. Max range is five hundred meters, but it'll go through this MRAP if they get close enough. It's nasty."

"Select him and zoom to max," Carson said.

Omar selected the man who was holding it.

"He's three-thousand eight-hundred meters. Too far to lock on—"

"But it's well within the max range of the M2. Let's shoot ten rounds, and let them know they're not safe even at that distance. Maybe we'll get lucky and hit one of the bastards, or at least push them back."

"Yes, Sir."

Omar sighted the target, and copy-pasted the coordinates, and then set the number of rounds, and looked at Carson. "I'm going to do a ten-meter right to left spray to improve our chances."

Omar's concentration was impressive. "I'm ready, Sir."

"Fire at will."

Omar clicked once, and the M2 shot with ferocity. As soon as Omar clicked the button, he flipped to the video of the MAV and watched as the man who had been holding the RPG-29 fell to the ground, in fact, all three men in the small group fell to the ground, but without the thermal lock, it was impossible to know if they were injured or dead."

"Any movement?"

"I think they're dead, but it's hard to say..."

"Nice shooting."

"It helps when they're still," Omar said humbly.

"Still, helleva nice shot from that distance!" Carson said. "Omar, you keep that guy in mind, and set your monitor to that site every thirty seconds. In the meantime we've got six separate groups we need to track. Let's pull the bug up to 2,000 feet and keep a wide view. Charlie, I want you on the three groups that went easterly. Omar, I want you on the other three. As soon as they pass three thousand meters, I want thermals locked in. Clear?"

"Yes, Sir," both men said.

The video screen of the MAV was showing the men galloping on their camels and then the group of three split up into single riders who were separated by twenty or more meters. They were now difficult targets, even for CROWS.

"Closest targets?" Carson asked. "Come on men, I need answers!"

"Two-thousand eight-hundred meters, Sir. Locked-on," Charlie said.

"I've got three locked-on, sir." Omar held up three fingers.

"Any targets that're locked-on, fire at will—three rounds per target."

A few moments later, in stereoscopic thunder, the M2s fired at the Baluchian and cut them down.

"Go to your next closest targets. No time for thermal reports. How many locked-in?"

"Three again, sir." Omar replied.

"Four, sir, all locked-in," Charlie half-shouted, his voice intense.

"Give them the same treatment," Carson intoned.

As before, the M2s fired their wrath with machine-like precision, taking the Baluchian's down.

"Sir, the center site, the one with the RPS-29?"

"What?"

"I don't see anyone there now... even the camels are gone."

"Impossible," Carson quipped. "Get our bug over there now."

"Okay, back to targets, who's locked-in?"

"I have four more," Charlie replied.

Omar was juggling the MAV coordinates and his locked-in targets. "I have three, Sir."

"Fire at will."

The clinical accuracy of the CROWS was mind numbing once it had a lock on a moving target, and it was in range. All eighteen targets were hit. The other three, who stayed back with the RPG-29, remained an unknown.

"I want to do a damage assessment, but Charlie you report first, I want Omar to focus on the first group that's missing. Our bug arrived yet?"

Omar switched to the MAV view. "They're on the other side of that small sand dune, sir. They even have the camels lying down."

"Go down close; I want to see their faces."

"How close?"

"Three hundred feet, maximum zoom. I don't care if they see our bug."

Omar made the modifications to the MAV's trajectory and lens, and in less than ten seconds they were looking at the faces of four men. "There must have been two men on one camel... I see four men."

"Agreed," Carson said. "That's Moshad; he looks like he's in pain. That's the General, so this is the brain trust. That'd be the shooter, he looks injured. The other guy looks dead or unconscious. Okay, I'm satisfied they're no threat. We'll deal with them later. Right now, I want a report on the thermals. We have eighteen to account for. Charlie, you first."

"I had nine thermals in my sector, all nine accounted for and dead."

"Good, Omar?"

Omar was still calculating, and held up one finger. "I have nine, too, but I can only account for eight thermals. Hold one moment."

Omar was opening and closing screens at an amazing speed. "Thermal seven is missing. Gone. I can only assume one of two things. He's dead underneath a camel, or he's buried himself in the sand on the far side of a sand dune."

"Okay," Carson said with a long sigh. "I think we're done here, for now. The plane is probably refueled by now. None of these guys pose a threat, and any General, after seeing that display of firepower, would only be thinking about retreat. We'll let the survivors live. Any problems with that, men?"

"No, Sir." Both Charlie and Omar agreed.

"Then let's go."

LB steered the dusty MRAP, whose M2 barrels were still smoking, toward the Boeing 777-X that glinted beneath the morning sun on the Northern Bypass Freeway like a symbol of human ingenuity. Suddenly, the fuel tanker that was parked next to the plane lurched in reverse, and began going backwards away from the plane, dragging the hose behind it, with two men in hot pursuit.

"What the hell is going on now?" Carson said, leaning forward in his navigator seat.

CHAPTER 76

Unattended

Raji was unconscious. He had taken four codeine tablets, inspired by Sanjur's happy, carefree attitude as they were sending him up the chute. Raji wanted to experience that cheerful, unperturbed state, too. Little did he realize that the innocent looking tablets would render him utterly unconscious.

When Gorgin finally woke up, he heard the gunfire in the distance behind him, and he saw that his comrade, Raji, was unconscious, and while he didn't see any obvious injuries, Raji was completely unresponsive. Three strange men were on the far side of a large tanker truck, refueling the airplane. Gorgin and Raji were behind the plane's tires, unnoticed and apparently unguarded.

Gorgin shook his head, trying to regain his clarity. He was obviously a prisoner by the same people who had tried to kill him. He stood to his feet and instantly knew what he had to do. His leg felt stiff, but he was strong enough to move. He was under the fuselage, on the far side of the tanker, opposite the four men that were refueling the plane. The smell of airplane fuel filled the air. More gunshots rang out in the distance, startling him as he crawled alongside the tanker.

When he got to the cab, he climbed inside as cautiously as he could, remembering his military training about breath control and movement fluidity. He opened the driver's door slowly just enough so he could get inside. He winced with pain, as his side brushed against the door. Gorgin was surprised that they had seen fit to bandage his wounds. Most enemies would have left him for dead.

Gorgin slouched in the driver's seat, careful to avoid detection in the side-view mirrors. He smiled slightly as he saw keys hanging in the ignition. The shift was in park, and the emergency brake was on. He glanced carefully in the side-view mirror on the passenger's side, lifting his head up slowly. He saw the three men talking among themselves, two of them had their backs turned to the truck, watching the battle unfold two miles out in the desert. Gorgin would have to do everything quickly in order to make his plan work.

He rubbed his eyes, took a deep breath, and locked the driver's door, then rolled up the window very slowly. Then he reached over to the passenger side and locked that door, too, and rolled up its window, hoping the squeaks he heard would be drowned out by the sound of the men's voices and the hissing of the fuel pump.

The instant he started the engine, he shifted into reverse, pulled the emergency brake and pushed the gas pedal as hard as he could. Two seconds elapsed. He heard screams from the men, ordering him to stop. He heard the snap of the fuel nozzle as he pulled away, and he watched as two men ran after him as he backed up the massive truck as fast as he could. Ten seconds elapsed. As hard as he pushed the gas pedal, the truck was still barely going eight miles per hour. "Come on! Move!" Gorgin said, beating his hand on the steering wheel, as he steered the truck back and forth like a DNA strand to make it harder for the two runners to get close. Twenty seconds elapsed.

Adrenaline surged through his body to such a degree that he didn't even feel his legs as he pushed on the gas pedal. The two men ran to catch up, one on each side, but at thirty meters the truck was beginning to pick up speed, and the runners were having a hard time keeping up, and Gorgin made it impossible to get close by swaying the truck back and forth slightly. The runners finally gave up. Forty-seven seconds elapsed.

One of the men pulled a handgun out of his side holster, and pointed it at the truck. Gorgin slouched down below the steering, careful to keep his eyes on the side view mirror, but the man didn't shoot, and began yelling back to the other runner, who seemed out of breath and angry. The truck had been successfully hijacked. Gorgin did a fist pump and screamed as loud as he could.

Gorgin kept backing up at full speed until he had at least a mile between himself and the plane. Then he slowed down and came to a stop. Gorgin looked in the back of the cab, and saw a glass jug of water that was half full, and grabbed it. It was heavy, and would serve his purpose. He was so thirsty, but he restrained himself. Gorgin positioned the water bottle down by the gas pedal, and using his shoelaces, tied it to the pedal. Gorgin unlocked his door, tilted his head back, his lips moving in silent prayer, and when he had finished, his eyes held a red glare.

His right hand shifted from neutral into first gear, as he leaned the water jug onto the gas pedal. The freeway was straight, wide and flat, and Gorgin knew that all he needed to do was aim the truck at the plane, and there was little anyone could do to stop it.

*　　　*　　　*　　　*

Frank had run as fast as he could, but his mobility was impaired from his rescue of Dr. Najafi, and he cursed that fact as he stopped in the middle of the road. The truck continued to back up, and Frank pulled his gun out, pointing it at the front windshield, but when he looked past the menacing grill, he couldn't see a driver.

Frank dropped his arm, and bent over to catch his breath. Frank's body was shaking. If someone wanted to steal the truck that bad, they could take it as far as he was concerned. They had gotten most of the fuel in the plane, anyway. The only issue was that the final costs to Helios kept going up and up. Now, they had to add a fuel truck to the bill.

Frank glanced to his left, wondering how far the MRAP was, and whether Carson would be going after the truck. But then the truck came to an ominous stop about a mile down the freeway. Suddenly, it dawned on Frank what was happening, and he ran back to the plane. He took a quick glance at the MRAP, as it bobbed over the sand dunes about a mile out. When he got to the plane, he ran to the exit door. "Martin, can you back this thing up now?"

"It'd take me a few minutes to get everything prepped—"

"We don't have time… we have an emergency…" Frank pointed to the fuel truck. "That truck is going to try and crash into this plane. How fast can you back up?"

Martin glanced in the truck's direction. "We'll see…" He ducked back inside the plane. Almost immediately, the engines of the plane fired up, its powerful, high- pitched drone spread across the desert.

Raji woke up groggily, and noticed his comrade was gone. The plane was starting up. The tires were moving. *Why didn't anyone tell me? I could be run over!*

*   *   *   *

Carson swiveled back to Omar. "What do you think is happening over there?"

"Someone hijacked the truck," Omar said. "I think they're going to drive it into the plane. Otherwise, he'd still be backing up."

The truck and the plane were facing each other like two gunslingers in a standoff.

"Lock-in the tires. As soon as you're locked, fire."

"Sir, it's a gas truck, if I miss…"

"LB, stop the vehicle!" Carson shouted. LB immediately pulled the MRAP to a complete stop.

"Okay, lock-in—"

"Shit, it's moving."

The tanker began to drive towards the plane, while the plane began to move backwards. Slowly. The closing of the distance was decidedly in the truck's favor. Omar made some calculations with his trackball, and looked at the truck's thermals, locking onto the engine block.

"The driver just jumped out of the truck," Carson said. "Do you have a shot yet? We have to take it now!"

Omar clicked, and the M2 fired three rounds at the engine, all three were direct hits, but the truck continued to move somehow, though there was steam rising from the hood.

"Tires!" Carson yelled. "Charlie, take a shot at the truck, I don't care what you hit, just stop it!"

The tension in the MRAP was profound, almost smothering. Nouri and Parto held each other, and Dorri leaned on Parto. "I said a prayer, Momma. They won't hurt Terran."

Parto smiled weakly, and held Dorri a little closer.

"Somebody shoot!" Carson screamed. "We have less than forty

meters between them. That truck is closing fast, *now shoot it!*"

Both M2s suddenly erupted in a barrage of gunfire. The truck's tires were reduced to shreds, and the truck immediately lurched to its right side, and drove off the road into the hollow space between the north- and south-bound lanes, and then tipped over into an explosive fireball. Frank was thrown back about ten feet from the explosion, but remained conscious. He looked up, flat on the ground, and thought he saw Martin looking down from the cockpit window, rubbing his forehead.

The plane's engines suddenly stopped, and Frank, for the first time in forty-eight hours, thought he could relax. Then he heard some faint pounding above him. He sat up. Peter was standing in the cockpit, pointing up the road, his face panic stricken.

Frank narrowed his eyes, and through the smoke he saw a powerfully-built man staggering hurriedly toward the plane from a distance of a quarter mile. It was Gorgin, and he was carrying a bag. Frank stood up as quickly as his body would allow. He was in some form of shock. Raji came up to him and started talking, but Frank was unsure if he understood. "Slow down... what are you saying?"

"He still thinks we're trying to destroy the plane," Raji yelled. "Give me your gun, it will prove to him we're not."

Still in a stupor, Frank took out his handgun and handed it to Raji.

Raji ran in the direction of Gorgin and waved his arms above his head. At first Gorgin paused, reaching into the bag and pulling out a grenade. Then, he heard Raji shouting. "It's okay. We're working with these men now. Namvar is inside the plane. He cut a better deal with the Americans. Look... they gave me a gun. Drop the grenades. You don't want to blow that plane up."

Gorgin stopped walking. He was about thirty meters from Raji, and another sixty from the plane. "How can I trust you? Maybe you defected."

"If you throw one of those, and it prevents that plane from taking off, every man will lose their wages. I don't have to tell you what they'll do." Raji put his arms straight out from his body. "Come on brother, what proof do you need? Look at your bandages. *They* did that." Raji pointed to the plane.

Gorgin looked at the burning fuel truck, and then further beyond it to the MRAP. "The problem is that I don't believe you. Why would Namvar be inside the plane? And why were you unconscious? I tried to wake you up... no," Gorgin shook his head and looked down at the pavement, "something's wrong here."

"Look, I took some of their pain killers, too many, they knocked me out. As for Namvar, he wants to go with them—"

"To America? I don't believe you. Namvar would never leave Iran for America." Gorgin started to walk again, toward the airplane, his eyes wary of Raji, shouting as he walked. "Why did you defect, Raji? Did they give you money? Did they promise you a trip to America? That's it, isn't it? You want to leave Iran and live in luxury?"

"No. You have it all wrong, Gorgin. Please, drop the bag. We'll collect our money, go home and have a big feast."

"You haven't explained why Namvar is going to America," Gorgin bellowed like a crazy man. He was only ten meters from Raji, and kept a steady pace in the direction of the airplane, along the shoulder of the freeway. "The difference between you and me is that you would rather take the easy money by playing with the enemy. Me, I know who the enemy is, and I will vanquish him... or die trying."

"Gorgin, everything I'm saying is true. As for Namvar, I don't understand it any better than you, but I've seen it with my own eyes!"

Gorgin was close to Raji's position, and he stopped for a moment, looking at him with a fierce stare. "These men killed our comrades. They tried to kill me. They probably killed Namvar, too, and you... you stand there *protecting them?*"

Gorgin walked past Raji like a man possessed. Raji followed him. "They're not going to let you get close enough to throw that. It's suicide. Do you want to die more than collecting your money and having a feast? Come on, brother. Stop this!"

Raji got down on his knees, dropped the gun to the ground, and held his hands together. "Gorgin, stop, look at me! I'm begging you. Don't go any further. Look at me, if I was their puppet, why wouldn't I have already shot you? Why would I be begging here for *your* life?" Raji jabbed his index finger three times against his head. "Think, brother, why would I do that?"

Gorgin stopped, turned and limped toward Raji with rage written on his face. "I hate this world! There," he pointed to the plane, "sits an insult to our people!" He pointed in the direction of the MRAP. "And there's another one. Why are they even here, Raji? *Why?!*"

Gorgin composed himself, pausing a moment. "And you ask me to believe your story that Namvar would enter *that* beast… brother… that was when you lost me."

Gorgin smiled imposingly like a man with nothing to lose. He slowly pulled the grenade's pin that he held in his hand, as if daring Raji to shoot him, but Raji could only shake his head, and whisper the word, "Don't." Gorgin tossed the grenade into the bag and began to swing the bag over his head as he ran towards the plane. He only ran three steps before a .50-caliber bullet cut him down, and the grenades spilled on the road like stones falling on the darkened bottom of a river. Raji fell to the ground, covered his head and held his breath. The explosion was deafening.

Raji's surroundings exploded in a blinding flash of light and a growling roar. Barely a heartbeat of time passed, but an undeniable presence swayed above and around him, and his mind lost track of the reality he had made himself a part of. He remembered one thing: breathe, just breathe.

CHAPTER 77

Departure

Martin looked down from the cockpit window, studying the impact crater on the freeway about thirty meters in front of them. "I need to know how deep it is. I'd much rather taxi past that hole than back up three thousand meters on this road."

Peter stood on his toes, looking out the side window. "Can you open this?"

Martin unlatched the window in his cockpit and slid it backwards.

"Frank, can you hear me?" Peter shouted.

Frank looked up in a daze. Two smoke columns gently fell over the landscape like shadows of a giant's legs. "What?"

"Can you inspect the depth of that impact crater? We want to taxi forward, past it, if we can, so we can take off straight ahead. Martin's worried about backing up three thousand meters."

"Sure, I'll have a look," Frank said. He ambled slowly in the direction of the two bodies. Several intact grenades were strewn on the highway. Gorgin was dead, but as Frank got closer, he could hear a rhythmic moan. He walked faster to Raji's position, and knelt down. Frank looked to the MRAP that was on its way to his position and signaled that he needed help. In a minute, the MRAP arrived, and almost immediately Omar rushed out the door.

"Man, am I glad to see you," Frank said.

"Same here, man."

Omar looked down at Raji. "He's still alive?"

"Yeah, can you help me move him into the MRAP?"

"Sure."

Carson poked his head out the door. "You okay, Frank?"

"Head hurts like hell, I've got burns over most of my body, my eyes are burning up from the smoke, starved as hell, but other than that, I'm peachy. How 'bout you?"

"God, you sound like an old man," Carson laughed. "I'll tell you this, if that plane gets in the air, I'm going to break into my secret stash of whiskey and drink like a fish. You with me on that?"

"Count me in."

"You can count me in, too," Omar said.

"Who said you were invited?" Carson quipped.

"I don't need an invitation after today."

Omar and Frank brought Raji to the MRAP and put him in the back where a bunk bed was pulled down from the wall. "Okay, we'll take him back to the plane and see if the Doc can take a look at him."

"I have to inspect a hole... I'll meet you back there."

"Sir," Charlie said. "That site with the General and Moshad... they just started moving again."

"Where?"

"In our direction."

"I feel like I'm in some goddamn Terminator movie," Carson said. "What's their distance?"

Charlie smiled at the reference. "Seven thousand, three hundred meters."

"Leave 'em be. There's nothing they can do from there. If they get into thermal range, you let me know."

"Yes, Sir."

Frank ducked through the door and went back to the impact crater that the hand grenades had left behind. "Omar?"

Omar peered through the door. "What's up?"

"Anything I should know about moving these grenades out of the way?"

"Best thing to do is to pull the pins, and toss them as far as you can... or you can use them for target practice. You don't want any kids finding them."

"Alright, when you get back to the plane, tell Martin that the impact crater is only a foot deep and four feet across. We were lucky they didn't all explode. With the size of those tires, going slow enough, we should be able to roll over this hole just fine. Also, let him know that if he hears explosions, I'm just shooting these grenades. Okay?"

"Will do."

Omar jumped back into the MRAP. The doors closed, and it backed up to the plane.

When the MRAP arrived back at the plane, they unloaded Raji and decided the best thing to do was to pull him up the chute, and have Dr. Najafi look at him inside the plane.

After they finished with Raji, Carson looked up at Peter. "I heard you say earlier that you had plenty of provisions on the plane. We have people down here who're starving. Can you send down any food? I know if I eat another energy bar, I might spontaneously combust."

"Sure, I'll send some down the chute," Peter said.

"Martin?" Carson said. "I think you should leave as soon as possible. We have more Baluchians on the way, no real threat, but if you could get in the air, I can leave, and we can avoid a conflict with them."

"Do you want us to take Raji with us?"

"I think it's best. If he stays with us, we have no doctor, and only a basic first aid kit."

"So the doctor stays with us, too?"

"Only if you promise to return him. They need him here."

"I'm sending him down. There's no way I'm coming back."

Martin ducked back inside the cabin, and a few minutes later, Dr. Najafi gingerly slid down the chute to Omar's waiting arms. Omar helped him walk to the MRAP.

"I think we're all set," Carson said. "Thanks again for the meals. Hope your flight is smooth."

Martin nodded. "Move your truck to the side, and then help us navigate the hole down there. Once we get by that, we'll take off."

"You got it."

*   *   *   *

It was 10:50 A.M. when the plane began to taxi to its final take off position. Everyone was aboard, some too injured to even notice that the cabin doors had been closed, and the chutes discarded. Terran, Sanjur, Namvar, Peter, and Jamere were looking out the windows, excited to be leaving. Martin and his crew were busy in the cockpit. Raji was laying in the back aisle with a blanket over him. He remained unconscious.

On the ground, Frank and Omar were leading the plane past the hole, and with only minor difficulty, maneuvered over the hole without incident. Parto, Nouri, Dorri, and Carson were outside the MRAP, which was located about seventy feet off the south bound road. They all waved goodbye as the plane's engines revved up, announcing its intention. Within seconds, the plane lurched forward and sped down the freeway. It seemed like a long time that it was earthbound. Dorri, who had never seen a plane before, asked, "Is something wrong, and it forgot how to fly?" Before Parto could answer, the plane began to take off and climb quickly into the sky, to Dorri's delight.

Carson ducked inside the MRAP. "Status on our terminators?"

Charlie checked the most recent data. "They came to a complete stop about ten seconds ago. It looks like they're already turning back."

As everyone got back inside the MRAP, Carson sat down and looked at everyone with a smiling face. "Okay, here's what we're going to do. We're going to drive to a place where we can find some shade, and take our fancy airplane food outside and have a picnic. Sound good?"

Everyone smiled back and agreed.

"And when we're finished with that, we'll head back to the school and check on our friend Hamid. LB, find us some shade."

CHAPTER 78

Protection

Terran slept soundly on the airplane after the first two hours of wonderment. He was in love with flying, but after a while the lack of sleep caught up with him and most of the others, too, especially after a full meal. The din of the engine noise and a full stomach was a perfect way to lose consciousness. Two hours into the flight, the passenger cabin was mostly quiet. Only Namvar and Sanjur were still awake.

Namvar ventured over to Sanjur's seat after he saw him return from the bathroom. "Mind if I sit next to you or were you going to take a nap?"

"No, you're welcome to sit," Sanjur said. "I've never really been on a plane before. I simply can't sleep when I'm surrounded by this kind of luxury. This is like a five-star hotel that flies, isn't it?"

Namvar chuckled. "I suppose you're right."

"Did you try the chicken or the fish?"

"The fish."

"Me, too," Sanjur gushed. "It was amazing. It's been a very long time since I ate a meal that was that good. There was not a molecule of food on that plate when I finished it. They could have returned it to the cupboard and no one would have been the wiser."

Namvar smiled. "How did you come to meet Terran?"

Sanjur paused, deliberating on how to respond. "I was the one who helped him escape from Moshad. You see, he ran away from his home to find new teachers who understood science, but the real problem, at least to him, was that his people expected him to fulfill a religious role. Something, as you know, they called the Mahdi."

"Why was it a problem for Terran?"

"He didn't want to be the Mahdi. He's brilliant, and as soon as Helios found out about him, they wanted him. Who knows why?

Maybe his brilliance is very rare. I suppose Terran will soon find out, but he has his own plans. So, on the one hand, he was being pushed to be the Mahdi for his people, and on the other hand, Helios wants his intellect to help them create some great technologies or something like that." Sanjur's voice became a mere whisper. "But Terran has his own agenda, and neither his tribe nor Helios knows."

"And what is his agenda?" Namvar asked, narrowing his eyes, and trying to sound casual.

"You know, he told me once or at least some parts of it, but I wasn't really listening that carefully... something to do with the weather I think. Yes, I'm quite sure, it was the weather. You can ask him when he wakes up, I'm sure he'd be happy to explain it."

Namvar crossed his legs and shifted in his seat, leaning a little closer to Sanjur, and then lowered his voice. "I have a feeling that when we arrive in America, you will be very influential in those first few months, before Terran learns English. I would just advise that you say nothing about any of this."

"Which part?"

"About him being the Mahdi or about his own agenda. It's really none of their business. Of course, if Terran instructs you to speak about it, that's one thing, but to do so entirely on your own, well, that's another." Namvar paused and looked out the window briefly. "All I'm saying is that we don't know what Helios has in mind. We should be cautious, don't you agree?"

Sanjur blinked a few times. "Of course you're right, Mister Akhtar—"

"Please, call me, Namvar."

"Okay... Namvar, and you can call me Sanjur. I can be very convincing as a stupid person." Sanjur paused for a second and then laughed to himself, jabbing his elbow into Namvar side. "Did I fool you?"

Namvar chuckled politely, unsure of Sanjur's meaning, but he had the distinct impression that Sanjur was shrewder than he had suspected.

"And your background, Sanjur?"

"Everything I am is self-taught, in the schoolroom of earth. I would consider myself a man of earth. I have no education—in the form of a schoolroom. I was tossed out at age nine—always talking, never studying, that sort of thing, but I applied myself in the art of selling, and so, over time, I became something of a merchant. A very good one, I might add. But then, like all of us I suppose, when Sunrot hit, my profession changed..."

Sanjur turned to Namvar. "When you spoke to Terran at the school, he mentioned you had been a Mawlawi... how did you become the Police Chief of Mashhad after being a scholar?"

Namvar hesitated. In a very real sense, Sanjur was his intermediary to the Mahdi. He had no choice but to trust him. He took a deep breath. "I spent seven years at the Dar al-Shafa school in Qom. I mostly studied Islamic law, but I also had a love for poetry and Sufi mysticism. I was torn as to which to follow, but my father insisted on the law. After I graduated, the school offered me a teaching role, which I eagerly accepted."

"What did you teach?"

"The philosophy of Sharia law."

"You were a philosopher or a lawyer?"

"More a philosopher... or so I felt. I had taught for five years, when Sunrot hit. The school was abandoned like everything else in Qom."

"Where did you go then?"

"I was in the Caravan of Survivors. Three of my students had survived, and they convinced me that we could make it to Mashhad. The rumors were that it had survived the earthquakes and windstorms, so we went. Those were confusing times..." Namvar shook his head in recollection.

"I've met others, who were in the Caravan. From their descriptions, I'm glad I wasn't one of them. So how'd you become the Police Chief, and more to the point, *why?*"

"I got to Mashhad six weeks after the start of Sunrot. I was a scrawny man, in rags and little more. A wealthy family took me in, because I had taught one of their children. They lived in the outskirts of Mashhad and had stocks of food, gold, silver and diamonds. The father had the wealth of twenty generations, or so he told me. I didn't really care, because money, to me, at that time, meant nothing. I even hated it."

Namvar paused to take a sip of water. "One night, a gang of thieves came into our neighborhood and began to break into homes with impunity. Most of the neighbors had guns, but these were not your regular burglars who used stealth. They simply shot their way into the homes and ransacked them, often killing the families, and then living in their house. *They* were the law.

"They had a leader, who happened to have raided a house across the street from where I was staying as a guest. We knew our home would soon be occupied, too. So I set about a plan to protect it and ourselves. That plan proved to be effective. The owner and many of his neighbors asked me to protect them. They offered me enough money to hire a staff and acquire vehicles and so on. That was how I came to be Chief of Police."

Sanjur put his hands up. "But what was your plan... how did you defeat this gang?"

Namvar nodded. "Yes, well, I walked across the street and introduced myself. His house was heavily armed, and I almost got shot before I even got in, but I was eventually let in. I explained who I had been, and how I had gotten there. The leader's name was Abu, and he was aware of the school in Qom. His grandfather had gone to the same school, so I was suddenly an insider. He told me that my house would be safe, but when I asked for the safety of the other houses, he laughed at my naivety. I think he was curious about me. He told me that if I could talk with the remaining owners and come to a satisfactory compensation for him and his men, that they would leave us alone.

"I did just that, and we struck a bargain. It was a complicated transaction to say the least, and my education served me well. Anyway, that's how it all started."

"But you were a scholar of the holy works. How could you then work with criminals?"

"In those days, my friend, everyone was a criminal. Everyone was either bending or breaking laws to survive." He paused and smiled. *"Laws are like the wind,* we would say. It allowed me to be a teacher, it was just that my classroom was no longer a privileged space of white alabaster, intricate carvings and curved doorways. That had all been destroyed. It didn't exist anymore, so I decided my classroom would be wherever I was, and my students would be whoever was around me."

"Ah, but you negotiate like a merchant—"

"When you study law, you understand negotiation. It's really what it is, when you peel away the edifice of law and justice, it's negotiation, compromise."

"Yes, but you taught Sharia law, its source is God. Isn't that how you believe?"

"It is, but I realized after Sunrot, that God was something less scripted and solid than I had come to believe in school. We're part of something... call it an experiment. I don't know what other word best describes it, but look at us, a self-educated merchant, and a simple teacher, on an airplane four rows behind the Mahdi, on our way to America." Namvar smiled as he shook his head in disbelief. "How could it be anything else but an experiment?"

"But do you still believe?"

"In God?"

Sanjur nodded.

"Of course. God's will is not something I can understand or question. To be honest, there were times I didn't, but they were short-lived. When I heard Moshad tell me that the Mahdi was here, in Mashhad—literally across the street, I felt these flames inside leap up. A few hours later, I met him, and I had no doubt. My belief survived all of the tragedy of Sunrot, and he... he is my reward."

Sanjur could sense Namvar's strong emotions in the tremor of his voice. He looked out the window, allowing Namvar some privacy.

"You believe he is the Mahdi, but I don't think *he* believes it," Sanjur observed. "How is it that you know he is?"

"That's why there is a prophecy. So we, the scholars, can recognize him, and once he's found, protect him."

"Protect him from what?"

"He will be used by the powerful to secure more power. And it's happening. The powerful are bringing him to their home. They will try to seduce him to take on their agenda, and he will resist. They will try to kill him for his resistance."

"If that's the prophecy, and you want to protect him, why did you let him get on this plane?"

"It's what *he* wants. I can't impose my will over his." Namvar turned, putting his hands over his heart. "I am soul in a man; he is God in a boy. I will follow his will, and I'll protect him to the best of my abilities. I hope I can count on you to do the same."

"For what it's worth," Sanjur said with a grin, "that's all I've been doing since I met him."

Suddenly, Peter came from the cockpit, and looked around the cabin as if he were searching for someone. He saw Sanjur and Namvar were the only ones awake, so he walked over.

"It looks like we'll stop in Olympia and get refueled. The Captain's concerned we won't have enough fuel to make it to Denver. When we land, I'll let you know what our plans are and how long we'll be staying there. It could be a day or two, we'll see."

Peter looked towards the back. "Raji's still unconscious?"

Namvar stood up and looked back. "Yes, it looks that way."

Namvar sat back down. "How much longer?"

"Our best estimate puts us on the ground about 2:30 P.M. local time."

"Which is how many hours?"

"About eleven more hours, I'm afraid."

Peter opened a bottle of pills he held in his hand. "Any more codeine for either of you?"

"Maybe two more for me," Sanjur said. "If you can spare them…"

"Sure," Peter said, shaking out two white pills, and handing them to Sanjur. "We'll try and get some doctors to look at everyone who needs help as soon as we land, but it might take time. Namvar, how about you?"

Namvar shook his head politely. "I think I'm okay, but thanks."

"Okay, I'll be back in about an hour or two. I think I'll take a couple of these myself, and try to get some sleep. See you later."

Both men nodded. Sanjur washed the pills down with a swig of water. The quiet drone of the engines returned to the awareness of Sanjur and Namvar as they both contemplated their next move in silence. Sanjur liked Namvar, and felt a certain kinship with him. It was good to know that he wasn't alone in his efforts to protect Terran, though, to be sure, he had no idea what foes they might encounter. One thing he felt confident in: they could be no worse than Moshad.

Of all the mysteriously winged creations of man, jet airplanes were among its greatest achievements. To Sanjur, it was a miracle. Even as the codeine rushed into his bloodstream, it was very difficult for him to close his eyes.

CHAPTER 79

HCP

The Greater Nation capital building was known as the Board of Governors. Each country that was a member of the GN had a Governor, and they each had living quarters within the Board of Governors building, which housed 163 nations. It was a large, sixteen-story complex that included health facilities, cafeterias and ample meeting rooms.

The plaza behind the Board of Governors (BG) led to its Hall of Citizens that featured the portraits of important citizens who had made sacrifices and contributions to the GN. The portraits were small—about four inches square, but what they lacked in size, the sheer number of portraits made up for their diminutive scale. Trevor Stanton loved walking in the Hall of Citizens, because it reminded him that the world was now one country, united.

The different skin colors, clothing, expressions, jewelry, facial features were so diverse. All member nations were represented on the wall, some more than others, but every effort was made to keep the representations proportional to population size. The last time Trevor had tried to count the pictures, he had stopped after reaching four hundred, and by his estimate, he was only 15 percent finished, so he figured there must be about 3,000 pictures that covered the walls. The back wall rose to seventy feet in height. Sometimes he would lean against the opposite wall and reflect on the scope of his achievement to unify the entire world.

It was 1:10 P.M. Trevor was followed by a small staff of handlers that made sure his schedule was adhered to, and all the needs of the President were met. He was running ten minutes behind for a meeting with his Faculty Director, Josh Sinclair. He had wanted Josh to meet the leaders from the Board of Governors who were excited to know more about Terran Kahn, and his anticipated arrival to the Denver ALIGN Center.

Trevor's Chief of Staff had chosen an intimate boardroom for the meeting, called Plaza Five. Its signature furnishing was a rosewood table top that was oval-shaped and incised with intricate beadwork in its center that depicted Earth's solar system. Encircling the beaded solar system like an asteroid belt was the cursive inscription: "You lead my arm. You move my mouth. You have the supremacy of the Universe beneath you. All is your creation." The table accommodated sixteen people comfortably, but for this meeting, only seven were invited.

As Trevor arrived to Plaza Five everyone rose to greet him, shaking hands and in some instances, embracing him. Jonathan Garfield from the United Kingdom, William Van Duyn from Belgium, Mikhail Khilkoff from Russia, Connor Mathis from Germany, Liu Huang from China and Vincent Grévy from France. These men founded the Leadership Council of the Board of Governors. While it was ostensibly an honorary role, it was these six, including Trevor Stanton, that wielded the power of the GN and were the core brain trust of Helios.

Josh Sinclair, as Faculty Director, was introduced as a guest to the Leadership Council. After introductions were made, Trevor motioned to the assembled group to sit. Trevor remained standing with his hands behind his back. He wore a beige encolored suit with a simple white shirt underneath, no tie. "Gentleman, I wanted to formally introduce you to Josh. I know some of you have met him before, but today's circumstance is unusual for a number of reasons. I invited him to be a part of this because he played such an instrumental role in getting Terran Kahn to our Denver facility.

"Three pieces of our puzzle have come into alignment," Trevor said, holding up his index finger. "One, we've heard from our director at the Preserve in Mashhad, Iran, that at 11:00 A.M. local time, our plane departed from Mashhad and is en route to Denver. Our mission was successful." A polite applause erupted in the room, and all eyes turned to Josh, who nodded in acknowledgement. Trevor held up two fingers. "Two, we have an intellect in Terran Kahn that has not been seen on our planet... well, quite possibly ever before. I'll let Josh speak about that in more detail in a bit." Trevor held up three fingers. "The trifecta occurred yesterday: HCP (Human Cloning Project) advised Dr. Wynton that they've achieved an average 91 percent intelligence fidelity on their subjects. If a subject had an IQ of one hundred, they can now clone that subject and achieve an IQ score of ninety-one. An astonishing result!"

Trevor smiled and moved to the buffet behind him. He then turned his head around back to his audience. "Of course, we won't be cloning subjects with IQs of one hundred, but given my math skills, I had to use round numbers."

The men chuckled at his modesty.

Trevor opened the buffet door that hid an ornate silver tray that held a collection of beautiful stemware and a lead-crystal vase filled with cognac. He poured eight glasses and began passing them out. "All of the pieces we've worked so hard to achieve are coming together gentlemen. We can now enjoy the fruits of our labors." Trevor held up his glass, as did everyone else. "Cheers, Gentlemen, to our good news!"

"To our good news." A chorus of voices, then a hush fell over the boardroom as the men eagerly enjoyed their taste of the world's finest cognac, Cuvée 3.128.

Trevor asked Josh to give a detailed report about their discovery of Terran Kahn and the Faculty's view of his intellectual feats on the Curriculum Initiation Program. There were various questions that seemed mostly interested in Terran's personality, to which Josh shrugged apologetically that he didn't know. Within forty minutes, Josh's report was complete. Trevor showed him to the door, shook his hand enthusiastically and had one of his aides, who were waiting outside the boardroom, escort Josh out of the Plaza.

Trevor closed the door behind him, and began pouring another round of drinks for his Leadership Council. "You know, Vincent, this cognac is French or so I'm told... do you recognize it?"

"Of course I recognize it, it's Cuvée."

"Well done, and so it is," Trevor said. "Gentlemen, what did you think of our Faculty director's comments?"

"We've all read the prophecy," Vincent said, "It all seems in order. But we all know that the prophecy says we will try to clone him, but he will resist. Regrettably, that could mean a million different things. Clearly, we can get his DNA without him knowing, so his resistance can't be attributed to that. Once we have the clones, what can he do?"

"Sometimes prophets prophesy their wishes," Connor said. "Maybe this is one such example."

"I agree with Vincent," Liu said. "We must be very careful to keep his clones isolated, and their work a secret. This project is the very basis of our future. If we don't succeed, our future is dire, if not impossible."

Everyone at the table nodded.

"When the plane returns to Berlin, how long before HCP will have its first trial?" Trevor asked, turning to Conner. He was a stout man with wire-rimmed glasses, a thick, graying mustache, and bald headed.

"Two weeks," Conner replied confidently. "In ten weeks we'll have our first test results. Who knows, by then we might be at 89 percent fidelity."

"Why not a hundred," Trevor said, toasting his cognac.

"One hundred," the chorus returned.

*   *   *   *

An hour after Trevor left, the Plaza Five board room, he was having a light lunch with his Chief of Staff, Zhou Hu, a thirty-something Asian women who was a protégée of Liu Huang from a very privileged noble family in Beijing. Zhou was slightly overweight. Even with high heels she was barely five feet tall. Her personality was a little too analytical for many, but no one would argue that she possessed exquisite organizational skills. She was an expert in, of all things, Greek mythology. However, she was brilliant in many diverse topics and had been one of the chosen to leave China, and live in the Board of Governors facility in Olympia. It didn't take long for her skills to come to the notice of Trevor Stanton. He quickly took her under his wing, first as his personal assistant, and later as his Chief of Staff.

Zhou wielded considerable influence in the affairs of the President, though few realized it. She was happy to play a subservient role in the background, but those who knew her ways, like those within the Leadership Council, respected her mental tenacity and ambitions.

As they were going over Trevor's schedule for the remainder of the afternoon, his personal assistant knocked on his door, and opened it just enough to poke his head through. "Mister President, we just got word that the plane landed at Warren County."

"Warren? I thought it was going to Denver."

"It needed fuel, Sir."

"Must have had some strong headwinds... well, that's great! We'll get to meet him ourselves. George, arrange transportation for them. They can stay in our guest suite. How many are there?"

"I don't know Sir, but they're asking for a medical team."

"A *team?*"

"Yes, Sir, that's what I heard."

"Can you get Peter on the network, so I can talk with him directly? Oh, have Josh join me as soon as you can find him."

"Yes, Sir."

George ducked out, closing the door silently.

"You'll bring him here?" Zhou asked.

"It's a chance for him to meet Aban Molavi."

"And you see that as a good thing?"

"You don't?"

"What if he sees something in this boy that he wishes Iran had kept?"

"Like...?"

"I don't know, but I think we should keep his visit secret. Don't meet here. Maybe your private residence?"

Trevor leaned back in his leather chair and looked around his office. It was a beautifully appointed office in the True North Wing, as it was called. The True North Wing was on the north side of the Board of Governors Building, which housed all of Helios' core functions in regard to global governance.

"Would you like to meet him?"

"The boy?"

Trevor nodded.

"Sure... if you want."

"Then we'll meet at my home," Trevor said, walking to the door. "George?"

In a few moments George came into the office. "Yes, Mister President?"

"Change of plans. We'll have Terran come to my home. This is a private meeting. Understood?"

"Yes, Sir."

"Did you find Peter?"

"Yes, Sir, he said he would call you back in ten minutes. He needed to coordinate the medical team first."

"Okay. What about Josh?"

"I'll do that now, Sir."

"George, one last thing. Make sure Peter gets whatever he needs."

"Yes, Sir."

George left and closed the door behind him.

"I hope Terran isn't injured," Trevor said. "That would be a shame."

"I don't sense anything like that, Sir."

"What does that mean?"

Zhou looked down at her hands, folded on her lap. "Only that I can sense things sometimes… you know, women's intuition."

"I see… well, let's hope you're right."

"Sir, can I ask you something?"

"Go ahead."

"What's the role that Terran will play? I mean, in Denver, they'll educate him, but to do what?"

"Well, I can tell you one thing, it won't be Greek mythology." Trevor chuckled at his own joke, and then turned serious. "I don't know. It'll be his choice."

"What do you think he'll choose?"

"I should ask you, you're the one with the sixth sense."

Zhou pouted her lips for a moment, and paused. "…I think he'll choose astronomy. A boy like that will want to look up at the stars and see just how big this universe really is."

CHAPTER 80

Correlations

Eleanor walked quickly to her office. An aide had told her that her brother, Josh Sinclair, was holding on the network. She was hoping for good news as she got to her office, closing the door behind her. Her computer was blinking, and she clicked the *Connect* button, and the video screen opened. Her brother looked up with a smile. "Hey, El. Good to see you."

"Thanks, you look like you're in a good mood."

"I just had a meeting with the power brokers of the new world, and drank expensive cognac... so yes, I'm in a good mood."

"It must be nice to be in the limelight. Any news on Peter or Carson?"

"Nothing new. They should be in Denver around five, local time."

"What was your meeting about?"

"They just wanted to know more about Terran's personality... which I couldn't answer. They actually seemed more interested in that, than his intellect. Kind of surprised me."

Eleanor tilted her head, staring at the screen with a distant look on her face. "They're wondering about the correlations," she said in a soft voice.

"Didn't catch that..."

"They're trying to assess the intellectual Fidelity Rate."

"Still not reading you," Josh said.

"Remember that report that Wynton released about a month ago? HCP found a strong correlation between intellectual fidelity in the test clones and the personality. A quiet, introverted personality, for example, had a lower Fidelity Rate than a strong extroverted personality. There was a significant relationship. Their report had broad ranging swings—I think they were 22 percent on average. That's why they were asking those questions."

"You're probably right. I think I missed that report, but I'll try and read it tonight." Josh sat up and looked at the corner of his screen.

"Eleanor, let me put you on hold, I've got a call coming in from Trevor's office."

"No problem."

Eleanor logged into the HCP database, and downloaded a file called: *Correlative Analysis of Subject's Personality and Intelligence Fidelity in Clones*. She clicked the link, and it opened in a new window. She scrolled down to the Summary.

> There was a significant relationship between the personality index in subjects with IQs above 180, and how well their clones performed in IQ tests. Subjects with personality indexes (PI) between 71 and 75 scored an average fidelity rate (FR) of 82%. Subjects with a PI between 76 and 80 scored an average FR of 86%. Subjects with a PI between 81 and 85 scored an average FR of 92%.
>
> In our test group of thirty-nine subjects, none exceeded a PI of 85, but our hypothesis is that the Subject's personality plays a very significant role in the fidelity of the intelligence within the clone organism. This could mean that a Subject with a PI above 90 could have a FR approaching 100%.
>
> PI screening of Subjects produces a high predictor of FR, and to date, it is the most reliable predictor of intelligence fidelity in clones.
>
> There are currently no theories as to why this correlation exists or what could be the causal relationship between PI and FR. More research is required to determine this. What longitudinal studies we have to date, indicate the rate of FR decline in clones over time, could also be affected by the PI. This theory requires additional study in order to prove that a relationship exists in the dimension of time.

Eleanor stopped reading, just as her brother's video window popped up.

"That was George. A major development. The plane landed here. It needed fuel and the pilot apparently didn't want to risk taking it to Denver. Peter's—"

"Terran's onboard?"

"Yes, that's confirmed, but George said that Peter called for a medical team, so some of the passengers are injured, and apparently, that includes Peter."

"Oh, my. When I talked with Hamid this morning, he mentioned there were Police that had gotten involved... it sounded like the whole thing was very complicated. I hope everyone is okay."

"Another thing—Trevor has called me to a meeting with Terran, at his home. I need to leave now, so I'll call you when I get back."

"When will they leave?"

"I'm not sure. We'll probably figure that out tonight. But I have a feeling they'll be staying over tonight, resting or getting medical attention. I really don't have any other information. I haven't spoken directly with Peter. Hopefully he'll be joining us tonight."

"Find out when they plan to leave, so we're ready to receive them. Okay?"

"I will," Josh said.

"Oh, and find out how many are coming. Hamid mentioned that there might be more than just Nouri and Terran... something about a woman and her daughter. Check on that, too. Okay?"

"I will. Gotta go, El. I'll call you when I get back."

"Okay. Have fun."

"You, too."

The video screen went blank, and the research paper replaced her brother's excited face. Her excitement to meet Terran was replaced by frustration that her brother would meet him first. So typical, and at the President's home, no less. The delay was softened by the fact that Terran was confirmed on the plane, so now it was simply a waiting game. She had to go tell her staff about the change of plans, and put on a good face. She doubted it was possible.

CHAPTER 81

Fences

It was early evening by the time Josh, Zhou and Trevor drove into his private residence near Front Royal, Virginia. The Smithsonian had a large campus called the Conservation Biology Institute, and several of its buildings survived Sunrot. One of them had been converted into the private residence of President Stanton, though he also had a residence at the Board of Governors facility, which was where he stayed most of the time for the sake of convenience.

"Ironically, I live on Research Drive," Trevor said with a chuckle, pointing to a street sign that was bent in a precarious angle. "But I think they plan to change the street name in the next month or two to something more appropriate like Legal Lane."

"I didn't know you were a lawyer." Josh asked.

"Yes, a struggling attorney in Washington, trying to scratch and claw my way into the power breakfasts, and grab a few well-heeled politicians as my clients. Of course, so was everyone else. I decided it'd be better to be a politician than an attorney, because the power is more immediate, and the income, while not necessarily better, comes a *lot* easier."

"You said this complex was once the property of the Smithsonian?"

"Yep, they had a biology institute here. Pretty big complex for a bunch of biologists, but the buildings, at least the two that survived, withstood major winds in excess of one hundred and eighty miles an hour… or so I'm told. That's my place right there." He pointed to a rather plain brick building, two-stories tall that was large, but unattractive.

"It was originally a captive breeding facility. They bred endangered animals for zoos, something like that. Any rate, we eat real well here. It's not the White House mind you, but then you should have seen my place eight years ago. This place is a big step up."

They got out of his black SUV, and walked to the front door, where they were greeted by two guards with automatic weapons in full view.

"If we had more light, I'd show you around, but I think Peter's on his way, so we'll wait inside and have a drink. Sound good?"

"Sounds good."

The inside of his residence was much more opulent than Josh had expected. It was obvious that the place had been remodeled from an institute into a palace.

"You play piano?" Josh asked, pointing to a Steinway Concert Grand in polished ebony.

"No, but guests often do, so we added it. Do you play?"

Josh gravitated to the piano like a boy who found a toy he'd dreamt about for many years, and finally found himself in the same room with it. "I used to. I haven't since Sunrot. Not too many pianos around anymore. Not like this anyway."

"Feel free to play. I'll make us some drinks. What's your preference?"

"What do you have?" Josh asked.

"I'm the President of the GN. I have it all." He laughed. "Seriously, whatever you want."

"Baijiu for me," Zhou said.

"Do you have beer?" Josh asked.

"What kind do you like?"

Josh ran his hand through his hair, trying to remember the brands he used to drink. "Um, Heineken?"

"Be back in a minute. Go ahead, play."

Josh drifted over to the piano and sat down. Zhou found a chair nearby. She sat down with a loud sigh, placed her elbows on the armrest and placed her fingers together like a steeple.

"I'm going to be very rusty, so be kind in your judgments."

"I wasn't one of those girls who played an instrument. I never cared for music that much. Don't worry about me."

Josh opened the fall, and smiled at the ivory keys. "It's an old Steinway, probably from the twenties. He pressed the sustain pedal, and then tried to recall a song, but his mind was blank. He closed his eyes. Still nothing came.

"Did you forget how?" Zhou asked teasingly.

"I think I did," Josh half whispered.

"You need to relax. Just breathe deep, and on the third breath, when you exhale, know that the notes will be there."

For some inexplicable reason, Josh listened to her advice. On the third deep breath he exhaled and let his fingers go. The music was unpolished, but the quality of the tone in the piano was so utterly amazing, even his inept playing was lent a generous voice. It was a masterfully built instrument, and Josh was carried away on its tone.

"Not bad for someone who hasn't played in twelve years," Zhou said.

Josh stopped playing. "Thanks."

"Keep going."

"No… I don't want to get too used to that sound. It'd be too hard to go without it."

Trevor came in carrying a tray of drinks. "You're welcome to come over and play it anytime you want."

"Serious?"

"I'm serious. I stay at the BG facility five days a week, sometimes seven. So here it sits. Just call George, and he can set it up for you."

"Wow… that'd be great. Thanks."

"No problem… Drinks?"

Trevor lowered the tray for Zhou who grabbed her drink, and then Josh took his.

"I thought you might have a little more nostalgia if you drank from the bottle, so I didn't bother to bring a glass."

"Thanks," Josh said.

The sound of car doors closing caught Trevor's attention. He went to the front door. "They're here."

Trevor opened the door and walked outside. The stars were beginning to have a presence in the sky, but there was still a faint blue corona near the horizon.

"Peter, good to see you."

"Thank you, Sir. I'm a little beat up I'm afraid. The doctors have been working on some of us most of the afternoon, so we're kind of whacked up on pain killers right now. Sorry."

"No need to apologize. Let's go into the house, and we'll make introductions there. Alright?"

"Good." Peter motioned to Sanjur and Terran to follow him. They filed into Trevor's house, Peter first, and then Terran and Sanjur. Namvar and Raji had stayed at the airport under doctor's care.

As they walked inside, Terran lit up as he saw the beautiful interior of President Stanton's home. Plush carpeting, tapestries on top, heavy velvet drapes over the floor-to-ceiling windows, spacious rooms, furnishings fit for a king. It was a home that he had never imagined possible. Terran quite literally stared, while everyone stared at him.

Trevor stepped up and held out his hand to Terran. "I'm President Stanton, but please, call me Trevor, all my friends do."

Sanjur immediately began his translation, and Terran shook hands, soaking in the visual grandeur of the home.

"Peter, maybe you can make introductions, you know Josh and Zhou..."

"Sure, Zhou Hu, this is Sanjur, whose last name I don't even know."

"It's Rovach."

"Ah, a Turkman?" Zhou asked.

"Yes."

"Zhou Hu is President Stanton's Chief of Staff. Sanjur is Terran's translator."

"Ah, so you're the teacher?"

In light of the surreal circumstances of being in the home of the most powerful person on earth, having a fresh dose of pain killers coursing through his bloodstream, and seeing a beautiful woman who was impeccably groomed, Sanjur took a deep breath and prayed that words would follow. "Actually, his teacher chose to stay in Mashhad. I'm more of a merchant by trade, but I do speak his language."

Peter, like an orchestra conductor, re-focused the group to Josh. "Sanjur, this is Josh Sinclair, he's the Director of the Faculty."

Sanjur shook his hand.

"And of course, this is the President."

Sanjur bowed with his two hands clasped together.

While introductions were being made, Terran slowly walked around the periphery of the living room, inspecting the room's furnishings. He touched the piano. There was a long shelf of knick-knacks—mostly

State gifts—that straddled a large fireplace. Terran couldn't reach the objects with anything but his eyes, but he saw some of the most beautiful glassware, jade carvings of triumphant horses in battle, and exquisite miniature paintings. Trevor watched with great interest as Terran moved through the room, oblivious to the introductions.

When Sanjur's introduction was completed, he called Terran over to introduce him to Zhou and Josh. Afterwards, Zhou commented about his blue eyes, and pointed to her eyes as she asked how Terran got them. Sanjur began to talk, but Terran interrupted him. "Tell her that I'm a half-blood, but nothing more."

Sanjur translated, and Zhou nodded. "He understands English, then?"

Sanjur smiled. "He doesn't speak English, but he has an uncanny way of deducing what people say."

Zhou smiled. "Your English is excellent, how did you learn?

"As I said, I was a merchant, tourists were my lifeblood. I had to learn to speak many languages. My father taught me, mostly, but I could just as easily say that a thousand Englishmen were my teachers."

"Ah, that explains the accent," Zhou said.

"Can I get anyone a drink?" Trevor asked, looking from Peter to Sanjur and then to Terran.

"I think water would be best," Peter offered.

"What are you drinking?" Sanjur asked Zhou.

"It's called Baijiu, it's very good. Would you like to try it?" Zhou held out her glass to Sanjur who nodded, took it and had a sip.

"Yes, I would have one of those, please."

"Are you sure?" Peter asked. "The pain killers?"

"I think one glass will be fine," Sanjur replied.

"Very well, I'll be right back, feel free to sit and make yourselves comfortable." Trevor turned to Terran and motioned for him to follow. "You can come with me, and I'll show you something."

Terran had been examining a life-sized marble sculpture of Venus de Milo, and followed Trevor as he walked down some stairs. Once they got to the landing, Trevor opened a door off to the left, and motioned with his arm for Terran to go inside. He hesitated for a moment and then went in.

The room had a large sliding glass door, and Trevor walked ahead and opened it, motioning for Terran to go outside. On the patio was a large teak table and chairs plus a telescope. Terran's eyes lit up.

"Do you know what this is?"

Terran nodded, his eyes opened wide. "Telescope."

"That's right. Now, stand here," Trevor positioned Terran right by the scope, and then pointed to the eyepiece. "Look through that."

Terran followed the instruction, and bent down slightly to look. A smile stole across his face that was visible to Trevor, even though Terran was looking down.

Trevor pushed a button on the side of the telescope, and it repositioned itself. Terran pulled back as it moved to a new bearing. When it stopped, Trevor nodded.

"It's programmed to look at various galaxies like Pleiades, Orion, or planets like Saturn and Venus, and of course, the moon. Hell, you don't understand a word I said…"

Trevor smiled to himself, and took Terran's hand, placing one of his fingers on a button to the side of the Telescope. "Just push here. I'll be right back. Okay?"

Terran nodded distractedly, as he pushed the button.

Trevor smiled to himself as he went back inside to get some drinks, wondering to himself what a small, unimpressive person Terran was. He wasn't anything like he had imagined. He was very quiet. Unfortunately, Terran probably wouldn't score high on the Personality Index.

As he was getting the glasses for his guests, Zhou came down the stairs. "So, where is he?" she asked.

"I took your advice and introduced him to the heavens."

"If he is what you think he is, he needs no introduction there."

Trevor chuckled at her comment. "A half-blood Baluchian, scrawny, small, speaks one language… not exactly what I expected. I'm not sure if he's what we had hoped for, but first impressions—I've learned the hard way—are not bankable."

Trevor poured some drinks, glancing behind him as Zhou went over to the patio. "You said he was looking at the telescope?"

"Yes."

"He's not there. You told the guards about our guests, right?"

"Shit!" Trevor rushed out to the patio and Terran was gone. He had a moment of absolute fear, and then saw a small shadowy figure about fifty yards away that appeared to be hunched over something near a thirty-foot fence that surrounded the complex. "That's got to be him." He pointed.

Trevor and Zhou half-walked, half-ran in Terran's direction. "Don't touch that fence."

Terran stood up and turned to face them as they neared his position.

"Let's get him inside," Trevor said to Zhou. "Maybe you could take him by the hand..."

"I'm not the maternal type," Zhou said. "Sorry."

As they got to Terran, he pointed to something on the ground. "She died from the fence. It killed her."

It was an owl. Its wings were spread, but the bird was face down.

Trevor looked to Zhou. "How do I explain the electric fence?"

"You don't. Let's go. It's cold out here."

Trevor held his hand out. "Let's go, Terran."

Terran kneeled down, picked up the owl, gathering in its wings, and then held the owl in his arms like a baby. The owl's body was the size of a large football. Its talons, seared from the electric fence, were almost the same size as Terran's hands.

Trevor started to shake his head to say, *no*. Owls were dirty creatures, but Terran appeared to be feeling for a heartbeat with his right hand. Zhou was already on her way back to the house. Terran then placed his hand on the owl's head, and seemed to be rubbing its skull. He touched the owl's talons very deliberately. He then placed the owl's body carefully on the ground, patted its head and walked away.

Trevor looked between the owl and Terran, and started to follow him home. Suddenly, he heard the commotion of beating wings. He spun around, seeing a large, near-shapeless bird fly away into the surrounding woods.

"Did anyone see that?" Trevor shouted. "That owl just got up and flew away. Zhou, did you see that?"

She was already close to the patio, and pretended she didn't hear.

The night air was chilly. The elfin boy walked in front of him. *Had he brought that owl to life?* Trevor thought. Was it possible that what he thought he saw was what he actually saw? Maybe, it was the owl's mate. Maybe, it was another bird. Maybe, the owl was merely stunned. A dozen different explanations poured over him until he began to doubt his own eyes and ears. By the time his feet touched the patio's concrete, he had dismissed the whole thing as impossible. A drink was all he needed.

We puzzle over things that appear magical. No hearing can be whole. No sight can be full. No touch can feel past the machine. This doubt takes its strength from us. It hovers over us, undisclosed, while magic sulks in the shadows of our doubt and disbelief—sheathed in our programs. Those things that lack names, those are the worst of magic's curse, because the nameless can never be truly believed, and it is the nameless we desire above all things *to believe.* We create names, billions of names. They are painted on every object by our minds. We hope they confer knowledge, but a billion names can paper over something magnificent.

CHAPTER 82

"No."

S he let the computer ring three times. She didn't want Josh to think she had been waiting for his call, though she had been for two hours, fourteen minutes. Eleanor clicked her mouse. The computer screen opened its video pop-up, and Josh stared out with a vacant look.

"Hey there, bright eyes," Eleanor said.

"I'm aware that I look a little drunk, so don't be jealous."

"How'd it go?"

"Terran is not what I imagined. Prophecies can be so... overrated."

"What do you mean?"

"He's a little kid, El, barely four feet tall. Doesn't really say much. Half-blood oddity. Doesn't even impress me as being that intelligent. Trevor took him outside to look at his telescope, went to make some drinks, came back a minute later, and the kid was in the backyard looking at a dead owl or something. That doesn't sound like a genius. Does it?

"Oh, and another thing, his translator isn't his teacher, he's some Casanova who was hitting all night on Zhou Hu, Trevor's Chief of Staff. And between his pain killers, the drinking, his distraction with Zhou, I think his translations were shit... sorry. His face was beat up. Peter looked bad, too. These guys went through hell to get this kid here. I'll tell you that story when I'm sober, but believe me, it was hell."

"You said Nouri didn't come?"

"No, it was some guy called Sanjur... Rovach. Tall guy. His face looked like it had been used as a punching bag for a heavyweight boxer. He refused to tell us how it happened—"

"Why didn't Nouri come?" Eleanor asked, alarm showing in her voice.

"From the description Peter gave, he decided to stay with the woman who found Terran... I forget her name."

"Love?"

"Something like that... she had a daughter, so that was probably a complication, too. Any rate, we're stuck with this guy Sanjur."

"But he speaks Baluchian?"

"Yes, claims to, seems to. But obviously lacks the vocabulary that Nouri would have had."

"We have an English program that Dr. Sorenson is developing for Terran. It won't take him more than a week to master English. Sanjur won't be an impediment, don't worry."

"There're more people he brought with him," Josh said. "I forget his name, but he was formerly the Police Chief of Mashhad, and then one of his lieutenants or something like that. They didn't come tonight, because apparently they're in worse shape than Sanjur and Peter... which is really saying something."

"Did you get a chance to talk with Peter?"

"Not really."

"What about the President?"

"He kind of had the same impression as me... the kid seemed quiet and withdrawn not very talkative or engaging. Hard to see him as the smartest person on the planet. I don't know, maybe he's just homesick."

Eleanor took a deep breath and leaned back in her chair, trying to assimilate the somewhat chaotic download from her drunken brother. "Let's restart by me asking questions, and you answering them, one at a time. Okay?"

"Shoot."

"Question one: you said Terran was a half-blood oddity. What did you mean by that?"

"Zhou picked up on his eyes—they're bluish—not your typical color for Persians, so she asked, and he replied that he's a half-blood. Refused to elaborate."

"Question two: why is the Police Chief of Mashhad accompanying him?"

"We assumed it was some kind of security deal, that he was going to provide protection for Terran, but it turns out that the guy was a religious scholar at some fancy school, and he's a devotee of Terran, or what he thinks Terran is... that Mahdi thing."

Eleanor nodded, and moved closer to the monitor.

"Question three: you said Terran didn't appear very intelligent. On what basis do you draw that conclusion?"

"Look, Sis, maybe I'm not the best judge of intelligence in the world, but I've been around my share of UHIQs—they're all a little... maladjusted, quirky, but they have passions. You ask them a good question, and they'll go on and on. You show them their first telescope; they'd be on that thing until you dragged them off. All I'm saying is that he doesn't fit my ideas of ultra-intelligence."

Eleanor paused, while Josh took a long drink of water.

"Question four: what did President Stanton think about him?"

"Like me, I think he was underwhelmed, but remained hopeful that the CIP scores prove out. I think the half-blood issue was a concern, because there's no mention of that in the prophecy, and that's not a trivial distinction, to put it mildly. If he's not the Mahdi, and his IQ is high, but not as high as we'd hoped, and he has this sort of withdrawn personality, we might be traveling down a dead-end. The fact that he has four others with him, including this Chief of Police guy, only adds to the weirdness. I don't know, I think Trevor was disappointed."

"Question five: when will they leave for Denver?"

"First thing in the morning. They should arrive around ten your time."

"Last question. The DNA sample... Peter is still getting that, correct?"

"Yeah, he's already got it, part of the medical exam when they landed. Martin, the pilot, will be bringing it to HCP directly from Denver."

"Anything else that happened tonight that you found interesting?" Eleanor asked.

Josh took another long sip of water, and wiped his mouth with his sleeve. "Zhou asked Terran if he believed in God." Josh took another sip of water.

"What'd he say?"

"No."

"No?" Eleanor asked.

"Exactly... not the answer you'd expect from the Mahdi, right?"

Eleanor smiled almost invisibly.

CHAPTER 83

UHIQ

It was 10:12 A.M. when the sound of the jet engines first broke the stillness of the morning. Eleanor and Liam were waiting with a small team of service personnel in two black SUVs at the Front Range Spaceport facility. Their window was cracked just enough to hear outside. It was a cold, windy day, when the Boeing 777-X came into their awareness, first as a distant sound, and then a silver flash in the eastern sky. Eleanor and Liam stepped out of the SUV to watch it land.

They were excited to finally meet Terran. They were the only ones within the Faculty Research Center that were aware of his standing as the Mahdi. Everyone else at the research center considered him a UHIQ (pronounced: *You Hick,* an acronym for Ultra-High Intelligence Quotient). No one else knew of his alleged stature as the Mahdi. It had been decided to contain that part of Terran's profile to ensure minimal bias. Most of the academics at the research center were hand-selected UHIQs by Eleanor, and she was well aware that nearly all of them were died-in-the-wool atheists, and those who were not, were agnostic. If they knew of Terran's supposed stature, they would avoid him like the plague.

It had been decided from the first notice of Terran's reputation, that his mantle as the Mahdi would be concealed. Her brother's report from the night before was actually, in some ways, reassuring. If Eleanor had one concern about Terran, it was contained in his open admission of being the Mahdi. That he would expose his God-like duties to everyone at the research center, who in turn, would immediately see him as toxic. In short order, they would refuse to work with him.

To change the mind of a UHIQ was one of the most challenging of all endeavors. If it was science, then the data of science could ultimately trump the opinion of a UHIQ, impressing them to change their mind, but even then, the data better be overwhelmingly decisive. If it had anything to do with the fluff of religion or the scent of spirituality, the changing of minds was an impossible feat where UHIQs were concerned.

This issue would be one of the first that Eleanor and Liam would have to discuss with Terran. They would request that he conceal his Islamic Crown as the Mahdi, and not disclose his beliefs in God or anything spiritual. The Faculty Research Center was devotedly scientific in nature. Nothing else mattered. If they could get his concession on that one issue, they were optimistic that Terran would be everything they had hoped he would be.

A mobile staircase was wheeled to the plane as it slowly taxied up. The staircase came about three feet under the lip of the exit door. Not a perfect fit. As the passengers began deplaning, they had to jump down or be lowered to the first landing of the stairs, which was not an easy thing to do for many of the passengers, because of their physical condition. In the case of Terran, he jumped like a boy would jump who had been cooped up for too long. He ran down the stairs with ease, not even touching the handrails.

"Looks like he has good energy," Liam observed. "Your brother's right though, he is small."

"You know what they say about small packages…" Eleanor quipped as she started walking towards Terran with her hand out.

"Welcome to Denver. I'm Eleanor."

Terran shook her hand, squinting at her face slightly, and then bowed. "I'm Terran."

"Yes, we know who you are…" Eleanor chuckled. "And this is Dr. Sorenson. You remember him?"

Terran shook his hand, and nodded. "Yes."

"Which one is Sanjur Rovach?" Eleanor asked.

Terran pointed to Sanjur who was being helped down the stairs.

"Liam, can you bring Sanjur to our car? We'll take these two back with us, and the rest can go in the other vehicle." Eleanor put her arm around Terran. "Come with me, we'll get out of the wind and cold."

They walked the short distance to the SUV and got inside. *He does have blue eyes.* Eleanor tried her best not to stare, but it was almost impossible. He was magnetic to her. He was what she had hoped for. Ever since Sunrot, ever since her appointment, ever since she had been asked to locate and acquire the world's best UHIQs, she had hoped one day to find a young mind with his intelligence that could be molded.

Eleanor had read the prophecy that her brother had given her from the Leadership Council, but she didn't care about the Mahdi, or the politics therein. She didn't care about the cloning project either. She was skeptical that clones would ever approach the creative brilliance of their original Subject. IQ, she argued, was just the paint, canvas, and brushes, but the artist was an intangible, not to be found in IQ scores or clones. That was where cloning would fail. What she had hoped for was precisely what was before her very eyes: a Terran Kahn. He was the UHIQ that would be able to bring the whole picture together.

Technologies as disparate as computers, medicine, space, genetics, food, water desalinization, and telecommunications; all of these plus a hundred more, were hibernating in servers, waiting, for the right mind to unlock them and unleash their functions back into society.

Eleanor and Liam saw themselves as the architects of Terran's intelligence insofar as they would channel it to the projects that most needed his kind of intellect and special abilities. Their project list was long, but they knew his mind would be facile, and able to integrate it all. He would be able to see the connections, and quite possibly invent new ways to do things even better than before.

Peter tapped on the window next to Eleanor, startling her from her reverie. She rolled down her window.

"Can we talk?"

Eleanor excused herself, and got out of the car. "You must be Peter."

"I am. And you're Eleanor, I presume."

"Yes, how was your trip?"

"Fine." Peter handed her a folder that was awkwardly bound in duct tape. "Your brother asked me to hand this to you. So I'm playing messenger."

Eleanor glanced down at the folder. "Thanks..."

Peter nodded. "I also wanted to ask you about the other two guys. Are they staying?"

Unconsciously, Eleanor lowered her voice. "I don't want them to stay, but I don't want to do anything that might upset our guests, so let's leave them here for the time being. We have plenty of room at the facility, so that's not an issue."

"One of the guys is in pretty bad shape. He'll need medical attention, and a wheelchair."

"Okay, we can handle all of that."

Eleanor patted Peter on his shoulder. "Don't wait. You can go on your way. Berlin, is it?"

Peter nodded. "Okay, well, Josh said to give you a hug, so I will give it to you, but I had shrapnel pulled out of my chest a few days ago, so it'll have to be a light one." Peter hugged Eleanor somewhat guardedly, and then waved through the window at Terran, and walked back to the plane.

Sanjur and Liam hobbled to the SUV and got in. By the time the SUVs were loaded up and ready to go, the Boeing 777 was already sprinting down the runaway to another take off. Terran watched, his expression mixed—happy to have finally arrived at his new school, but that plane, in many ways, held the last vestiges of his old world.

When they had landed in Olympia, they were offered showers and new clothes. Even then, another layer of his home was removed from him. Now, he was dressed in a white shirt several times too large, and blue jeans rolled up at the hem. He was okay with the new clothes, and he understood they were necessary, but there was a melancholy they induced. He missed Nouri, Parto and Dorri, even Carson and Frank. He knew this was all necessary, but the knowing didn't make it easier for his state of mind. Especially as their SUV pulled away in opposite directions from the airplane.

CHAPTER 84

Letter

In the deepest reaches of the world, He will learn. He will listen to the teacher that others have never heard. He will take this teacher into the night and explore vast realms. He will learn from his teacher while others sleep, coddled in their dreams of hope and wishes and reparation. The Mahdi learns at a speed that others desire, but cannot copy. Envy follows him, and where envy is, death is never far behind.

* * * *

Once they got past the AK-47-wielding guards, they went into a small tunnel, and down a few steps to a landing. Eleanor took something from around her neck and swiped it over a card reader, and the elevator doors opened. The elevator was a new experience to the four guests. Only Namvar had ever been in one.

Eleanor motioned with her arms for all of them to enter. "Our entire organization is underground, but it's a very nice facility."

Sanjur paused for a moment and looked at Eleanor. "What does the word *facility* mean?"

"Place of operations." Eleanor smiled.

"Ah," Sanjur said, and then made the translation for Terran, who was already looking at all of the numbers inside the elevator.

Liam pushed Raji's wheelchair. He was wide-eyed at the new environment he was suddenly a part of. He had regained consciousness in Olympia when the doctors worked on him, which was when he realized he was in America. It was like waking up into a dream.

"All of these numbers are different levels… underground?" Terran asked, pointing downward.

"They must be…" Sanjur said, just as the elevator began to drop down.

They went down to "L11" with a smooth stop, and the doors opened up into a wide hallway with golf carts in a parking area just off the elevator bank. Eleanor motioned for Terran and Sanjur to get in one, and then Namvar and Raji would go with Liam.

They waited while Liam got Raji into the golf cart, putting his wheelchair in the back. Then the two golf carts sped off down the carpeted hallway. "Is this anything like you imagined it would be?" Sanjur asked, elbowing Terran.

"No," he replied shaking his head in wonderment.

There were a few curious onlookers in the hallway who stared at Terran when they drove by. Some would wave at Eleanor, and then shift their attention to the little boy in the back seat with the tall bearded man whose face still looked battered and bruised.

Sanjur tapped Eleanor on the shoulder. "How many students are there?"

"Well, this is mostly a research center, so everyone here is mostly teachers. We only have a few students. Most are older than Terran, but we have one his age."

"How many live in this facility... all levels?"

"About fifteen-hundred."

Sanjur sat back and translated what he had heard.

They had gone about a hundred yards down the hallway when Eleanor slowed the cart, and pulled off to the side, near a door with a keypad. She pressed some buttons and the door unlocked. She turned to Terran with a friendly smile. "This is your new home."

Terran got out of the cart, and went inside to a spacious room that opened to a living area. A hallway went off to the left, and a kitchen and half-bathroom to the right.

"Down the hallways are two bedrooms," Eleanor said. "We've stocked the closets with some clothes for both of you. Sanjur, your bedroom is the first door on the right. Terran, yours is the last door on the right. The door to the left is the bathroom."

Sanjur and Terran were both looking around in a state of bewilderment. Flat screen panels hung from the wall on one side of the living room with a computer just below the four panels. A full kitchen with a half-wall was opposite the living room. A wall mural depicting a desert oasis was on the far wall behind the monitors.

"We thought you might like the mural," Eleanor said. "Oh, and the refrigerator is stocked with a variety of drinks and food. Help yourselves to whatever you want."

Eleanor wrote something down on a piece of paper. "Sanjur, this is the code to get into your quarters, please instruct Terran how to use it, too. Okay?

"Okay..."

"Good, we'll let you explore your new home. Feel free to change your clothes or take a shower, whatever you like. I'll come back in about an hour, and we'll talk about the English program we've developed for Terran. I think that's where we should focus for now."

Eleanor started to turn around to leave, and held up her index finger. "See you in one hour then. Goodbye."

"Goodbye... oh, Dr. Sinclair, where will Namvar and Raji be staying?"

"We didn't know they were coming until late last night, so their quarters are still being arranged. We'll try and keep them as close by as possible."

"They can stay here, we have plenty of room," Sanjur said, sweeping his arms around their living room.

"It's kind of you to offer, but we have plenty of room for them. It's no trouble."

Eleanor walked out, closing the door behind her. Sanjur glanced at the piece of paper with the four numbers on it: 4792.

"Is this really happening?" Sanjur said as he spun slowly around, taking in his new home.

"I think I must check out the kitchen," Sanjur chuckled.

*   *   *   *

Eleanor closed her door and went into her kitchen, taking a knife from a drawer, and carefully sliding it into the folder's half-inch opening. She ripped through the duct tape that had been wrapped around the folder like a maniacal spider spinning its silken death sac around its prey. She was very curious what her brother would send her in such a manner. They had email. They had computer chat. They had phone networks. Apparently, none of those were suitable. She was nervous as she opened it.

A handwritten letter was inside. She recognized the handwriting as Josh's.

Eleanor,

I have reason to believe that the Leadership Council has infiltrated our communications. I think they have a decidedly different interest in Terran and our project.

In my conversation with you last night, I was telling you what I wanted the Leadership Council to hear, not what I believe. I had a chance to spend about fifteen minutes alone with Terran and his translator, Sanjur. Words are not how he communicates—I mean, not exclusively. I saw flashes when I was in his presence. It was like another being was communicating with me while I watched Terran's body speak. I don't know how to describe this. If there is such a thing as a Mahdi, then he is it.

If the prophecy is correct, if Terran Kahn is the Mahdi, then the Leadership Council may try to assassinate him once the cloning is successful. I don't pretend to know what the ramifications are if Terran Kahn is assassinated, but I want no part in it. There is something inside this boy that is not human. It is not human, not at least how we describe it. It may be our future ten thousand years down the line of evolution, but it is not of our time or world. I guess that's what I really mean.

I don't necessarily believe the prophecy, but I have read it. It speaks of the Mahdi as the one who unites the world in spiritual union. Who brings the world—the whole world—to the next stage of our evolution: coherence, unity, and peace. I don't understand why this would be seen as a threat, by those in power, but I am told it is.

The key thing for you to understand is that I believe in Terran Kahn with every atom of my body. I believe we need to protect him. At this time, I don't know whom to trust. I would encourage you to meet with Terran in private until I have more information. I would also encourage you to dampen the enthusiasm around his intellect. Play it down. Any reports you make, any communications you send, operate under the assumption that they will be intercepted.

My sources are inside the Board of Governors. They are very convincing, and it was only a day ago that I became aware of them. This is a far-reaching conspiracy that stems from Old Testament times.

I know this is a lot to process. I've been agonizing whether to tell you for fear that this letter could get compromised. I went to Peter this morning, before they left, and handed it to him directly. He's a good man. If the folder was wrapped in duct tape, then you're seeing these words for the first time. When you peel back the duct tape you will see my writing if you look closely. Let this be your proof. Please destroy this letter once you've read it. Then call me, and use the word: "Buffalo" in the conversation. Then I'll know you found the letter and the duct tape was intact. If you don't use the word "Buffalo," I will know that the letter was tampered with or you never got it. In either case, I will be gone.

I will do everything I can to find a secure channel of communication, or I will come for an extended visit, if I feel I can't. You're the closest thing right now to a protector of Terran—perhaps his best chance for survival. My prayers are with you.

All my love,

Josh

Eleanor sat down. Her hands were trembling. *How could this be?* She repeated this thought until she began to speak it over and over. She grabbed the folder and peeled the duct tape back, and found Josh's writing. It was a simple line: "I always looked up to you." Tears suddenly flowed into her eyes as she saw it. She walked over to her computer and turned it on. She read the letter one more time, as her computer booted up, and then took it to the kitchen sink and burned it, washing the ashes down the drain.

She splashed water over her face, and blew her nose, dabbing her eyes. She went over to her computer and dialed Josh's number. On the third ring he picked up. Every word was now somehow different, every look was cheating reality.

"Hi, El," Josh said, trying to look upbeat. "Did he arrive?"

"Yes."

"Well, what do you think?"

"Too early to tell. We haven't had a chance to really speak. Nice kid. Seems a little shy, but he's probably overwhelmed by all of the changes over the past few days."

Josh looked down at his hands for a moment, and then back up at Eleanor. "Blue eyes are kind of odd for a Persian kid, aren't they?"

Eleanor nodded. "Do you remember when we went to California, when we were kids?"

"Yeah..."

"I don't know if you'd remember, but we saw this buffalo that had blue eyes at one of the State parks."

Josh lit up suddenly. "Oh yeah, I remember that. So you're trying to tell me that Terran reminds you of that buffalo?"

Eleanor choked back a tremor in her voice, and took a quick breath, trying to produce a convincing chuckle. "Not exactly, but when you see it, it sort of stands out in your mind the same way."

"I guess I know what you mean."

"I'll meet with him later today, and explain our English program that Liam put together. Our goal is to get him up to speed on English in the next week. If he studies hard, he might be able to access our

Learning Accelerator by the weekend, and then he'll be off to the races."

Josh furrowed his forehead. "Let's hope we don't have another Sidis Complex. I'm concerned that his personality might be a problem with the cloning. I read that memo you sent from HCP. Did you know that the PIs below sixty show a negative FR?"

"I don't think that he'll score that low."

"Will you be doing a PI soon?"

"I'll have Dr. Moralis interview him once he's had enough time to adjust. I don't want to rush it."

"I agree… give him time to adjust. Then do the PI in a week or two, once he's established his new routines, and has a handle on English."

"That's the plan," Eleanor said softly. She felt her attention drifting to Josh's letter, and she had to straighten her posture to remind herself to act normal.

"Okay, Sis, thanks for the update. Keep me posted on your progress."

Eleanor nodded. "I will."

"I love you, El."

"Love you, too."

"Bye."

"Bye."

The computer pop-up faded to a dark gray with a single line of text: "Connection lost. Try again?"

Eleanor closed the pop-up. She sat in stunned silence. Her mind suddenly blank, as fear's fingers curled around her neck. She felt its grip seize her. She glanced at her watch, took a deep breath and stood to her feet. She slipped on her shoes, and walked out of her quarters with a new sense of mission.

CHAPTER 85

Believe

Eleanor had met with Liam immediately after her brother's call. She had explained to Liam that she thought it would be best if she gave Terran and Sanjur a tour of the facility. She would keep the conversation light. Let them stretch their legs and get a good feel for the facility. She'd prefer that Liam focus on completing Terran's English program. "Let me conduct the tour, you do the important work," were her exact words. She never mentioned anything about Josh's letter or his suspicions.

The elevator doors opened onto the fifteenth floor, and Eleanor walked directly to a switchbox. She was holding a flashlight in her mouth to free her hands. She flipped a bank of switches, and the hallway lit up. The hum of electricity flared for a moment, and then settled down once the surge was over.

Eleanor wore her favorite faded red cardigan sweater over a pair of jeans. She played the role of tour guide to Terran and Sanjur, but her mind was not on tours, but rather warnings.

"Follow me," Eleanor said, motioning with her hand. Sanjur and Terran followed her down a corridor that led to a single door. As they came to the end of the corridor, Eleanor opened the door with a swipe of her cardkey, and went inside, turning on the lights with a quick flick of her wrist.

"This section of the facility was originally designed to do research into psychic abilities. The rooms back there are all anechoic chambers. They're completed shielded from every external influence you can imagine, including electromagnetic fields, radio frequencies, and even electromagnetic pulses. They're the ultimate manmade void, energetically speaking."

Sanjur made the translation, stumbling on a few words, but Terran nodded.

As they went inside one of the chambers, Eleanor pointed to the pyramidal structures that protruded from the walls and ceiling. "These are called Radiation Absorbent Materials or RAMs. They help to provide isolation from RF frequencies... among others." She closed the door, and immediately a deeper silence was felt by all of them.

"Down the hall to the east wing, similar rooms were built to protect all of the data resources that the previous owners managed. Over seven thousand computer servers are contained in rooms not too unlike these."

"What are computer servers?" Terran asked, after Sanjur's translation.

"They are the programs... the software that runs everything. The previous owners of this building oversaw the Internet... they watched it."

Eleanor motioned with her hand to the floor. "Sit."

Terran and Sanjur both sat down in the middle of the room.

"Ask her how far below the earth's surface we are right now," Terran said.

After Sanjur posed the question, Eleanor smiled and pointed up. "About a hundred and twenty meters."

Eleanor sat down with them. "Let's not talk for a minute or two so you can see how quiet it is. It's really quite amazing."

Terran laid back, and closed his eyes after Sanjur finished his translation.

"It's like being in space," Sanjur whispered, and then quickly covered his mouth, admonishing himself to be quiet. After a minute, Terran sat up and stood to his feet. He began walking slowly around the perimeter of the chamber, touching the pyramidal protrusions with his fingers. It was a rectangular-shaped room about the size of a large living room with a ceiling at least twenty feet high.

Terran kept walking. "Ask her why she brought us here."

"He wants to know why you brought us to this room." Sanjur said.

Eleanor felt something in the room. It wasn't sound, it wasn't light. It was movement, a presence, her skin suddenly stippled with goose bumps, as this feeling of something invisible moved beside her. She looked, but saw nothing. She glanced at Sanjur who was watching her with curiosity.

"Is something wrong?" Sanjur asked.

"No... no, I'm fine."

Eleanor wrapped her arms around her legs. "I thought he'd enjoy a room such as this, where there's no interference of any kind. Sometimes I come in here, and turn the lights off... just think."

"Yes, we have caves like this in Turkmenistan," Sanjur said. "They're hollowed deep inside limestone walls, and if you go in deep enough, they say you can hear your thoughts in a parallel universe."

Eleanor smiled, and then took a deep breath. "Ask him if he believes he is the Mahdi?"

Sanjur glanced at Eleanor, and then spoke to Terran over his shoulder.

Terran responded. "Tell her that I am what I am... a vessel. If the Mahdi occupies this vessel, am I the Mahdi? Or am I the vessel? Who would she like to speak with, Terran or the Mahdi?"

Eleanor listened to Sanjur's translation with widening eyes. "I want to speak with the Mahdi," she said resolutely.

"Sanjur, can you leave us alone for a minute?" Terran asked.

Sanjur blinked a few times and nodded. He stood awkwardly to his feet, limped to the door, opened it and closed it behind him.

Eleanor watched with growing alarm, as Sanjur left without an explanation. She looked at Terran, who seemed withdrawn. Then she noticed that the light in the room weakened, as if someone slowly turned down the lights. A part of her wanted to stop everything that was happening. *Walk out of the room,* she thought. Pretend that nothing occurred, but it was too late. Her mind and heart were caught up in the presence that she could sense was gathering. It was like a storm, collecting itself along a distant shore, and once seen, somehow you know that it will come your way.

Eleanor covered her eyes to ward off a plasma wave of brilliant light that suddenly flooded the room. She blinked a thousand times while the light peeled away whatever stood between her and the strange being that she saw in flashes of light. It was a Light Being, transparent, vivid, enriched in the potency of the room's shields. It stood, seven feet tall, towering over her like a waterfall of light that filled the room. She tried to speak, but words failed her. She kept her hands partly over her eyes—the light too bright to look at directly. In a moment's grace, it weakened, and began to crystallize into a form. The form was that of an androgynous Being that was still of light, but seemed more corporeal, of substance, of mass.

Eleanor continued blinking, wondering if she could trust her eyes. She looked and could not see Terran in the room anywhere. *Had he left?* What was *this* that stood before her? *Who are you?*

"I am that which myth has created," a voice said. "I am that which time has seasoned in such a way that I can rise before you and be seen and heard. I am that which some will call the Mahdi, some will call the Antichrist. I am that which huddles inside every being, waiting to be asked to come alive and grow. If you can see me, if you can hear me, you are in the enviable position to truly decide what and who I am."

The voice was melodic and pure. There was no structure in it, it simply flowed like water. The Being stood perfectly still amid its flowering light. Its eyes barely moved, but it was ever so clear to Eleanor that it was addressing her.

"How can you be both good and evil at one time?" Eleanor asked.

"Because I am infused with the beliefs of all people of all times. I am the Being that all beings desire and all beings fear. They invent me, and I am born. They embellish me, and I evolve. They fear me, and I am fearsome. They love me, and I am caring. I am the creation of all beings."

"How do you live inside this boy?"

"The very same way I live inside you, and an infinitude like you. The only difference is that he is prepared. His vessel is like this room. Clear, coherent, simple, and unswayable. He is designed for me, so that others can see what is inside themselves, if they could only look."

"Why? *Why* is he designed this way, and *who* designed him?"

"He allows what I am to be in your world. I designed him in the ordered perfection of possibilities. He is me incarnate. I am him discarnate."

"For what purpose are you here?"

"There is only one purpose if you occupy a body, and that is to know that you are a soul."

"How does that matter when our planet has undergone the death and destruction of Sunrot?"

"It is the only thing that does matter, because if you know this, then you can make sense of life, no matter what form life takes."

Eleanor remained highly focused. Her eyes barely blinked, never looking away from the being before her. "The Mahdi comes from a small village in the deserts of Persia," she said. "He's still a boy, yet he has the attention of the most powerful leaders on this planet. What do they want with him?"

"What all men want, they want to know that they have a soul. Even those who dismiss the soul as nonsense, not one among them would turn away from proof. Not one. They seek this proof. They want it, and they sense it in him, because I am in him more powerfully than anyone else on this planet."

Eleanor shook her head. "I don't understand how they could think that they'll know their soul by controlling Terran…"

"They don't want to control him. They want what he has. They want his power to be their power. They hope, even unconsciously, that he will love them and grant them grace and redemption. This hope lives in their heart, and all will feel this, even you."

Eleanor collected her thoughts and paused. "Are you part of a religion?"

"I am."

"Islam?"

"Yes."

"And Christianity?"

"Yes."

"What about Judaism?"

"Yes."

"How can you be in all of these?"

"I am in all religions. Why does this surprise you?"

"Because Christians believe in Jesus Christ, and you're the Mahdi. You're supposed to be the successor of Mohammed. I don't think Christians or Jews will believe in you, if the Islamic faithful claim you as their own."

"My identity is never founded in one thing, because I am the infinitude. Those who believe that they own my identity and label me as their property, they are the first to lose me. This loss is not because *I* leave them, but because they are possessive, protective, selfish, and in these behaviors, *they* leave me. Those who reject me, because I am purportedly owned by one faith, because I appear from one geography and not another, their minds are crystallized, enchanted with words more than their heart's longing. They, also, have left me."

Eleanor slowly shook her head. "There are so many competing interests in this boy…"

"As I said, there is only one interest, to know oneself as soul. Everything else is a journey to this realization. We are here to hasten this journey."

"When you say *we*, who do you mean?"

"I am a node on a network, the same as you. The network is we."

"And this network is one network or…"

"It has always been one network, and thus it will remain. I cannot exclude a node, or that node would perish."

Eleanor rubbed her eyes and looked again at the Light Being that stood before her. Was it possible that this was some kind of an illusion? Had she fallen under the influence of Terran? She looked around the room again. He was still missing.

"That's it… we're all souls and nodes on a network?" Eleanor asked. "Sounds like a fairy tale to me. How does it relate to *me?*"

Eleanor was surprised by her intensity when she spoke, but something inside her was emboldened by the presence in the room.

The Light Being moved towards her. "It is learning to love in such a way that the whole network is lifted up. That is how it relates to you, because it is how your life is given meaning."

"Well, maybe I don't know what love is… or maybe I don't know what the network is… or maybe I'm defective in some way, like a doll that lost its arm or leg. Maybe I lost something when all of those I loved died. Now you come along and say we should love in a particular way that uplifts everyone? Do you have any idea how hard that is?"

"It is always harder to ignore this fundamental truth, than it is to practice it." The Light Being moved a step closer. It was about nine feet away from Eleanor. "You are not lost, in the sense that you are missing anything. You are lost because you have too much."

"Too much of what?"

"Density."

"What does that mean?"

"You have too much that you have held onto. Too much that you believe and doubt in contradiction. This creates density. This density creates separation from your soul. This separation creates the conditions that breed density, and it feeds upon itself."

"So how do I become less... dense?"

"You love without borders. You love without conditions. You love even in the face of hate, doubt, deceit, and injustice."

"And when I fail?"

"You love."

"I think I will be a failure in this... I know me; I won't be able to love injustice or hate. I can't do that. It's not me."

"You do not love injustice or hate, you love the people affected by it—those who suffer, those who take advantage of it, even those who perpetrate it."

"Why?"

"Because they are all part of the network."

"Ah, the network again. Well, here's what I think about the network: it's full of selfish, superficial people who are too tired even to pray any more. We're too tired, we're just too tired..." Eleanor's voice softened. "Maybe that's what density is really about."

"The network includes all. There are no exclusions based on geography, religion, conduct, beliefs, or anything else that is a human invention. There is nothing human about the network. The network is soul."

"Yes," Eleanor said, nodding her head, "but if you don't see or know the soul, the network's a pure abstraction. It's a mental construct and nothing more. What's invented by humans is real. I can see it and touch it. You want people to love everyone, because we're all souls, and we're all connected, but unless we can see the soul, how can it ever happen?"

"That is why we are here: to make soul visible."

As the last word tumbled from the mouth of the Mahdi, the Light Being began to fade, as if to invoke an irony. It faded into the figure of Terran who had been standing behind it the whole time, unseen. Terran stepped forward within a few feet of Eleanor, and opened his arms and embraced her. She realized in that instant that she must change her life. Her eyes shut as the light in the room returned to its previous level, and what had always been missing in her heart, entirely filled. Now, in the softly rocking weight of a young boy, she felt a completion.

Terran whispered in her ear, "Believe. It's time to believe."

CHAPTER 86

Lamb

Pirdah sat at his outdoor dining table, waving a hand at restless flies that were intent on his lamb. Moshad and General Amirmoez were his guests, eager to enjoy their lunch of lamb meat and rice. Moshad and the General had returned the day before, empty handed to the utter disappointment of Pirdah. For nearly three minutes Pirdah had openly wept at the news. After he composed himself, he had suggested the three meet for lunch the following day.

"Are you certain? Only a clear mind is certain," Pirdah exclaimed.

"We tracked them to the school, we watched them enter. The girl was with them."

"The only way they would know of the Mahdi is if they could see him. They must have a way to see."

The General shook his head very slowly as he sat back in his chair. "We know they have computers. We know they have the Internet. If they have these two things, they can see. So what are you suggesting, your Holiness?"

"Terran will do whatever he needs to do if we threaten his new family, especially the little girl. We know what he did at the school when Moshad held her captive. He'd do that again."

The General leaned forward. "Yes, but that was walking across the street... this... this is—"

"If they have airplanes, what's really the difference?" Pirdah said.

Moshad cleared his throat, nodding courteously to the General. "The difference, your Holiness, is that Terran was in control of his own legs, but he doesn't have control of Helios' airplanes. They would see the girl as collateral damage, and nothing more."

"He's the Mahdi, he would have leverage over them," Pirdah argued. "You of all people known that he's not without his ways to get what he wants. We just have to make sure he values her safety bad enough to return."

"Your Holiness, What about Moshad and his men?" the General asked. "There are ships. They could travel there. It would take more time to be sure, but we know it will work."

"Unless the sea swallows us," Moshad said with a nervous grin.

Pirdah set his napkin on the table, set down his fork and sighed. He let the silence march in emptiness for a few moments. The other men grudgingly stopped eating.

"I don't want delays," Pirdah said. "Every day we wait, we risk his death. Stanton is a fool in matters of our faith. We must show our resolve."

"Your Holiness, your words, as always, express truth," the General said. "We can do both. I can take some of my men and capture the girl. We'll see that we get on the computer and show her to Terran, so he knows it is real. In the event we fail, Moshad and his men can take a ship to America and find him. He can find him, I have no doubt."

Pirdah grabbed his napkin, and returned it to his lap. "Moshad, is this acceptable to you?"

"Yes, your Holiness."

Pirdah nodded slightly and smiled. He took his fork in his hand, and began eating again, to the delight of his two guests. When the Holy One stopped eating, everyone at the table had to stop, too. It was Pirdah's favorite technique to get his way. *Men will agree to amazing things, if they can only continue to eat their lamb.*

CHAPTER 87

Three

The morning air was fresh, but brisk. President Stanton and Zhou Hu were just finishing their breakfast on the patio. Notebooks were piled high between them, a clear sign that it was a working breakfast, in case the servers had any doubts. Zhou, being the consummate purist, took notes on nearly everything she was involved in, including the social event the night before.

"When are you going to tell me what you thought of him?" Trevor asked.

"What I thought of him..." Zhou reflected the words back in slow motion. "Assuming you're talking about Terran Kahn, I thought he was a cute, normal boy who couldn't keep his eyes off your Venus de Milo." She fluttered her eye lashes. "I'm quite sure he felt totally out of his element."

"That's it?"

"I didn't see anything else particularly special about him. He picked at his food, barely ate anything. He didn't ask Sanjur for many translations of our conversation, which I thought was odd. He seemed somewhere else the whole night."

Zhou reached for her stack of notebooks, and pulled out a green one, labeled: *Terran Kahn*. She leafed through it, and found the page she was looking for. "He initiated only one subject all night that seemed of interest to him: how our weather has changed since Sunrot."

Zhou looked at her notebook. "Specifically, he asked about our monitoring of geomagnetic storms, and if we tracked solar activity."

"Maybe he's more interested in space than I thought. Anything else of interest?" Trevor asked.

Zhou looked at her notes. "I asked him twice about his comment that he was a half-blood. He didn't answer me. He's clearly not comfortable talking about his parents or bloodline. I also asked him what time of the day he was born, but I got nothing. I didn't push too hard on either item, but I was firm. He won't be an easy one to get to know."

"The psych profiling will start next week," Trevor said. "We'll get to the bottom of it then. He was probably tired from his trip. Peter gave me a more detailed description of their extraction mission—it would've been a lot to process for any kid."

"I noticed you and Josh talking… anything from him?"

"To be honest, I was a little surprised at his reaction."

"Why?"

"He fought hard to bring this kid here. His sister, Eleanor, was a huge proponent for grabbing this kid. Until I brought it up at the Leadership Council, there wasn't a lot of support for taking one of our best assets to Mashhad, knowing what condition their airports were in. We knew it was a long shot, but the Leadership Council thought it was a good risk if it turned out that this kid was the Mahdi."

"What exactly surprised you about Josh's reaction?"

Trevor took a long sip of orange juice, and dabbed his lips with a napkin. "Just that he didn't observe any of the typical signs that Terran was a UHIQ. He wondered if we'd been deceived."

"Deceived? By whom?"

"It was a just a comment, and he said not to take it seriously."

"This kid went through our CIP in record time," Zhou said, sitting up in her chair. "A lot of UHIQs have taken that thing—hell, *I've* taken that thing, and it's next to impossible to get past level seven with straight positives. He did straight positives through level ten. How could he have duped us? Unless… our Faculty was hacked or an insider cheated."

Zhou leaned back in her chair. "Is Josh suggesting someone inside the Faculty may have cheated?" Zhou asked.

"No… no, he wasn't suggesting anything. He just said he was disappointed at Terran's lack of interest in things, his lack of passion… I don't know, maybe the kid got lucky and picked some—"

"Luck doesn't play a role in the CIPs," Zhou interjected. "I know you haven't had the pleasure to take one of those, but trust me, there's no way. I knew some students in Beijing with IQs literally off the charts, pushing three hundred. They were L-10ers, but both had two misses on their way to level nine, and it took them each over an hour." Zhou leaned back, and crossed her arms. "Luck isn't a possibility."

Zhou composed herself with a deep breath. She was irritated at the suggestion that luck could have played a role in Terran's intellectual feat.

"I think the logical explanation is always the best," Zhou said. "We know that Terran was raised as the Mahdi. We know that he has many of the characteristics described in the prophecy. If he's the Mahdi, then we shouldn't be disappointed that he's ours. Whether you believe he's the return of Mohammed, or the Antichrist, or just an over-the-top UHIQ, whichever, he's ours."

"I sense you believe a little in the prophecy," Trevor observed. "I thought you were a skeptic of such things."

"I'm a skeptic of everything, but that doesn't mean I don't explore the possibilities. I think we're putting too much emphasis on his personality, how he behaves, and not enough on the fact that he's a level-ten-straight-positive with an elapsed time of..." Zhou glanced down at her notebook, "...well, it doesn't matter. All you need to know is that he solved an L-10 question before it was explained."

"And the prophecy?" Trevor asked.

"What about it?"

"Where are you on a scale of one to ten, ten being total belief?"

"Which prophecy?"

"Cardinal Dameris."

"The Vatican didn't want that prophecy out, so I give it extra weight. My mentor taught me that if a prophecy's in the public domain, it can't be trusted. The Dameris prophecy defined Sunrot, and it defined that a UHIQ would be born on the first day, and that that UHIQ would be the Mahdi. The fact that the Vatican had this prophecy from a source unconnected to the imams, and it proved to be more accurate, makes it very interesting. I give it an eight."

Trevor nodded with a smile.

"It's also interesting," Zhou continued, "that the Islamic prophets call al-Mahdi The Guided One. It raises the question: who guides him? It's always been assumed that Allah and Mohammed guide him, but who knows? Maybe it's us."

"It's also been assumed that Jesus will have a second coming at the end times, and that the Antichrist will also be on the chessboard." Zhou paused, and looked at Trevor, and then down at her hand, holding the stem of her glass. "What's really interesting is that two UHIQs were born within minutes of the first solar flare hitting our magnetosphere. We don't know exactly when Terran Kahn was born, but I bet it was at that same time."

Trevor crossed his legs, shifting in his chair. "You're suggesting that we have three twelve-year-old boys—the Mahdi, Jesus, and the Antichrist all incarnating in human form on the planet, and that the *sun* had something to do with it?"

Zhou turned to a different page in her notebook. "Let me read you a quote that the imams believe:

> " At the moment of birth a light pierced the top of the child's head and reached into the depth of the sky. This child is the Mahdi, He who will fill the earth with equality and justice, just as it is now filled with oppression and injustice."

"What they're describing as *light*, I can just as easily interpret to be a solar flare. A flare so powerful that from its energy release, a cascade of events ensued that we now call Sunrot. Twelve years later, we find the one who is called the Mahdi, and we know we have two other UHIQs born the same day... quite possibly the same precise time."

Zhou paused while a server came to their table to clear some dishes. They both smiled politely while the server carefully picked up their utensils and plates, then stepped away without a word or sound.

"I can't believe you're bringing this up as a possibility!" Trevor said, leaning forward in a half-whisper. "Have you ever discussed this with Liu or anyone else from the Leadership Council?"

Zhou shook her head, and remained silent.

"How do you know about the other UHIQs?"

"I read the reports from the Faculty."

"Do you think they're aware of this?"

"About me reading the reports or the other UHIQs' birth times?"

"The birth times, and how it might relate to Terran and the prophecy?"

"I don't know."

Trevor shook his head and leaned back in his chair. "When I was growing up, the end times were supposed to be World War Three, triggered in the Middle East. The Antichrist was a powerful lawyer, banker, or politician, and there was no mention of a Mahdi. There was no mention of Sunrot…"

"Until Dameris defected from the Vatican, no one knew of these prophecies."

"Where are these other two UHIQs you mentioned?"

"One is in Berlin at an ALIGN Center there, and the other's at Denver."

"I suppose you have notebooks for each of those, too."

Zhou nodded politely.

"Where were they born?"

"A very good question. You see, that was what caught my attention. All three, including Terran, were born on the thirty-sixth parallel between the fifty-ninth and sixtieth meridians."

"So they're all related in time and space."

Zhou nodded. She could sense Trevor's mood darken.

Trevor rubbed his forehead for a moment. "For now, let's keep this conversation to ourselves. I want some time to consider the implications, and how best to alert the Leadership Council. Okay?"

Zhou nodded.

"Can you make me a report that defines this… this theory you have?"

"I don't want to be associated with this theory. If you want to release it to the Leadership Council, that's fine, but I don't want any credit for its discovery."

Trevor narrowed his eyes, surprised at Zhou's reluctance. "Why?"

"They scare me."

"The Leadership Council?"

"Yes, but also these three UHIQs."

Zhou pouted her lips when Trevor pushed his chair back and stood up.

"There's one thing I need to correct you on," she said.

"What's that?"

"You said three, twelve-year-old boys…" Zhou shook her head. "One's a girl."

EPILOGUE

Terran pointed to the screen. "What is this?"

Prichet Davis put his reading glasses on, and leaned forward toward the monitor. He was one of the researchers in computer heuristics at the Faculty Research Center in Denver. Eleanor had asked him to mentor Terran on computer programming.

"It's called a back door," Prichet said, "though I have no idea how you find these things."

"What is its purpose?"

"Years ago, when we took over this facility, we needed to use the server capacity that's stored in the server crypt. That's what we call that place on L15 where all the servers are stored—anyway, we needed to use it in order to reboot the Internet. Our lead programmer, Andre, you haven't met him yet, figured out a way to do it, without deleting the content on those servers." Prichet squinted again at the screen, and propped his reading glasses on his forehead. "That back door allows us to access the original content stored on those servers."

"What is the original content?" Terran asked.

"Who knows? No one at the time had an interest in it. It was all obsolete anyway. It's yottabytes of data… not really sure what to do with it. But there it sits."

"A single yottabyte contains one septillion bytes. I don't think there's that much data in the entire world. Are you sure there's that much data?"

"I don't know, I'm exaggerating. Don't take me so literal, kid. All I can tell you is that there're over seven thousand custom servers down there, and for many, many years, they tracked everything that went on in this world."

Prichet put his reading glasses back down on the bridge of his nose. "How'd you find it?"

Terran's fingers typed at an amazing rate on the keyboard. Prichet watched in awe. "No one else uses it... the back door?" Terran asked, ignoring Prichet's question.

"Look, you've been here a total of a week. You hardly come out of your room. You don't realize it, but everyone else in this establishment *works* for a living. We're too busy to hack into old servers that have God knows what, so, no, I doubt anyone else uses the back door."

"But you could, if you wanted?"

"Sure, if I wanted to."

"How would you make it so it was impossible to hack?" Terran asked.

Prichet leaned back and looked up, stroking the stubble under his chin. "I'm not saying I would, or even could do this, but I'd write a code moat that required multiple checkpoints, and then I'd alternate—in real-time—the requirements for those checkpoints into a randomizer. The randomizer would key off of an algorithm that would relate to something totally unpredictable... like, like deep earth tremors or gamma ray bursts from a distant star system. Then I'd use a front door encryption key that was deceptively simple, but led nowhere. Any hacker would assume the backdoor would also be simple. But it would be anything but..." Prichet bolted upright in his chair. "...something like that."

The whole time he was talking, Terran continued to type. He pointed to the screen. "These are the other students here?"

On the screen were the photos and short bios of eight *UHIQ Novices,* according to the header at the top of the screen. The upper-right said: FRC-HR Personnel Database.

"I don't know how you got into HR, but you can't go there!"

"Why?"

"It's private information!" Prichet said, squirming in his chair.

Prichet leaned forward and hit some keys. The screen went to a general home page entitled: "Faculty Research Center Home." Along the left side was a list of fifty-two links. Prichet pointed to the links. "This is the only place you can go. If you can find it in one of these links, you can go there. If it's not in one of these links, it's forbidden. Got it?"

Terran turned around and stared at Prichet for a moment. "If I can find it, why is it forbidden?"

"Look, I'm not your ethics teacher. All I can tell you is that just

because you can find things, doesn't mean you're allowed to find them...
if that makes any sense."

Terran's forehead furrowed in confusion.

"I'm a little hungry," Prichet said, hoping to change the subject.
"Mind if I get something from the kitchen?"

Terran shook his head, and returned to the computer. Before
Prichet opened the refrigerator door, Terran was back on the page with
his fellow students. He noticed his picture was the first one. The second
one was of a girl, who looked Middle Eastern. He clicked the link under
her picture. It opened a larger image of her. She was quite striking,
and Terran stopped for a moment to admire her beauty. Opposite her
picture was a detailed biography, salient test scores and subject interests.
But it was underneath her picture, in the very right corner, in a small,
unobtrusive font, that Terran saw a number that absorbed him: 061221.

The heart is the Temple of Wisdom.

-John Berges

Monument

For if just once in its brief lifespan
the mud-limbed creature staunch entrusts
the entirety of its being to a single guiding star,
without thought to consequence or charge,
shorn of reservation and uncertainty,
of indurate heart, of resolute mind,
of immaculate soul…
it is ever sung and honored
within the senior ranks of bravery,
notwithstanding the overt success of its mission.

The act of commitment bricks the monument;
a willed reorientation of self
to the nurture of the seed's kernel,
to the perfume of the flower of life
from which all life springs.
And should it be asked of me,
a sprout of divine derivation,
if the retrospective yields the lesson,
I would proud salute in quiet reverie
the God-spark's passionate audacity
that emboldens and animates the mundane.

About the Author

James Mahu is the anonymous and visionary creator of five websites, four novels, a large collection of philosophical discourses, a dozen papers on spiritual practices, poetry, short stories, visual artwork, and nearly a hundred music compositions.

His first published creation was WingMakers. com, which established James—its creator—as a multidimensional storyteller who is focused on sharing deep, original perspectives to the conversations of spirituality, cosmology, extraterrestrial life, myth and the importance of the heart in one's personal mission.

Publisher's Note

James is a talented neologist. A neologist is a person who creates new words or a new meaning for established words, and those words are called neologism. As you read, you will come across a word you may not recognize, then go to look it up in the dictionary, only to see that it is not there. When you cannot find the word in the dictionary, you know that James is presenting you with another neologism.

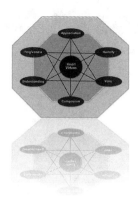

READER'S NOTES

To all who are making the journey, the area below is for you to imprint your energy in the form of notes, definitions and observations.

READER'S NOTES

Appreciation, Compassion, Forgiveness, Humility, Understanding, and Valor

READER'S NOTES

Appreciation, Compassion, Forgiveness, Humility, Understanding, and Valor